PRAISE FOR SUZY ZAIL

'Zail has caught the despair of those without a voice . . .
I Am Change is not a book for the faint-hearted but it is
a book that needs to be read, mulled over, and discussed'
Magpies Magazine

'A confronting but gripping novel . . . a powerful
story of hope, adversity and redemption'
Junior Books + Publishing

'Zail's story is as gut-wrenching as any Holocaust tale . . .
The haunting, matter-of-fact tone of Hanna's story will
likely resonate with teens learning about the Holocaust'
Booklist

'This is a must read for any teenager or adult
interested in the past, the tragedy of war or what
happens when humans believe they are superior'
Kids' Book Review

'An elegant, disturbing portrait of one of history's bleakest
moments, offset by the subversive power of love'
Publishers Weekly

'An excellent library and resource book that will
help open the conversation with young teenagers
about this dark side of modern history'
ReadPlus

For my father

Inkflower
First published in 2024
by Walker Books Australia Pty Ltd
Gadigal and Wangal Country
Locked Bag 22, Newtown
NSW 2042 Australia
www.walkerbooks.com.au

Walker Books Australia acknowledges the Traditional Owners of the country
on which we work, the Gadigal and Wangal peoples of the Eora Nation, and
recognizes their continuing connection to the land, waters and culture.
We pay our respect to their Elders past and present.

 A catalogue record for this
book is available from the
National Library of Australia

ISBN: 978 1 760659 39 4

Typeset in 11 pt Sorts Mill Goudy
Printed and bound in USA by Sheridan Books, Inc

10 9 8 7 6 5 4 3 2 1

The author and the publisher thank Sue Hampel, OAM, Co-President, Melbourne
Holocaust Museum and and Member of the Australian delegation in the Education
Working Group to the International Holocaust Remembrance Alliance, for her
generosity and expertise in reading and advising on *Inkflower*.

INKFLOWER

SUZY ZAIL

WALKER BOOKS

AND SUBSIDIARIES

LONDON • BOSTON • SYDNEY • AUCKLAND

CHAPTER 1

NOW

There are a mountain of lessons you learn at school. You won't find them in textbooks, and no teacher will ever quiz you about them, but you commit them to memory because you want to survive. Mr Prescott is looking at me, like I'm stupid enough to put up my hand. Putting up your hand to answer a teacher's question without being called on breaks at least a dozen of Glenrock High's unspoken commandments including: Don't suck up to teachers. Never admit you've been listening. And don't be too smart. There are other lessons: Don't be too stupid. Don't ask stupid questions. Don't ask too many questions. Don't ask questions your teacher says is a *good question* or you'll wind up the teacher's pet. Don't speak in a foreign language or wear jeans from Kmart or have a weird name. Don't try too hard to be cool (but *be* cool). Don't *take* notes in class – *pass* notes – and don't get caught, but if you do, eat the evidence.

So, no way am I going to put up my hand to answer a question. Especially a question about sex in Sex Ed class. Because there's no coming back from that.

"Abstinence," Mr Prescott sweeps a strand of dyed black hair back over his bald spot, "is the safest course of action." He stops at my desk and drums his fat fingers on the wood. "Anyone disagree?"

I want to die. His beady black eyes which were, moments ago, scanning the room for prey, have zeroed in on their target. Me. Possibly, the least qualified person to debate the point. I pick up a pen and write the word *abstinence* in my notepad, hoping that will satisfy him. I pretend that twenty-seven heads haven't turned to look at me, that twenty-seven sets of eyes aren't watching me sweat through the armpits of my shirt.

Prescott circles my desk, fingers steepled over his stomach, chins wobbling. "Good," he says, a screwed-in smile poking out from under his handlebar moustache. "Because if you have sexual relations, you'll get pregnant, and die." He doesn't actually say the last bit, but he wants to. 10th Grade sex education is about *not* having sex and he wants to be sure we get the message.

He adds two more words to the board – *self-control* and *chastity* – and tells us that sexual intercourse should only occur with God's blessing. I don't believe in God, but I'm not about to tell *him* that. Just like I didn't admit to not needing one of the brick-shaped feminine hygiene products Mrs Worthington was handing out in 7th Grade Sex Ed. (I got my period in 8th Grade, at a pool party. It was horrible.)

I focus on disappearing – *nothing to see here!* – and finally, after what seems like a decade, Mr Prescott returns to his desk, crossing his thick arms over his belly. "Any questions before the bell rings?" He chews on his moustache.

Paul's hand shoots up. "Why don't we just pick partners ... and practise?"

I catch Adam's eye and he grins. The class erupts. It was hot in here to start with. There's no air-conditioning in these concrete-block classrooms, but it's not just the late November heat of an Aussie summer, it's the heat of a mixed Sex Ed class and the heat coming off our sixteen-year-old bodies, especially Adam's, which sparks on contact, spreading like a wildfire inside me whenever he's near.

"Mr Marsh!" Prescott barks over the bell, shaking his finger to mark his words. "Principal's office. Now."

We grab our bags from our lockers and head to the oval.

"It was worth it, just to see Prescott's face." Paul joins us at the smokers' pit behind the huge jacaranda.

"Ouch!" Adam says, staring at the red strap marks on the back of Paul's legs. "How many?"

"Seven." Paul pulls a crumpled cigarette packet from his pocket.

"No thanks," Adam says. No-one on the soccer team

smokes. Paul shakes the packet at me.

"Dad would kill me," I say. "He has this thing about smoke ..." He hates the smell. Cigarettes, bonfires, barbecues. Leaves the room if one of his friends lights up.

Deb waves away the offer. "Smoking's bad for the skin." So is the sun but Deb has yanked down the straps of her tank top so she doesn't get tan lines. The final bell rings and Paul takes a last drag, letting out a ripple of white smoke. He tosses the butt into the pit, a sad hole some kid carved out in the dirt so the teachers wouldn't find out half the year was addicted to nicotine.

"Sleepover Friday?" Deb sweeps a handful of purple flowers from the grass and tucks one behind her ear.

"Sure," I say, hooking an arm around her shoulder. "But can we sleep at your house?"

Deb has a puppy. A yellow, floppy-eared labrador called Elle. As in L for Lowe. As in Rob Lowe. We're not allowed a dog. She also has a double bed and a phone in her room. The walls are plastered with posters of a half-naked Christopher Atkins on the beach in *The Blue Lagoon*, and her mom serves burgers for dinner, which we wash down with Coke in front of the TV. Her mom is cool. She doesn't fire questions at us about school and there's no dad in the picture so there's no let's-all-sit-down-to-eat-together. There's no ten o'clock-lights-out or you're-too-young-to-read-*Cosmo*-magazine, so we get to stay up late, studying the sealed section's bedroom tips to fill in the blanks.

I glance back at Adam, leaning against a tree, arms crossed, face sun-browned. He sees me watching and shoots me a smile.

"Call you later?"

"Sure," I say, like it's no big deal that I'm dating Adam Winter. It's been two months but it still feels surreal. Adam Winter is the type of boy girls write songs about. The type of boy who reads books and likes girls who spend way too much time in their heads and who aren't ready to have sex, not yet. A boy with electric green eyes and his own private voltage.

I want to stay, but if I'm not in the carpark when Dad gets here, he'll park the Honda and start wandering the halls, calling for me. Dad doesn't have a mouth, he has a megaphone, and an accent you can't pin down, but it's not from around here. I unhook my arm from Deb and race to the carpark.

"Hey, pineapple!" Dad waves me over. He's not in the car. He's standing on the steps, chatting to a shirtless man bent over a bush with a pair of a pruning shears. "This is Bill," Dad says, introducing me to a man in sagging overalls and a crumpled straw hat, "but you probably already know that." He turns back to the man. "How long did you say you've been the gardener here?" The hat looks up.

"Ten years in December." Bill squints in my direction. "Hi Bill," I whisper-croak.

We walk to the car.

"No time!" Dad says, pulling me away from Elle, who's straining at her leash for a pat.

"So where are we going?" I open the door and sink into the brown bucket seats of the hulking Honda. Dad reaches for the volume button on the stereo and cranks it up. Frank Sinatra croons through the open window.

"Dad?" I interrupt Frank. "I've got stacks of homework. Do I have to –?"

"It won't take long." Dad exits the carpark. "I've just got to smile for a few photos. It's not every day I get to open a retirement home."

"Mr Mayor!" A man in a pinstripe jacket waves from the steps of the Sunnyside Home for the Aged. There's a plaque bearing Dad's name and the date of last week's official opening, 14 October 1982.

"Why don't you come in?" Dad says, grabbing my backpack. "They have a cafeteria." He reaches into his pocket and pulls out a two-dollar note. "Buy yourself something cold."

The reporter points the way.

The hallways are long, the walls tiled and washed in fluorescent white. Every few steps there's a door opening onto a room with somebody in it. Silver-haired women and toothless men with empty eyes and trembling hands.

A wrinkle of a woman stands behind the cafeteria glass. She wears a hairnet and is spooning mashed vegetables onto plates.

"You the mayor's kid?" she says, when I step up to the glass. "Bless, you look just like your father."

"Thanks," I say, pointing to a can of Fanta. "I get that a lot."

My mother has movie-star looks – killer cheekbones, almond-shaped eyes and jet-black bouncy hair – but no, I look like my father.

I walk back through the sad corridor, past the high-care ward, which gives me the creeps with its moaning and shrieking and flashing lights, past men slumped in wheelchairs and nurses carrying bundled sheets. A woman in a silk slip, wearing a string of pearls, stops muttering when she sees me.

"Veronica!" She smiles a gummy smile and slips a spindly arm through mine. "I thought you'd forgotten your little sister's birthday."

I try to back away. "I'm not Ver–"

"Well, don't just stand there, Ronni." She shuffles on slippered feet. "Come help me do my hair."

Wrinkles frame her mouth and eyes.

"You want me to do your hair?" I ask, peering into rooms for one that might be hers.

"Well, I can't very well turn up to my seventeenth birthday party looking like this, especially since –" she brings her face close to mine, "– Robert has promised to come." She points the pale pink tip of a manicured finger at a bed in a room with not much else in it. There's a small sink with a single tea cup drying on the rack, an empty vase and a pink cardigan with pearl buttons folded neatly on the single bed. The room smells like a toilet.

"Here." She pats the bed next to her. "Grab the brush. They'll be here soon."

"Who?" I ask, draping the cardigan over her shoulders. I don't ever want to grow old, not this kind of lonely, dried-out old, when you talk to strangers as if they're family and forget to get dressed.

"Well, Mother, Father ..." she rattles off names, "... and Robert of course." She reaches for a small silver frame, bones creaking. "Handsome, isn't he?" She shows off a man in a bathing suit. He has a curling moustache and slicked back hair. "I think he might propose today."

"There you are!" Dad sweeps into the room, grinning. "I see you've met Mrs Montgomery. Nice cardigan, Edith." Dad winks at me. "You ready to go?"

I should stay and help her pick the perfect outfit. But it's all too awful: her faraway eyes, the smell of the sheets, the sterile walls, and her pencilled-in eyebrows that dance when she talks.

"Yep, let's go." I return the brush to the table and follow Dad out. "Just a sec," I say, stopping at the door.

Edith looks up and smiles through watery eyes, her bony fingers still clutching the frame.

"The red dress would be nice," I say, pointing to the closet, "and the sparkly shoes with the heel."

CHAPTER 2

NOW

Mr Curlew calls the roll. There are usually twenty-eight of us, but today there are three absences. Phillip has lice, again. Jason has a stomach bug. No-one knows why Denise is away, so we make stuff up. She's probably pregnant, is the general consensus. We just had Sex Ed, so babies are on our mind.

"So, who wants to go first?" Mr Curlew parks himself on the edge of the scarred walnut desk, feet stretched out in front of him. His pants ride up, past his ankles. Smiling avocadoes dance across the tops of his socks. It's his second day as an English teacher at Glenrock High and his face is still hopeful. He has small, scared, pinned-back ears and closely cropped hair. We stare at each other across the classroom.

"I can work my way down the class list but I thought it might be more fun to do your oral presentations this way," he says, "you know, let the zeds go first?" He releases a brittle laugh.

The clock above the door ticks like a time bomb. It's painful to watch. *No-one's going to put up their hand*, I want to tell him. But I don't, because that would involve *me* putting up my hand.

Mr C's shoulders droop. He drags the class list from his desk and runs a thin finger along the line of names.

"Isn't that your mom?" Deb tugs at my shirt and points to the door. My mother is standing in the corridor outside our classroom, her eyes huge in the fluorescent light. She sees me, lifts a limp hand and waves and I don't think, *Why does she look so pale?* I think, *Maybe if I don't look at her, she'll go away.* But she doesn't. She stands in the hallway looking lost and sad and I'm not a good person because all I can think is, *If I don't get to the door before Mom knocks, everyone will see her and want to know what's up.*

I adjust my face into a smile. "Yep," I say, my face burning. "That's Mom. Better go."

"Is something wrong?" Deb watches me pack my things.

"No," I say too fast. "I must've forgotten my lunch or something. I'll be back."

I *had* to be back. It was Deb's birthday and there was a cake sweating under the lid of my desk and balloons shoved into my locker. I jump out of my seat, momble an apology to Mr C and race for the door, hoping no-one can see past me to my mother, who doesn't look like my mother because this woman's mascara is smudged and her hair hasn't been brushed.

"We're doing our orals. What's up?" I say, trying to

keep my voice low, steering my mom away from the window so we don't have an audience.

Her mouth opens and closes. She reaches for my hand and the hallway is empty so I let her feed her fingers through mine, and we stand there, like we used to when I was six and scared of school.

"We have to go home," she says, blinking hard, and I can hear the panic in her voice but I'm still thinking about the cake and how long whatever this is will take and whether I'll make it back in time for recess. We hurry through the carpark, neither of us saying a word until she unlocks the car door and we slide into our seats. She reaches for her seatbelt and her hand is shaking.

"Mom, what's wrong?"

She can't look at me.

"Mom, you're scaring me. What's happened?"

"I'm sorry," she says, grabbing the wheel. "I don't know how to do this."

"Do *what?*"

She swats away a tear and kicks the car into reverse. "Can we just wait until we're home? Dad will explain everything. Your brothers are already there."

And now *I'm* scared because she's driving with one hand and scraping away tears with the other and I get the feeling that as soon as I walk through our front door whatever this is will only get worse.

Dad is sitting on the couch between my brothers with an untouched cup of tea in front of him. Jack is wearing a polo shirt with the collar turned up under his lab coat. Tom looks like he stepped out of a Duran Duran video, in a studded leather jacket and acid-wash jeans. They look like they always look, Jack preppy and serious, Tom a rock-god. But something's off. Jack's gnawing on a fingernail and Tom doesn't know what to do with his hands. No-one's talking. Dad smiles when I walk in, but it's not his usual smile – his lop-sided, half-smile. It's a smile with both sides taped up at the corners. Tom scoots over and I slump down next to Dad. I want to say something to splinter the silence but I've never been one of those people who can speak their fears out loud. So I wait, my face turned away from Mom's.

"We're all here now," Jack says, and Dad reaches for my fingers.

I feel like I'm five again, my small hand safe in Dad's, both of us in the garden staring up at the sky. *Isn't it beautiful?* he used to say, hoisting me onto his shoulders. *All that blue sky, and all of it ours?*

"Dad, please, tell us what's going on." Jack sounds scared.

Finally, Dad speaks and all the other sounds – the birds outside the window, the garbage truck idling in the street, the midday news on the radio – are sucked out of the room and all I hear is: *I'm dying.*

"I'm dying," Dad says, and the world tilts.

Dying, he says, the word soft, an apology.

"We've just come from the specialist. I have amyotrophic lateral sclerosis."

Jack's face warps. I've never heard of amyotrophic lateral sclerosis, but Jack is in his fourth year of medical school and he's shaking his head. Tom is in first-year med and he's crying, terrible tears dripping down his chin.

"But you're not sick," I say, pulling my hand from Dad's. "There's nothing wrong with you. You *can't* be dying." Dying doesn't make sense. My father's too young to die and I'm too young to lose him.

Dad blinks and clears his throat. "I was having trouble lifting my arm," I hear him say over the thumping of my heart. "So, I went to see the doctor. He referred me to a specialist. They've done all the tests."

"No!" I shake my head.

I make him tell us he's dying again and I can see how much he hates saying it, but it's not sinking in. He was supposed to grow old and shuffle around the house in slippers. He was supposed to lose his hair, and his hearing. I slide my hand back into his. It's clammy and alive and I think of all the maybes. Maybe they got it wrong. Maybe he'll get better. Maybe they'll find a cure. Dad pulls his glasses from his nose and wipes at his eyes. I've never seen my father cry. Not when he was lying on a trolley waiting to be wheeled in for open-heart surgery. Not when his sister died of cancer. Not ever. That's how I know it's real, and it undoes me, and then I'm crying and Mom unravels and Tom is sobbing and Jack's face is hidden in a wad of wet tissue. Hundreds of thoughts race around my head but mostly, *He's going to die. He is going to die and I won't have a father and there's absolutely nothing I can do about it.*

"How long did they give you?" Jack's voice is hoarse.

"Six months," Dad says.

My father has to do all his living in the next six months.

Gray light seeps through the window. My brothers speak in the space between silences but I don't hear what they say. I'm pulling apart my father's words and putting them back together, trying to make sense of them.

An hour passes. Or maybe it's three. *Stop!* I want to yell at the spinning world. *Stop. I want to get off! I don't know how to do this.* That's what Mom said in the carpark and now I know what she means. Dad's dying is the first bad thing that's ever happened to me and I don't know how to feel, what to say. How do you comfort someone who's dying? I don't have the words. I never learned them. We don't have deep and meaningful conversations in our house. We don't do moody, angry or sad. We don't talk about the messier parts of life – sex, death, loneliness, jealousy. If something bothers us, we don't talk about it. We deal with it, or ignore it. We were raised on the *If you don't have anything nice to say, don't say anything* school of parenting. *Smile,* Dad always said, if he caught us in a frown. *Smile.* So, I smiled. No-one is smiling now.

Dad wraps an arm around my shoulder. Tears glaze

his face. "My muscles are going to weaken and I won't be able to do some of things I'm used to doing," he says, "but amyotrophic lateral sclerosis doesn't affect the brain or the memory so I'll still be *me*."

I scoop my heart off the floor. *He is going to die.*

I lie on my bed in the dark, a mixed tape the only weapon I have against the escalating noise in my head. I crank it up loud but Madonna is no match for my wild mind. What if this sadness changes me into someone my friends don't recognize? What if Mom remarries? Will I have to share a room with her new husband's kids? Will I have to change schools?

Why does he have to die? I bury my face in my pillow. Why him? Why now? I'm sixteen. *Sixteen.* And we're just getting to the good bit where he teaches me to drive and watches me graduate. I don't want to be a girl without a father. I don't want a sad family and a sad story; I like the story I have.

The door creaks open. "Dinner's on," Jack says.

I don't lift my face from the wet pillow.

"You okay?" The mattress dips and Jack's hand is on my back.

I want to say, *Dad has a terminal illness. So no, I'm not okay.* But I don't. I fling my arms around my brother and bury my wet face in his polo shirt and cry until I could wring the tears from it.

"If you don't have anything nice to say, don't say anything, right?" I say, looking up at my brother.

He shrugs, neither of us admitting that we're terrified out of our skulls.

"So, dinner?" he says, standing to go.

"I'll be there in a minute. Just got to make a quick call."

The thought of calling Deb and having to say the words, *My dad is dying*, out loud makes me want to claw off my skin, but I have to call. It's my best friend's birthday and I wasn't at the cafeteria at recess with cake and balloons and I didn't drop in a gift and I won't be joining the Cartmans for dinner. If I don't call, *she* will. I punch her number into the phone.

When she answers – on a birthday sugar-high, her voice fizzing – I know I won't tell her about Dad. Not because I don't want to bring her down (I don't) but because telling her won't make his illness go away, it'll make it bigger. If I tell my best friend that my father has amyotrophic lateral sclerosis, I'll have to admit he is dying. And then there'll be no stopping it. And there's a part of me that still hopes it isn't true.

I try to make my voice sound cheery. "Happy birthday to you, happy birthday to –"

"Okay. Please stop." Deb laughs. "That's the most pathetic happy birthday I ever heard."

"Sorry. Dad's sleeping." My voice wobbles. Deb and I have known each other since forever. She always knows when something is up, so I tell her what I can. "Dad's sick and Mom's out tonight so I won't be able to come over. So, what did your parents get you?"

Soon she's telling me about her new Walkman, and for a moment I'm in the room with her, stuffing Cheezels into my mouth and tearing at wrapping paper, not here in this sad house with the walls falling down.

"So, I'll see you tomorrow?" Deb asks.

Tomorrow. I think of all the tomorrows I have that Dad doesn't. And then I think about school and everyone seeing through my skin to my breaking heart. I'm not used to being the person other people feel sorry for. I'm the friend you come to when your boyfriend has dumped you or your parents have split. I can listen to a sad story for hours; listening is my happy place. I'm okay with uncomfortable as long as it's someone else's uncomfortable. I picture walking through the whispering corridors of Glenrock High and Mr C asking how I'm doing and everyone wanting to hear what it's like to find out your dad is dying.

"Maybe," I say, the lie burning a hole in my brain.

My brothers stay for dinner and it's like old times, when the three of us were still at school and they were living at home. I eat, but I feel empty, because back then death was a different planet and now it's in our house. Dad is talking about having their friends over – he wants to be the one to tell them – and Mom is nodding but her smile is broken. She runs a hand through Dad's dark hair and then she's crying again and she stands up so fast, her chair falls backward and she's running, howling into the backyard. I follow her there. The sun is setting and the sky is red like its bleeding.

"I want to go with him," she says and, at first, I don't understand.

"With him? Where?" And then I realize what she means and I want to be sick.

She looks up, her eyes huge in the dim light.

"No," I say, grabbing her hand, "you don't." I picture a cemetery and my parents' twin plots, the gravestones bearing the same date. "You don't want to die. You don't, you *can't*." I'm begging now. "Please," I whisper, hounding her for a promise. "Say you'll stay. *Say it!*"

She promises, wiping at my tear-smudged eyes and we sit without speaking, our sadness spilling out of us as the sky turns black.

The phone rings for what has to be the twentieth time. I know it's Adam. He's the kind of guy, the kind of *boyfriend* (I'm still getting used to that word) who calls when you're not at school to see if you're okay. I haul myself out of bed, pad down the hallway, and lift the handset from its cradle. I can't ignore him forever.

"Hi," he says when I pick up. "Missed you today."

Normally the boy on the other end of the line and those words – *I missed you* – would make me smile. That was before. This is after.

"Yeah, sorry. I had to come home. Dad's not well and Mom had to work, so ..." My words dry up.

"Want me to come over? I know it's late but ..."

There's a click. Mom has picked up the phone in the kitchen. "Lisa, it's late." She doesn't sound angry, just tired.

"I won't be long," I say. "Just catching up on what I missed at school."

Mom is weird about me using the phone after ten and even weirder about boys.

"Okay," she says, "but be quick."

"So, I guess I'm not coming over?" Adam says when Mom hangs up.

"Sorry, I think I'm coming down with something." It's the easiest excuse. "I wouldn't want you to catch it."

I feel shitty lying to Adam but it's too early in our relationship for tears. He's never seen me cry and I'm pretty sure if he wrapped his arms around me I wouldn't be able to stop.

I put down the phone and pick up one of the brochures Dad left on the side table and read it front to back. Motor neurone disease. ALS. No remissions. No treatment. No cure. My father will need a wheelchair, a feeding tube and a machine to talk for him. He'll end up paralysed. Then his lungs will give out.

My dad is unmistakeably, unstoppably dying and it makes me want to punch a hole through the wall.

The clock on my bedside table glows 1.04. I can't sleep. I wrap my comforter around my shoulders and tiptoe down the hall to my parents' room, the moon like a spotlight. The door isn't locked. I ease it open. Dad looks like he's dreaming and I wonder where he is. Maybe he's visiting yesterday, before his world was blown apart. I drop to all fours and crawl to the foot of their bed where I lie, like I used to when I was small. When I was curled up like a question mark at the end of their bed the dark couldn't hurt me. "Nothing bad is going to happen. I won't let it," Dad used to say, picking me up off the floor and returning me to my bed. Dad *used* to say ... I'm already thinking of him in the past tense.

Days pass in a blur. I don't go outside; the sun is too pushy, the sky too blue. I'm not sleeping well. I have this recurring dream. I'm at school and everyone is staring and pointing as I walk down the corridor. My arm is looped through Dad's and he's wearing a hospital gown flapping open at the back.

I cry a lot, mostly in bed. It feels wrong to break down in front of Dad. When I tell him I'm too tired to go to school he doesn't argue but he makes me do my homework and that's a relief. All those formulas and dates and words take up space in my brain. If I was him, I'd want to stay in bed all day. I'd want to sleep the disease away. But he's up every morning, dressed and ready for the day.

"You coming to the park?" he asks, but it isn't a question. "I'll grab the ball. You get dressed. Your brothers will meet us there."

He steers me back to my room and after that, to the park at the end of our street. The tears are gone and my father is back.

"I don't know why I got this disease," he says, picking up the soccer ball and packing his sadness away, "but I know how I want to spend the next six months." He sets the ball down. "I want to spend it with you guys."

He takes aim and sends the ball flying, past Tom who's nodding, tears hanging on his lids, and Jack who's standing guard at the goals. It misses by a mile but my father is smiling and this one is real.

I shake off my sadness. If Dad can do this, so can I. I'll cry later; when he's dead.

CHAPTER 3

NOW

"Shnitzel!" Dad says, lifting his plate from the table to inhale the smell of crumbed veal. My dad has a huge appetite, so it's not a slice, it's a stack.

"Impressive!" Tom says, admiring the slab. "What's the record? Three? Four?"

"Seven," Dad says, wiping crumbs from his mouth.

"Seven in under ten minutes." Mom passes the peas. "What was the name of the restaurant?"

"The Schnitzel Master." Dad smiles at the memory. "There was a prize for whoever could eat the most schnitzels in under ten minutes."

"Gross," I say.

"It was actually very professional. There were rules. If there was any food on the table or in your lap, you were disqualified. You weren't allowed to go to the bathroom in case you threw up. And it wasn't just the schnitzel you had to eat. There were sides – chips, sauerkraut, potato salad."

"And the liter of beer," Mom reminds him.

"What did you win?" I ask, feeling queasy.

"Nothing," Dad says, reaching for the mashed potato. "Eat more than anyone else and you got a free schnitzel."

Dad excuses himself from the table and returns with a bottle of red wine. It looks expensive. "No point saving it," he says, his smile so wide you can see his gums. He is joking about dying and everyone is laughing and then the laughter trails off and the tears start.

Dad pulls a handkerchief from his pocket and passes it to Mom. "Life's not always about the happily ever after," he says. "Sometimes it's just about living the best you can with what you've got. Sometimes it's just about not giving up." He smiles at Mom and she smiles back, a weak imitation. "I'm not going to lie in bed and cross days off a calendar. And neither will you guys. Lisa, on Monday you're going back to school." He plants a kiss on the top of my head. "Boys, no more days off university. You can visit at night and on weekends. I'm not going to let this disease ruin more than one life." He tries for a smile. "And I'm not going to spend the next six months crying. We have a lot to talk about. There are things you should know about my childhood." He blinks and clears his throat. "About what happened."

There's a long silence and then his words fill the room. "I want you to know who I am. I want you to know where I come from and what they did to us."

I can't hear what he says next because a bomb has gone off in my brain. My father wants to tell us who he is.

23

I know who you are, I want to say. *You're my dad, and soon you won't be, so I really, really don't want to spend our time talking about a past that's already dead. A past you kept secret. A past I never asked you about because we had a deal: I wouldn't ask and you wouldn't tell.* I don't remember the first time I asked Dad about the war. He must've clammed up or changed the subject. I don't remember him being angry but I must've known it was *the thing we didn't talk about.* And that was fine by me. I knew the story had a sad ending; I didn't have grandparents. There was a war and Dad had survived it and come to Australia. That's all I needed to know. All I *need* to know.

Secrets are never good and I'm just holding on here, so please let's not do this, I don't say, but my eyes must be telegraphing every word, because Dad has put down his fork and is reaching for my hand.

"One of my jobs as your dad is to tell you stories about my childhood." Dad hangs his head. "I never did that and now it's too late to show you where I grew up and why I left, but I can *tell* you those stories so one day you'll understand where you come from. I owe you that."

No, you don't, I think. *You don't owe us a sad story before you disappear. The past makes people sad and we have enough sad in our lives right now.*

Jack is six years older than me and Tom is four, so they say things like, "Of course, Dad," and "How should we do this?"

"You're here every Friday night for dinner," Dad picks up his fork and spears the last of his schnitzel, "so I was thinking we could start tonight and continue next Friday and we'll just keep going for as long as it takes? Let's meet in the living room in five minutes."

Everyone nods but as soon as Dad's left the room, I turn on Mom.

"Do we have to do this now? I'm supposed to be at Deb's."

"Your father is sick." Mom stares at me across the table. She doesn't use the word *dying*. "And this is something he wants to do." She sets her fork down. "This is not about *you* or what *you* want."

"No ... I know," I say, feeling terrible.

I know she's right but I just want to go to Deb's after dinner, like I always do. I want to spend Friday nights watching cheesy videos and reading trashy magazines and talking till three without feeling like I'm a terrible person for wanting to be with my friend. Dad said no more tears, and the only way I'm going to pull that off is if I get out of this house.

"No, I mean, does it have to be *Friday* nights?" I say, and Mom looks disappointed.

I look over at my brothers, hoping for support. They were as quick to leave after dinners as I was. As soon as dessert was done, we'd scatter – me to Deb's, Jack back to his flat to spend the night with his girlfriend and Tom to a pub near university that served cheap drinks.

Jack leaves the room and comes back with Dad's video recorder and an empty tape. "Is it okay if we tape this?"

Dad nods.

"Great idea," Tom says, shrugging off his leather jacket. "Lisa, do you still have that cassette recorder?"

I find a blank tape in my desk and write *Dad's story. Part 1. 28 October 1982* in tiny letters on the small rectangular sticker, knowing that as soon as I press record the door to my old life will slam shut.

Everyone has secrets but I have the feeling ours are worse than most.

Mom is sitting on the couch, sipping lukewarm tea from a small cracked cup. Her eyes are red. Dad is sitting next to her. They are holding hands. My parents are always holding hands, which is pretty embarrassing when you're in your fifties, but now it's just sad. Behind them, through the open window, the sky is flat and black. Tom is on the floor, long legs stretched out in front of him. I'm sitting on Dad's left. Jack is facing us, waiting for the story to begin, but story is the wrong word. This isn't going to be a once-upon-a-time and a happily-ever-after.

"It began with a …" My father shakes his head. "I was five when …" He starts and stops, struggling to work out where to begin, what words to use to make us understand. His eyes rake the room, looking for answers. "I don't know where to start. There's so much I haven't told you."

"Start at the beginning," Mom says. "Start with your childhood."

Tom grabs the cassette recorder from the table and presses record. Jack trains the video recorder on Dad's face. Soon a three-hour VCR tape is all we'll have of my father.

Dad nods and clears his throat and we wait for an introduction to a boy we've never met.

My dad looks nervous. My dad never looks nervous; I can't remember ever seeing him sweat. He loves an audience. But now he's pulling a handkerchief from his pocket and wiping the sweat from his upper lip.

"We don't have to do this," I say, offering us all a way out.

But Mom says, "I want to know. Please." It's the way she says it, begging almost, that gives her away. She doesn't know. Dad kept this a secret from her too.

Dad nods and wades into the past. "There were good times," he says, and I breathe out for what feels like the first time in a long time. I'm not ready for where my father is taking us and am thankful for this small reprieve.

"Eating apples dipped in honey to bring in the new year, hiking in the hills, finding two *kneidlach* in Mamme's chicken soup. It wasn't *all* bad," he says, shifting in his seat.

There are five of us in the room, more if you count the ghosts, and I wonder if it's Willie, Dad's dead brother, that he sees. I don't know much about Dad's past but I know he had a brother called Willie who died in the war. Tom was named after him – Tom William Keller.

"There were happy times," Dad says searching for a memory he can't pin down. "It's just, when I think back, all those happy times are crowded out by the bad times ... the hunger and lice, the smack of a fist –" his voice is so faint I have to lean forward to catch the next words, "– the knives and guns."

The words tumble out, new and terrifying. My dad is speaking, but I see a little boy who is scared and I realize I don't know my father – don't know him at all.

"Guns?" I say, blinking hard, and the boy retreats and my father comes back to us from far away.

Dad's face shuts down, and something inside him turns stony. When he opens his mouth to speak again it's without feeling. He tells the rest of the story from the outside looking in.

CHAPTER 4

THEN

I was a lonely kid. In Czechoslovakia, kids didn't play with Jews. They spat at us and called us dogs. I didn't look like the other boys. I thought that was why they picked on me. So one morning before school, after I was sure Tatte had left for work and Mamme was busy in the shop, I shoved my skullcap under my pillow and grabbed a pair of scissors.

I had *peyot* like my father and Tatte had shown me how to twirl the hair so it fell in spirals in front of my ears. He told me they brought us closer to God but all I saw in Mamme's mirror was a weapon kids used to wrench me from my chair and lead me around the schoolyard like a dog on a leash. I grabbed a curl and chopped it off, then quickly hacked off the second and ran to school.

They beat me up at lunchtime, like they always did. As soon as I stepped onto the soccer field, they tackled me to the ground. I wrapped my arms around my head and curled up tight. Someone kneed me in the head. Feet and fists battered my back. I can't remember my classmates' names or their faces, but I remember the taste of blood in my mouth, and the teachers who turned away and pretended not to see. Maybe it was my fault. The other Jewish kids warned me to stay inside. They said I was asking for trouble. They said I *was* trouble.

Tatte didn't punish me when he saw the cuts and bruises. He sat me down, and in his quiet way, tried to explain hatred. "Emil," he said, running his fingers through his beard, "you can change your clothes, your hair, even your name. It won't change anything. To the boys at school, to the rest of the world, you'll always be a Jew. You'll always be different."

He was proud of that difference. He hoped, one day, I would be too. I just wanted my turn on the soccer field. And I wanted Tatte to tell me to crack the boys' heads open, but he never did.

"This is not what I meant by being proud of your difference," he'd say looking up from his prayer book at a black eye or a blood nose. "You can't talk these people out of hating you. Not with your words or with your fists. This is just the way it is here. What matters is that you know you deserve better."

Tatte was right – I couldn't talk them out of hating me, couldn't stop them from hissing and spitting and booing – I just had to wait until they grew out of their meanness. In the meantime, I'd learn. They could pin me down and beat me up but they couldn't control what I knew. I was smart, smarter than the rest of them, and I worked twice as hard. Knowledge was my way out of that town and, more than anything, I wanted out.

I didn't know what I'd find if I stepped beyond the forests that skirted our village but I knew there were cities with paved roads and cars. There were buildings that touched the clouds and libraries bigger than our school. My primary teacher, Mr Lukacs, told me about the skyscrapers whenever he found me alone in the yard. His is the only name I remember and the only face I can bring into focus. Brown slicked-back hair. A moustache. Brown eyes. Maybe because he was kind.

Mr Lukacs also told me that my father had big plans for me. "You won't be here forever," he'd say. "Your tatte is saving to send you to university to study Law." Law! Tatte thought I was smart enough to be a lawyer. I pretended not to know, but from that day on, I studied doubly hard.

It wasn't hard keeping things from Tatte; he wasn't around much. Tatte bought and sold livestock and traveled the country to find the best horses and cows. And when he wasn't away, Tatte was at the synagogue hiring Hebrew tutors for the poorer children or settling petty arguments between our Jewish neighbors. In our village and the surrounding hamlets, Aaron Rosenfeld's word was law.

I missed him when he was away and longed for Friday to come around. On Fridays Tatte would come home, and when the first stars appeared in the sky, Mamme would bless the candles and Tatte would bless the wine, passing the cup between us so we could each sneak a sip.

There was always someone new at the table. In Porubka, you were either poor or very poor. We lived without gas or electricity. We drew our drinking water from one of the town's four wells and wore hand-me-downs, but we had a horse and cart and we wore shoes.

"We're luckier than most," my father would say, shuffling over to make room at the table for a hungry guest.

Mamme would set an extra plate but she'd always leave enough to pass me a secret second helping under the table. My brothers and sisters had legs like tree trunks and I was scrawny and in need of fattening up.

On Saturdays work and study were forbidden, so Willie and I were free to explore the forest or wade in the creek, catching trout. We'd raid the neighbors' plum trees or play stickball against the stable wall, returning just in time for lunch. Our house always smelled of freshly baked *challah*. The smell hid in the corners of the rooms. It clung to our clothes. It must've been lifted by the wind and carried downstream to the poorest parts of town because as soon as it hit the table there would be a knock at the door and Mamme would be handing not half the loaf, but all of it, to a toothless man or a woman in rags.

"There's enough for everyone," Mamme would say, tipping out the flour to knead another roll.

Mamme never sat down. She was either making dinner, darning socks, helping us with homework or tucking us into bed with a story or a song, and when she wasn't doing that, she was in our small general store, where she stocked the shelves with anything our neighbors couldn't make or grow.

Because our parents were busy we were expected to help. After school and on Sundays, after we studied with the Hebrew tutor, we were expected to chop wood to feed the fire, sweep out the house and roll up our sleeves to dig up dinner. It was my job to feed the animals. We had a horse to pull our cart, a cow for milk and a goat to keep the garden neat. I named them all and made them my friends, but the cow was my favorite.

Minulka was skinny and would vacuum anything from my open palm – eggs from the henhouse, leftover *matzo* balls, the sugar cubes I stole from the store when Mamme's back was turned. I was the youngest of five. My brothers and sisters were in high school in Ungvar, half a day away by horse and cart, so I told the cow all my secrets and she never laughed once, not even when I told her I was going to be a lawyer.

I saw things a ten-year-old boy shouldn't see, things I'll never be able to unsee. I saw soldiers force a family of five onto their hands and knees to lick the sidewalk clean. I saw them string a boy in an army uniform to a tree.

"You still feel sorry for those Jewish pigs?" they asked one of their own, winding a length of rope around his wrists. I heard the sickening snap of bone, ran around the corner and threw up.

I'd always fought to be noticed. Now, all I wanted was to be invisible. Walking to school and *shul*, between boots and batons and rifle butts, I tried to make myself small. I stopped fishing at the creek and spent more time at home.

I saw Tatte cry for the first time that year. He came home late one night, later than usual, his eyes swollen and red. My parents always spoke in whispers in Hungarian or Yiddish so I wouldn't understand, but I'd picked up a few words. His best friend, the kosher butcher, had been beaten to death for being out past curfew.

After that Mamme didn't allow me outside past dusk. I didn't argue. I was tired of pretending I didn't care when kids called me a filthy Jew. I was tired of feeling like I'd done something wrong, like *I* was wrong, because I was Jewish.

I thought when I turned twelve and started cadet training, things might change. We were all in it together, helping to win the war. I didn't realize *we* were the enemy. My classmates were given guns; I got an armband with a yellow star.

I hated that star. It was an angry yellow, the size of a fist, with the word *Jude* – Jew – scrawled across it. Seeing us branded made my classmates meaner, and braver. Kids who'd disappeared into class when the bigger boys hunted me down now joined the hunt for the yellow star.

I came home day after day with black eyes and split lips, thinking things would get better. Tatte told me they would. He told me to focus on my studies. If he was scared, he didn't show it. If he'd heard rumors about broken shop

34

windows and burning books, he didn't let on. If he knew about the deportations, he never told.

"It's okay to be scared," Willie would say, curling my hands into fists. "Just don't let them *see* your fear." He'd bob and weave around the garden, pointing to his chin. "Aim here," he'd say. "If you land the first punch, you'll have time to run."

A week before I turned thirteen, Tatte took me to Ungvar to be fitted for a suit. I climbed onto Tatte's work-cart and patted Bessa.

"If you want that new suit, we'd better get moving." Tatte handed me the reins.

I'd never been allowed to steer the horse. I cracked the worn leather straps before Tatte could change his mind and Bessa lurched forward.

After a while, Tatte closed his eyes and asked me to sing my bible portion, just as I'd sing it for the congregation on my *bar mitzvah*. I sang the first prayer, my voice shaky, and then my father smiled, so I sang some more. I sang all the way to Ungvar, steering Bessa home four hours later, a brown paper package resting between us. Tatte didn't talk on the way home; he sat with his prayer book open on his lap. I didn't mind. My head was buzzing with everything I'd seen – the tubs of buttons in the tailor's shop, the streets choked with people, and Ungvar Castle, four storeys high, looming over the River Uzh.

I don't remember much of my actual birthday. I don't remember if I was nervous singing my *haftorah*. I don't know if the synagogue was crowded, but I remember where I sat, squeezed between Tatte and Willie. If that synagogue was still standing today, I could go straight to our seats. Walking to synagogue with Tatte every Friday, dodging the rocks our neighbors hurled, I'd close the heavy wooden doors behind us and sink into my seat. Aside from home, it was the one place where I felt safe and loved. The room was cold and the wooden bench seats hard, but I could sit there for hours, feeling important just being near Tatte. He'd concentrate more on his prayers than on me, but sometimes he'd draw me close and let me warm my hands in his pocket. And if I prayed hard, and sat very still, he'd smile at me, a lopsided half-smile, and call me by my pet-name, Elyuka.

The next time he used that name – Elyuka – it was March 1944, the last night of Passover. Mamme was with my sisters, Dita and Sari, washing the Passover dishes in the creek when the Hungarian officers pounded at our door. My oldest brother, Max, had been gone for months, ordered to dig ditches on the Russian front, but Willie and I were home. Tatte sent me to my room.

"What is it, Tatte? Is it about Max?" I crept into the kitchen as soon as the soldiers left.

Tatte was holding a piece of paper. He looked so sad.

"It's an order, Elyuka." He grabbed Willie's shoulder to steady himself. "It's from the Hungarian Military Command. We have to gather at the synagogue tomorrow.

36

We're going on a trip. Now run, get your mother."

Tatte had called me Elyuka. We weren't in *shul* and I hadn't done anything to make him proud. Something bad was about to happen.

"We have to be at the synagogue at 8 am," Tatte said when I returned with Mamme and my sisters.

Mamme started crying and pulling things out of draws – plates and cups, pots and pans. Tatte dragged a bag into the kitchen and I stood in the doorway watching Mamme fill it with potatoes and jars of duck fat and left over *cholent*. She was running from one corner of the kitchen to the other, snatching things up and putting them down again – tablecloths and candlesticks and rugs and books.

Tatte stood in the corner of the room bent over his prayerbook.

"We should leave," Willie said. "Tonight. Once it's dark. We can avoid the main road and head through the forest."

"It's too dangerous," Tatte said, eyes returning to his prayer book.

"How do we know what's out there isn't *more* dangerous?" Willie tore the book from Tatte's hands. "You have money. We can pay someone."

Tatte gently pried the prayer book from Willie's clenched fists. He didn't raise his voice or send Willie to his room.

"No-one will hide us. It's too risky and even if they could," he shrugged, "where would they hide six of us? And how would they account for all the extra food? Go pack, Willie, and take Emil with you. Get some sleep."

I didn't have much to pack. A few pairs of underwear, pyjamas, a shirt. I pulled my *bar mitzvah* suit from its hanger and folded it into my bag. I'd heard whispers in *shul* about Jews being sent to work. If I looked smart and showed the German officers my report card, maybe they'd put me to work in an office.

I woke early the next day. In the half-light I could see Tatte still praying. I padded to the kitchen where Mamme was bent over the stove cooking sugar into cubes.

"Sit. Eat." She lifted a slice of veal from a pan and slid it onto a plate with some beans and a carrot.

I wasn't hungry. Dita didn't have a smile for me, Sari looked terrified and Mamme had pulled my soccer ball from my bag.

"Why do we have to leave?" I blurted. Tatte's head was down, his eyes half-closed. "And what about Minu?"

Tatte didn't look up. I tore through the back door, across the garden, panting when I reached the stable. We couldn't just leave her here, not like this. I pressed my cheek to her swollen flank and ran a hand across her belly.

"She'll be okay." I turned at the sound of Willie's voice. "Cows give birth all the time." He dragged a bucket of water and a bin of hay into Minu's stall. "We'll see her again." He clamped a hand on my shoulder and guided me back to the house. "And you'll meet her calf and we'll name it together, soon as we get back."

"And how long with *that* be?" I stepped into the kitchen and turned to my father. "When will we be allowed back?"

"In a few days, God willing." Tatte zipped up a bag.

Mamme stared at the pantry shelves, at the bottled jams and boxes of teas. "I need more time." She pulled a jar of pickles from the shelf, put it back, then picked up a hairbrush.

"Can I take my schoolbooks?"

Tatte shook his head. "We're only allowed one bag each." I waited for him to tell me not to worry, to say that God had a plan, but he just smiled a sad smile, stuffed his prayerbook into his pocket and lifted a suitcase from the floor. "We'll lock the house up and your books will be here, exactly where you left them."

I forgot about maths and Minu as soon as we rounded the corner and saw the town square swarming with people. Mamme took my hand. There were guards holding guns and officers on horseback and they were shouting and forcing everyone into a line. Mamme dragged me forward. Her hands were clammy and her hair clung to her face in matted strips.

"We mustn't lose Tatte!" she said, hurrying to catch up to him.

All the Jewish families in our village were there, coats half-buttoned, loaded down with bags – the cobbler, the fishmonger, the toolmaker and the hatter. Small children hung onto their mothers' coats; older kids tried to look brave. We found Tatte standing in line behind the fishmonger's wife.

"I need another blanket," she complained to the fishmonger when the baby she was cradling began to cry.

Tatte reached into a bag and pulled out his prayer shawl. "For the little one," he whispered.

"Emil!" I heard a familiar voice call out. "Emil! Over here!"

I swung around to see Mr Lukacs pushing through the crowd, an officer on his heels. He was staring straight at me and waving something in the air. A book.

"*Halt! Geh nicht weiter!*" A uniformed guard pulled his gun from its holster and Mr Lukacs froze, his eyes still on me.

I pictured the young Hungarian officer in his ragged uniform, swinging from a tree by his wrists, and ran. I found Willie at the back of the line and slumped down next to him. A man holding a bowl of half-finished soup nudged me with his shoe.

"Keep moving," he said, "or we'll all get shot."

"We're all going to die anyway." An old woman hauling a bucket of milk stopped behind us.

"Lower your voice!" Tatte appeared. "There are children here." He reached out a hand and hauled me to my feet.

We found Mamme, Sari and Dita at the front of the line, which I could now see snaked its way toward three open-air trucks. A bent man with a silver beard stood at the steps of the truck, his head bowed in prayer.

"*Los! Schnell!*" A soldier in a black SS uniform pointed a gun at the man's head.

The old man didn't look up; he didn't move. A wet circle darkened the front of his pants but he went on praying. Tatte pushed through the crowd, took the man's arm and lifted him onto the truck. Mamme hurried forward, tears coursing down her cheeks.

I slipped my hand into hers and lied to her for the first time. "Don't be sad, Mamme," I whispered, "it'll be fun on the truck."

CHAPTER 5

NOW

I've never met my grandparents or my Uncle Willie. Until now. What am I supposed to do with them? I don't know these people. And it's *their* sad story, not mine. It's not even Dad's. It's too far back in the past, all of it happening to a boy I don't know. A boy with a yellow star and blood on his jumper, a boy who's climbing onto a truck headed somewhere bad.

I should say something now that Dad has stopped talking, but no words come. Outside the moon disappears behind cloud. Someone turns on a light. Mom slips from the couch and walks to the bathroom. I hear water running, then her soft footsteps padding back to us. She passes my father a glass of water and waits for him to drain it.

"Why didn't you tell us before?" Jack lowers the video recorder.

"I didn't want you to be marked by my memories. I mean, how do you explain hate to a six year old? How can a kid understand what I went through? *I* still can't fathom it. And I didn't want you to."

I pick up a pen and scribble a few words on the pad Tom dropped into my lap when we first sat down. I was supposed to get Dad's words down in case the recording stuffed up. I write: *Yellow star. Cattle train.* I don't write: *You must have been scared. I'm scared too.* I don't want to see my father's soft side. I need him to be strong, to keep being him ... until he's not.

"When you got on that truck," Tom says, "did you know where you were headed?"

Dad shakes his head. "Maybe I should have, but my parents spoke in whispers. We didn't have a radio or newspapers. Mamme kept the curtains drawn and Tatte had God on his side. He told us hate was like a storm; you just had to keep your head down and wait for it to pass."

"Rosenfeld," Jack says, confused. "You said your father's name was Aaron Rosenfeld, but we're Kellers?"

"I changed it," Dad says.

"Changed your name?" It's the first thing I've said since we sat down. "What do you mean *changed* it?" I feel like I'm suffocating. Like my name is a lie. I'm not Lisa Keller. I'm Lisa Rosenfeld. Lisa *Rosenfeld.* I stare at Dad.

"I changed my name," Dad says, like it's no big deal, "but that's another story, for another night. I think I'll head to bed." Dad shakes off the memories and kisses us goodnight.

I watch Mom and Dad walk from the room, holding hands, her head on his shoulder. Jack pulls the video tape from the recorder.

"It's probably safer if we leave these here." He hands me the recording. "I'll pick up some spare tapes before next Friday."

Tom grabs his keys. "That was heavy, but so much makes sense now."

I stare at him. "Like what?" *Like why Dad forgot to mention our last name was a lie?*

"Like why Dad was so disappointed when we quit soccer and how he's always going on about how lucky we are to go to university."

Jack nods. "And that weirdo smile he got from his father."

My brothers look at me. I can feel my face burn. I have the same hand-me-down half-smile. And I hate it. At least I *did*, until Adam told me it was one of the things he liked best about me. "It's like you don't want to rub your happiness in people's faces," he'd said, "so you turn down the wattage. Like last week when you got that A+ in English Lit. You do it every time I say you're beautiful."

"And the curfews," I say, because I shouldn't be thinking of Adam's arms or his mouth.

My brothers' faces are blank. "Curfew?" Tom says. "What curfew? We never had one."

"*You* never had one. *I* have to be home by ten."

It wasn't because my brothers were older; it was because they were boys. The male species has an easier time in our house. I know it's not because Dad loves my brothers more. I'm his *little piece of pineapple*. But I'm a girl and that means helping Mom with the dishes and *we're having a conversation, young lady* when I'm caught kissing Adam in the living room, but an arm slung over a shoulder and a proud smile when Jack lost his virginity at the same age. It means never being asked my opinion at the dinner table. And it hurts.

"Makes sense," Tom says, and I hurl a cushion at his head. "No, I mean the curfew and why Dad didn't want Mom to go back to work until we were all in school and why he ran for council, why he wanted to be mayor."

"Just like Tatte," Jack says.

"I get it," I say. "It doesn't mean I have to like it."

Deb's not answering the phone so I head to my room, tip my Converse High Tops from their box and throw Dad's tapes in, wondering what it's like to dig up all the smashed pieces of a life.

A few hours later I'm still not sleeping so I drag the shoebox out from under my bed, grab the videotape, shove it into the recorder and press play.

Dad's face fills the screen. I search for the scrappy boy my father described – an eight year old with a purple bruise on his cheek. I can almost see the grazes and the cut on his top lip but I can't make out his eyes or his gap-toothed grin. That boy didn't grow into my dad. That kid was broken; my dad is invincible. He doesn't walk into a room, he fills it. He doesn't speak, he booms. He is the *opposite* of invisible.

45

I wake up to a washed-out blue sky, to the same yellow and orange trippy wallpaper, the same shaggy brown rug. I want to slide my feet into my Reeboks, pull on a pair of shorts and go for a run, but I'm staring at the walls and thinking about Dad waking up in this house he built twenty-seven years ago, this house he will die in.

I force myself out of bed, pull on my shorts and duck out the back door and I know it's stupid but I'm surprised by the trees; that they still exist. The sun is dangling in the sky and people are talking and laughing and I want to scream, *Don't you know my dad is dying?* But I don't because:

1. The thought of people seeing me meltdown makes me break out in hives.

2. Someone might actually *ask* me what's wrong, and then ...

3. I'd have to tell them. And now it's not just Dad's disease. It's his beyond-awful childhood and the fake name and the fact that I now have grandparents and an uncle, and they're *all* going to die.

I don't scream, I run. And after that, there's a tennis lesson and piano practice, which Dad won't let me skip, and honestly, I don't mind. When I'm practising scales or lobbing the ball over the net, I don't have to sit at the kitchen table and listen to Dad's friends tell him how unfair this all is and how anything would be better – a heart attack or a car accident – than this slow death he's facing. I can't handle the women's wet kisses and the men's sad eyes. Neither can Dad.

"Sorry," he tells them, "I promised Lisa a driving lesson." He grabs Mom's keys.

"So, that wasn't just a ruse to escape the hugs and the hand-holding?" I ask, fixing a Learner plate to the windscreen. "We *are* driving today?"

Dad nods and reaches for the seatbelt. "I'm probably not the best person for the job, but let's give it a crack."

I swing the car onto the street. It's Saturday afternoon, the shops are closed, so the roads are quiet. "What do you mean you're not the best person?"

"Well," Dad laughs, "it's not like I don't *have* my licence, it's just that ... back in the fifties, they did things a little differently."

"Differently?"

"Let's just say I didn't have a lot of lessons before I sat the test."

I raise an eyebrow.

"Your Uncle Carl taught me."

I don't have any uncles, at least not in Australia, so Dad's friends became our uncles and aunts, their kids my cousins.

"He taught me in a weekend rental, driving circles around a carpark. I sat the test the next day. I mounted the kerb twice and went the wrong way down a one-way street. The cop sitting next to me made me pull over. 'Well, you obviously can't drive,' he said. 'Lessons are two pounds each. You'll need at least ten, but how about we save everyone a lotta trouble? Instead of paying twenty pounds to a driving instructor, pay me the twenty, and I'll pass you on the spot.'"

Dad points to the fuel gauge. It's close to empty. "Let's stop at the next gas station and I'll show you how to fill up." He doesn't say, *Because I won't be here to teach you once you start driving on your own.* Instead he says, "When I bought my first car, I *still* had no idea how to do a three-point turn or park the thing, so I asked Carl to pick it up from the car yard for me. I must have washed that car ten times before I got the guts to drive it out of the garage."

He lets me park the Mazda in the carport next to his Honda. "So, we're still good to drive on Saturdays?" I ask. Religious Jews don't drive on Saturdays. I know this because Dad's friend Mark is religious and Dad explained the driving thing when I asked why Mark never came to the football.

Dad nods.

"So, you're *not* planning on becoming religious and growing a beard?"

"No," Dad laughs, and I slump back in my seat, but then I remember the name ...

"We're not changing our name back to Rosenfeld, are we?" I have to ask. "Because that would be *really* complicated at school. They'd have to change the class lists and I'd have to rename all my books."

Dad shakes his head. My smile must be a thousand watts because Dad says, "Your grandmother had a smile like yours that lit up the dark." He swings the car door open. "You know I named you after her?"

"What?" I say, my heart beating hard. *Was Lisa a lie, too?*

"Pepi." Dad smiles. "It's your Hebrew name."

My smile sags and his does too, and I know what he's thinking: *To the kids at school, to the rest of the world, you'll always be a Jew. You'll always be different. Be proud of that difference.* What he doesn't know – and what I can't tell him, not now, not after the story he's told – is that no-one at school knows I'm Jewish, not even Deb. It's not that I'm hiding anything; it just hasn't come up. I mean I'm not *really* Jewish. I don't go to synagogue or keep the Sabbath. I go to a public school and I eat pork. But now I have a Hebrew name. And a grandfather who is practically a rabbi.

We sit at the water's edge, the white sand like a smile hugging the water.

"I used to come here all the time when I first came to Australia. It's where I took your mom on our first date."

I should *want* to hear this happy story, but I'm tired of stories so I change the subject. "Who wants a swim?"

Dad gets to his feet, tugs off his T-shirt and walks to the water's edge.

Tom dives headfirst into the break but Dad stays in the shallows, his arms already thinned by the disease. Mom takes photos – Dad walking, Dad smiling, Dad waving at her – and we have lunch. We don't talk about Friday night. We don't mention the truck and where it's headed. Instead, Dad wants to know where we see ourselves in ten years.

"I'm thinking about specializing," Jack says. "Maybe surgery."

"And Sharon?" Dad asks. "Is it serious?"

"We've only just moved in together ..." Jack squirms. "Maybe."

Dad waits and Jack gives in. He's going to have to do this. We all are. "We'll probably end up together, and in ten years I'll be, what, thirty-two, so, yeah, maybe we'll be married and have a kid or two."

Dad's smile stretches from ear to ear. "What about you, Tom?"

"A job in medicine," Tom says. "I'm thinking in a hospital, maybe paediatrics? Hopefully by then I'll have saved enough to put a deposit down on a house." He's on a roll. "Somewhere near you guys, close to Mom."

Dad is beaming. It's easy for my brothers to tell Dad their plans. They're both studying medicine. They've both moved out. I'm in 10th Grade.

"Your turn." Dad looks at me. "Weren't you planning on traveling with Deb after you finish school?"

I nod.

"Her uncle has a van, right?"

I'm so awed by the fact that Dad actually remembers our plans to convert Mr Cartman's old work van into a luxury five-star hotel on wheels that I forget what *this* is, this crystal-balling a future Dad won't live to see, and I start babbling. About the van and the beaches we'll sleep on and the places we'll see. I have no idea where I'll be in ten years but I hear myself say, "And after that, I'm thinking about studying Law."

"Do you want me to drop you at school?" Mom hands me a piece of toast and scoops her keys from the bench.

"No, that's okay." I shake my head. "I'll walk with Deb."

I'm not ready for the circus. I want to turn up to school late to avoid the hellos and the air kisses and the where-were-you-Saturday-nights but Deb has drama first period and she's the lead in the school play so she wants to get there before the bell. Drama is the only elective we're not doing together. I don't do drama because I don't *do* drama and the thought of emoting up on stage in front of an audience makes me want to throw up my breakfast.

The doorbell rings. I pull my backpack on and sweep Dad's pills and bottles of herbal medicines from the kitchen table into a drawer.

"Hey, Mrs Keller!" I hear Deb say. "Just here to pick up Lisa."

"Hey." I sprint from the kitchen. "I'm ready. Let's go."

But Deb is standing in the hallway with her hands on her hips. She's wearing an electric blue shirt-dress and slouchy boots. Her hair is huge. Disco-queen huge.

"So, what do you think?" She struts down the corridor, spins and sashays back. "It was either this or pastel tights and pink leg warmers. Mom killed it this year with the birthday presents. Even got the Jane Fonda workout video. Hey, Mr K." Deb flashes my dad a sympathetic smile. "Hope you're feeling better."

"Bye, Dad!" I say, dragging Deb out the door, relieved

when she says, "So, what did my bestie get me for my birthday?"

"Here," I say, pulling out a mixed tape. "It's all your favorites – Donna Summer, The Go-Go's, The Pointer Sisters."

"Oh my God! I *love* their new song!" She grabs the tape and shoves it into her Walkman, and I think, *Why did I give it to her here, where everyone can see us?* But I laugh, because this is Deb being Deb, jiggling her hips and shimmying down the sidewalk, singing song lyrics at the top of her voice.

An old man wheeling out his trash can looks up. A woman pushing a pram stops. Two boys cycling past wolf-whistle but Deb can't hear them. I reach for the Walkman and hit stop.

"There's one more thing." I hand her a photo album.

There's a picture on the cover of the two of us in 7th Grade wearing white rollerskates and matching denim jumpsuits, but inside it's glitter and love hearts and Hollywood hunks torn from our favorite magazine.

"Oh my God! Rob Lowe!" Deb plants a pink kiss on Rob's cheek. "He's got a movie coming out. Can you imagine that face on the big screen, up close? I am going to die!" She grabs my arm. "Literally, die. There's–" but I don't hear what she says next because *why does my dad have to go and die?*

I try not to look like I've just been smacked across the head with a textbook. If only I could time travel back to last week, the day before the disease planned its attack, when all I had to worry about was getting an A on my Maths test and how I could sneak Adam into our family room without my parents finding out.

"I love it!" Deb says, cramming the album into her bag and slinging an arm around my shoulder.

And then we're at school and it's too late to tell her about Dad. Or the war.

"Gotta bounce! See you in History!" Deb shoves her bag into her locker and runs to beat the bell.

I throw my locker open and snatch up Deb's shriveled balloons, wishing I could climb inside and hide in the cool dark, but the bell's ringing and I don't want to walk in late.

Mr Harrison, my Maths teacher, must be seventy. He has hair growing out of his ears and wrinkles like lines on a map. It takes him half a day to walk between our desks to hand back our assignments. He's got decades on my dad. I stare straight at him and focus hard on his words, wishing he'd talk louder than the voice in my head that's asking, *Why Dad? Why not him?*

Next class is History and I'm sitting next to Deb, and she's passing me notes like nothing has changed even though I'm about to lose a dad. I look around the room and kids are laughing and joking and doodling on their textbooks and the classroom looks exactly the same as it always does, and I can finally breathe because the ALS-monster lives at home, not here at Glenrock High.

"You like?" Deb is holding out her hand, her fingernails orange from polish. We're sitting at our usual table in the middle of the cafeteria.

The dipsticks who have the table next to us are still giving the new Vietnamese girl a hard time. "Hey, *flied lice*," they call out to her, pulling out their pens and holding them like chopsticks. "What's for lunch?"

"Psychos," Deb says, turning back to her nails. "So, what do you think?"

"Very glam."

I pull my Vegemite sandwich from my lunchbox and take a bite. I learned the rules early. Lunch should contain a white bread:

A. Vegemite sandwich

B. peanut butter sandwich, or

C. cheese and lettuce sandwich.

Preferably in a lunchbox. A paper bag means you're poor. It's the same for jeans. Wear bogus Kmart denim and no-one will speak to you, except other kids in the Fraternity of Sad Jeans.

"But you love *cholent*," Mom said the first time I returned home with a full lunchbox. "I just want a Vegemite sandwich and a cheese stick," I told her. "No more *cholent* or pickles."

Karen and Tracey slide into the seats we've saved for them. Tracey's crimped blonde hair is pulled back into plaits but her fringe sticks straight up, battling gravity.

"Whoa!" Deb says, laughing with her head tipped back. "How much hair gel did *that* take? And as for you,

Miss K ..." She reaches out to touch Karen's new short, feathered hair. "Very Princess Di!"

"Really?" Karen beams. "I couldn't decide whether to leave it long like Brooke Shields, or go royal ..."

"What's up?" Tracey says, popping a pink Hubba Bubba bubble. "You missed most of last week, Lis. You okay?"

The three of them turn to look at me. *My father isn't dying*, I tell myself. *The doctors didn't sit him down and tell him he has six months left to live, because my father is not dying.*

"I'm good," I say, blinking hard. I'm not going to tell Deb or Karen or Tracey. Not until I have to. I've never dumped anything on them before and I don't want their pitying looks and their sad words. People are scared of sick, and they're scared of sad, and I don't want Deb calling Karen or Tracey for advice about boys because I have *bigger things to worry about*. Or because, if she calls me, she won't know what to say.

"Dad had the flu and then I got sick. I'm totally fine now. Oh, look!" I jump up. "There's Adam! Gotta go."

Adam is standing against the wall, feet crossed at the ankles, laughing at something Paul is saying like he doesn't have a care in the world, like nothing bad has ever, or *will* ever, happen to him, and I wonder if I'll ever be as casual as that again, just standing around making conversation.

"Hey," I say, and Paul turns to leave.

"Hey, you!" Adam smiles, all dimples and teeth.

He scoops his hair out of his eyes and there it is, that flash of green; those eyes. And those black, blinking lashes. And for the millionth time I think, *No-one looks good in a school uniform. How does he pull it off?*

Adam wraps his arms around my waist, his face so close to mine, I can smell the Juicy Fruit on his breath. And I let him. Here in the cafeteria, where everyone can see us. I'm not into public displays of affection, so this is big.

"Looks like you missed me," he says, and he smiles that killer smile and he has no idea that my father is dying and *by the way I'm Jewish and I'm sorry I didn't say anything but I come from a long line of secret-keepers.*

"Looks like you missed me too," I say, grabbing his hand.

We wander into the corridor and lean against the lockers. He wants to kiss me, but he won't because he knows I'm not the kind of girl who'll let herself be kissed in front of the entire student body of Glenrock High. So *I* kiss *him*. Because kissing Adam Winter is like having a zillion butterflies inside you and because kissing him is my best chance at forgetting. So I kiss him harder and for a moment the world stops and I'm not the girl whose father is dying. I'm just a girl, kissing a boy.

The bell rings and we pull apart.

"Suppose we've got to go," he says, looking puppy-dog sad.

He has no idea what sad feels like.

Deb talks the entire way home from school and I like how her words beat back the noise in my head. It's easy with Deb. She talks and I listen.

"I hear things were hotting up in the hallway today? Damn." She laughs and throws back her head, her ponytail bouncing. "I can't believe I missed the action. I want a play-by-play!"

I blush, tell her it was nothing, and ask her about her latest crush.

"Hey! Earth to Lisa." Deb is standing in front of me, waving her hands in front of my face. "Where did you go? I mean, I know I do most of the talking but when I mention a new boy's name I normally get a grilling." She pouts, sticking out her bottom lip.

"Sorry," I say, swimming up from the dark. "Tall or short?"

"Tall."

"Blond or dark?"

She cocks her head and waits. I *know* her type.

"Okay, so he's blond," I say.

She nods.

"11th Grade?"

"Twelfth."

I keep her busy with questions until we get to the bit where she says this boy is the most beautiful human she's ever laid eyes on. And then we're at my gate and Dad is at the front door, pulling his keys from his pocket. Deb waves.

"Good to see you're feeling better, Mr K!"

"Good to see you too, Deborah."

Dad waits for me so we can walk inside together. He wants to know how school was.

"Fine," I say. "I got an A minus on my History project." I grab a juice box and stab it with a straw.

"Deb doesn't know, does she?" Dad rests a hand on my shoulder.

I don't look up at him.

"You can tell your friends, Lisa. It's not a secret."

And now I'm angry, because who the hell is he to talk about secrets? My dad has lied to me his entire life. And now he's coming clean. *Now*, when he can't stick around for the fallout. I shake off his hand, tramp up the stairs, fling myself onto my bed and turn the music up loud.

"You can't ignore your dad back to health," Mom says the next day. "We don't have forever, so you have to take whatever he's offering you now."

She's right about the disease. It's not going away. But I can ignore it. I can go to school. I can do my homework. I can practice piano and do laps of the park. I can study for exams. And I can kiss Adam Winter until the anger wanes and the big feeling that took up all the space in my chest is just a small stone I carry around.

And then it's Friday and Mom is making chicken soup and Dad drives to Carlisle Street to pick up a *challah*. The kitchen table is dressed in a tablecloth and there's a pair of silver candlesticks on the table next to a small silver cup. Tom arrives for dinner first, kicking off his Converse and pouring himself a beer. Then Jack joins us and we all sit down. Mom strikes a match and bends to light the candles.

So, we're doing the Jewish thing now? The *challah*, the candles, the wine, the prayers. Isn't this what got Dad into trouble in the first place? I'm not big on religion. I get that people in the Dark Ages had to reach for something to explain a world they couldn't understand, but now we have science. All religion seems to do is separate people.

Dad runs a hand across his bristled chin. I've never seen him with the beginnings of a beard. It makes him look older and I wonder if his arms are already betraying him; if his hands are too weak to run a razor across his face. He picks up the cup of wine and mombles something in Hebrew that I don't understand and the others begin to eat. I just move the food around on my plate.

"Let's sit in the living room," Dad says after dinner.

Jack tears the packaging from a new videotape and Tom picks up my cassette recorder.

Dad's smile slips. "I think when I finished up last time we were being herded onto a truck?"

CHAPTER 6

THEN

I didn't mind living in the brick factory at first. As long as you stayed away from the fence and the prowling Hungarian guards you could walk around without being afraid that some kid who was bigger than you would pin you to the ground and take a slug at your head. We were dirty, we stank, we slept in our clothes, but we were all Jews. So for the first time in my life I didn't feel different. I was part of something – something awful – but I wasn't alone.

And then the food ran out and people got sick and every so often someone would walk past pushing a wheelbarrow and I'd see an arm or a leg poking out. More trucks came to the brick factory, and with them more Jews. You had to be careful walking around. Everywhere you looked there were pots and pans and clothes and toys and old people without teeth and kids with grimy faces. I was always tripping over someone's feet or coming to a sliding stop in front of a body lying in the dirt. The guards weren't so careful. They stomped on beds and shook out blankets and bags. They slit pillows with their knives and overturned pots searching for jewelry and money. I once saw them punch a man in the mouth to get his gold tooth.

Mamme cried a lot. She cried when she had to give up her winter coat, the one with her wedding ring sewn into a shoulder pad. She cried when she saw Tatte stripped to the waist, washing himself over a bowl of soapy water. She cried when she opened her bag and found that all we had left was one piece of cheese and a pickled cucumber. But mostly she cried at night in Tatte's arms.

Willie had found us a disused brick kiln to sleep in. Mamme smoothed a rug over the cement floor and we curled up under a woolen blanket that still smelled of home. I tried to sleep but it was cold in the kiln, with its roof blasted open and bricks scattered everywhere, and I didn't have a pillow and I could hear people groaning and begging for food. One night I heard Mamme whisper to Tatte: "We've been here for weeks." Her voice dipped and I had to listen hard to catch what she said next. "I think they mean for us to stay here, Aaron. I think they mean for us to –"

I rolled over and pulled the blanket over my head. I didn't want to hear my mother say we were going to die.

Tatte prayed day and night. Sometimes I slipped my hand into his and stood next to him, pretending to pray. It was hard to stay hopeful. There were more bodies in wheelbarrows, more people who'd rushed at the barbed wire and been shot. You couldn't escape the sound of babies crying. Everyone was hungry. One day Willie disappeared with Mamme's candlesticks and came back an hour later with a loaf of bread.

The next time he slipped away I followed him, past a man sobbing into his prayer book and a woman in her underwear, until I stopped just feet from a stretch of barbed wire where a makeshift market had been set up. There were no tables, just a mess of blankets on the ground covered with precious objects that people living in a ghetto had no use for – clocks, mirrors, silverware, prams.

Willie sat down in the dirt and held out Mamme's gold hatpin. A woman plucked it from his hand and dropped two plums into his lap. The next day he traded Mamme's crystal vase for a boiled egg and a slice of roast veal. I think Tatte realized how he came by the food when our tablecloth went missing, but he didn't say anything, not until Willie mentioned the rumors about men escaping.

"The escapes – they are just gossip." Tatte marched Willie behind the kiln. "It's giving people false hope. We're surrounded. Every inch of that fence is patrolled."

"Not at night," I heard Willie say. "There's less of them then. I could volunteer for one of the crews that pack up Jewish valuables, get my hands on some garden shears. We could cut the wire and squeeze through. We'd be safe in Ungvar. We have blue eyes, we could pass as *goyim* if you shave your beard."

"I forbid it." Tatte's voice was steely.

"You forbid it?"

"Willie," Tatte said, his voice softer now. "I've been meeting with the other village leaders. They know things."

"What things?"

"Well, like the fences are lit up at night and if anyone goes near them the army has orders to shoot." I heard footsteps and saw Willie and Tatte standing at the opening to the kiln. Tatte had his hands on Willie's shoulders. "And also," he said, trying for a smile, "the war will be over soon. The Russians are close."

After three weeks at the brick factory we were told to pack our bags. I knew we weren't going home. Willie was convinced we were being sent to work camps.

Tatte shook his head. "If they were putting us to work, why would they take babies and old men? No," Tatte said, "they need to stay a step ahead of the Russians, that's all. They'll move us to another ghetto, the Russians will win the war and you'll be back in Porubka, to celebrate the end of the school year."

I wanted to believe him. It was the middle of May. I'd missed three weeks of school, but I was smart. I could catch up.

They marched us through the gates of the brickyard, a snaking line of Jews – thousands of us – hauling suitcases and sacks. We traveled lighter this time; no dishes or valuables. Instead of food, we walked out with the crumbs in our pockets. I was tired and thirsty but I didn't complain. There was nothing Tatte or God could do to make the guards put down their guns. Mamme started singing a folk song, but I didn't join in. We needed more than songs and empty promises to make it back home. Maybe if Mamme had spat on her hand and wiped the dirt from my face or pulled out a comb I might have believed her when she sang of better times. Mamme had never let me out of the house without patting down my hair and tucking in my shirt, so I knew we were headed somewhere bad.

We stopped at a railway shunting. The guards shouted something and everyone dropped their bags.

"Leave your bags on the platform," Tatte whispered. "They'll load them on another train."

I looked around. There weren't any trains, just wooden cattle cars. I stepped into line behind Tatte and we inched forward slowly, staring at the planks of flaking wood and the worn floorboards. The people who had climbed in before us were crammed inside, standing shoulder to shoulder, their eyes huge. There were no seats and no windows, just a bucket on the floor.

I stumbled forward, confused. "Surely they don't mean for us to –" I began, but the swell of the line carried me up and in, after my parents.

Dita, Sari and Willie piled in after us, and others, too, dozens of other people, pressing us against the walls. The cattle car groaned and when they couldn't stuff any more of us in, the guards closed the door and bolted it shut from the outside. It was pitch black – so dark you couldn't make out faces – and deathly quiet, until a kid started crying. She was begging her mother to turn on the lights. I was scared too but I didn't admit it. Willie had told me it was okay to be scared, as long as I didn't let anyone *see* my fear. I figured it was time I started practicing.

I reached out, feeling into the black space around me. "Tatte, is that you?"

An elbow dug into my back. "Mamme, where are you?"

Someone's fingers grazed my face. There was a jolt and the train began to move. I shut my eyes and tried to focus on the rhythmic pounding of the wheels to stop myself wondering where we were headed and when we'd go home. I didn't want to think about how thirsty I was or how I'd sleep standing up. And what was that smell?

I remember when it dawned on me that the bucket in the corner must be the toilet. I shoved my way to the corner of the wagon, took my pants down and crouched over it. After a few days I didn't bother. I was too weak to push my way through the wall of bodies. I went where I stood. The smell was awful. But it wasn't just that. It was armpits and vomit, and after a day or two without water or food, the stink of dead bodies. I slept on one, after Willie checked for a pulse and declared the man dead. I didn't know if he was a stranger or a family friend and

I didn't care. I was tired and weak and his belly was softer than the floor.

There was nothing to do in the carriage except stare at the railway tracks through the worn floorboards and listen to people bicker. By the second day the carriage had grown quiet, the silence occasionally broken by loud sobs and people pounding on the door, begging to be let out. Willie stood in the corner of the wagon reaching up toward the roof.

"What are you doing?" I asked him.

Ever since I was a kid, I was *always* asking what he was doing or where he was going, and could I come. He was five years older than me – so much smarter and braver – but he never said no, never told me to leave him alone or go play with kids my own age.

Willie hoisted me onto his back. "See those slats?" he said, pointing to a row of small ventilation slots that sat high on the wall. "You can see the sky through them. Take a look."

I brought my face close to the vent. I couldn't see houses or trees, just a blur of green and blue.

"Do you still think they're sending us to work?" I whispered.

Willie shrugged. "Wherever we're headed it has to be better than this. Okay, hop off. It's my turn." He wrapped his arms around my neck. "I reckon you're big enough to take my weight."

I think I might have smiled then, feeling bigger and stronger and closer to being a man than I ever had, but then Mamme called out.

"Stay close," she said. "We have to stick together."

"Hush, Pepi," Tatte said, getting to his feet. "The boys need to sleep. Come, Elyuka, lie down. I guarded your spot. Close your eyes and, God willing, when you wake the doors will be open."

Tatte blew his nose and bent over his prayer book and soon all I could hear was the clunk of the wheels and Tatte's whispered prayers.

I prayed too, that someone would hear him.

Three days after setting off, the train's wheels ground to a halt and the door was thrown open. Mamme squinted into the light, except she didn't look like Mamme. Her hair was a mess and her dress was crumpled and dirty. She blinked at the sky and then at the guards who were shouting at us – "*Geh raus! Schnell! Schnell!*" – but she was too slow. Two guards leaped into the carriage, grabbed Mamme by the arms and dumped her onto the platform.

"Get up!" Tatte stared at me, wild-eyed. "Get up, Emil!"

But I couldn't. My legs were shaking and the light was blinding and Tatte's hair was stuck to his head in matted clumps and he looked like a beggar and there were so many dead bodies. A man in a ragged striped jacket and drawstring pants climbed into the wagon and pushed past me to pluck a small girl from the floor and tip her into a wheelbarrow.

"They are going to kill us," someone shrieked.

A dog barked and bared its teeth. More men climbed into the wagon. A guard cracked his whip and then Tatte was scooping me up and the next thing I knew I was standing between Tatte and Willie on a platform under a sign that read *Auschwitz*. Dita, Sari and Mamme stood behind us, my sisters' arms looped through Mamme's to steady her.

I'd dreamed of this moment, of the carriage doors being flung open and taking in lungfuls of air, but the sky stank and everything was gray – the faces of the ragged men in striped uniform, the watchtowers, the barracks. It was like all the color had been leached out of the place. I stepped closer to Tatte.

"I want to go home." I longed to slip my hand into his pocket, but this place was not for hugs or handholding.

Mamme shook her head. "The world's gone mad. Why are they all screaming at us?"

Tatte swept the wet hair from Mamme's face, but he didn't have an answer for her. Every few feet an SS guard stood with a gun, its long barrel following us like a huge eye. I stared at the officer closest to me. He was tall and his boots shone. He looked like he'd had a good night's sleep and a big breakfast. But now he was opening his mouth and his face was turning red.

"*Zu funftantreten!* Rows of five!" he yelled, spit gathering at the corners of his mouth. He waved his gun in the air and we scrambled forward. Above us a loudspeaker blared: "Women, children and the elderly to the left, Men to the right! *Schnell! Schnell!*"

"Aaron!" Mamme's eyes were as big as moons.

"We will see each other soon, Pepi." Tatte took her hands in his and whispered something, then turned to Sari. "Look after your mother." He kissed her forehead. "Stay together if you can." He pulled Dita close, then turned to me. "Be brave," he said. "You're the man of the house now." He slipped his prayer book into my coat pocket. "Mamme likes to hear me *davening* at night. Pray for her." He bent to kiss me. His lips were cracked and his stubble stung.

"Men to the right! *Mach du schnell!*" an officer yelled.

I pressed my face to Tatte's chest, tears dripping down my nose.

"It will be okay," Tatte said, peeling my fingers from his neck. "They won't hurt children here. You'll have an easier time. Willie and I will see you soon." And then they were gone.

"Was that your father?"

I turned to see a man with a shaved head pointing in the direction Tatte had disappeared. He wore the same striped rags as the men who were dragging bodies into wheelbarrows. I looked past him to where the men were gathering in rows of five and nodded.

"Listen carefully," the man whispered in Yiddish. "Go to your father. You'll be safer on the right, with the men. You're small," he spoke quickly, his words tripping over each other. "Stand on his feet. You'll look taller. You'll need a profession. Tell them you're a carpenter or a bricklayer. Now go! Run!"

I ran, only realizing when I reached Tatte's side that I hadn't said goodbye to Mamme or my sisters. I turned to call out to them, to wave and mouth the words *goodbye* and *I love you*, but there were swarms of people, and I couldn't find Mamme's eyes or Sari's green dress or Dita's red hair.

Tatte frowned when he saw me. "Why aren't you with Mamme?" He looked worried. "If they catch you ..." He drew me close, his eyes darting between the line of SS officers standing to our left and right.

"It's okay, Tatte," I spoke in whispers. "I met a man. He spoke Yiddish. He said I had to come here, to *this* side. He said it was safer."

I stopped talking, because Willie had spun around and they were both staring at me, mouths open, and I suddenly realized what I'd said. We hadn't known which group was safer. Willie had guessed the men would be working hard labour and the women would be assigned lighter work.

We stumbled forward, in silence. *Mamme is smart*, I told myself. *Sari is strong and Dita is the bravest girl I know. They'll be put to work like us.*

Tatte gripped my hand. "What else did the man say, Emil?"

"He said I'm too small and that I should stand on your feet." Tatte stuck out a foot and Willie did too and I climbed onto their shoes, my left foot on Tatte's, my right on Willie's. We walked like that, past guards and SS officers plucking boys from the line and marching them away.

"He also said," I whispered as we drew close to a group of men in white coats, "that if anyone asks, we should tell them we have a profession, like a farmer or a carpenter."

We decided that Willie would go first and when the men let him pass, I should run fast as the wind past the doctors and under the sign up ahead that read *Arbeit Macht Frei*.

A man with perfectly parted hair and a gap between his two front teeth looked Willie up and down, and with a flick of the stick he was holding, waved him to the left.

The doctor looked at me. I puffed up my chest, sucked in a big breath of air, and ran fast as my legs could carry me, past the dumbstruck doctor and the men in white coats shouting, "*Sofort Aufhoren! Halt!*" I heard a gunshot and dogs barking but I didn't look back, not until I was through the gate on the other side, buried in the crush of men slated for survival.

And then they grabbed Tatte.

CHAPTER 7

NOW

Dad reaches for a glass of water and gulps it down. His shirt is stained at the underarms and his face is shiny. I don't know if it's the close warmth of the room or the heat of the cramped cattle car, but I feel it too. I jump up and open a window to let in some fresh air.

I think about my father at thirteen, searching for his mother so he could say goodbye, and I think about saying goodbye to Dad. I picture him in a hospital bed, the curtains drawn around us. I look over at Dad finding his way back to us, and Mom looking at Dad, at this man she thought she knew, and realize the send-off has already started. Dad's storytelling is one long goodbye.

"I'm so sorry," Mom whispers, reaching across the couch to find Dad's hand. "It must have been awful being separated from your mother."

"I didn't realize it would be the last –" Dad suddenly stops as if he meant to say something else, but the something got stuck.

I squeeze my eyes shut to stop myself crying. If Dad can rein in the tears and tell us about sleeping on a dead man without flinching, as though he'd slumped onto a beanbag and not a *dead body*, then I have no right to cry. I breathe out, a long slow exhale, and readjust my face so the shock doesn't show.

I don't want to be here. I want to run to the bathroom and hide, or escape to the beach and dig my toes in the sand, to remind myself that I am here under a star-blistered sky in Elwood, Australia and it's 1982 and the war's been over for decades. But I stay. Because my dad has had enough shit in his life and I don't want him to hurt any more than he's already hurting. But I wish he'd stop. Or fast-forward, so we can all move on and talk about something else.

"Did you ever find out the name of that prisoner who saved your life?" Tom ejects the cassette tape and grabs an empty one.

"No." Dad swallows hard. "And I didn't know that's what he was doing – saving my life. Not at first. I never saw the chimneys coughing up smoke. No-one told me about the –"

But I don't hear what he says next because I'm thinking about the stranger. Dad didn't know the man was saving his life. I didn't know about *any* of this, and I didn't ask him to tell me. But now he has, and no matter how hard I try, I don't think I'll ever be able to un-know it. And there's a giant-sized hole in my heart because I've lost a grandmother I've never met, and now I feel like I know her, know that if she was still alive, she'd make me chicken soup, sing to me, and tell me about my aunts who looked just like me when they were sixteen.

Dad searches for the right words to explain Auschwitz. "Maybe if I hadn't been as hungry and tired, I might have paid attention," he says. "I might have noticed the flames or the black sky or the ash that settled on everything."

I mash my face into my pillow.

When Mom comes in to say goodnight I turn to the wall so she can't hug me. *She* lied to me too. Mom always told me there was no such thing as the bogeyman. That evil existed in storybooks, not in the real world, not in *our* world. "There's no such thing as monsters," she'd said when I was small, flinging the closets open. "See? You're safe," she'd promised, tucking me in and turning on the night-light. "It's just your imagination."

But it wasn't. Monsters were real.

"What's up?" Deb asks when I phone her. "I got back from dinner last night and saw your message on the machine. That's twice you've skipped our Friday sleepovers." I'm about to apologise, but she's speaking again. "It's okay, I forgive you, as long as you promise to come over tonight so we can get ready together."

"Together?"

"For Paul's."

"Oh ... sure. Of course." I pretend I haven't forgotten.

"And after the party, I can sleep at yours."

"No," I say, hunting for a reason she can't come over. "If we sleep here, we'll have to be home by ten. I'll sleep at your place. Sorry, I've got to go. Dad's taking us out for brunch." I groan. "The Pancake Parlour."

Deb snorts. "Your dad knows you're not five years old, right?"

"Not sure," I say, "but that would explain the no-phone-after-10-pm rule and the curfew."

Deb laughs and I cling to that laugh for as long as I can, because it feels like the past. Like the old me. The *old* us.

Dad slides into a booth and I squeeze in next to him. Tom, Jack and Mom sit across from us. The Pancake Parlour is cheesy – fire-engine-red walls, black vinyl seats, wood paneling and chequer-board floors – but it's where we celebrate all the big Keller milestones. Learning to ride a two-wheeler, finishing primary school, graduating. I'm not sure what we're celebrating today.

I scour the menu and settle on a triple stack with vanilla ice-cream, hot chocolate fudge and sprinkles. "I'll have the Alice in Wonderland," I say, and I might as well be five.

Dad orders a breakfast stack with eggs and bacon. The air-conditioning isn't working and the table is sticky with maple syrup but Dad's smile is huge. He beams at the syrupy pancakes stacked high on his plate and the waiters in cheap suits and the children on the next table licking whipped cream from their fingers.

"So what are we celebrating?" Tom asks. "Jack hasn't popped the question. No-one's graduated. Did Lisa get through a driving lesson without pranging the Mazda?"

I poke my tongue out at him.

"I'm selling the business," Dad says between mouthfuls of egg and bacon, "unless any of you have changed your minds and want to become jewelers?"

My brothers shake their heads. Both of them worked at Keller Jewelers during the university holidays, doing deliveries and answering the phone. They learned to melt gold, hammer it into strips and fuse the ends to make rings, but neither of them wanted to spend their lives at a bench. I preferred collecting the shiny baubles Dad brought home – a small velvet box to hold my baby teeth, a silver L for my ninth birthday and a gold bracelet with tiny diamonds for my sixteenth. "I'll wear anything you want me to, I just don't want to sell the stuff," I told him the first time he suggested I spend my school holidays at work.

"I know we're a disappointment." Tom lowers his head in mock shame. "You're getting two doctors and a lawyer ..."

Dad spears a piece of bacon with his fork. "And all I wanted was for you guys to drop out of school and take over the business."

He laughs, and the laugh becomes a hacking cough and Dad's face is turning purple and then he's choking. Mom screams and Jack yells at me to move and I scramble from my seat to watch Jack drag Dad from the booth and wrap his arms around Dad's middle. He jerks hard and a small square of gristle falls to the floor.

"The muscles in your throat are getting weaker," Jack says in the car on the way home. "You should probably cut your food into smaller pieces."

Mom and I look at each other and we're thinking the same thing – *this is happening* – and the thread of hope I'd been clinging to, that Dad might defy the odds, that the doctors might have gotten it wrong, suddenly snaps and I'm freefalling.

"Hey," Dad says, "no long faces. Today was about celebrating."

"Celebrating?" I stare at Dad. "Celebrate *what*?"

"My retirement," Dad says, turning the key to lock the car. "But after what happened today, maybe ... just life."

Deb and I walk into the party and everyone's there, Adam and Paul and Karen and Tracey. 'Tainted Love' blares from a boom box. It's Saturday night and Paul's parents are away so the kitchen is an open bar and the living room a dance floor. Deb swipes a bottle of malibu from the kitchen counter and I follow her out. Paul has shoved the living-room furniture against the wall and turned down the lights and there are people everywhere waving their arms in the air and shouting out lyrics. And I shout too, because my life sucks and sometimes screaming at the universe helps.

Deb empties the bottle into our cups, even though she knows she'll end up drinking mine. I don't drink. I'm the one who holds back your hair when you're leaning over the toilet bowl, the one who walks you outside to get some fresh air, the one who stops you from pulling off your top because *it's so hot in here.*

I don't drink because I don't want to say or do anything I might regret. But tonight's different.

"Let's do this!" I say, taking a swig.

"Well, *this* is a historic moment," Deb laughs and raises her cup.

I take a second sip, hating the taste. What I like is the fire it lights inside me, so bright it shuts out everything else. I empty the glass. Someone hands me a bottle of vodka and I take a swig from that too, and then people are hooting and clapping and offering me bottles but I shake my head *no*, and escape to the toilet, afraid of what I might tell them if I have any more.

I tip the rest of the vodka down the toilet and walk back into the beery air. Adam is waiting for me in the hallway. He circles his hands around my waist. It's dark and I'm tipsy.

"Hey," I say, launching myself at him.

His mouth is warm and tastes like sunshine. He pulls away to say something, but I don't want to talk, I don't want to think, so I kiss him again. And again. And again. Until I'm not sure where I end and he begins; until we're just lips and tongues and teeth. He tugs my shirt from my jeans and slides his hand up my back and my skin is thrumming, and I wonder if anyone can see the small starbursts of color where his fingers graze my skin.

"You're amazing," he whispers, kissing me on the neck, and I know I should be happy, because maybe he's falling as hard as I am, but there's this voice in my head saying, *He doesn't really know you.*

Adam is waiting for me to say something but my brain is being held hostage. *Adam wouldn't be here, holding you, if he knew the truth,* the voice taunts. I don't look any different to the kids at Glenrock High. I have my dad's sea-blue eyes and fair skin but I can't shake the feeling that if Adam found out I was Jewish – if anyone found out – it would change how they saw me.

None of it makes any sense. I grew up on jelly sandwiches and Oreos, a thousand miles from the gates of Auschwitz. My father never talked about his fractured childhood. I've never been called names, but still, there's some part of me, way down deep, that knows it's not safe to be a Jew. *I was tired of feeling like I'd done something wrong, like I was wrong, because I was Jewish.* Dad's words loop in my brain.

"You okay?" Adam says.

"Must be the drink. I'm not feeling great." I'm lying again because … I'm a liar. "I think I'll head home."

"I can walk you?" He turns to grab his jacket.

"No, that's okay," I say too fast. "You stay. I'll call Mom."

"Whatever." He shrugs and downs his glass. "Guess I'll see you Monday."

I leave Adam standing in the hall with his empty glass and find Deb on the dance floor. Cybotron is on the boom box and Deb's doing the robot.

"Sorry, I'm not feeling great. Must be the vodka," I yell into the space above her head. "I'm going to head home."

She freezes, robot-style, one arm by her side, the other swinging at the elbow. "Call. Me. Tomorrow," she says in her best robot voice.

I wait for Mom on the nature strip. When she pulls up to the house a few minutes later I climb into the car, wishing the seat would swallow me. Mom's more sad than angry, and maybe that's worse.

"I don't understand," she says, her voice small. "You're not a drinker. Of all the times –" Her eyes search my face. "You choose *now*?"

Now is *why* I'm drinking, I want to tell her, but I don't because the drinking hasn't worked. My head hurts and everything is blurry and death is still here, in the car and on this street. It's in the clouds and the sky. It's everywhere.

"I'm sorry," I say, "I won't do it again."

Dad shed his old life, like a snake sheds its skin. I'm going to have to grow a new skin; a tougher one.

I join the track team and sign up for the school newspaper. I owe it to Dad to live like time is running out, I tell myself, but I know it's just an excuse to get so busy that I won't have time to think.

Mr Curlew hands back our English homework. I get a B. I'm not great at creative writing. Give me Shakespeare or Bronte and I'll analyse the hell out of them, but ask me to write about my life in five hundred words or less and I'm flailing. I don't know Mr Curlew and he doesn't know me, and he's not going to in five hundred words or less. I look down at the words scribbled in red ink below the B. *Your writing is strong, Lisa. Great use of vocab, but you were supposed to write about home and what it means to you. I know what your house looks like, but where are you in this house? I couldn't find you.* I stuff the essay into my bag and head to the cafeteria.

"So, what's the goss?" Tracey asks when Deb and I sit down, and for a moment I think about telling them.

But then I see the new girl, hugging her lunchbox, wandering between the tables looking for a place to land. There's plenty of spare seats but no-one waves her over. No-one smiles and shuffles over to clear her a space, and I think, *Thank God for Deb and Karen and Tracey.* And I think, *I'm not messing this up.* Because the thing about high school is, you're only as good as your last outfit or haircut. Sit with the wrong people at lunch, forget someone's birthday or keep something from your best friend (like your father is dying or your grandparents were murdered) and you're dumped. Banished. *Persona non grata.* It's true.

Just take a look around Glenrock and you'll see someone being rammed into a locker or a group of girls huddled in a corner, laughing and pointing.

I don't want them pointing at *me*. I've gotten through ten years of schooling without a scandal because I fly under the radar. I have friends. Enough to always have someone to save me a seat at lunch, but not too many to start a turf war. I'm an A average but I don't get dissed because I don't give them ammunition. And I want to keep it that way.

We sit with our heads tilted close and I listen to my friends complain about their bodies and boys and homework. And I laugh when I'm meant to and I ask the right questions. And hold on tight to the stories I can't share.

Apart from the B, it's a pretty good day. I don't let myself think about Dad, not till the bell rings. Deb and the others are meeting Paul and Adam at the skate center but I say Dad's promised me a driving lesson and head home.

Dad is in the living room, sitting cross-legged on the floor opposite a man wearing tie-dye pants. The man's feet are dirty. I can see them because he's not wearing shoes. Or a shirt. He is old – a thousand years older than my father – and he's chanting. It's been like this all week. On Tuesday I came home to find my father lying facedown on the couch, his back like a pincushion, a dozen thin needles piercing his skin. Wednesday was a massage with hot stones. Thursday, suction cups. My dad sees neurologists, physiotherapists, dieticians and a dozen other 'ologists', but he also sees Chinese medicine doctors and energy healers. He swallows strange-smelling liquids and handpicked herbs. *It's your back, your shoulders, your liver that is to blame*, they tell him. *You have to expel the negative energy.*

Dad doesn't have negative energy. He's the sunniest person I know. He also doesn't do alternative medicine. He doesn't meditate or do yoga or take vitamin C because *why pop a pill when you can suck on an orange?*

"What's going on?" I whisper to Mom as we peer from the door.

Dad's eyes are closed, plumes of sandalwood and sage drifting up from the incense burner smoking at his feet. In each of his hands he holds a crystal. Mom shakes her head.

"He'll try anything," she says, tears sliding down her cheeks. "He's got nothing to lose."

Friday night rolls around again and we're doing the whole nine yards – chicken soup, schnitzel, the wine, the candles.

Mom holds out a box of matches. "Do you want to light them?"

I shake my head. "No, I'm good."

Mom watches Dad cut the schnitzel into tiny pieces.

"I'll be careful," he says. "I promise, no choking."

Mom's face is moon-pale, her smile tight. I stare at my plate – at the leftover beans and the untouched veal – while my brothers discuss my father's medication and Dad looks for a way back into his story.

I try to imagine what it was like. The guards with guns. The dead in wheelbarrows. I can't. And I don't want to.

CHAPTER 8

THEN

I watched from the other side of the fence as a guard pinned Tatte's arms behind his back while another officer pointed a gun at his head. I couldn't make out what the officer was saying but when he finished talking Tatte shook his head.

The man's smile vanished. Then the guard with the gun was marching Tatte under the sign that read *Arbeit Macht Frei*, cutting a corridor through the masses of frightened men, straight toward me.

"Find your boy." The guard pressed his gun to Tatte's head. I slipped into a huddle of men and hid, too scared to look up, too scared to move. Minutes dragged by and more prisoners joined us. And then there was a hand on my shoulder and a voice whispered, "Emil?" I looked up and saw Willie, his face flushed with relief. He pressed a finger to his lips and then he stepped aside, and there, a few feet away, stood Tatte, smiling his lopsided half-smile. I knew not to hug him.

We stumbled forward, away from the guard who'd meant to kill Tatte. I was dizzy with hunger.

Tatte told me what happened. "After you ran, the guards grabbed me and told me to find you. I was next in line so they must have guessed you were my son. I told them I'd never been married and didn't have a son. They threatened that if *I* didn't find you, *they* would, and shoot the both of us but they must have got bored of the search, or maybe they believed me. Anyway, praise God, they let me go, and here I am."

I marched after Tatte, down a long concrete corridor into an enormous room. There must have been close to a thousand of us. Our clothes smelled of piss and our fingernails were caked with dirt. I thought of the boys in my class who had called me a filthy Jew. I couldn't argue with them now.

"*Ausziehen! Schnell!*"

Men started to fumble with their zips. We'd been ordered to strip naked. Shoes clattered to the floor, and glasses and watches piled up on benches.

"Will they let us come back for our things?" I pulled Tatte's prayer book from my pocket and left it on the bench.

I didn't hear his answer because a man in a black jacket with a yellow armband was shouting something about a shower and then people started wailing and the man next to me leaped onto a bench and cried, "They're sending us to die!" A guard clubbed him on the head.

When I turned back to Tatte he was praying. "*Yisgadal, veyiskadash, shmey raba.*"

Tatte had recited the mourner's prayer every day for a month after burying his best friend but I'd never heard him whisper it *before* someone had died. Tatte bowed his head and prayed for us.

I unbuttoned my shirt and squirmed out of my underpants.

"Ignore them," Willie said, falling into line. "The Germans wouldn't shower us if they were planning to kill us."

"Okay," I said, but I couldn't look him in the eye. Willie had always been my hero, and not just because he was older than me. He was different to anyone I'd ever met. He had big plans to live a big life. He didn't let fear or hate get in the way. Every day was an adventure, kicked off with a smile. He made our lives seem huge and our problems small. There was no-one like him, and I didn't want to see him stripped of that; just another shivering Jew surrounded by guards.

"I won't go," a man said, tightening his belt around his coat.

A German with a machine gun pulled the trigger, tearing holes in the man's coat where his heart would have been.

A guard at the entrance to a concrete chamber poked my ribs with his rifle. "Get in."

I lifted my eyes to the ceiling and saw showerheads hanging from a network of pipes. People pushed past me, arms and legs brushing against my skin. I didn't know where to look, so I focused on Tatte. He wasn't crying. Maybe he thought God would save us; maybe he held back his tears so *we* wouldn't be scared.

The guards bolted the doors and people started sobbing.

"Aren't they happy to get clean?" I asked.

Tatte didn't answer.

The man next to me sang a Hungarian song and then the water pelted down, spattering my arms and legs. It tasted like mud but I swallowed it down and a few minutes later we were spat out into the cold night.

From there we were ordered to run, dripping, to another brick building. A prisoner in a striped uniform grabbed Tatte and lifted his razor, shearing off Tatte's white beard, and then all the hair on his head. He looked strange with a chin where his beard had once been.

"Arms up!" the man shouted, scraping the blade under Tatte's armpits.

I watched, horrified, as the hair on Tatte's woolly arms and legs floated to the floor.

I was hairless, so the guard's razor was fast.

"*Raus! Raus!* Out! Out!"

We were running again, this time to a row of wooden troughs. One by one we clambered into the green-gray liquid, closed our eyes, held our breath and ducked our heads under. The disinfectant stung the cuts on my scalp, but I didn't cry. I marched past a table buried under a mountain of rags. Behind the mountain sat a prisoner who flung scraps of cloth at me; a blue and white striped pair of drawstring pants, a flimsy striped jacket and a cap.

My pants were too big and my top was missing a few buttons. I wasn't given socks or gloves or a coat. Someone hurled shoes at me, a pair of hard, wooden clogs. People dressed quickly. I was glad when Tatte covered his nakedness, but he looked so sad.

"I barely recognize the two of you," he whispered.

I looked across at Willie, at his shaved head and the nicks on his chin and his dirty striped shirt, and realized what I must look like.

"It's me, Tatte, Elyuka."

"Yeah, and don't you ever forget it." Willie winked. "We might all look the same, but no-one in this room can handle a soccer ball like you do and I bet none of them know how to ride a cow. But *most* importantly," he pulled on his cap, "you're the only one who can boast you're my little brother."

We were loaded onto a truck and driven past row after row of identical brick buildings, past men without names and women without hair. The sun sank in the sky and lamps flickered on.

"That's where they'll put us to work," Willie whispered, pointing to a distant chimney coughing up smoke.

A whistle blew and the truck stopped inside another perimeter fence.

We climbed out and were told to wait in line. I stared at the parade of hairless men in blue and white striped pyjamas. Men with empty eyes and stick-thin legs. Nothing belonged to us any more, not our shoes, our clothes, our houses or our hair. Tatte had lost his wedding ring, his prayer book and his glasses. They'd stolen Willie's watch. Next were our names.

"Emil Rosenfeld?" A man wearing a bloodied apron stood next to a chair. He looked more like a butcher than a German guard. "*Sitzen*," he said. "*Linker arm*."

He pinned my left wrist to the armrest and lifted his pen.

"This is your new name."

I read the number drawn on my skin. *Ein sieben sechs drei neun*. A7639. He put the pen down and lifted another one from his desk, except this was no ordinary pen. It had a wooden handle and instead of a nib, a sharp pointed needle that he drove into my skin, over and over, puncturing the number with ink.

"This is your barrack," a man with a sharp slit of a mouth said, "and I'm your block *alteste*."

He herded us inside a two-storey brick building. There was a long walkway in the middle and either side of it were rows of bunks, but they weren't really bunks, they were just planks of wood. The men on these shelves didn't sit up to look at us, they just lay there, hardly moving. There must have been a thousand of them, maybe more.

Another whistle blew and we were told to line up. The block leader walked between us, a whip in his hand. I stared up at the timber slats. There were no mattresses or pillows. A few of the men slept under blankets, but mostly they just lay there in their clothes, spooned against each other. I wanted to join them, wanted to curl into a ball and sleep. When would they let us sleep? My eyes started to droop.

"Elyuka," Tatte whispered, nudging me. "Stay awake."

"I am only going to say this once, so pay attention!" The block leader turned to face Tatte. "I don't care if you live or die but if you *want* to live," he clamped Tatte's lips between his fingers, "you'll keep your mouth shut and do what I tell you. It's my job to keep this new home of yours in order." He pinched Tatte's nose between the fingers of his other hand.

I could hold my breath underwater for at least half a minute; Willie even longer. It was a game we played whenever we swam in the creek. We'd never played it with Tatte. The block leader kept talking. *Twenty-five, twenty-six, twenty-seven.* Tatte's face was turning blue.

"I could kill you right now," the block leader said, "I can do whatever I want, because I am your ..." He waited for us to answer.

"Block *alteste*," I called out, quick as I could, my eyes fixed on Tatte, who was buckling at the knees.

"That's right," the block leader said, pulling his hands from Tatte and wiping them on his shirt.

Tatte opened his mouth and breathed in hard.

"When you're inside the barrack, I want to be able to hear a pin drop. I want to be able to hear the rats crawling under your blankets." He whipped a blanket from an inmate and shook it out. "And if there's anything hidden under there – an apple core, a prayer book or a piece of soap – watch out! You'll be fed three times a day." He clicked his fingers and a prisoner darted between us, handing out battered aluminium bowls and spoons. "You lose your bowl or spoon, you don't eat."

Another inmate scurried around dropping needles, thread and bits of cloth onto bunks.

"Take two triangles and find the scrap of cloth with your number on it. Sew the triangles together so they form a star and stitch your number under it." The block leader wore a green triangle on his jacket. Ours were yellow. "Keep the block clean and try to keep yourselves clean too. I mean, look at you," he said, his face hard and sneering. "You're filthy. You Jews have no self-respect."

A7639. I handed the scrap of material to Willie so he could sew it onto my jacket.

"I'm sure they'll let us sleep soon," Willie said when the block leader left. "Hey." He swiped a tear from my cheek. "We'll survive this." He reached for a yellow triangle. "Someone has to, and that someone will be us."

"Criminals wear green triangles." A boy with a slashing scar that ran from his neck to his chin sat up in bed.

92

His bony ankles poked out from under his blanket; his feet were wrapped in rags. "Gypsies wear black triangles, Jehovah's Witnesses wear purple, red is for political prisoners and pink for homosexuals. My name's Rudy," he said, extending a bony hand.

"So the block *alteste* is a criminal?" I could feel the drumbeat of my heart.

The boy nodded and leaned closer. "Murderers and thieves make good block leaders and *kapos*." He looked at us and sighed. "The *kapos* are the guys with the yellow armbands. They run the work units. If you're a *kapo* or a block leader you get extra privileges." He pointed to a room at the far end of the barrack. "The block leader gets his own room, more food, cigarettes."

He looked around, pressed a finger to his lips and unbuttoned his shirt, holding it open to reveal a pocket sewn into the lining. It was yellow, a bunch of hastily stitched together triangles. He pulled a sliver of bread from the pocket and slid it into his mouth.

"When you get fed tonight, you'll want to wolf it down." He re-buttoned his shirt. "Don't. Cut the bread into thin slices, have some and save the rest. You'll only get coffee and a bowl of soup tomorrow and it has to last till dinner."

Willie grabbed a handful of triangles and stuffed them under his cap. I grabbed a needle and a spool of gray thread.

"How old is your little brother?" the boy asked through rotting teeth.

"Old enough," Willie said, getting to work on our pockets. "So, where *are* we? Germany?"

The boy picked at a scab under his nose. "Poland."

Poland? I looped my arms around my knees. We may as well be on the moon. There was no way to escape Poland. There was nowhere to run, nowhere to hide and no-one to help us get back home.

"*Achtung!*" A man in a black uniform barked directions and we marched to the latrines.

I was hungry and tired, but mostly I just felt lost, especially without Mamme to sing me to a happier place. I missed her with an ache that was even worse than my hunger. I shuffled forward in step with Willie and Tatte, picturing Mamme reaching out to take my hand and drop a piece of food into it. A plum picked from our garden or a slice of cheese.

"*Scheissen!*" the kapo yelled.

I found an empty hole in the concrete slab and yanked my pants to my ankles. It was hard to shit on command with so many bodies so close and the kapo walking between us swinging his stick, but I didn't know when they'd let us back again, so I sat and tried, watching the men at the sinks trying to scour the dirt from their bodies. An older man who looked Tatte's age stood over a rusted basin, scraping a piece of cut glass across his stubbled cheeks.

"What do you think?" he asked the man next to him.

"Not a day over forty." His friend smiled. "You'll pass."

"Pass what?" I tugged at Willie's shirt and pointed to the old man.

Willie shrugged and pulled a piece of yellow cloth from his pocket to wipe himself.

"Wash, Elyuka," Tatte said, stripping to his waist and bending over a basin. He twisted the tap and brown water gushed into the cracked porcelain.

"What's the point?"

Tatte turned off the tap and reached for my hand. "Elyuka, I don't know what this place is, or what God's plan is, but these people can't tell us who we are. I'll wash because it makes me feel like me, it's something to hold onto. Call it dignity, call it whatever you want, they can't take it, because it lives *here*." He tapped my chest. "This is where you live. It's where God lives, where your memories and your sense of right and wrong live. Do as they say, bend when you have to, but never lose sight of who you are."

The sky was black by the time we lined up for roll call. Floodlights illuminated the square. We were ordered to line up in ranks of five. Willie was on my left, Tatte on my right. Every time my eyes grew heavy or I listed to one side Tatte or Willie would tug at my sleeve and I'd wake with a shock because this wasn't a dream, I was really here, and none of it made any sense. If the Germans needed us to work then why make us stand in the cold for hours. Why beat us and starve us if they needed us strong? And why play music?

I thought I'd been imagining it, but no, there was definitely a violin. I cocked my head to one side – a violin and a flute – and then more prisoners trudged in, their feet marching in time to the beat, hundreds of men with their heads bent low. Some of the men wore boots, some hobbled in clogs and some, like Rudy, walked with their feet wrapped in rags. The stronger ones carried the dead on stretchers, tipping them out and stacking them like wood.

"*Achtung! Mutzen ab!* Caps off." An SS guard pulled a rubber baton from his belt and we sprang to attention, pulling our caps from our heads. "*Mutzen auf!*"

No sooner had we exposed our shaved heads than we were pulling our caps back on again. Over and over for what seemed like hours. Arms up, arms down. Caps on, caps off. There didn't seem to be any point to it, but then a boy two rows up from me collapsed and I realized maybe that *was* the point. I snatched my cap from my head and shoved it back on.

The guards began to count us – those who still stood, those who'd collapsed and the dead who'd been dragged in from work detail. Soot drifted through the air covering our jackets with ash and my eyes grew heavy.

"*Ein sieben sechs drei neun!* A7639!" A German officer in a black uniform stopped at the end of our column. "A7639!" the officer repeated my number and reached for his gun, ready to shoot if there was no response.

Willie elbowed me in the ribs, jolting me from my stupor.

"*Yavol!*" I leaped forward.

"A7640!" The officer slid his gun back into its holster and Tatte stepped forward.

Another long hour passed, and then a whistle sounded. Roll call was over.

I didn't listen to Rudy. As soon as I got my hands on my ration I devoured it on my bunk. First the stick of cheese, then the brick of hard black bread, small enough to close my fist around. I meant to save some for the next day but I was so hungry it felt like someone had grabbed a shovel and dug out my stomach. I tore at the bread, and before Willie could stop me there was nothing left of it, except for a few crumbs that had fallen onto my lap. I swept up the scraps and ate them too, watching the fight that had broken out below.

The block leader had tossed scraps of food to the floor and the inmates tore at it, digging their nails into their bunkmates' arms, scratching and biting and kicking and shoving while the block leader gnawed on a sausage and laughed. I rolled onto my stomach and shut my eyes. I could hear Tatte praying.

"How can you?" I turned to him. "After all that's happened?"

"I pray because I still believe. You've got to hang on to hope, Elyuka." He touched my arm. "It's all we've got."

The lights went out and I started crying. Willie reached into his shirt and pulled out a sliver of bread.

"I'm sorry," I said, taking it from him, "I'm just so hungry."

"It's okay." Willie swatted away my tears. "The only way we'll survive is by helping each other. You've just got to stop crying." He dropped his voice even lower. "As soon as they sense weakness, they'll –"

"*Wer wagt es zu reden?*" A torch clicked on. The block leader walked from one end of the barrack to the other, sweeping the beam of his torch along the top tier of bunks. "I heard you talking. It will be worse if you don't own up."

I squeezed my eyes shut.

"Get down!" The block leader swung his torch at the timber planks. He swung it again and I heard a dull thwack and a man cry out. The shelf bowed again as the man climbed to the ground. "This is what happens when you don't follow the rules."

The block leader flicked the lights on and dropped his torch onto a table, sitting the prisoner down and angling his chair so we could all see the man's face prickled with sweat and his eyes big as saucers.

"It wasn't me. It was –" The prisoner looked up and narrowed his eyes, and for one heart-pounding second I thought he was going to say *Willie*. But he couldn't have, because we didn't *have* names. The block leader grabbed the metal torch and swung it at the man's head. He swung it again, harder, and the man slumped.

"*Alle Augen auf mich,*" the block leader hissed.

Men from the farthest bunks gathered around to watch. Anyone caught averting their eyes would be next, the block leader warned. I didn't shut my eyes or reach for Willie's hand. I watched a man die. It could have been Willie. It could have been me.

"Show's over," the block leader said, ordering the two closest inmates to drag the body outside. "Oh, and one more thing." He flicked the lights off. "For those who just arrived, there's a bucket near the door. If you prefer the latrine, be my guest, but just so you know, there's a pack of dogs outside, and they're hungry."

I lay down next to Willie. His eyes were closed, his arms wrapped around his shoes, his head on his tin bowl. My left arm was numb but there was no way to turn over without everyone having to roll over so I lay there awake, listening to Tatte pray to, and plead with, God. I squeezed my eyes shut and slowed my breath to match Willie's.

"*Alles Raus!*"

I woke to the sound of shouting.

The block leader was battering the timber bunks with his torch. "*Steh auf!* Get up!"

The hammering dragged Tatte and Willie from their dreams. I didn't ask who they'd spent the night with. I'd spent it with Mamme. We were back home and I was in the bath, my soccer boots on the floor, my dirty clothes in a heap. Mamme had run the kettle to heat the water.

I don't remember what we talked about but I remember her sitting on the edge of the wooden tub, rubbing soap into my hair.

I didn't tell Tatte about the dream. I knew it would make him sad to think of me missing her. I swung my legs over the bunk. I didn't need to get dressed; I'd slept in my clothes. A whistle blew and we ran to the latrines. Another whistle sounded and we lined up for breakfast, a cup of murky water some of the men called coffee.

"Remember," Willie said, grimacing, "no matter what they give us, you *have* to eat." He raised his bowl to his lips and gulped the bitter brew down.

The sun appeared in the sky as another whistle sounded and the barrack emptied for work detail. It must have been six in the morning but no-one came to get us. Not until it was time to line up for lunch. I held out my bowl and drank the slop down. Two men dived to the floor to capture a potato peel that had escaped the barrel while a third sucked at the dirty floorboards, his cheeks dark with dust.

"Let's hope when we get work it won't be carting rocks or digging trenches," Willie whispered at roll call.

I worried I was too small to be put to work. I wanted to work. The sign over the main gate read, *Arbeit Mach Frei. Work Brings Freedom.*

Our block *Schreiber* – an inmate tasked with keeping track of our numbers – ran his finger down a clipboard. "*Einer fehlt.* One missing," he shouted into the wind.

The sun sank and we waited in the square – caps off, caps on – until two SS officers appeared with the missing inmate, blood streaming from his nose.

"Hiding under his bed," one of the officers reported, pulling out his gun and shooting the man in the head.

Days passed, or maybe it was weeks. I can't remember. I know that I stopped crying in Auschwitz. I stopped dreaming too. It was better not waking from dreams to find Mamme gone. I got used to her absence, got used to the smell of the latrines and the dead at our door. I was always hungry and thought about stealing food from one of my bunkmates, but Tatte's words gnawed at my insides, *Remember who you are.* Instead, I learned that the soup was thicker at the bottom of the pot.

"There's turnips and bits of meat if you wait," I whispered, dragging Willie and Tatte to the back of the queue.

I learned other things too. I learned to tuck my blanket around my body to stop others pulling it off. I learned not to rush at the latrines because sometimes the guards used it as an excuse to crack a few heads. I learned to take up as little space as possible, and I learned why the older men shaved.

"They line everyone up for a selection once a month," Rudy told us. "They're not selecting us for work," he shook his head. "They're watching us for weakness. If you limp, cough or can't keep up, they send you away. They look for stooped backs, rashes, a sweat – anything that signals you're not strong enough to work." He glanced at Tatte and stopped talking, but later that night he slipped

Willie a piece of glass. "Tell your father to shave every day. He'll look younger."

Rudy taught us other things too – sometimes in return for a stick of cheese or a nub of sausage, sometimes for nothing. He taught us to march in the middle of a group, beyond the sweep of the guards' batons and how to trade soup for bread, and bread for cigarettes.

"I don't smoke," I'd said.

Rudy had laughed. "It's for the block leader," he'd whispered. "You need to stay on his good side."

And then there were all the things I had to *unlearn* – the sound of laughter, the comfort of a hug, the sleepy, warm feeling you got after eating a meal. I couldn't play hide-and-seek with Willie to cheer myself up or slip my hand into Tatte's pocket to feel less alone, but the three of us did what we could to look out for each other. If one of us had extra soup, we shared it. If someone needed a shot of hope, we'd tell stories from home. We checked each other for signs of sickness and promised that no matter how hungry or exhausted we were, we'd drag ourselves to roll call because we were going to make it home.

CHAPTER 9

NOW

Dad's words dry up. The only sound in the room is the drumming rain. He sinks back into a cushion but he's not here, he's in Auschwitz standing at roll call, pulling his cap on and off his head. I uncross my legs and pad to the window to close it. The rain looks like ash.

"You must have been so scared," Jack says.

The word feels wrong, too small for what my father went through, and how do we even try to understand words like *scared*, *hungry*, *dirty* and *skinny* when they mean one thing to my father and another thing to us?

"How did you do it?" Tom asks. "How did you get past the guards on the platform? You hadn't eaten in days. You must have been exhausted."

I wait for Dad's answer. I used to think he was a superhero when I was little. He was stronger and faster and could jump higher than I could. He could float across the water on two planks of wood and send a golf ball so high it disappeared behind clouds. He was telepathic too. He knew when I'd done something naughty before I even owned up. But then I grew up and stopped believing in superheroes.

"How did I do it? I don't know." The surprise is still there in Dad's voice. "I guess I just didn't want to die." He clears his throat. "I had dreams."

He is getting tired and I don't know if it's the weight of the story or the disease wearing him down, but when he lifts the cup of tea Mom pours him, he uses both hands to guide the cup to his mouth.

"Your tattoo," Tom says, glancing at the purple ink on Dad's arm. "I always thought it was something you did on a dare. I actually thought it was cool."

Dad offers his arm so we can all see the faded flowers. I'd asked him about them once. I'd found a unicorn tattoo wrapped in plastic at the bottom of a cereal box and asked if he'd also found his in the Rice Krispies.

Dad rests a wide-knuckled hand on Tom's shoulder. "The tattoo artist who did it *was* kind of cool. What was his name?" Dad's eyebrows knit together. "Oh, that's right, Dave! His name was Dave. He worked in a dingy shop called the Black Ink. I was sick of explaining the number to everyone I met. I couldn't stand the sight of it, so I asked him to remove it. Dave took one look at my number and said it must have hurt like hell but he couldn't get rid of it. 'That number's not going anywhere,' he said. 'The ink's too deep. Bloody unprofessional, whoever did it.'"

Dad stares at the slanting rain as Mom works her way through a small hill of tissues. I don't know if she's crying because of the story, or because Dad never told her the things he's telling us now.

"It just felt wrong," Dad continues, "because I *wasn't* a number. I wasn't that boy. Not anymore. Dave told me I had a choice. I could either pay a plastic surgeon to do a skin graft or cover the number with another tattoo. He handed me a sketchbook of skeletons and motorbikes. I politely declined. I wanted to draw my own."

"Why flowers?" I ask.

Dad shrugs. "I guess I just wanted something beautiful to cover up the ugliness. It could have been anything. I just needed it gone."

I pick up the phone in the hall but only get as a far as my bedroom door. The cord is stretched taut. I *really* need my own phone.

"Deb?" I need to hear my best friend say something – anything – that's not sad.

"So, is this a regular thing ... you staying home on a Friday night?"

I know she is hurt but I don't know what to do about it.

"Sorry," I say, sitting cross-legged on the floor. "I'm as bummed out as you are but now that Tom and Jack have moved out, Mom's gotten weird about us spending time together, so ..."

She must know I'm lying but she doesn't push.

"That's cool," she says.

But it's not. I'm hiding from Deb and she doesn't know how to find me. "What about we do our homework together on Sunday?"

"Sure," she says, the smile back in her voice. "I've got to ace the next English assignment. Got a C on the creative writing piece. I'm guessing you killed it? You were writing paragraphs in 1st Grade while the rest of us were still on the alphabet. You're basically Hemingway."

"I did okay."

Mom has materialised and is standing over me, tapping her watch. It's after ten.

"Bedtime," she says, pointing to the phone.

I mouth *okay* and wait for her to leave.

"Is that Adam?" Deb trills. "You could've told me. I get it. If *I* had a boy in my bed, I'd be ditching me too."

"Yeah," I say, when Mom disappears. "It's Adam. He's sleeping over and Mom's going to make us breakfast in bed."

Deb snorts.

"It's ten," I say. "I better go before she comes back wielding a club."

It's the shortest conversation we've ever had. The longest was four hours, thirty-seven minutes. (She timed it.) I pull my essay from my backpack and head to bed. Mr Curlew wanted us to tell him about our homes, but I couldn't, because then I'd have to imagine our house without Dad in it, and his desk empty of papers, and his side of the bed empty.

I flip the page over, pull a pen from my bag and write down all the things I don't want to forget about my dad:

1. The bony bump in his nose.
2. His big walrus laugh.
3. The gap between his two front teeth, large enough to slide a coin through. (We tried.)
4. The way he reacts whenever he sees me, like he's just walked into a surprise party.
5. His huge hands.
6. His size 11 shoes. I'd climb onto them when I was small, wrap my arms around his middle, and we'd stomp around the house like a two-headed monster.
7. Skiing between his legs.
8. Sleeping outdoors on hot summer nights on mattresses he'd dragged into the back garden.

I stick the list in the shoebox with tonight's tapes and bin the other pages of my essay. If my dad was a house he'd be haunted and there'd be trapdoors and secret rooms and a skeleton in every closet. And me? I'd be the wiped-out home you read about in the news, built on shaky foundations too close to the sea, washed away by a freak storm.

I climb under my blanket, the warmth and the dark slowing the fast up and down of my chest. The room blurs and Willie appears beside me. His scalp has been shaved and it's covered in cuts but he looks just like Tom – blue eyes dropped into a pale, round face. *Hey*, he whispers, swiping fat tears from my cheeks. *We'll survive this. Someone has to, and that someone will be us.*

Dad played his last game of golf yesterday. I know because he didn't drag his bag into the laundry to clean his clubs and there was no talk about how close he came to a hole in one. There was no talk at all, just a flare of irritation when I asked about the game and the heavy thump of his study door closing. He stayed locked in his study yesterday, and most of today, and he still hasn't come out.

I practise piano, do a lap of the park and crank out some homework. It's 5 pm and I only have an hour to get ready; my Saturday nights start early because I have to be home by ten. I wash my hair, and there are clothes everywhere – on my bed, the floor, my desk, the chair. My favorite Fiorucci T-shirt is laid out on the bed: two winged angels wearing sunglasses against a striped blue and white backdrop. I can't do blue and white stripes. I grab the top and aim it at the bin.

I join Mom and Dad in the bathroom. Mom is brushing her hair, black waves dancing down her back.

"Can I borrow some mascara?"

She opens a drawer. Dad is leaning against the sink rubbing shaving cream onto his skin. He sees me and smiles. I stand between them, the three of us side by side at the bathroom sink. Dad pale and freckled between two big ears. Mom with honeyed skin and glossy black hair. Jack has her amber eyes. Tom has her strong jaw. But there's not a hint of her on me; I'm all Dad. Braces fixed my gap-toothed grin but you can see him on me. The long lashes and long fingers. The thin arms and long legs splattered with freckles. The big feet and blue eyes.

Dad winks at the mirror. "My little girl's all grown up," he says, scraping at his bristles, "but you're still my little piece of pineapple." The wonky smile is back, but his hands are shaking as they grip the razor. "I love you, pineapple."

I love you. He's been saying that a lot lately.

"How much?" I ask.

It used to be our favorite game. *I love you to the fridge and back,* he'd tease. *To the milk bar. To 2005.*

"I love you halfway across the universe," he says, splashing water on his face, "to Saturn and back."

"Love you too, Dad," I say, kissing his wet cheek.

He towels his face dry, but when he's finished there are still patches of gray on his cheeks, bits he has missed. He sits on the edge of the bathtub, exhausted.

"Do you want to cancel?" Mom asks. "Ernst and Barbara will understand. We can eat dinner at home."

Dad shakes his head. "I'll be okay. Maybe I'll just lie down for a minute."

I finish my makeup and poke my head into his room. Dad's sitting on the edge of his bed, grappling with a shoelace.

"I just wanted to say bye," I call from the doorway.

"Lisa," he says, giving up on the shoe. "Sorry about being a sad sack today. It was just ... having to give up golf. It was hard. I just needed a little time." He smiles and the skin around his eyes crinkles. "Say hi to Adam."

Unlike my parents, Adam's are cool about us hanging out in his bedroom with the door closed. As soon as the door clicks shut, I climb onto his bed.

"Dad says hi." I kick off my shoes.

Dad says hi? You are in this beautiful boy's bed and the best you can do is *Dad say's hi*. Do you actually *want* him thinking about your Dad right now?

Adam grabs my hand. "Come here," he says, vacuuming up any awkwardness.

I shuffle close and lie down. I think I might love him. Of course, I haven't told *him* that. I'd rather eat my own eyebrows than say the L-word first.

"Why so quiet? What's going on up there?" He sweeps a stray lock of my hair from my forehead.

"Nothing," I say. *Everything*. My eyes start to fill.

"Lis, what's wrong?" His voice is low, his face so close to mine, I could play dot-to-dot with his freckles.

Breathe, I tell myself. *Think*.

"It's nothing. It's stupid." I blink away tears. "It's just, you know, that B Curlew gave me for our home essays. I really need to stay on an A if I'm going to get into Law and he didn't say it had to be deep. He should've graded me on what I wrote, not on what he *wanted* me to write."

Adam reaches for the tissue box on his bedside table but I wave it away. "He said he couldn't find me ... in my house ..." I roll my eyes. "The writing was good, but he wanted me to give him more. What does that even mean ... *giving more?*"

Adam is staring at me, not saying anything. Why isn't he saying anything? Maybe my psychotic rant about Mr C has freaked him out. I brick up my face. "Normally it wouldn't get to me," I say, "but I had a crap night's sleep, so maybe it was that."

He buys it. "Screw Curlew," he says. "*I* know who you are."

And I don't think, *No, you don't*. I think, *Please kiss me*. And he does, and there's only this bed and his hands on my body. And at last I can breathe.

He feeds his fingers through mine and we kiss until it's dark outside and then we kiss some more. He kisses me on the shoulder, the neck, my mouth, and it's an eight on the Richter scale. And that's what I need right now, a mind-blowing kiss. Then his hands are under my top and he's reaching for my bra. The air crackles between us.

"Do you want to?" he asks, his fingers at the clasp, and I nod because I want to feel this good – this lost – forever, but the red light on Adam's digital clock is flashing 9.42.

"I should go," I say, even though I don't want to.

He walks me the three blocks home and we kiss at my door. He's staring at me.

"So, how's soccer going?" I ask, shifting the spotlight.

"Good. Great. The new coach is awesome. He's a soccer tragic, like your dad. I reckon we're a chance for the finals this year. If we get in, I'll grab you some seats."

"The finals, when's that?"

"End of the season, four or five months."

Four or five months. Dad will be in a wheelchair. He'll have a feeding tube and a machine to help him breathe. I try to keep my face from imploding. I can't kiss away this conversation.

"Maybe," I say. "I've got a lot on."

Adam shrugs. He's smiling but it's the ghost of a smile. He unwinds his arm from my waist. "Sure," he says, "it's just soccer. No big deal."

Mr Curlew is droning on about gerunds and past participles. I try to stay awake but I'm so tired I could sleep for a week. I'm normally a good sleeper. The walls could be falling down and I'd still be comatose. But lately every time I close my eyes, I see yellow stars.

"Miss Keller!"

What? Where? I blink my eyes open. It takes a minute to realize I'm sitting at a desk in a classroom.

"Sorry," I whisper, my cheeks flaming.

I can feel twenty-seven sets of eyes burning a hole in the back of my brain. I force myself to look up into Mr Curlew's small brown eyes. His hair is greased down and he's wearing a pale yellow shirt, the same color as his skin.

"What's going on?" he asks, his voice quiet. "It's not like you to fall –"

Someone sniggers in the back row.

"Get back to work," he yells.

It's the first time I've heard him raise his voice and I feel like applauding. But this can go two ways – I tell Mr C why I'm snoozing or I avoid social suicide. I choose option B. I turn, so everyone can see me stretch and yawn. I move my lips silently. *So boring*, I mouth. Deb nods and Tracey laughs and then everyone's talking and Mr C is throwing up his hands.

The bell rings and I rush for the door.

Deb loops her arm through mine. "Oh my God," she whispers. "I can't believe you fell asleep!"

Mr C stops me at the door. "Can I have a word, Lisa?"

Deb gives me her best eye-roll and follows the rest of the class out.

"Is everything okay at home?" He parks himself on the edge of his desk. There are ducks on his socks.

"Yeah, of course," I say.

He has that I-don't-believe-you look on his face, but it's better than pity. "Because if there's anything you'd like to talk about ..." He is staring at me like he's trying to burrow under my skin. "Anything at all, we can –"

"No, I'm good," I say, and because I feel bad – because he is trying – I say, "I just haven't been sleeping well. Sorry about before. It wasn't the lesson ..."

There's nothing else to say, so I stop talking.

"Okay, then," he says. "Sure, you can go."

There's a note in my locker from Adam. Not a grubby one torn from an exercise book. This note is on pale blue stationery and his writing is careful. *Meet me outside the library.* I picture him kissing me behind the stacks, because the last time we were in the library we kissed. Behind the stacks.

But when I get there, Adam is not in the library. He's waiting for me outside. He grabs my hand and we skirt the library, turn a corner and scale a low stone wall.

"Happy anniversary," he says, pulling a chair out for me. It's just him and me, and a desk and two chairs set up on the hot asphalt, our own private restaurant.

"Did you actually –" I point to the desk.

"Yep, dragged it from chem lab." He flips open the lid and pulls out a package. "Cinnamon, right?" He hands me a box of Downyflake donuts. "Two months putting up with me. I figure I owe you." He grabs a donut and tears it in two. "To us," he says, handing me the bigger half.

I take a bite. I am a horrible girlfriend. Adam wakes up early so he can pick up my favorite donuts and break into a classroom to steal a desk, and I can't even remember it's our anniversary.

"To us." I cram the donut into my mouth so I don't have to say anything.

"You forgot, didn't you?" He licks the sugar from his fingers. "That's okay but I expect big things for our third."

I turn at the sound of footsteps. It's the Vietnamese girl and she's blushing more than I am. She's wearing the same outfit she wears every day – a white polo neck, a navy skirt that comes down to her knees and long socks with flip-flops.

"Sorry. I thought this was the way to the library." She hugs her books closer to her chest and now her cheeks are tomato-red.

"It is," Adam says. "Just head around that corner." He jumps up, pulls a donut from the box and balances it on top of her stack. "We got plenty."

"Come on, spill," Deb says, as soon as I sit down.
I open my lunchbox. Tracey and Karen huddle close.

"Spill?" I swallow hard.

Deb sighs dramatically. "Are we not best friends anymore? Because besties tell each other everything."

Shit. She's onto me.

"It's not a state secret. Paul told me ..."

"Paul?" I haven't told Paul about Dad. I haven't told anyone.

She digs a Twix bar out of her bag and rips the wrapper open. "Paul helped Adam with the desk. Whatever," she says. "You're no fun anymore."

"Oh, *that?*" I say, red creeping up my neck.

Maybe I *am* avoiding her. I feel a pang of guilt, and sadness too, that my best friend knows everything about me – where I was the first time I got my period and how badly I want to beat my brothers' senior year grades – but now there's this huge thing she doesn't know. This thing

I still can't tell her. Not here. Not like this.

I tell them about the note, the donuts and the desk. "You'll have to help me come up with something awesome next month."

Deb smiles and Karen claps her hands.

"Oh my God, I love a good romance. It's just like Charles and Di."

Tracey is only half-listening. Her eyes are tracking a tall, blond boy across the cafeteria.

"What about you?" I turn the spotlight back on Deb. "How are things going with Jason?"

"Darren," she says. "You're forgiven. Jason was last week; I got bored."

She drops her voice to a whisper and we all lean in. "We got to third base on Saturday night."

The girls high-five her.

"So, what do you think?" Deb asks, running her fingers through her hair. "I'm thinking I'll dye it pink."

"Yes, yes, yes!" Karen yelps.

Tracey adds, "That'll be super cool."

And I know I should be nodding my head frantically. I know my small smile will disappoint. I know I should tell Deb about Dad and our Friday night storytelling, but if I tell her, *I'll* become the story, and why can't I just be me?

So, I throw my arms around her and hug her instead.

Deb laughs. "I'll take that as a yes."

At school, people open their lockers and change into gym clothes and run to beat the bell. At home, Dad swaps his knife and fork for soups and smoothies. In between appointments and friends' visits and card games and dinner parties, he sleeps on the couch with a book splayed on his chest.

Today he's snoring and Mom is sitting next to him staring at the black square of the TV screen.

"Hey, Mom." I flop onto the couch.

"I always thought it was too good to be true." She shakes her head. "We were *so* happy ..."

"Oh, look at the time!" I jump up. "Jack and Tom will be here soon. I can set the table? Where do you keep the prayer book?"

Dad stirs, smiles and points to a drawer and I think about all the things I don't know about my father, all the questions I never asked and all the ways I've ignored him. All the Friday night dinners I cut short to sleep at Deb's when I could've stayed and asked about Auschwitz. I knew about the Holocaust. I'd studied the Second World War for a week in 9th Grade but I never asked him about it. How screwed up is that? I knew my dad had lost half his family and I'd never asked how. Or what that had done to him.

CHAPTER 10

THEN

My home for the next eight months was a coal mine in Jawischowitz. They drove us from Auschwitz in open-air trucks. It wasn't far. There were no seats on the truck so we stood watching the peasants dig fields and the farmers tend cattle. In Auschwitz there was only gray – mud, concrete and smoke – but here, minutes from the camp, was green grass and blue sky. And food, real food. I watched a boy pull a potato from the ground, drop it into his basket and bend to pull another one.

"I hear it's a work camp," Willie whispered as we approached the main gate. "Things will be better here."

They weren't. The camp wasn't as sprawling as Auschwitz but it was ringed with the same barbed wire. Different camp, but the same ugly barracks. The same floodlights and guard towers. The same tangled heap of bodies by the high-voltage sign. The gate swung open and our truck drove in.

We were shaved and handed a pair of underwear,

clothes for work, and a thin scrap of linen to towel ourselves dry after we washed. I stuffed the towel and the musty underwear under my cap and grabbed the bowl and spoon the young guard offered me. The guards were mostly young and German, boys around Willie's age, with cropped blond hair and round, ruddy cheeks. They wore their pants tucked into boots. We were from two different planets.

They made us line up for their boss, the director of the camp, a man with black hair and weasel eyes. He wore a carefully pressed uniform and stood facing us, looking bored.

"*Ausziehen u lass die hosen runter.*" He scraped a pocketknife under a fingernail and we slipped off our jackets and dropped our pants. "*Dreh dich um.*" We turned around so he could look us up and down.

A tall, thin-lipped guard stalked from the director's side. The guard reached out a gloved hand and next thing I knew I was being yanked from the line and marched away. I was shoved through a door and thrown at a bunk.

"Wait here," the guard said, closing the door behind him.

The barrack was dark and empty, a wooden shed with splintering shelves. I don't know how long I waited before the doors were flung open.

"Welcome to the youth barrack!" A boy who looked a lot older than Willie crouched down beside me. "You're really young, aren't you?"

"I'm old enough," I said.

"And I'm Andor." He smiled, showing off a full set of teeth. He kicked off his clogs and climbed onto the bunk above mine. "I'm twenty. Lied about my age to get in here," he peered over the edge of his thin mattress, "so we have *that* in common."

I turned away from him. I was alone, completely alone. I didn't know if Willie and Tatte were in the next barrack or on a truck back to Auschwitz.

"I know it looks bad," Andor said, "but trust me, if you saw the other barracks, you'd be smiling right now. This barrack is their showpiece, the one the Germans show visitors. There's about sixty of us in here. Same size barrack, next one over, has two hundred men, maybe more."

I rolled onto my back. I hadn't slept on my back for weeks. I'd have a whole bunk to myself here but still, I knew I wouldn't sleep. I was too worried about when I'd see Tatte and Willie again.

"Do you think my father and brother might be in the next barrack?" I looked up at Andor.

"Maybe," he said, jumping off his bunk and reaching a hand out to pull me from mine. "Want a tour? There's still a few minutes before roll call." He pointed to a trough. "That's where you wash your underwear and work clothes. They'll swap your stripes for a new uniform every two months. You were in Auschwitz," he said not waiting for an answer, "so you know the deal with food. The *kapo* is an asshole," he lowered his voice, "not as *big* an asshole as some of the others but if he asks you if you want a red coffee, say no. Last guy who held out his cup was smashed over the nose with the ladle and stood there, dripping blood into his cup."

Andor boasted that he saw his father every day, sneaking into his barrack to give him a piece of bread or a sausage he'd filched from the kitchen. "If they catch you," his fingers found a fading yellow bruise on his cheek, "they'll beat the hell out of you – or worse – but my dad's sick, so I don't really have a choice."

A whistle sounded and Andor bolted for his bunk. I lined up next to him. A fat man with a green triangle and mud-colored eyes swept through the barrack. He held a long stick in his stubby hand which he pointed straight at me.

"*Du bist neu?* You new?" He prodded my chest with the stick.

I nodded.

"Well, you won't be here for long." He slid a cigarette between his lips. "Four, maybe five weeks before someone scrapes you off your bunk and dumps you outside."

We attended roll call, same as Auschwitz, and then waited in line for dinner, same slab of black bread and bowl of soup. Shuffling back to the barrack I passed Tatte and Willie in the line and almost smiled. But a smile could get you killed so I buried it in a place the guards couldn't reach – the place Tatte had said my memories lived.

Willie's hand shot up when he saw me, but he thought better of waving and dropped it to his side. Tatte blinked twice, slowly. *I love you*, the blink said. *You'll be okay.*

We ate inside the barrack. I gulped down the soup but tore the bread in two, so I could trade half for a cigarette to stay good with the *kapo*.

"Hi." The boy on the bunk next to me extended his hand. "My name's Isaac," he said, accidentally spitting a piece of bread out with his name. He plucked the soggy crumb off his lap and slid it back into his mouth.

"Emil," I said, making another friend.

I'd convinced myself that I didn't need friends – I had Willie. But Willie was gone now, so I shook Isaac's hand.

"That's Joseph," he said, pointing to the boy beside him. "We look out for each other; the boys who sleep either side. We mind each other's shoes and bowls, make sure no-one steals our blankets. You in?"

I nodded.

"Do I look sick to you?" Joseph asked.

"Not again, Joe," Isaac pleaded. "They're going to catch you." He turned to me and lowered his voice. "He does this every few weeks. Tells the room orderlies he has a fever or the shakes, and when they shove a thermometer at him, he rubs it between his hands when their backs are turned." Isaac wagged a finger at his friend. "They're going to get wise to you."

"When *you're* working the mines and *I'm* here in bed, I have the whole day to pray to God," Joseph swatted away Isaac's concern. "He'll look after me."

The lights went out and we scrambled into bed. By 6 am the next morning I was on a truck bound for the Brzeszcze coal mine. By 6.20 I was standing to attention next to a long gray conveyor belt. Armed SS guards flanked the wire fence. German shepherds strained at their leads.

"Listen carefully, new boys!" The *kapo* brandished his stick, his voice spitting and mean. "You are the youngest and smallest here. Your job is to use those tiny fingers to pull stones from the coal that comes out of that shaft." He pointed to a black hole where the belt began. "This belt will start up in a few minutes and if you miss a stone or a rock – if I see even one shiny white nugget make it onto that truck at the other end of the belt – your rations will be cut." He smiled a snake smile. "I don't care if your legs get tired or your fingers ache. The only reason to stop work is if you're dying."

Our other jobs were to sweep the ground and clean the coaldust from under the conveyor belt. It was easy to get your fingers caught in the exposed metal. Isaac must have got too close to the cogs because one day it dragged his fingers in with his cleaning cloth. I rushed to turn the motor off but I was too late. His arm was ripped clean off his shoulder. The *kapo* ordered someone to prise it off the cogs.

A woman stopped at the belt, where I stood watching Isaac being loaded onto a stretcher. She was Polish and dressed neatly. I'd seen her before, serving sandwiches to the guards, but mostly walking the length of the belt, inspecting the load. She carried a clipboard and scribbled notes that she handed to the *kapo*. Sometimes he'd look up from her report and nod. Sometimes he'd wrap a hand around the foreman's throat and yell at him to increase production. "What are those *Judenhunde* doing down there?" The *kapo* would aim his stick at the shaft. "Taking a holiday? You tell those scum, no food tomorrow unless they speed things up."

The woman leaned over my shoulder, taking notes as she talked. "Don't expect your friend back."

She stopped by again later that day. "Be under the belt in five minutes."

She wasn't SS and she didn't have a gun but she had some sort of power because the *kapo* showed her respect, so I did as she said. A few minutes later a pair of leather shoes with a small heel tramped past and a shiny, red apple fell at my feet. I grabbed it, finishing it off in a few greedy bites, wondering what I'd done to deserve such kindness. Every day after that I ate under the churning wheels. Rye bread, pears, pickles – whatever the guards left on their plates. Whenever I saw the woman's hands I imagined my mother's, slipping me an extra slice of meat under our kitchen table.

Once, my Polish friend – she never told me her name – joined me in our secret restaurant. In between bites of herring and sausage I told her about baking *challah* with Mamme and collecting plums to make strawberry jam. I told her about Sari's crooked teeth and Dita's wild hair and how Tatte wanted me to go to university. She didn't talk much, but she listened like my stories mattered, like *I* mattered.

"You're so small, the smallest boy here, you should eat," she whispered. "Tomorrow I'll bring you bread."

Her kindness let me believe there was still goodness in people and that one day it might be put right, if I could just hold on.

I was sure Tatte, Willie and I could survive standing in the hot sun over a conveyor belt. It wasn't hard work; not like digging ditches or splitting rocks. When I finally spotted Tatte and Willie marching through the gate, I wanted to shout, *You were right, Tatte, we'll be okay*! Instead, I watched them shuffle past the belt and disappear underground.

I couldn't ask Willie what it was like in the mine shaft but Andor told me. His father worked there too.

"There's a lift that takes them hundreds of feets down a black hole. They blast coal and load it onto carts in the dark. It's dangerous work and if they don't fill four hundred wagons a day, the *kapo* keeps them under for a double shift."

"But how can they see what they're doing?" I whispered, imagining Tatte and Willie stumbling around in the dark.

"They get lamps. Without a light you're dead. There's no way to make it through the maze of corridors and even if you did, you wouldn't last long. Soon as you climbed out, the guards would shoot you for losing your gear. A few of the men who worked with my father –" Andor stopped short, but I begged him to go on. "They threw their lamps away."

When our shifts overlapped, I'd watch Tatte and Willie emerge from the mine, coughing up coaldust – Willie, bow-legged and blinking, his face powdered black, and Tatte bent over like an old man. Tatte's cheekbones jutted out, his arms were thin as matchsticks and his face vacant, but every time we locked eyes he'd blink and stare so intently that, marching away, I'd feel like we'd just had a conversation.

Willie was doing better than Tatte but he couldn't stand straight. I was getting fed under the belt and they were starving. I had to do something. So I snuck into their barrack. Willie was angry, at first. Said he wouldn't eat my food.

"It's too dangerous," he said. "*I'll* come to *you*."

Then he carved up the potato Andor had stolen for me, and he and Tatte wolfed it down.

Willie came every week to reassure me Tatte was still alive. He never asked for food – even after I told him about my Polish friend – but I always saved something for him. I was starving. If a blade of grass had grown in the soil of Jawischowitz, I would've torn it out and eaten it, but Willie and Tatte were hungrier. Their barrack was also more crowded and they had a meaner *kapo*. Willie didn't like to talk about him but I saw the bruises and black eyes.

"I don't want you to come anymore. It's too risky," I told him the next time he snuck into my barrack. "Promise," I said, handing him a week's worth of smuggled food. "Unless something bad happens to Tatte. Then come right away."

Days turned into months. I turned fourteen. I knew it was my birthday because Tatte stepped out of line as we were marching to roll call and shuffled toward me.

"Happy birthday, Elyuka," he whispered drawing me close, *happy* so out of place in that barbed-wire hell. And then he was gone.

Willie snuck into my barrack later that night with a present – a brick of bread with a matchstick shoved into it. He visited again, on a Sunday. Sunday was our day off in Jawischowitz. That meant cleaning the latrines and the barracks instead of working the mines. Every fourth Sunday Dr Mengele came to visit. I recognized him even without his stick. He was one of the doctors who stood at the podium at Auschwitz, choosing who would live or die. I guessed he was doing the same thing here. He'd have the *kapos* select a group of men – anyone who was weak, had a fever or a limp – and then make them run up and down, do star jumps and touch their toes. If they couldn't, they disappeared.

The Sunday after my fourteenth birthday, Tatte was ordered outside to join the selection. I was cleaning toilets at the time. Willie told me what happened. He'd watched the whole thing. He'd promised not to visit unless something bad happened so when he snuck to my barrack after lights out I knew he was bringing me terrible news.

"Is it Tatte?" I asked, when he woke me. "What's wrong?"

"They were all told to hop across the square." Willie's voice was hoarse. "Fifteen yards on the right foot, then

fifteen yards on the left. It was when he swapped feet."
Willie stared at his hands.

"What *about* his feet?" I wasn't whispering any more.

Willie slapped a hand over my mouth. "Tatte slipped on ice when he was younger. He broke his ankle, but back then no-one saw doctors. It healed by itself." Willie lifted his hand away cautiously. "Tatte hopped on his left foot, his bad foot, and buckled. He failed the test."

"Where is he?" I grabbed a fistful of Willie's shirt. "Can I see him?"

"They loaded him onto a truck and drove him away."

"Where? Where did they take him?"

"Mengele told them they were being taken to a sanatorium, but I think he just wanted to shut them up and get them on the truck."

"So Tatte's dead? You think they killed Tatte?"

And suddenly it was too hard to hold it all in – all the tears I'd held back since climbing off the cattle train – and I started to bawl.

"Shh." Willie grabbed me and pulled me close. "Don't cry." He patted my back. "I didn't say Tatte was dead, only that he's not in some resort recuperating. He's probably here, in the hospital, or at another camp."

We wrenched apart at the sound of footsteps. A lamp clicked on.

"I've got to go." Willie pulled away. "Tatte will be okay, he's strong, he *wants* to live."

The *kapo*'s door swung open and Willie ran from the room.

Tatte will be okay, I repeated the words in my head, repeated them over and over, as the *kapo* stalked the bunks. Over and over, until I believed them.

I learned to hate that day. I'd never really hated the boys at school. I just thought they were stupid. But Hitler wasn't stupid. The SS weren't stupid. The guards who put bullets in boys' heads weren't stupid.

I learned to hate without showing it, learned to cry without tears and speak without saying anything. We were so hungry it hurt, so thirsty we lifted our faces to the clouds and opened our mouths to catch the rain. Even with the extra scraps from my Polish friend I got so skinny I could close my thumb and third finger around my forearm. All anyone talked about was food. The hunger was different to any hunger I'd known. Different to the cattle train and the brickyard and even those first days in Auschwitz. The hunger built over months. I watched my muscles disappear and my stomach cave in. I was always hungry. It was a kind of torture to feel a stump of bread in my pocket, and only break off a crumb so there'd be something for later.

After Tatte was taken, everything turned a darker shade of gray. I watched Willie disappear into a mine shaft every day and had to fight to stop from wanting to disappear too. There was no escaping camp. There was the electrified wire and dogs and guards, and even if you were willing to take the risk – say by jumping from the truck on the way to the mine – you couldn't do it without taking a dozen people down with you. If I'd jumped and disappeared into the forest, the rest of the boys in the truck would've been shot.

The best revenge was to stay alive, to sleep with your food tucked under your head and slip the *kapo* cigarettes to buy his sympathy. Every night I'd knock on the *kapo*'s door and give him the cigarettes I'd bought with the guards' leftover sandwiches. Our *kapo* was mean. He'd beaten nearly every boy in the barrack. I'd escaped a beating, but I knew my luck couldn't last.

He was a drunk, and whenever he drank, he got more violent. One night he made us walk home from the mine.

"Walking's good for you," he said, pulling his flask from his jacket.

Everyone was on edge. It didn't take much to unleash his rage – a smudge on your face or a streak of dust on your arm, you walked too slow or looked at him wrong. By the time we got back, we'd missed dinner. I snuck to his room before lights out. He'd come to expect my little gifts and if I didn't show up, he might have come looking for me. The door was open so I went in.

"I won't keep you," I said, talking fast. "I just wanted to give you this." I held the cigarette out.

He staggered toward me and grabbed my arm. "Sorry ya mizzed dinner," he slurred, swaying as he spoke. His breath smelled like Tatte's kosher wine. "I know how much you like soup, Janek." He took my face in his sweaty hands and pressed his wet, reeking mouth to my forehead. "Next time I'll give you two bowls." He burped. "Don't be cross with your father."

I always thought the cigarettes were the reason he never hit me, but apparently it was because I looked like his son. I'd never thought of our *kapo* as someone's father. I couldn't imagine him warming a little boy's hands in his pockets or teaching him right from wrong. I couldn't imagine him beating his own son to death either, and that made me feel better. At least for a while.

CHAPTER 11

NOW

Dad has five months left to do all his living. And he's doing it here, back in the camps. I don't want to spend our last months in Jawischowitz.

"Can we get away this weekend?" I ask him, but he doesn't hear me. He's still in 1944.

"I stole food once," he says to no in particular. "Tatte had told me to remember who I was but I could barely remember the sound of my own name. And I wasn't Emil Rosenfeld, the smartest boy in school, anymore and I wasn't Tatte's son, the future lawyer. I was a stranger, a skeleton, a boy without a name. I'd been watching a boy who slept a few bunks up from me," Dad says from inside the nightmare. "He had food piled under his mattress: mouldy turnips, apple cores, bits of bread."

My mother pulls a tissue from the box on the table and blots my father's forehead. For years he couldn't find the words. And now they won't stop. Remembering must feel like walking on broken glass.

"One morning I noticed he wasn't moving. The *kapo* was banging the bunks, but the kid just lay there, not breathing. I knew by the time we reached the mine his bunk would be stripped, so I reached under his blanket and swiped his food."

"It's late," Mom says, consulting her watch. She holds her wrist out so Dad can see the time. "We can continue next week." She doesn't want to hear the things my father was ashamed about. Neither do I.

"I'm nearly done," Dad says. "I just need a drink." He looks at the peppermint tea Mom has poured into a cup.

"Oh!" she whispers, realizing.

I look away as she lifts the cup and holds it to his lips.

"I didn't eat the food right away," Dad ploughs on. "I waited a few days. I remember I used to write things on the floor, in the dust, after lights out. Kind of like a diary. I didn't have pens or pencils; I just used my finger. I drew letters. Names mostly. Dita. Sari. My own. Just to remind myself I wasn't a number. The day I swallowed the dead boy's food I wrote to Mamme. I told her the food would have gone to waste." He shakes his head. "Mamme hated waste."

"What happened to the boys in your barrack?" Tom asks.

"We became friends. It was easier to survive if someone had your back." Dad's voice is flat, a little less alive. "None of them survived."

Dad doesn't shed tears for his teenage friends. His voice is even and I wonder if his grief is buried next to his smile, in the place Tatte talked about where right and wrong live, and all of the other things that could get you killed.

"What about Andor?" Jack asks.

"Andor wouldn't listen." Dad shakes his head. "I told him to be careful. I begged him to be good. 'I'd rather see you alive than share another stolen meal with you,' I'd tell him, but he'd creep into the kitchen when the guards' backs were turned and stuff his shirt with scraps. He gave most of it to his father and the rest he shared with me. He was fearless. He'd slink in and out of lines of men, snaking his way to his father's hut and slip inside when the guards weren't looking. One night, after lights out, I heard him drop to the floor and tiptoe out. He never came back."

"What about the Polish lady who fed you under the conveyor belt? Did you see her again?" I dive in with a question, searching for a tiny spark of light in Dad's dark past.

"I was marched out of the camp a few months later." Dad frowns. "I never got to say goodbye. Or thank you."

I'm standing in the doorway of Mom and Dad's bedroom. Dad is sitting on the edge of his bed with his back to me, a small dumbbell in each hand. He curls his left arm, bringing the hand weight to his shoulder, exhales, then pulls up his right. "Five, six," he counts under his breath.

Sweat prickles his skin. He lowers the dumbbells, fills his lungs and tries again but his arms are trembling. Dad swears under his breath and drops the weights. I step into the room and scoop them from the floor. They are ten pounds each.

"Oh, I didn't see you there. What's up?" Dad says, hauling himself to standing.

"Nothing," I say. "Just wanted to say goodnight."

"Goodnight," Dad says, trying his best to hold out his arms.

I fall into his hug. "Is it hard?" I whisper into his neck. "Talking about the camps?" It's been five weeks and it's only just struck me how hard it must be.

"It's fine," Dad says, peeling me off him.

My eyes are superglued to the floor. "I just don't get how you're not angry. You know, about what they did to you."

"I'm not angry about *that*." Dad stares at the weights. "It's my arms and my voice and ... just give me a minute." He drops onto the bed and closes his eyes. When he opens them again his face is shuttered. "You were asking about the war." He blinks and clears his throat. "I'm not angry about that. Every day since the war has been a bonus. There were days I was convinced I'd never make it out, never get to see the world or dance with a beautiful girl or sit at a desk or swim in the sea. I got to see the circus. I learned to ski, I married that beautiful girl ... and I had you." Dad's smile warms the room. 1944 is back in its box. "So, are we driving tomorrow?" He shuffles to the bathroom and I follow him in.

"Sure," I say, picking up a hairbrush.

"I thought we could head up the freeway and then next week maybe we'll start you on *real* lessons."

The brush snags on a knot. "Like with an instructor?"

Dad grins like he's handed me a gift, but I know why he's quitting.

"Great," I say, yanking the brush through my hair.

Dad stares at the toothbrush Mom has left for him by the sink. It's already loaded with toothpaste.

"Okay, so I'll see you around ten?" I back out the door as Mom comes in, and I wonder if she's also thinking about all the taps and handles he won't be able to reach. All the switches and shoelaces and zips between now and sleep. And all the people in the world with two working arms.

Dad's friends visit. He greets them without a handshake. They tiptoe around, their faces smudged by shock. No-one mentions the D-word. Dad excuses himself, saying he's tired, but he's locked the study door and it's been hours since he's come out. When Mom knocks gently to tell him they've gone, he doesn't answer.

"Ernst brought your father's favorite shtrudel cake and he couldn't eat it," Mom explains. "He couldn't shake their hands and his voice wasn't loud enough to cut through the noise, so he just stopped talking. He'll be okay. He just needs time."

Time. The *one* thing Dad *doesn't* have.

I pull my headphones on and turn up the volume so Irene Cara is louder than Mom. I head to the kitchen, mouthing the lyrics to 'Fame', drop a piece of white bread into the toaster and open the fridge. Irene is gushing about heaven and fame and no-one forgetting her name. What does *she* know about death and eternity?

I kick the fridge door closed and stab the Walkman's eject button.

Dad just held a pen for the last time. He tried to sign his name on the school form I shoved in front of him but the pen kept slipping from his fingers.

"Why don't *you* sign it?" he said. "I reckon half the kids in your class have forged their parent's signatures. Go on," he nudged me with his shoulder, "go grab my wallet. You can copy the signature on the back of my licence."

I grab the licence and pick up a pen but I can't do it. They stole Dad's name in Auschwitz. I can't steal it a second time.

I find Mom at the kitchen table and hand her the form. "Can you sign it? It's permission to try out for the athletic leagues."

Mom takes the pen from me.

"I'm such an idiot," I say. "I just asked Dad to sign it." I look at Mom. She has dark rings around her eyes and her hair is stringy. "Can you check if he's okay?"

"Why don't *you* ask him? He's right there."

Dad is standing at the door. "Ask me what?"

I can't look at him. Three days pass. Or maybe it's a few seconds. "I'm sorry," I say. "Asking you to sign ... it was ..."

"It's okay," Dad says, lowering himself into a chair. "I knew it was going to happen. My hands have been getting weaker. It's a pain in the ass but I'm okay. Really," he says, comforting *me*. "Last week I could feed myself soup with a spoon." He speaks softly. "I spilled more than I ate and I hated mealtime but now I can't lift the spoon so Mom has to feed me. I've learned my lesson. Next month I might not be able to swallow so I'm going to accept every spoonful gratefully. I'm going to enjoy every mouthful."

My father motions me to scoot closer. I lean forward. We're so close our knees are touching.

"Celebrate today," my father whispers.

It's Saturday night and Tom, Jack and I haul mattresses outside so the five of us can sleep outdoors under the stars, like we used to when we were small. Before Jack got busy with university and Tom became too cool to do sleepovers with his sister. I wait for Dad to find something hiding in the sky and call out its name so we can race to be the first to find it – a dragon, a castle, a bear or a fish.

Instead, he says, "Feels like you could reach out and touch it, doesn't it?" He is staring up at the moon. "Thing is, it's more than almost two hundred thousand miles away, and because it takes time for the moon's light to reach us, right now what you're seeing is the past."

I wonder if he's trying to tell us something about other worlds, about how far apart we are from the boy in Jawischowitz. Or maybe he's just talking about the moon.

"Are the stars different here?" I picture the stars shivering above Auschwitz.

"In Australia?" Dad pulls himself up onto an elbow. "Brighter, definitely." His eyebrows knit together. "I don't know ... maybe their twinkle depends on where you are. In my village, stars in the night sky on a Friday meant the Sabbath had arrived and that meant time with Tatte. On the ship over here, the stars looked like sparklers." His smile stretches into a crescent moon. "And the stars that were out on the night of our first date –" He looks at Mom. "Do you remember, Eva?"

Mom nods and slips her hand into his.

"She thanked me for the stars." His eyes light up at the memory. "I couldn't afford a fancy restaurant, so I packed a picnic and we caught a tram to St Kilda beach. And at the end of the night she thanked me for the English words I'd taught her and for the stars and the moon."

"And the cheese," Mom laughs. "You brought good cheese."

Mom suggests we pack a picnic for Sunday.

"We could go to St Kilda beach?" Jack suggests. "Go for a walk, have a swim. I'm not on ward duty."

"I'm off too." Tom waves away a mosquito. "Why don't we make a day of it and cap it off with dinner?"

We fall asleep under the slanting moon and wake to a lavender sky. Mom packs a picnic basket and we head to the beach. We walk the foreshore, arms looped through Dad's so he won't tumble on the uneven sand. Today he doesn't seem to mind being held up, and we laugh and talk, even though his arms feel brittle. When we reach the shoreline, Dad sits on the wet sand, waves lapping his legs as he watches us swim. Mom has packed sandwiches for us and a thermos of soup for Dad. We stay all day, until the sky turns pink-gold and the sun slides into the water. I forget to call Deb.

Dad's smile is framed by a beard. Mom slides a spoon of breakfast into his mouth and asks me to grab a tissue. She's still in her nightgown, still hasn't showered or eaten. *Help her*, the walls whisper, but I don't.

"I've got to get to school early. We're training before class."

I toss her the box. I can't pick bits of egg from my father's beard or blow his nose. And I don't want to watch her do it either.

"Kiss?" Dad says tilting his head.

History repeats itself.

Dad watched Tatte wait for death and I'm watching Dad.

Tatte was refused food. Dad can't feed himself. Tatte got so weak he couldn't hop. Dad's arms don't work.

We have shared a similar hell, Dad and I, watching our fathers grow weak and silent. I bend to kiss Dad's cheek. At least I get to say goodbye.

I shake Dad's ghost off at the school gate and walk onto the quad. Kids are huddled together on the hot concrete. I spot Deb and the others in a cluster of gossip and run to join them.

"So, he never called me back." Tracey is frantic. "I mean, I called him twice. I don't understand. We had an awesome night Friday night. *You* saw us. He was all over me."

Karen is nodding like a crazy person and Deb is reaching for Tracey's hand.

"I stayed home *all* Saturday." Tracey chews on a flaking fuchsia fingernail. "But he didn't call. So, I called him on Sunday and his mom said he wasn't home." She spits a wedge of nail onto the hot asphalt. "I *know* he was home. Maybe he thinks I'm a dork?" She breathes out.

"Really?" I say, except I hadn't meant to say it out loud. It comes off sneery, like, *Really? Is this what you're wasting our time on? My dad can't feed himself and you don't hear me monopolising Monday.*

Tracey's pink mouth is an O. Karen is shaking her head and Deb is looking at me like I'm a walking personality disorder.

"I mean, look at you," I backpedal. "You're gorgeous, a total hottie. He's a spaz if he doesn't know how good he has it."

"No shit, Sherlock," Deb says.

"Okay," Tracey says, rummaging in her bag for makeup. "So, what I'm hearing is ..." She swipes metallic orange eyeshadow across her lids. "I can do better."

We nod frantically.

"So much better," I say.

Tracey smiles and slips her arm through mine. "The new girl, she'd be kind of pretty if she grew her hair." She points to a bench where the new girl sits eating cold noodles from a bamboo box.

"Mai," Karen says. "Her name is Mai. She's in my French class."

"Well, Mai might as well have a giant red X taped to her back," Deb says. "Do you think we should tell her about the flip-flops with socks thing?"

"And the chopsticks," I say. "We could leave a note in her locker?"

But by recess Mai is yesterday's news. All anyone's talking about is Gavin Brown's dad, who's been spotted sleeping in his car.

I heard he goes to AA.

He lost his job.

I hear they're separating.

Poor Gavin.

I skip the cafeteria for the track. It's quiet out here, just the pounding of sneakers on bitumen and my in-and-out breath. I run at lunchtime too. Every day up to the athletic leagues trials. I don't picture snarling German shepherds chasing me or faceless men in SS uniform. It's just me, trying to outrun time.

"Hey, you."

I look around the track, shielding my eyes with my hands. "Hey," I say, finding Adam leaning against the fence that rings the track.

"It's lemonade." He's holding out a popsicle. "Your favorite."

I lunge for it.

"Uh-uh," he says, pulling the popsicle away. "You gotta pay up front."

I'm sweating. Big, dark, oval patches under my arms and down my back. "You really want to kiss *this*?"

He nods like a bobblehead.

I lean over the fence and kiss him and it's clammy and warm and I reek of sweat but he's smiling when I pull away.

"That's better," he says. "I was getting withdrawals. Haven't seen you all week."

He hands me the popsicle and scoops the hair from his eyes. The sun's hitting his face and his eyes are electric. "So, want to catch up Saturday night?"

"I'd love to," I say, shoulders drooping, "but I can't. We're going away Saturday morning."

"I could come?" Adam's mouth pulls into a smile. "Not for the weekend. For dinner Friday night."

I shake my head. "Uh, I'm, we –"

"Don't worry about it," he says, the light gone from his eyes. "I forgot I promised ... I said ... I'd ..." His words trip over each other. "I told Mom I'd stay home. She's making my favorite – bolognese – so, yep, I forgot. Sorry." He swallows his hurt and walks away.

You can't tell him the truth now, at school, with everyone watching. You did the right thing, I tell myself, tamping down the guilt. *It's just a weekend.* I head to the quad. *You can make up for it by telling him next week. No, not next week. Maybe the week after.*

"Congrats! You made the team!" Deb waves me over.

She's wearing a sweatband. We *hate* headbands. She's sitting with a group of girls I don't recognize and wearing a yellow jumpsuit I've never seen before.

"Thanks," I say, dropping down next to her.

"So, I was thinking," I say, "it's Dad's birthday next week and Mom is dropping me at the shops after school so I can buy him a present. Want to come?"

A girl in legwarmers with Olivia Newton John-wannabe hair leans in to the conversation. "We've got rehearsal after school," she says, pulling a tube of lip gloss from her bag and offering it to Deb. I watch, horrified, as Deb spikes her lips with cherry-red gloss.

"Oh, sorry," Deb laughs, "Lis, this is Kim. She's an insane actor."

An actor. Great. The drama kids in our school are God-like and as close to celebrities as you get. She's probably tried out for *Sons and Daughters*.

"Oh my God," Deb says, turning back to Kim. "That scene you did with Will yesterday. You killed it."

They're talking a million miles a minute, their hands diving into the same Cheetos packet, and I momentarily lose my mind because I'm waving and saying in a voice I don't recognize, "… and I'm Lisa, Deb's best friend."

Kim smiles and Deb says, "Sorry, I can't come shopping, Lis. Maybe next time. Say happy birthday to your dad."

"Sure," I say, trying to act cool.

I tip my head back and drain the last of my Fanta. I'm only half-listening to the drama gossip when Deb mentions a new boy. Jeremy someone.

"What happened to Darren?" I try not to sound shrill.

"Dumped." Deb rolls her eyes. "Too needy."

"He was hot," Kim says, "but clearly missing a frontal lobe. I mean calling you *every* night?"

"Crazy, right?" Deb looks at Kim, and Kim looks at Deb. No-one looks at me.

I slide Deb a note in class when Mr C's back is turned.

Who's the new boy?

Jeremy Carruthers.

Tall?

Basketballer, so that's a yes.

Blond?

Beach blond.

12th Grade?

Yep. Kim introduced us.

You like him?

Big time.

I'm drawing a baseball pitch, marking out the bases with little check boxes for Deb to tick, but I change my mind and rub it out. *Are we okay?* I write instead.

I wait for her answer.

I was going to ask you the same thing.

I look up at the clock. Three minutes till the bell.

Deb lobs another note. *You've been kind of a space cadet.*

I'm okay, I write. *Sorry. Just a lot going on.* I toss Deb the note.

She reads it and shrugs. "Like what?" she mouths.

The bell dings and we file out of class.

"Is it Adam?"

"Adam?" I wheel around to face her.

"I don't know, he went to Leanne's party on Saturday night. He only went because you were busy," she says, but it comes out like a question.

"Yeah," I say. "I was."

We head for the lockers. I don't tell her that I didn't know Adam went to Leanne's because it's not a big deal. And if I tell her, she'll make it a big deal.

"So, what's going on?" She stops at my locker.

"Nothing." I sweep books into my bag so I don't have to look at her. "I've just been swamped with training and trying to get my driving hours up."

"Long as you're good," she says, scanning the hall.

"I'm good." I smile and point to my face. "See?"

But she's not looking at me. She's waving down Kim.

Dad's turning fifty-two and I have no idea what to buy him. I stare at the men's colognes lined up on the shelf like

146

soldiers. And beyond the wall of bottles, men's shaving kits, socks, wallets and ties. I swat the tears from my cheeks. Cologne, a new tie, cufflinks, what's the point? I can't give Dad what he really needs.

I leave the bright lights and leathery smell of the men's floor of the department store and catch the bus home. There's a cupboard way up high in my parents' bedroom packed with the story of our lives – Mom and Dad's wedding album, our birth certificates, school reports, sports trophies and old birthday cards. I grab a stepladder and, balancing on the top rung, open the cupboard and reach in, feeling for a box I haven't touched in years, relieved to find, when I open it, dozens of carefully labelled super-8 films. Using Mom's markings, I order them by year. There's nothing before 1950. No footage of my father's village and his tumbledown house. No home movies of a small boy in a worn coat with a yellow star. No smiling, ragged teenager with toothpick legs, just back from war.

I creep into the study where Mom keeps the photo albums. There has to be something here – a stack of faded black-and-white photos or an old album that traveled with Dad on the ship. I pull album after album from the shelves until I'm sitting cross-legged on the floor surrounded by all the moments he didn't want to forget, starting with a photo of Dad clutching a small suitcase. I turn the photo over. On the back, in Dad's no-nonsense handwriting, are the words *Port Melbourne, January 1950.*

I'll never meet the boy with the yellow star on his

jumper. I pull an album from the floor and open 1972. There's me, snowploughing between my father's skis, my mittened fingers wrapped around his legs. There's Dad in bathers, his feet strapped into waterskis, lifting a hand to wave at the boat. Jack in a karate uniform holding an orange belt. Tom and Dad in a three-legged race stumbling toward the finish line.

I free a handful of photos from their plastic pages and go back to the start, pulling pictures from 1950, working through the years until I reach 1982. I pick up the small tower of photos, wind an elastic band around Dad's life, and slide the stack into a backpack with the film reels. I've read the ad taped to the window of our local electrical goods store, so I know that for a small fortune they'll convert Dad's life to a VHS videotape. I grab my bank book, feed my arms through the straps of my backpack and head out.

Dad sits at the table, in the small spill of light cast by the candles. A checked dishrag is draped over his pants. Mom sits angled opposite him, feeding him soup. Swallowing is hard. He coughs a lot. He has to chew his food to a pulp so it goes down. When he asks about our week, his voice is soft. I've become used to his dissolving words, his dying language.

Tom tears at the *challah*. Jack carves up the chicken.

"Let's start," Dad says.

He's smiling but I know the sad is somewhere there inside him, behind all those walls he's built between 1944 and now. I think I'm ready for the detonation; ready for the last of the walls to blow. I'm almost seventeen. Dad was thirteen when they shoved him into that cattle train. And if I don't do this now, I might not get another chance. I lean in. Dad is about to disappear into some dark room in his head and I want to walk in with him. I want to see everything he is seeing behind those blue eyes.

"Winter arrived," Dad begins, and the room fills with ghosts. "The days were short and the nights freezing."

I picture my dad on a bunk, teeth chattering. I picture Willie in the snow, pulling his cap off his head with frostbitten fingers. Tatte might die tonight. Willie too.

I take a deep breath and step into the story. *It's okay to be scared*, I hear Willie whisper, *just don't let them see your fear*.

CHAPTER 12

THEN

Winter arrived and the cold made the guards meaner. Our workload was doubled and our food rations halved. My hands and feet stung from the cold, my lips were blue and my fingers numb. The only time I stopped shivering was when I wrapped my hands around a bowl of hot soup or crawled into bed between two bodies.

By the end of November, we were digging ditches for the German army every night after work. They gave us secondhand boots and thicker uniforms but we didn't get gloves or coats, even though the temperature dipped below zero and we spent our days hacking at the frozen countryside. We were trucked out to work alongside prisoners from a neighboring camp. The Buna Monowitz inmates knew more than we did. They told us about other camps and what the SS did with Jews who failed selection.

I scooped a handful of snow into my mouth and swore I wouldn't give up on my family, not until I was freed

and back in Porubka, and could see for myself who had
survived, and who hadn't.

By January 1945, we were on the move again. We weren't
told why we had to leave or where we were going.

"We're being evacuated tomorrow," was all the *kapo* said.

The barrack erupted. Men jumped from their bunks,
pelting him with questions.

"Where are we going?"

"Will we be fed?"

"How long will the march last?"

The *kapo* cracked some ribs with his stick and the
crowd dispersed. "All you need to know is that we leave
in the morning."

He pointed his stick at a pile of blankets and told us to
grab one. "Take your bowl and anything else you can get
your hands on."

A second guard stood at the door, his beard covered
in ice, a hand on his gun. I climbed onto my bunk and
looped my arms around my knees. A boy two bunks down
draped a blanket around his shoulders, and tied it at the
waist with a piece of rope.

"Got to stay warm," he whispered, packing mattress
stuffing into his new coat. "You need those boots?" He
turned to me. "I can trade you a cap for them?"

I shook my head. With or without boots, we weren't
going to survive the march. Not in the snow. Not without

food or shelter. *Food*. My stomach twisted. I climbed off the bunk and on my hands and knees I combed the floor for a crust of bread or a corner of cheese that I could save for the march, but it had been licked clean.

"What if we hid?" the boy next to me wheezed. "The *kapo* might not count us? The Russians are coming. We could wait for them."

"No," the boy in the blanket said. "I've heard the guards talking. They have orders to kill anyone left in the camp. In a couple of days this place will be a graveyard."

At first light we were forced from the barrack into a snowstorm. We marched, our fingers and faces numb. The storm was a blinding white, and yet somehow Willie found me. He told me not to look down, but I'd already seen them; the boys who'd refused to walk and the men who'd collapsed. It was impossible not to see the bodies in the ditches, leaking blood onto the snow. I lifted a wet boot and pushed my tired legs forward.

I was hungry and my shoes were full of snow. It was at least ten below zero but I just kept walking. I walked all day. When I stumbled, Willie's arms caught me. When he slipped and fell, *I* dragged *him* to his feet. We marched for hours. All you could hear was the crunch of boots and the occasional shot exploding into someone's chest. But then, every so often, the sky sparked red and the guards lowered their guns. Something was on fire. Maybe Jawischowitz was burning?

A rumor slipped through the line of men – the station where we'd been heading was under Russian control.

We were ordered off the road through a snow-covered field in a different direction. It must have been midnight before they ordered us to stop. We'd come to three stables. Two were already crammed with prisoners and the third was filling up fast. I was about to push my way in when a guard stepped in front of us and barred the way.

"That's enough of you in there. The rest of you, lie down." He clubbed the man next to me with his rifle butt, sending him reeling into the snow.

I lay down fast, pulling Willie down next to me. "I'm sorry," I whispered. "If I'd walked faster, we'd be warm."

It was still half-dark when I woke the next morning. Prisoners were flooding out of the third stable, climbing over each other, frantic to get out. An old man collapsed beside me. He rocked backward and forward, his eyes glazed, his mouth whispering his son's name. The boy had been sleeping next to him when the loft above them came crashing down. The old man had escaped with a shattered knee, but his son had been crushed.

I waited for Willie to open his eyes, then I hugged him. "There's coffee," I whispered, dragging him to the back of the line.

We drank the coffee they gave us and gnawed at the block of frozen bread that would have to last us all day.

"*Alles raus!*" the guards shouted. "*Vorwärts marsch! Eins, zwei ...*"

I dragged myself on. Every few steps, someone buckled and a shot rang out. After a while I stopped noticing the bodies. I passed boys with frozen stares and men buried under snowdrifts, and felt nothing. It was like I was on autopilot. My head and heart had stalled but my legs were still moving.

Even when the voices in my head got loud – *Die and you can rest. Stop and you can sleep. Give up and you can stop fighting.* Even when I found myself imagining the sweet relief of resting my head on a snowdrift, I'd force my eyes open and talk to myself. *You don't want to die, you don't want to die. Not now, not after all you've been through.*

Hours passed. Willie would shake me every time my head dipped and I'd stare at him, confused, my legs moving, my mind numb. Snow clung to his eyebrows and the stubble on his chin.

He shook me again. "The Russians are coming," he whispered, shoving snow into my mouth. "They're on their way. Just hold on a bit longer."

The Russians are coming, I whispered to the trees. I tried to keep my eyes open, tried to lift my legs.

"I can't." My knees buckled and Willie caught me. "I can't stay awake. I'm sorry." I tried to wriggle from his grip. "I'm slowing you down. I'm putting you in danger. Go," I begged Willie. "Please. Just go."

Willie turned to his friend Jacob and shouted something into the wind, and then they were either side of me, hauling me up by the armpits and dragging me forward. Something exploded and the sky glowed orange.

"The Russians are close. Maybe they'll come tonight?" I heard Willie say.

"They better hurry," Jacob whispered. "He hasn't got long."

Willie pressed his mouth to my ear.

"We're going to make it home, Emil. All I need you to do is stay with me. Can you do that?"

I wanted to say yes but the word froze in my throat. I wasn't cold, just tired; so tired. *Sleep, Elyuka, you're exhausted,* I heard Tatte say. I let my head drop and my arms hang by my side. *I'll take care of you.* Tatte smiled his crooked smile. Then he turned out the lights and the room went dark.

I woke from a dazed sleep, expecting to see snow, but instead I saw the wooden slats of an open cattle car. I swept my hands over the boards and tried to remember how I got here.

"He's awake!" I heard Willie's voice. "Here, take some snow, Emil. Eat. You need strength."

I sucked on the ice my brother scraped from the carriage floor and huddled closer to him to keep **warm**.

"Is it over?" I whispered. The last thing I remembered Willie saying was that the Russians were coming.

Willie shook his head. "The bastards are taking us to another camp."

I looked around the carriage. It was hard to tell the living from the dead. "How did I get here?"

"Jacob helped." Willie rubbed his hands together, his breath fogging in the frozen air. "We dragged you between us and hauled you onto the train. You've been asleep for three days. I fed you snow and stole clothes from the dead to keep you warm." He pointed to the jacket I wore over my shirt and the pants he'd wrapped around my neck like a scarf.

The carriage stopped and someone started shouting. "*Raus! Schnell!* Out quick!"

We climbed out of the carriage and followed the guards through a set of gates. There were thirteen of us. The rest of the prisoners stayed in the wagon; some too weak to climb off, most of them dead. It was my third concentration camp. I was so used to dogs and guns and barbed wire that when I walked through the gates of Buchenwald, I barely registered the surroundings.

"*Los! Funferreihen!* Rows of five!" A *kapo* reached for his stick and we scurried forward.

We were shaved again, dunked again, shoved into showers. I gave my number to a fat man who sat behind a desk.

"Juden!" he spat, and someone flung a jacket at me. It had a yellow upside-down triangle and a new number; my new name.

By the time I stepped through the door of my new barrack – a huge dilapidated shed beyond the main camp – my uniform was covered in a dusting of black ash. There must've been more than five hundred boys crammed into that barrack, a tangle of bones and rags, packed so tight you couldn't see the bare boards under them. I squeezed between Willie and a man who didn't talk on the third tier of a four-storey bunk bed, staring across the wide passage at the boys on the other side, hoping to see a familiar face from Jawischowitz.

The barrack stank and the bunks were crawling with lice. I didn't recognize any of the worn-out faces staring back at me, but I could feel Willie's breath on my neck. Most of the boys here were alone. We'd all lost our homes, our names and our mothers but I had a brother. Here, right next to me. A brother who shared his food with me and dragged me to roll call. A brother who had the same wide nose and freckled skin I had; someone I could look at when I started to forget who I was.

"There's no work for you in Buchenwald," they told us at roll call as we stood in the dark with snow up to our ankles.

Our job was to clean the barracks, the latrine and the small yard in the *alter lager*. If we were caught outside our block, we'd be shot. Escape from Buchenwald was impossible.

I looked up at the white sky and wondered what it would feel like *not* to be frightened.

"Do you remember what it feels like?" I asked Willie, knowing I shouldn't, knowing we weren't allowed to talk. If they caught you, the *kapos* came at you with their batons. I'd never been struck so maybe I'd got sloppy.

"What *what* feels like?" Willie whispered.

"Being happy. Not being scared. Feeling full. Being warm."

Willie's eyes flew open. He shook his head, but I didn't see the *kapo* until it was too late. He brought his stick down hard, the blast of pain so sharp I was sure he'd broken my back.

"*Nicht sprechen!*" I heard him yell as Willie dragged me away, a hand clamped over my mouth to stop me from screaming.

My skin burned where it had been sliced open and my back ached for weeks. After that I never spoke outside, out loud. I stood at roll call in the murderous cold and swallowed my coffee, but I wouldn't talk. All I could offer Willie was a blink to let him know I was okay; the same blink Tatte had offered me all those months ago in Auschwitz.

I stopped counting the days. I became numb to the cold. I stopped noticing the rats. The dead feeling was a kind of relief. Things hurt less. But Willie *wanted* me to feel. We'd seen the *muselmann* lying on their bunks, their eyes empty, their mouths slack.

"Once a prisoner looks like that," Willie had said, pointing to a man whose forehead was crawling with lice, "once they stop washing and getting out of bed to pee, you know it's the end."

Willie tried to get me to talk at night after the *kapo* was snoring behind his locked door, but I didn't know what to say. That they'd made us into animals? That we looked like lunatics in our mismatched shoes and threadbare uniforms? He'd only say that whatever we wore, we were more human than our captors could ever hope to be. I knew he was right, but still, God had abandoned us and chosen to give the Nazis guns. If a *muselmann* was someone who felt completely hopeless, then maybe I *was* a *muselmann*.

"You have to wash," Willie would scold me. "Clean your food bowl. Don't forget your cap!"

The weeks dragged past. I marched, I ate, I swept out the latrines, but I was dead inside. I knew I shouldn't give in to my sadness. To be sad was weak. If you were weak you died. I tried to hold on to hope, to picture Mamme's face, and Sari feeding Minu's calf, but the images wouldn't stick. I couldn't remember what milk felt like sliding down my throat. I couldn't conjure the smell of Mamme's smoked meat or remember the color of the suit I'd worn to my *bar mitzvah*.

I made elaborate plans to end my life – I'd run at the electric fences, I'd attack a guard, I'd break into the *kapo*'s room and someone would fire a gun and it would all be over. Or I could just walk. Walk out the barrack door and leave our block. Or I could talk, raise a hand, laugh out loud, ask a question. There were a hundred ways you could die in Buchenwald.

I imagined all of them, but when the time came, I couldn't do it.

"What's that?" Willie said, tugging at my collar.

I shrugged. It was a lump. I'd had it for weeks. It wasn't sore, so I'd ignored it.

"It might be a boil, let me see." Willie ran his fingers along the back of my neck. "It's the size of an egg, Emil. You need a doctor to drain it."

"Can't *you?*" I whispered. I'd heard the camp infirmary was death's waiting room. "The revier – the sick quarters – is where prisoners go to die," Andor had warned Joseph.

I reached back to feel the tender spot at the base of my neck.

"They don't feed patients," I said, pulling my collar up over the boil.

"Jacob's little brother works in the kitchen." Willie took my arm. "I'll get you food."

I let Willie take me. The snow was beginning to thaw but the wind was still icy. In the revier I wouldn't have to get up at 5 am and stand in the driving rain while they counted us. I could lie in bed and sleep all day.

The revier was cold; a narrow ward crammed with bunks. A wooden bench ran the length of the room, its pocked surface hidden under buckets of shit, balled tissues and discarded needles.

"This way." A nurse led me past a man with a sticking out stomach, and a prisoner lying naked on sopping sheets. None of the patients turned to look at me. They stared into space with glazed eyes, or slept like exhausted animals curled on their bunks.

We stopped at a door.

"Come in," the nurse said, offering me a tired smile. "Get undressed and climb up."

She pointed to a table topped with a paper pad spattered with blood. Under the table, on the floor, were four pieces of rope. I did as I was told, hoisting myself onto the table just as a man stepped into the room. He had bloodshot eyes and was clutching a kitchen knife, the type Mamme used for slicing beef. There was a sink in the corner of the room but he didn't stop to wash his hands. He stepped toward me, holding the knife, its sharpened edge glinting in the fluorescent light.

The nurse stuffed a rag into my mouth and turned me over so I was face down, my nose pressed to the stained bedsheets while she wound the rope around my arms and legs, fixing me to the table. I tried to lift my head, to beg them to stop, but the words came out muffled. The heel of a hand forced my head down and then there was an awful tearing pain, worse than any I'd ever known.

Nails tore at my skin. My neck was on fire. I clawed at the table. And then I passed out.

CHAPTER 13

NOW

We're at the beach in a brown brick motel with a wading pool and a view of the sea. Mom has packed all Dad's gear – measuring cups, medicine, his special toothbrush and pillow.

Dad's door opens and he steps into the sunshine. "Mom's unpacking. She'll join us for lunch. Are we still walking?"

The three of us nod.

"Let's go," Jack says, looping his arm through Dad's.

We head to the beach. It's warm. White clouds scud across the sky. The waves lap at Dad's size 11 feet.

"Do you mind?" Dad says, glancing down at his cardigan. "I didn't realize it was going to be this hot."

Jack works Dad's arms from the sleeves and knots the cardigan around his waist. Dad is wearing a T-shirt that was bought for a bigger man. It sits sloppy on his shoulders and gapes at the neck. I try not to stare at the pink, puckered scar.

We walk alongside the scalloped green ocean, everything so alive – the churning sea, the scuttling crabs, the wind rippling the spear grass.

"I'm sorry," Dad says, "can we stop for a bit?" His forehead is bubbled with sweat. "Crazy, that I walked through the snow for three days with no food, and now –" He sucks in air.

"The march from Jawischowitz?" Tom asks.

"The Death March," Dad corrects him. "That's what they called it in history books. We didn't give it a name. There weren't words for the things they did to us."

I imagine a book filled with strange new words, words that had to be invented for the things the guards did to my father; words to describe what happened at roll call and in the showers that weren't showers and the ovens that baked men.

Dad stares past us. We're a world away from winter, but I imagine him a pale, blinking boy, dragging his feet through the snow, thick snowflakes settling on his shoulders, the cold finding its way through the buttonholes of his shirt. How did a boy like that grow into my father? A man who chose to spend winter weekends in the mountains teaching his children to ski? We weren't allowed to stay indoors during the day, no matter how hard it snowed. "Put on an extra layer," he'd say, heading out. When our toes were numb, he told us to focus on our snowplough. When our fingers were stiff with cold, he warmed our hands in his pockets. How did the dead not crowd the slopes? How was he not haunted by the marbles of ice he pulled from my plaits? By the sight of his daughter, a snow angel collapsed in a drift?

Dad lets Jack guide him back to the pool and deposit him in a chair under the blunt shade of an umbrella. Mom joins us and we order lunch. She feeds Dad chicken and corn soup, plucking bits of chicken from the bowl so she can shred them.

"I'm going to hospital this week." Dad's smile becomes unstuck. "I'm getting a feeding tube."

The sun ducks behind a cloud. The birds stop singing.

"Dad's been losing weight," Mom says, her hands twisting and knotting. "His doctor was worried he wasn't getting enough nutrients and the swallowing's getting hard."

I stare into my glass. There's already so much less of my father.

"It's not fair," Mom says, and Dad shoots her a look.

"I won't be able to taste food but I'll still get fed," he says, "and *yes*, I suppose that's sad but if it means I live a bit longer, then it's a good thing, isn't it?"

I nod and try to keep up. Every week Dad casts off a bit more of himself. I'm trying to be okay with losing these little bits of him, but it's all happening so fast. And just when he's decided to start talking.

Sunday is Dad's fifty-second birthday. We fill the room with balloons and birthday banners and hunker around my father, reading our birthday cards out loud. Mom has spent the morning preparing Dad's favorite foods, blasting them in the vitamiser and delivering them in a cup. Dad can't eat cake so Mom burrows candles into a chocolate mousse and we hip-hip-hooray and help him blow them out.

Tom and Jack lug a box to the table and unwrap it for Dad – a TV for the bedroom. Mom unwraps a framed photo of Dad the day he was voted in as mayor. He is wearing a robe trimmed with velvet and silk, and a smile the size of Europe. I pull a video tape from my backpack and slide it into the motel VCR. Everyone moves to the couch to watch black-and-white footage of Mom and Dad walking hand in hand down a beach, Dad sitting at a workbench melting gold, Mom in a lace wedding gown stepping out of a car, the two of them exchanging vows in front of a rabbi.

Dad sits, warmed by the memories. I wish I could shrink us into the film, into that beautiful and happy world where Dad danced and hiked mountains and had time to spare.

Jack drives us home on Sunday night. I pull the video from my backpack and leave it on top of the VCR. I won't watch it again. I don't want Dad to be some guy on a video I tell my kids about. I want him to pick them up from school and buy them ice-cream and take them to the park. I never had grandparents to do that, and now my kids won't either.

The phone rings.

"Hey," I say, when I hear Adam's voice. "I was thinking maybe after school we could catch up?" I need to make up for all the nights I've bailed on him.

"Gran died." Adam's voice hitches. "Yesterday."

"Oh, I'm so sorry. I didn't know she was unwell."

"She wasn't," he says. "I mean she was old – seventy-eight – but there was nothing wrong with her." He blows his nose. "Anyway, I won't be at school tomorrow."

"Do you want me to come to the funeral?" I say, filling the awkward silence. "I will if you want me to –"

"No," he says, his voice flat. "It'll probably be small, just family."

I feel a wash of relief.

"There's a wake tomorrow night, at six, if you wanna come to that –"

"Of course," I say. "I'll tell Deb and the others."

"They already know."

"Oh."

"You were away ... so ..."

"No. Of course."

Mom picks up the phone and for once I'm glad. "Lisa, it's after ten."

"Okay. Getting off."

The phone clicks.

"So, I'll see you Monday night?" I try and think of something comforting to say. "She was lucky. She got to seventy-eight."

"Lucky?" he says, dully. "Yeah, sure, whatever."

Mr C is calling the roll. Deb is away, Karen too. When Mr C marks Tracey and Paul down as absent, he looks up from his clipboard to scan the room. Three boys from the soccer team aren't at their desks. Neither is Leanne.

"What's going on?" he says, fingers pianoing the desk. "Are the Beatles in town?"

It doesn't get a laugh.

Mr C clears his throat. "Okey-dokey, then. Let's get to work." He pulls *Romeo and Juliet* from the stack of books on his desk. "Reading aloud from the top of page 34. Who wants to be Juliet?"

I superglue my eyes to the desk. I'm hardly a candidate. Juliet would have gone to a Montague funeral. Even with all the Capulets hating on her. I count the empty desks. Seems like anyone who ever passed Adam in the hall or sat next to him at assembly is at his gran's funeral. Everyone except me.

Mai is waiting in line at the cafeteria. Two airheads from 9th Grade cut in front of her.

"They're all out of flied lice," one of them says to her. "But if you like long-dong-dik ..."

They crack themselves up. Mai studies her tray.

"Assholes," I whisper under my breath.

"Sorry?" she says.

"Ignore them," I say, "They're just –"

"– giant dicks?" She smiles and I smile back.

It's the flip-flops with socks, I want to tell her, *and the haircut and the noodles.*

"Lis!" Deb waves me over.

I stuff a dollar into the cashier's palm for my Cheetos and head to our table.

"What gives?" she says when I sit down. "You weren't at the funeral and *you're* the girlfriend."

I slump in my seat. "He said it was going to be small, just family."

"We're family," Deb says.

Karen and Tracey nod their agreement.

"So, do you want me to pick you up tonight?"

"I don't know," I say, getting flustered.

Mai is walking toward us, tray in hand, eyes smiling. There's an empty seat next to me.

"Can I have a sip?" I swipe Tracey's bottle of Sprite and suck on the straw. When I lift my head from the bubbles, Mai is gone.

"Okay, so I need some advice." Deb's eyes slide left, to a boy with shaggy blond hair wearing a faded Billabong T-shirt and pastel shorts. "Do you think he's hot? Hotter than Jeremy? I mean, he's hot, right?"

"His name is Chris." Tracey studies her shoes.

"Oh my God." Deb grabs her arm. "*You* like him."

"We've talked."

"Because I will totally back off if you like him."

"She likes him," Karen says, and Tracey elbows her.

"Okay then. Surfer boy is all yours." Deb adjusts her headband. "Jeremy's hotter anyway."

The bell rings and we clear the table and walk our lunch trays to the bin. I stare at the bruised tomatoes and soggy red pepper I'm about to ditch in the trash and think about Dad on the Death March sucking on ice to stay alive. Every day I tip half my lunch into the trash – crusts of bread, half-finished juice boxes, dry carrot sticks. I pick a tomato from my lunchbox and force it down.

I don't know how to dress for a wake. I spend hours in my room, pulling on clothes and ripping them off again. Are you supposed to wear black? Is a sundress too cheery? Do Catholics have dress codes? I wiggle out of my shorts. The wake starts in fifteen minutes. The walk to Adam's house takes ten. I climb into bed and pull the doona over my head.

The alarm wakes me at 7 am. I stand under the shower until the hot water turns tepid, pull a comb through my hair and scoop a pair of jeans from the floor. There's a note from Mom on the kitchen table. *Taken Dad to hospital. I'll be home for dinner.*

I go back to bed. I can't face Adam. What would I say? *I'm sorry, I just wasn't up for it.* The only way he'll understand is if I tell him about Dad, but I can't make this about me. It's *his* time to grieve.

I watch bad daytime TV and lie in bed flicking through old copies of *Cosmo*, my mind zigzagging between Adam and Dad. Adam with a hole in his heart the size of a grandmother. Dad with a hole in his stomach, wide enough to fit a piece of plastic tubing.

Mom comes home with a showbag from the hospital – foam supports for Dad's arms, more pillows and a neck brace. She's ordered an armchair with an electric lift.

"Dad's finding it hard to stand up once he's seated. This will make it easier," she says. "Can you help me move the furniture?"

We convert the house into a hospital. The kitchen table is littered with boxes of medication, liquid food supplements and antiseptic swabs.

There's only the two of us for dinner. We're in bed by eight.

Mom lets me skip school on Wednesday. I hate hospitals – the antiseptic smell of them, the desolate corridors and sad neon-lit rooms – but I want to go with her to pick up Dad.

I follow her onto the ward. Dad is resting against a pile of pillows surrounded by doctors but when he sees us come in, he blinks a hello. The same blink he used to send me when he was out of earshot, in the school auditorium when I was on stage, or on sports days when I was on the podium and he was in the bleachers. A blink that said, *I love you and I'm proud of you.* The blink Tatte gave him when words weren't allowed.

I blink back and when the doctors leave, Dad pats the mattress and I lie down next to him. His eyes are red but he doesn't look broken. There's a plastic hose sticking out of his stomach. A nurse explains how to remove the gauze and clean the wound, how to uncap the tube and grind Dad's medication and wash it down the tube with water.

"Can you open the curtains?" Dad says, his voice soft.

The curtains in our house are always drawn open. Dad likes to let the outside in. I drag them apart. The window is facing a brick wall.

I write my name and the date – 3 December 1982 – in the diary and wait for the school nurse to assign me an empty cot. I don't normally hang out in sick bay but I can't stomach the cafeteria, not after watching Mom uncap Dad's feeding tube and give him breakfast.

"I haven't seen *you* before." The nurse presses the back of her hand to my forehead. "You're not one of my regulars, so I'm going to assume you're not faking it."

I am.

"Stomach ache," I say, wrapping my arms around my middle.

"*That* time of the month, is it?"

The nurse pulls the curtain around my bed. I swallow the tablets she leaves me and lie down, wondering who

Deb is having lunch with and whether she's replaced me as her best friend. I get it. *I* wouldn't want to hang out with me. I'm the reigning champion of sad and I'm not a good person; I don't turn up for my friends.

The cafeteria is the last place I want to be, but I head back there at the end of lunch so I can walk into class with Deb. She's sharing a table with Kim and a few of the other 11th Graders but waves me over. I squeeze myself onto the bench.

"So?" Deb says. "What's the deal?"

I'm normally the one asking the questions. "The deal?"

"Where've you been?"

I shrug. "Sick bay."

She looks disappointed. "Not now. I mean, this week. You missed the wake and you've been kinda weird."

The table is quiet. Kim puts down her chicken sandwich. She's not looking at me but I know she's listening. They all are. I can't find the right words. I'm such a mess.

"Did I do something wrong?" Deb says.

"No!" I shake my head. "It's ... it's ..." My eyes flick to Kim. "Stuff's happening at home. I can't talk about it right now."

We sit without speaking. Deb's never gone quiet on me and the silence feels like a yawning hole.

"So, I have a spare ticket for Simple Minds." Kim hooks an arm over Deb's shoulder. "They're playing at Festival

Hall on Saturday. Wanna come?"

I spend the rest of lunch hiding in the girls' toilets and walk home at the end of the day with music in my ears. Deb and I are never going to be okay. We're never going to be *us* again. Not until I tell her what's going on.

But first, I've got to make it up to Adam.

Mom makes an exception and lets me go to Adam's on a school night. I stop at the shops on the way over and buy all his favorites – a Twix, jelly babies, barbecue chips and a Nesquik. I practise my apology; practise asking about the funeral without hyperventilating. I don't want to know what it's like to watch someone disappear underground, but I'll ask. And I'll tell him about Dad. *I wanted to tell you.* I test the words out. *It's just taken a while to wrap my head around losing him.*

Mrs Winter opens the door.

"Come in, Lisa," she says, blinking back tears. "Adam will be so happy to see you."

I follow her to the living room. Adam is sitting on the couch with his head in his hands.

"I'll leave you two alone then."

"Hey," I say, when the door closes behind her. "How are you doing?" I can't remember what I was meant to say next. The only thing working is my heart, banging against my chest. "The funeral. It must have been ... your gran, she was –"

173

"Where were you?"

I swallow a few hundred times. *Tell him. TELL him.*

"I'm sorry," I say. "I really wanted to come –"

He shakes his head. "Well, *that's* great."

It's two hundred farenheit in here and I'm sweating but I smile, because if I don't, I'll cry.

"I give up," he says, his face shut down. "I can't do this anymore. You're always busy on the weekends. You won't let me come over. Half the time you don't take my calls. You don't wanna hang out but you're too gutless to tell me." There's an edge to his voice I don't recognize. "So I'll do it for you. We're over."

He walks me outside. We have the dusk to ourselves and the first glimmer of a star-packed sky but I'd give up the moon if he'd just look at me.

"So, you're breaking up with me?" I try to memorize his face, the freckles on the bridge of his nose, the forest green of his eyes. *Of course, he's breaking up with me. I'm a horrible girlfriend.*

"You checked out a few months ago, Lis. I'm just calling it."

The words knock the breath out of me.

"And the worst part is," Adam's voice sounds ragged, "I was falling for you."

I take my smashed-up heart and head home. Walking away is the right thing to do. I can't make a contest out of our tragedies. I don't want to one-up his grief and I don't want him taking me back because he feels sorry for me. But still, it's hard. The horrible silence between us and Adam's boarded-up face and how close he was to loving me. It's summer everywhere, but I feel cold.

Mom doesn't offer me the matches on Friday night but I take them from her and light the candles. Jack pours the wine. Tom pops open a can and empties it into a syringe. Dad's dinner. He uncaps the feeding tube, attaches the syringe and depresses it. A thick white liquid disappears into Dad's stomach.

"Mmmm," Dad says. "Delicious. So, what was I up to last week?" He sifts through his memories.

"Buchenwald," I prompt him. "You were tied to a table in the camp hospital."

I realize how much I want to go back there. How it's the only time I'm yanked out of myself to a place that's not all about me. Adam was right. I haven't been there for him.

Because I'm here.

In Buchenwald.

With Dad.

CHAPTER 14

THEN

I woke in bed with a bandage wrapped around my neck, the first bed I'd slept in since I'd left home. I ran my hands over the sheets. *Sheets*. I had *sheets*. And a blanket! I pulled the scratchy wool up under my nose to hide the beginnings of a smile. The corners of my mouth had begun to curl up, not just because I was here, in a bed, getting better, but because I *wanted* to get better. *I want to live*, I realized, and that was huge. I'd thought about dying for so long, but when it really came down to it, I wanted to live. I wasn't a *muselmann*.

"I'm not going to die," I whispered into the blankets. "I'm going to get out of here."

"What are you in for?" an old Polish man called from the next bed. I'd got the hang of Polish under the conveyor belt in Jawischowitz, so I understood his whispered words.

"A boil," I said, still afraid of full sentences.

"Keep it clean," he said pointing to my bandage. "There's no medicine if it gets infected. Bastards." He fiddled with the gauze taped above his cheek. "I came in with a sore eye and they took it out. Left a dirty big hole." He hitched himself up onto his elbows. "Maybe it's for the best. I've seen things here I don't ever want to see again."

Willie snuck in to see me the next day with a potato filched from the kitchen.

"I'm meant to be discharged tomorrow," I told him, "but I think I'll stay a while."

The next morning when the doctor came to check on me I tried Joseph's trick, massaging the thermometer up three degrees while the doctor checked my wound. I stayed in hospital another four days.

On the eighth day I handed in my real temperature and the nurse called for a guard to escort me to barrack 4.

"Not four," I said, blinking. "I'm in barrack 36."

She rifled through some papers. "No, you've been assigned to barrack 4. Says right here." She tapped at the page. "Thirty-six must be full. Go get your things."

"But my brother ... I can't ... we've been together –"

The infirmary door swung open. "*Gehen! Verschieben!*" The guard wanted me outside.

I rushed to my bed to sweep up my things.

"Did they say barrack 4?" the Pole whispered.

I nodded and he grabbed my shirt and yanked me toward him, burrowing his face into my chest.

"What are you doing?" I tried to pull away, but he had the cotton between his teeth.

His eyes jerked up as he gnawed on the fabric. "You can't wear this," he mumbled, unpicking the stitching.

He tore the yellow star from my shirt and tossed it under a bed. "Barrack 4 is the Russians. If they find out you're a Jew, they'll eat you for dinner."

"*Vy chto-to ishchete?*" A boy around Willie's age, a huge hulking boy with hands as big as pillows, stopped me as soon as I walked through the door.

My eyes must have been big as bowls because there were boys everywhere – laughing, arm-wrestling and huddled in groups talking. They all wore the red triangle of political prisoners and none of them had that *muselmann* look; that empty-eyed stare.

I didn't know any Russian so he switched to a broken German that I understood.

"You looking for something?" He dug his fingernails into my neck and I winced. The nurse had taken off my bandage but the wound still throbbed. "What? You don't like the place?" The boy wheeled around to his friends. "He doesn't like the place!"

I liked the place, I liked it plenty. There were bedrooms with single bunks and mattresses and pillows. There was running water and a kitchen and a bench with bread *and* butter.

"So, let him leave." A boy doing a handstand sprang to his feet. "He's too young to be here, anyway." He stalked toward me. "You're not a political prisoner, you're no Russian, so why are you here? Let me guess. You've been sent to spy on us?" He squatted on his haunches to get a better look at me. "Actually, no. You don't look smart enough. Are you slow?" he asked, stretching out each syllable.

I heard the boys behind him snicker and guess at my crime. Was I a homosexual? Maybe a Jehovah's Witness? I waited for someone to uncover my secret.

"Let him talk," a German boy said, and the room went quiet. He reminded me of a whippet, lean and wiry. "What are you doing here?"

I squared my shoulders and forced out the lie. "My father is a communist. The Nazis couldn't find him so they took *me*. They won't find him, not ever, and every day they don't, he's doing something to hurt them." I tried to sound proud.

"You got brothers here? Uncles?"

I shook my head. "I did," I said in my best German. "I've got two older brothers, a mother and two sisters. They took all of us because we wouldn't give up our father. And now I don't know where any of them are, or if they're even alive."

My eyes must have got cloudy, because the boy threw his arm around my shoulder and led me to a room. "You can have that one," he said pointing to a bottom bunk. "The boys were just having a little fun. They won't bother you anymore."

They were all nice to me after that, Ludwig – the German whippet – made sure of it, but I didn't want to get too close in case I let something slip, so I kept to myself.

Willie had come to the revier the day after my discharge and, finding my bed empty, had asked the old Pole where I was. Ludwig and the boys welcomed him when he came that night.

"Your brother!" Ludwig cheered, steering Willie toward me. "He's here! He's alive."

I wrapped my arms around Willie and whispered in his ear, "We're communists. Tatte's in hiding. We're not ..."

"I know," Willie whispered, head dipped to where his yellow star had once been. Now there were just a few loose threads. "The Polack warned me."

Willie snuck to my barrack every few nights. We spent most of our time in the kitchen so I could sneak him food. I gave him what I could – bits of rubbery sausage, half a brick of bread, and something for Jacob. It felt good to be able to give Willie something after everything he'd done for me. Everyone in the camp was always telling me how small I was. Feeding Willie made me feel taller, but I was still scared. It was dangerous in the barrack. Dangerous because the boys were German communist sympathisers or Russians, and I was a Jew.

The hardest part was showering. I couldn't let them see I was circumcised, so I had to wait until they'd all showered before I dropped my towel and slipped into a stall. No-one ever saw me naked. They must have thought I was shy. I didn't wrestle or tell stories, I didn't talk unless someone talked to me first, but I *did* listen. I sat on the edges of conversations, smiling at the boys' jokes and nodding at their predictions that the war would end soon. It felt good to be surrounded by people who smiled, people who made plans for when they got out.

Their dreams were infectious, and pretty soon I was dreaming about what the future might look like when I got home. Willie listened to my wondering but he was too exhausted to dream, so I dreamed for the both of us while he sat slumped in the kitchen, gnawing on bread. I didn't want to know what was going on in his barrack, so I didn't ask. I didn't want to see men hanging off the gallows, so I stayed inside whenever I could.

Eventually danger found its way in. I'd come back from showering, wrapped in a towel. It was raining so the barrack was full. Boys sprawled on their bunks, restless and bored. I gripped my towel so it wouldn't slip and grabbed my pants with my free hand, trying not to fall while I stepped into them.

A boy on the next bunk smiled at me, his curiosity piqued. "What's the story, Emil? Do you think we fancy you? You're holding that towel so tight your knuckles are white."

Heads swivelled. The room grew hushed.

Heinrich, two beds down, jumped to his feet. "It's because he's so small." He pointed at the towel. "He's embarrassed because he has a ..." he searched for the right words, "... a microscopic dick."

Pretty soon I was surrounded. Boys were taking bets and guessing measurements.

"This big."

"No, *this* big!"

They were closing in on me. Heinrich snorted. "No-one's that small. He's not a newborn!"

I was backed into a corner, fingers reaching toward my towel.

"Come on, rip it off and prove us all wrong!"

My hands were sweating. I gripped the towel harder.

"What's going on?" I heard Ludwig's voice and saw the circle widen to let him in. And then he was next to me. "So, what are we doing here?" He looked around the group, saw the boys' big smiles. "Looks like fun. What did I miss?" He looked at Heinrich.

"The consensus is that young Emil here has a midget dick. And he was just about to prove our hypothesis."

Ludwig nodded, looked from Heinrich to me and back at Heinrich. The barrack grew quiet.

"Okay then," he said raising a hand.

I squeezed my eyes shut and waited to feel the tug of the towel but when I opened my eyes, Ludwig's arm was thrown over Heinrich's shoulder, his face dead serious. "Show's over, boys. We were all small once," he said, bending to stare at Heinrich's crotch. "Some of us still are!"

Winter retreated and the snow gave way to mud. Days rolled into weeks and April arrived. At night, when all the noises of the camp died down, we'd lie in our bunks and listen for the distant rumble of artillery, guessing if it was the Red Army or the Americans come to save us. Rumors floated through the camp – the Americans were close and Hitler wanted Buchenwald emptied before they arrived. The camp commandant confirmed the rumor the next day. Buchenwald would be liquidated. They would evacuate ten blocks per day – ten thousand inmates – and march us to factories outside the camp. Barrack 4 was close to the main gate, so we watched the straggly columns of men disappear into the forest, day after day, wondering when *our* turn would come.

A few days after the announcement Willie came to visit. "I'm leaving tomorrow," he said. "We march out in the morning."

"Tomorrow?" I asked, panicked. I needed to see Willie's face at roll call to get through the day. I needed our whispered conversations and the comfort of being with someone who knew me.

"We won't be apart for long." He lowered his voice to a whisper. "The Americans are close. We'll be together soon. And not in a camp or a factory." His eyes shone. "I'll be taking you home." He grabbed me in a hug. I could feel his ribs through the thin cotton of his jacket.

"Wait!" I called before he slipped out the door. I ran to my room and whipped the sheet from my bed. "Take it." I shoved the sheet down his jacket. "You can tear it into strips and wind them around your feet, like socks."

Thousands of prisoners trudged through the main gate the next day, but I couldn't pick Willie in the sea of blue and white. I was alone now. Completely alone. My whole family gone. I looked around the grimy barrack. It was darker and gloomier than it had been the day before. I curled up on my bunk and waited for the room to grow dark.

At sunset I found out I was to be reunited with Willie sooner than I'd thought – my barrack was slated for evacuation the next day. We were to be dressed and at the square by 8 am.

I woke early on Wednesday 11 April 1945, anxious to leave Buchenwald, but our *kapo* never came. Gunshots and grenades exploded in the distance.

"Get down!" Ludwig shouted and we fell to the floor.

Everything went quiet. Ludwig and a few other boys inched toward the window. I crawled after them and peered through the bars to see guards scrambling from the sentry boxes. An officer ran past, pulling on a blue and white jacket. Up ahead, a truck tore through an open gate.

Ludwig pushed the door open and I crept out after him. The square was deserted.

"Have they gone?" I asked incredulous. "Is it over?"

Ludwig lifted his fingers to his lips. "It only takes one."

We crept toward the square. Others joined us – an old man with a limp, a small boy wearing a striped jacket hanging down to his knees, and a group of men talking excitedly in German. Ludwig stopped to question them.

"The guards have deserted." Their eyes flashed. "The resistance have taken control!"

I stared at them, clueless. "The resistance?"

"The resistance fighters ... the underground. They have a short-wave radio," one of the men explained, raising his voice so others could hear. "The resistance has sent an SOS!" he shouted. "The Americans just answered. They said to sit tight. The Third Army are on their way!"

A man in a striped shirt sank to his knees in the mud. "*Baruch atah elohenu malakhe ha'olam.*" He looked up at the white sky and continued to pray. "Blessed be the God who sets us free."

"Free," I whispered, the word fizzing in my mouth. "I'm free," I said again, just to hear the words.

The news spread fast and within minutes the square was crawling with inmates. They came alone and in pairs – laughing, cursing, praying and whimpering. Mostly they wandered the square in a daze. One of the men Ludwig had been talking to found a ladder and broke into the office of the German camp command. We waited. My heart was drumming so hard I was sure Ludwig could hear it.

"No more guards!" someone whispered.

"No more selections!"

"No roll call."

A telephone rang inside the command tower. Minutes dragged by before the man who'd broken into the office climbed down the ladder, stopping halfway to raise a hand. The crowd hushed.

"That was Berlin. Gestapo headquarters just gave the order to liquidate the camp."

Boys bolted for the gate. People started panicking. The man kneeling in the mud got to his feet. An old man started wailing.

"Stop!" the man on the ladder shouted. "They don't know the SS have deserted the camp. They gave *me* the order."

"So, there's no-one here to carry it out," Ludwig shouted back.

The boys at the main gate stopped and wheeled around.

"There *will* be." The man raised his voice so that everyone could hear.

"A regiment of Hitler Youth are on their way. They have instructions to kill us, but we're not going to let them! Arm yourselves." The German leaped from the ladder to scoop a rock from the ground. "Search for sticks, guns, rocks, knives – anything you can find to defend yourselves."

Ludwig combed the dirt with his fingers and pressed a rock into my hand. *This can't be how it ends.* I closed my fist around the rock. *Killed in the final hours of war by a bunch of German schoolkids.*

Somewhere to the west, tanks rumbled past.

"The Americans!" Ludwig shouted, turning toward the roar of approaching tanks.

An airplane screamed overhead, dropping packages from the sky. A brown box thudded at my feet but I just stood there, dizzy with fear. What if the Hitler Youth got to us first? The end of the war was hurtling toward us. My future was being decided outside Buchenwald's main gate, and if the wrong side lost, I was dead.

CHAPTER 15

NOW

The rumble of gunfire and the chanting fades and the room is quiet. It's just us and Dad slumped in his chair. A thin string of saliva spills from his bottom lip. Mom reaches for the suctioning machine. It's been sitting in the corner of the room but it's the first time I've seen her use it. Dad opens his mouth wide and I push up out of my chair, but my brothers don't leave, so I sink back down. Mom flips the machine on and pokes the wand into Dad's mouth. She slides it around, vacuuming the spit from under his tongue and between his teeth.

I want to dive back into the story, back to 11 April 1945, when Dad still had a fighting chance. The machine stops gurgling. Mom pulls the wand from Dad's mouth and his white smile reappears. He threads his fingers through hers and whispers, "Thank you."

Dad's known terrible hate but he's also known love. I almost did too, but here's another way I'm nothing like my mom. She manages to feed, wash and dress Dad without making him feel small. I don't even have the courage to hold Adam's hand while they bury his gran.

It's almost midnight. I sweep a hand under my bed for the shoebox, but find my diary instead. Small scraps of paper flutter out; notes Adam passed me in class or left in my locker. I miss him. It's not one thing, it's everything – his gold-dust smile, the way he wears his stone-washed jeans, how comfortable he is in his own skin and the way he makes me feel ... like I've swallowed the sun.

I close my eyes and picture walking through the corridor on Monday, everyone pointing and whispering, waiting for me to crack. I've never had a boyfriend so I've never been dumped. I don't know how to do this.

"I'm fine." I practice the words out loud. "It was mutual."

Dad's best friends visit every Sunday with bagels and smoked salmon that Dad will never eat. Ernst pinches my cheeks. Carl asks how I'm holding up. They have tattoos and accents, and I wonder if they met Dad in the camps or on the ship over here.

"See you next week, *boychik*," Ernst says, kissing Dad's cheeks.

"You don't need to come to the front door," Carl offers, but Dad's hand finds the stair rail and he follows them downstairs to see them out. By the time he makes it back up, he's puffing and his face is slick with sweat.

"Too many visitors?" I ask.

"No," Dad says, shuffling to the living room. He presses a button on the electric armchair and it rises to catch him. "I love seeing people. I can't get outside on my own, so they bring the world in." His words start to slur. I tell myself that he is tired, but I know it's the disease.

"We talk, like we always have. I learn from them and they learn from me." He speaks slowly, careful to pronounce every syllable, fighting to keep his words apart. "They want to be a part of this and it feels good to let them."

He narrows his eyes at me. "So, how's Deb?"

"She's okay."

"She hasn't been here in a while ..."

"She's busy." I shrug. "*I'm* busy. I can see Deb anytime. I just want to spend time with you."

"I want that too," Dad says, "but you need your friends, especially now." There's a sheen of saliva on his lips. "Do you mind?" he says, glancing at the tea towel on the armrest. I must look panicked because he says, "Just hold it up close to my face. I'll do the rest."

I hold the tea towel so Dad can drag his mouth across it. He pulls away when he's done.

"Have you told her?"

I shake my head. I want to say, *It's your fault.* I want to say, *We're not talking because of* you. *You taught me to build walls so no-one could get in and now Kim is Deb's new best friend and Adam has dumped me.*

190

"It's hard," I say.

"I know," he whispers.

Adam is walking down the corridor toward me. It's been two days, eight hours and six minutes since we broke up. The sea of students part to let him through and everyone's watching and whispering behind their hands. He's walking in slow motion, at least that's how it feels. And this is exactly what I've always avoided – being the news story of the week.

I don't lose it. I never lose it. I mould my face into a smile and wait. His hair has fallen over his face and I want to push it back but I can't; he's not mine anymore. Adam is ten lockers away … nine … eight. He raises a hand to wave, smiles one of his megawatt smiles and I think, *Did I imagine the break-up?* And then he walks right past me. To Leanne's locker.

I pretend to rearrange my folders. If I could hide in my locker, I'd climb in.

"They're splitsville," someone says.

"She dumped him."

"Nuh-uh. He dumped her."

I shove my headphones on and head to class.

Mr C's not there yet and Tracey leaps from her desk to sit on mine. Karen squats down next to me and grabs my hand.

"We heard," Tracey says, offering me a soggy knot of bubblegum pulled from her mouth. "Sorry, it's my last one."

"You okay?" Karen whispers, rubbing my arm.

I'm not, but I'd rather lick a toilet seat than admit I'm hurting. I shrug off the bubblegum. And their questions.

"I'm good," I say. "It was mutual."

I hide behind my hair when Deb squeezes into her seat. If I look at her I'll end up a puddle on the floor.

The bell rings and Mr Curlew bounces in, dropping booklets onto desks. "Right-e-o," he says.

I peek at the socks poking from under his brown corduroy pants. It's become a habit. Today is jelly beans.

"Seeing as next year you'll be heading into 11th Grade, it's time to think about how many subjects you want to do in 12th Grade. Most of our students do five, but if you're averaging an A, you can do six. Let's run through the subjects."

I watch Mr C's mouth move but I'm thinking about Dad getting up every day – getting showered and dressed and fed and suctioned – when he could stay in bed and ask for a bedpan. When he could close the curtains and dim the lights. Refuse the pills and make the end come sooner. *Kellers don't take the easy way out,* I imagine Dad saying. Because that's what he always says. *Talent is not the point,* he said when I wanted to quit ballet. *Kellers aren't quitters,* he said when I tried to give up piano.

I think about his lost childhood and all the work he's put into mine, and the way he smiles when I practice my scales or come home, dripping, after a run. *Kellers don't take the easy way out.* I grab the 12th Grade form, pick up a pen and write *six* in the subject box.

"Psst." Deb pitches a note at my desk.

She's sitting across from me and she's dressed like she's expecting a talent scout to walk through the door – pale pink jumpsuit, shimmering blue eyeshadow and a side ponytail. I unfurl the note. Two words: *You okay?* I tear off a corner of the booklet and start scribbling an answer.

"Miss Keller!"

My pencil snaps. Mr C is standing over me, his hand outstretched, waiting for the note. I drop it into his palm. His eyes scan the words.

"I'll see you after class." He spins to face Deb. "This is your last warning, Miss Cartman. Next time it's detention."

The bell rings, the class empties and Mr C folds himself into Deb's empty chair. "What's going on, Lisa? And before you say, it's none of my business, when it affects your schoolwork, it is. So, do you want to tell me why my star pupil has tuned out?"

I study the woodgrain on my desk.

Mr C shakes his head and sighs. "You like writing, don't you?"

"Sure." I look up.

"Okay, how about we make a deal? I know there are things you don't want to talk about, and that's okay. Why not try funnelling your feelings onto the page?"

I open my mouth to object but he waves my thoughts away.

"This is not a punishment. I'm not going to grade you. I won't read it, if you don't want me to. I just think it might help."

That seems fair. As long as he doesn't read it, I can fill the pages any way I want. Song lyrics. A chocolate cake recipe.

I nod my agreement.

Deb, Tracey and Karen circle my locker.

"Sorry about the note." Deb offers an apologetic smile. "And I'm sorry about Adam."

"Just shattered," Karen says, pulling a crumpled tissue from her pocket and dabbing her eyes. "You two were my favorite couple after Charles and –"

Tracey elbows Karen in the arm.

"We're here for you," Karen says, passing me the damp tissue.

I let them hug me. No-one says Adam is a dufus, or that I can do better. Because I can't.

"I'll meet you on the quad," I say. "I need the toilet."

I lock myself into a stall and sit on the closed lid of the toilet. I'm crying into my hands when the bathroom door swings open. I don't recognize the voices on the other side of the stall. There are two of them. One talking from behind a toilet door, the other at the sink. I lift my feet onto the seat.

"You going to Heather's on Friday night?"

"Nuh. Been grounded. Craig saw me smoking outside Kentucky Fried Chicken and he told Mom. Little brat."

"Bummer."

"Oh my God, did you see what Cath's wearing today? She's such a poser."

"The neon mini?"

"And that hideous tank top. Do you think it has anything to do with Adam Winter?"

"Adam?"

"He's single."

"No way!"

"Yes way." A toilet flushes. "He dumped Lisa last week."

"I knew they'd split."

Water gushes into a sink and I hold my breath.

"I mean, please. He's a babe. He can do way better."

A door slams and the room goes quiet. I pad to the sink, splash my face with cold water and force myself to go outside, hoping the asphalt will swallow me up.

"It takes time." Kim stops to rest a hand on my arm. "It might not seem like it now –" the corners of her mouth droop in a performance worthy of an Academy Award, "– but, trust me, you'll get over him." She squeezes my arm.

"I'm okay," I say, to end the pity party. "It was mutual. We're good."

Adam is sitting at the next table so I smile and wave. *See, it's not weird.* He waves back and, of course *he's* fine because girls are lining up to date him. And he can do so much better than me.

The cafeteria is organised into its lunchtime cliques. I drop down next to Deb and let her pull off my headphones and shove them onto her head. Phil Oakey is singing the chorus, wailing about a broken heart.

"Really?" Deb stares at me. "Human League? I mean they *are* one of the all-time best bands but, Lis, it's a break-up song." She buries the headphones in her bag. "Seriously, are you okay?"

Nothing about my life is okay. "I'm fine," I say, managing a smile. "It's just bad timing. Both of us have too much going on."

Deb's eyes narrow like a cat's. "Too much going on?" She shakes her head. "Lis, you can talk to me. What happened? Was it ... " I follow her gaze to the next table where Leanne sits sandwiched between Adam and Paul.

"I'm fine," I say. "Maybe we can talk after school?"

I miss going back to Deb's place to make toasted cheese sandwiches. I miss lying on the trampoline and planning our gap year.

"I have rehearsal tonight. The school play starts Friday." She's looking at me as if I've crawled out from under a rock. I should know when my best friend's show opens.

I nod and pick the crusts off my sandwich. "Of course. Sure, we can do it another time."

"Sounds good. How about Saturday? I don't have to be on stage till seven."

Deb is allowed to skip class for the rest of the week to attend rehearsals, costume fittings and soundchecks, but it feels like she's still with me, propping me up.

When I get home there's a package waiting for me in the letterbox. I rip open the wrapping paper to find the latest *Cosmo* magazine with a note stuck to the cover: *The other fish in the sea.* Deb has attacked the pages with a red marker, circling the cutest boys. There's an arrow pointing to Michael J Fox and a giant X through Rob Lowe next to the words, *Hands off! He's mine.*

On Tuesday my desk is full of mini M&Ms. On Wednesday she leaves a mixed tape in my locker, *Best of 1982.* Side A is a dance party and Side B is a get-over-him compilation. She's written out the song lyrics to Gloria Gaynor's 'I Will Survive'.

I can't deal with Tracey's and Karen's sad puppy eyes so I skip the cafeteria for the library and demolish half the M&Ms while I write up the sports news for the school newspaper. Mai is at the next table. She's reading *The Color Purple*, one of my favorite books. I feel terrible about ignoring her last week, so I smile and lift a book from the pile I was about to return.

"If you like books that rip your heart out, try this." I slide *I Know Why the Caged Bird Sings* onto her desk.

She nods and rifles through the pages of the memoir.

I win my division for the 800 meters at the athletic leagues the next day, but no-one's there to cheer me on. Adam isn't waiting at the fence with a melting popsicle so I grab my trophy and walk home. I have Mr C's writing assignment to distract me from all the things that suck in my life. He wants to see me on the page so I pick one of my favorite recipes from Mom's cookbook – double fudge chocolate cake – and start copying down ingredients. I stop at full-cream milk. Mom has turned the suctioning machine on and I can hear its rattle through the wall as it sucks the spit from Dad's lungs. *Kellers don't take the easy way out*, I imagine Dad saying again. *Your teacher wants to know who you are. Tell him.*

I close the cookbook and grab *Dad's story – Tape One* from the shoebox. *You said you couldn't find me on the page, Mr C. That's because I was here, in 1945, with my dad.* I grab the pen, slide the tape into my cassette recorder and press play.

I was a lonely kid. In Czechoslovakia, kids didn't play with Jews. I write the words down. Dad's story. My history.

Mr Curlew stares at my spidery script. "I'm glad you took my suggestion seriously," he says, as the last students file out of class. "How many pages have you got here?"

"Thirteen." Tape one and tape two.

Mr Curlew smiles. "Did it help?"

"It didn't change anything."

The smile wobbles.

"But I'm going to keep writing anyway."

"That's great," he says, his smile resurrected. "You don't need to report back ... unless you want to."

"I'm good," I say, folding Dad's story back into my bag.

At home, the table is cluttered with gauze, tape and syringes. There are pills popped from their packaging and a pitcher of water. Dad is sitting at the table with his shirt open and his feeding tube uncapped, a tea towel draped across his lap.

"I'm home!" I sing out, dropping my bag, but Mom doesn't answer.

She's running between Dad and the stove, dropping potatoes into boiling water and dicing onion. It's Friday afternoon and my brothers will be here soon.

"Won't be long!" Mom calls to Dad.

I join her at the bench. "Want me to do the onions?"

She's about to hand me the knife but says, "Actually, could you feed your father instead?"

We both turn to face Dad. He's trying to walk his fingers along the table toward a box of pills.

"Sure," I say, swallowing, "but you'll need to show me how."

Mom picks up a clear brown capsule and shows me how to pierce its skin with a kitchen knife. I squeeze the gel into a measuring cup and she adds water and stirs. She shows me the list. Ambien, then vitamin B6. We take turns pouring medicine into Dad, peeling the plastic coating off capsules, crushing tablets, measuring morphine.

There are no pills for *our* pain.

"The pot's boiling over," Dad says. "Lisa can do it."

Mom looks from the stove to the tube in her hand.

"She'll be okay," Dad says, and now I have to be.

I take the tube from Mom, careful not to pull at his skin.

"You need to flush water down the tube before putting the cap back on," Dad clues me in.

I pick up the jug and try to steady my hands. I can't look at him.

"Good," he says. "Is the cap tight?"

I nod.

"Okay, now you can tape the tube back to my skin." He speaks slowly trying not to swallow his syllables.

I tear a piece of tape from the roll and carefully, gently, fix the tube to the soft, freckled skin on my father's stomach. I try not to let my fingers graze his skin.

"It's okay to need help." Dad waits until I look up. "I fought it at first, but then I realized we all do it as kids. We let our parents bathe and feed us. But then we grow up and suddenly being reliant is somehow shameful." He looks down at his shirt and waits for me to button it. "The first time your mom fed me, my pride was a little dented, but it wasn't destroyed. Asking for help isn't weak. We all need to be taken care of. Tell you the truth, I think all of this has brought us closer. Having you here, sitting with me – caring for me – it's nice. The secret," he tells me, "is to change how you see yourself."

"You mean pretend things are different?"

I lift the tea towel from the armrest and dab the sweat from his face.

"No, I mean, change the things you think define you. I'm not strong anymore, so I've let that go as a measure of who I am. I'm more than my body. More than my disease.

I'm more myself – or a better version of myself – than I've ever been."

I shake my head. How can you be a better version of yourself when you can't blow your own nose?

"I've learned patience," Dad says. "I've learned to let go of things. If Mom isn't in the room when I want to lie down, I just give up on the idea of bed and sleep in my chair. I've learned to accept help and ..." He searches for another silver lining.

"You've learned to listen," I say. My dad wasn't a fan of listening, or other people's opinions. He preferred his own.

"This illness has changed me for the better." He smiles. "That's how I can let other people undress and shower me without hating them for it. I still like myself. Maybe more than ever."

The doorbell rings.

"Whoa," Tom says, when he sees Dad's new stairlift.

"What is this?" Jack asks, taking a seat.

I press the green button on the armrest and the chair glides up the stairs on a metal track fixed to the handrail. When Jack reaches the top, he floats back down so Tom can have a turn.

We sit down to dinner.

"*I'll* do it," I whisper, taking the matches from Mom.

I light the candles and hold my hands up to my face to recite the prayer with her. Jack blesses the wine and Tom blesses the *challah*. We've practised every night this week, reading the Hebrew words Jack printed for each of us in English: *Barukh attah adonay eloheinu ...*

Dad tears up. It's the first time he's heard us speak Hebrew, the first time Jack and Tom have pulled on *kippahs*. I picture Dad as a kid, standing in barrack 4, clutching a towel around his waist, terrified his Jewishness might be exposed, and wonder if he passed that fear on to us.

He had a towel. We have our white bread names: Jack, Tom and Lisa. No-one would ever guess.

CHAPTER 16

THEN

The sounds of war died down. An American tank circled the camp. Someone scaled the gate building and hoisted a white flag. A defiant voice rang out over the loudspeakers.

"The SS have been overpowered. The Allies have won."

The war was over. A strangled cheer rose up from the crowd.

We were free. *I* was free. No more SS. No guards with whips. No dogs. No standing still in freezing rows. It was hard to believe.

"Can we leave?" I asked Ludwig.

"Whenever you want. The Americans have won the war."

The rock I'd been holding slipped from my hand and landed with a thud.

"You can go home," Ludwig laughed. "We can *all* go home."

I wanted to laugh like Ludwig. I wanted to whoop and cheer and follow him across the square to swarm the Americans who'd breached the barbed wire, but I just stood there, feeling empty and scared. Scared to go home and find no-one waiting. I wasn't the only one. A strange sorrow pervaded the camp. People were weeping. So many had died.

The soldiers stared at us. Some of them looked frightened. Mostly they looked sad. I don't know what they'd expected to find when they tore down the gate, but it wasn't scarecrows in filthy striped rags. It wasn't naked men wearing blankets like prayer shawls or girls with bald heads and scabby knees.

A group of prisoners tried to lift the soldiers onto their shoulders. Inmates pushed past me to shake their hands and take the cigarettes they offered. The hungriest stuffed them into their mouths. Someone scaled a ladder and wound the hands of the camp clock back to 3.15, then stopped the clock so the hands were frozen there, stuck up in surrender. Those too weak to walk lay by the huts staring into space, looking like dead men, except every so often one of them blinked.

A jeep rumbled into the square and more officers jumped out holding scraps of cloth up to their noses to block the smell. They walked around the camp, gigantic men with guns slung over their shoulders, but they didn't point them at us. An officer Willie's age pulled a knife from his belt and slit open one of the boxes that had dropped from the sky. I bent over the crumpled cardboard and pulled out a chocolate bar. I closed my eyes and blocked out everything else – my wobbly legs, my itchy scalp, the boy with the battered face waiting his turn behind me – to focus on the square of chocolate melting on my tongue. I'd forgotten what real food tasted like. It tasted like a miracle.

I grabbed another chocolate bar and stuffed it into my mouth, trying to ignore the pink-faced officer who was staring at me. He must've thought I was a creature from another planet, more bones than skin; a boy insane with hunger.

"What's your name?" he asked, first in Russian, then German.

"Emil," I said between mouthfuls, "but they don't use names here."

I rolled back my sleeve so he could see the tattoo. He was blinking fast and his fists were clenched, so I knew he was angry and that made me feel better; that he knew this was wrong.

"How old are you?" The question seemed to make him sad.

"Fourteen," I said, reaching into the box for another chocolate bar, surprised that after two, I still felt empty.

Ludwig grabbed my hand. "Emil, stop!" He snatched the chocolate bar and held it above his head. "You've got to give your stomach time to adjust."

I lunged for the bar.

"Emil, I'm serious. They shouldn't be feeding us this shit. It'll kill you. Start on bread and crackers. Stick to bland foods." He pulled a packet of dry biscuits from his pocket, offered me one and waited until I crammed it into my mouth. "Slow down," he said, "you've got to eat slowly. Chew."

"I'm Jewish," I said, because he still didn't know. There was nothing to tell us apart, nothing that screamed I was different to the other boys, nothing he should've picked up on, nothing he'd missed. We were all the same this side of the fence; all hungry and tired and scared and lost. Even Ludwig. I didn't apologise for lying. Or for being a Jew. I waited for him to curse or turn away but he didn't do either; just handed me the packet of crackers and said he'd see me back at the barrack.

I was used to following orders, so I left the box of chocolates to the boy with the bruised face. It was hard tempering my hunger while everyone around me binged on sardines and cream biscuits, but Ludwig was right. Half our barrack spent the night clutching their stomachs. They survived, but hundreds didn't. I saw the boy with the battered face lifted from the ground and thrown onto a cart. And with every day that slid by, more inmates died – of eating themselves to death – and of starvation, exhaustion, tuberculosis and typhus.

Of the twenty-one thousand prisoners the Americans found alive in Buchenwald, less than a thousand were kids like me. I was some kind of marvel, the officers told me, a survivor. I should've been glad – and I *was* happy to be alive – but I couldn't celebrate. Not until I found out what had happened to my family. *Home*. What would that look like, I wondered, as I wandered the camp. Tatte would be at the kitchen table bent over a prayer book and Mamme would be in the kitchen slicing onions for soup. Or not. Here in the camp no-one had heard of an Aaron Rosenfeld of Porubka. No-one knew where my mother or sisters were. *Check the lists*, they suggested, but I didn't. I didn't know if the lists tacked to the noticeboard contained the names of the living or the dead.

I headed to barrack 36, Willie's old barrack, hoping that if he hadn't made it back yet, one of his friends had. But the barrack was empty. I found my way to Willie's rotting plank bed and climbed onto the splintering wood.

"Hello," someone said from under a blanket.

"Willie?" I whispered. "Willie, is that you?"

I tore across the bunks, but when I whipped the blanket away Willie wasn't under it, just a man with yellow skin and rotting teeth.

"Sorry, I thought you were my brother," I said, climbing off the bunk.

"Maybe I know him?" The man pulled a potato from under the wool blanket and bit into its green skin.

"Maybe. His name is Willie. He left yesterday when the barrack was being evacuated. Do you know him?"

The man shook his head.

"Willie Rosenfeld." I pointed to my brother's bunk. "He slept over there. He's skinny. He has brown hair." Except we didn't have hair, I remembered, and everyone was skinny.

The man shrugged and took another bite of his potato.

"If you see him ... if he comes here looking for me – looking for Emil – tell him you saw me. Tell him I'm in barrack 4."

I walked out of the barrack and through a gate. It felt good to walk without being ordered to, without a gun at my back. I could walk quickly, or drag my feet, turn left or duck right. Or stop. Just stop and sit cross-legged on the ground to feel the sun on my face.

I didn't stop. I kept walking until I reached the hospital. I wanted to find my friend, the old Pole, and thank him for warning me about the Russians.

The nurse who'd looked after me stopped me at the door. "Sorry," she said, looking me up and down. "We're only taking typhus patients." She pulled a cigarette from her pocket and slid it between her lips. "If you want to be seen, there's a clinic set up near the main square." She looked at me closely. "I know you, don't I?" She lit a match and bent toward the blinking flame. "You were here, in the ward. What were you in for?"

"A boil," I said, impatient to see my friend. "I'm here to see someone. I don't know his name, he was Polish, and old. He didn't have teeth. He was in the bed next to mine. He had typhus."

Her narrow face disappeared behind a cloud of tobacco smoke. "I'm sorry," she said again when the smoke cleared. "He's gone."

"To Poland?"

She shook her head. "Nachum died yesterday."

I didn't cry. Willie wouldn't have wanted that. The old Pole was dead, but I was alive and so was Willie and the war was over and soon we'd be home.

"They'll be waiting for us," Willie had said the night

before he left Buchenwald. "Tatte will be talking to God full-time and Mamme will be stockpiling *cholent* and cake." I pictured my parents huddled around the kitchen table, their sleeves pulled down to cover their numbers, their hair growing back in uneven clumps.

"They're waiting for us, Willie," I yelled at the sky. "Where *are* you?"

I found out that afternoon when I visited one of the American tents set up in the square. I took the bread the soldiers offered and tore it in half, slipping the bigger half into my pocket.

"You don't need to save it," the soldiers said, "there's plenty more."

But I saved some anyway. Just in case. I walked back to my barrack, thinking about Mamme. I hadn't thought of home for so long. Now it's all I could think about ... who would be home when Willie and I got there.

"Emil?"

I heard Jacob's voice before I saw him. I'd recognize that voice anywhere. His whispered words had helped get me through the Death March. I spun around.

"Jacob!" I grabbed him by the arm and he pulled me toward him and we stood there hugging for the longest time.

"I just got back," Jacob said, pulling away. "There was an old man in my barrack, asking if my name was Willie. He said someone was looking for him and I figured it was you."

"It was," I said, looking past Jacob. "So where is he? Where's Willie?"

Jacob stiffened.

"What?" I stared at Jacob.

His face drained of color. "He's not ..." He shook his head. "Emil, he's not here."

"What do you mean?" I asked. "Is he still in the factory?"

"There *was* no factory."

"No factory? So where is he?"

Jacob hung his head.

"*Where is he?*" I shouted. "Jacob, what happened?"

Jacob crumpled to his knees. "We were on the same transport. We thought we were going to a factory but then the trucks stopped and they made us get out. We had to walk to a forest." Tears slid down his cheeks. "There was a clearing and in the middle a huge pit."

"No!" I said, shaking my head. "No. I don't believe you. You're lying. Why are you lying?" I didn't want to hear any more. Willie was coming back. He promised. "He promised," I wailed. "Willie promised he'd come back."

I squeezed my eyes shut and buried my face in my hands. Maybe when I opened them again this would all be a sick joke.

Long minutes passed.

"We made a pact," Jacob said, the light gone from his eyes. "If Willie survived, he'd find my little brother and tell him what happened, and if I survived, I'd find you. I won't tell you any more, if you don't want to hear it ..." Jacob rested a hand on my arm.

"No," I said. "Tell me."

Jacob mopped his tears with his sleeve. "They made us fan out around the pit, maybe three or four deep. I was standing right on the edge, furthest from the guards' guns. Willie was a few rows back." Jacob's hands formed fists. "And then the shooting started. I must've blacked out because when I woke up, I was in the pit. There were bodies on top of me. Blood everywhere. Dirt in my mouth. I wasn't bleeding so I figured I must've fallen in. I lay there for hours, playing dead till it was dark, till the trucks drove away and the forest went quiet. And then I crawled out from under the bodies and dragged myself out."

"So, you didn't see him?" Hope ballooned in my chest. "You didn't see him in the pit?" Maybe the bullets had missed Willie too.

"I looked for him, but it was dark and there were so many bodies." Jacob slumped against the wall. "Eight of us crawled out. We waited in the forest for two days to see if anyone else made it. No-one came." Jacob looked at me, waiting for me to understand. "There was no-one left alive in that pit."

He kept talking – something about eating grass until the Americans came – but they were just more words I couldn't make sense of. My head was too full of the horror of Willie's death – the dark forest, the yawning hole and Willie falling. Willie landing on a bed of bodies. Willie's last breath, his heart stopping. In those awful last seconds he'd have been thinking about me and how he'd broken his promise to take me home.

Jacob was talking again but I stared past him, at Willie's ghost. "It's not right," I whispered. "It's not fair.

You worked so much harder to survive. *You* deserve this, not *me*."

I wasn't as kind or brave as Willie. I wasn't as smart. It was Willie who taught me a mean left jab so I'd be safe in the schoolyard. Willie who begged Tatte to shave his beard and escape the brickyard. Willie who carried me through the snow and fed me ice. Willie who made me laugh when there was nothing to laugh about and forced me to believe in happy endings.

I didn't say goodbye to Jacob, or thank him for finding me, I just got up and ran. Ran until I couldn't run anymore. I stopped at an abandoned brick building and leaned against the wall, howling. I cried for Willie, for the old Pole and for Mamme, Tatte, Dita and Sari. If Willie was dead – strong, smart Willie – then maybe the others were dead too.

"*Yisgadal, veyiskadash, shmey raba.*" Someone was saying Kaddish on the other side of the wall.

I stepped into a dim room and saw a man staring into a furnace. I took a step closer to the ovens, to see what he saw. There was ash and soot but there was also bone. I felt the ground give way under me. The strange smog that hovered over the camps, the stink of rotting bodies, the smoke that belched from the giant chimneys – the SS had been burning bodies. And the dead stacked like rotting wood at the back of the building weren't waiting to be buried; they were waiting to be burned. How had I not seen it? The building was a few minutes' walk from barrack 4.

I stumbled outside. People died every day in Buchenwald. I knew that. But these weren't a few hundred bodies piled in a bony heap. These were half-dressed women and naked men stacked high as houses.

I lay in bed with my blanket drawn up to my chin. Ludwig had come to my room and slipped a piece of bread under the blanket and now a nurse was pressing the back of her hand to my forehead.

"I'll be back," she whispered, but I ignored her.

Willie was dead and the world had stood by and let Hitler kill him. Nothing made sense. Ovens baked men and chocolate could kill you and maybe there was no-one waiting for me back home.

I stayed in bed for three days, hiding inside sleep, dreaming of Willie and black holes.

Ludwig came and dribbled some water onto my tongue. "I'm not leaving until you get up," he said. "You survived this shit hole and I'm not going to let you –"

"Did you know?" I said, turning to face him.

"Know what?"

"About the ovens? And the showers?"

Ludwig nodded. "You didn't?" He looked surprised.

I shook my head, feeling small and stupid. "I never guessed that the chimneys ... the smoke ..." I shook my head. "I met a man at the crematoria." I swallowed hard. "He told me they packed people into showers and turned on the gas."

Ludwig had known. Willie must have known too. All those whispered conversations cut short when I was near. His warnings not to leave my barrack. He knew, and he protected me from it because if I'd known just how broken the world was, I would've given up.

I choked back my tears. Willie had taught me to fight; to never give up. My hands hooked into fists. "I won't let you down, Willie." I shrugged off my blanket. "I'll make it home," I promised my brother. "I won't let them win."

I was practised at keeping my feelings in check. I'd learned to stand still while nooses were knotted around men's necks. I'd learned not to cry when prisoners were beaten and to make myself dead inside, so they couldn't hurt me. I could do that now. I could pretend that my world hadn't exploded. I could pretend I was okay, until I *was* okay.

"I'm okay," I told Ludwig, trying to empty myself of feelings.

It didn't work. Instead of feeling numb I felt angry. I didn't beat it back. I let the anger grow hard. It felt good to feel something. To be *allowed* to feel.

I lined my pockets with rocks and joined a gang. The boys were around my age, all of us were angry and out for revenge. The townspeople in the nearby villages weren't happy to see us. No-one offered to feed us or give us clean clothes. Mothers covered their children's eyes and families locked themselves indoors, frightened at what we might say or do to them.

We didn't hurt them but we did some damage. We threw

eggs at farmhouses and trampled flowerbeds. We drove nails through truck tyres and tore down fences. I was the smallest in our gang but I pulled my weight, throwing rocks at car windows and driving cattle from their paddocks. I had so much rage and sadness inside me; it felt good to *be* the nightmare, not live in one.

We stormed villages for two weeks, freeing goats from their pens and kicking in car doors. I didn't feel guilty. We'd passed these farmhouses on our way to hard labour, we'd marched through these fields, a stone's throw from the camp. The people cowering in their houses must've seen the black smoke and smelled the rotting bodies. They would have known someone who delivered food to the camp.

I only stopped because the American Military Police told me to stop. "If you don't," they threatened, "we'll arrest you."

The day after we were set free journalists arrived, poking their heads into barracks to take photos and scribble notes; to see if what they'd been told was true. I saw a reporter throw up outside the latrines and a man in a three-piece suit escape to the safety of a waiting car.

Germans from the nearby villages were forced to tour the camp, staring at us in embarrassed silence, men with full heads of hair and stomachs spilling over their belts, women with curves.

"You are all witnesses," a man in a US military uniform told them as they stood stiffly in the middle of the square, studying their shoes. "Those piles of bodies you saw, those naked men, were farmers and accountants, shopkeepers and doctors. They had brothers and cousins. They had careers and homes. They married and raised sons."

Our stories mattered. Every small heartbreak and devastation. *Are you here on your own?* the men and women with notepads asked. *What's your name? How old are you?* Every time they asked my anger loosened, but I wasn't ready to tell them who I was or who I'd lost.

I was transferred to the SS officers' quarters where I slept on clean white sheets and watched a tent city grow up around me. Aid workers set up desks heaped with clothes and nurses disinfected wounds and handed out medicine. I had my body scraped for lice and dusted with pesticide while captured German officers dug graves to bury the dead.

After a few weeks the smell of smoke disappeared. People offered us smiles. They listened when we talked and called us by our names. I started to feel human again; maybe even hopeful. I still kept bread hidden in my pocket but I'd stopped hiding *myself* away. I wanted to trust the world again. I wanted to laugh out loud.

"How old are you? Ten? Eleven?" The American relief worker measuring me for clothes stared at my sticking out ribs. "You sure are tiny." She handed me the smallest pair of pants she could find.

I put them on and turned up the cuffs. My new shoes were three sizes too big and my shirt gaped at the neck. With my fingers hidden under drooping sleeves I looked like a clown, but I felt like a million dollars.

"I want to go home."

"Where's home?" the woman asked.

The words tumbled out, quicker than I could sort them. I told her about holding Tatte's hand in *shul* and baking bread with Mamme. I told her about the boys at school who wouldn't let me play soccer and the guards in the brickyard who stole Mamme's warm coat. I described the smell in the cattle train and my hiding place under the conveyer belt. I showed her my scar and told her about Willie. I told her everything.

I told my story again the next day and the one after that. I told it to anyone who wanted to hear it – investigators, rehabilitation officers, the military. And when I finished talking about the past, we talked about the future.

"We'll send you to Switzerland to recuperate," they said, "and once you're well, we'll fly you to the United States. We'll find a family to take you in and you can finish school."

I wanted to finish school. I wanted to climb into an airplane and cut through the clouds. I'd dreamed of living in New York ever since Mamme told me I had an aunt living there. Mamme's big sister, Merele, had moved to America before I was born and had married and had children – my cousins – who were big now, and had homes of their own.

"I'm sorry," I said, hoping I was making the right decision. "I can't go to America. Not yet."

"Leaving is your best shot at starting over," they said. "There's every chance there'll be no-one waiting for you back home."

"Maybe," I said, "but if there's a chance, I have to take it. Maybe a miracle is headed my way."

I was free and my stomach was full. That was a miracle. The day the prisoner on the platform told me to run to Tatte, that was a miracle too. The Polish woman telling me to duck under the conveyer belt, the *kapo* who thought I looked like his son, the US Army arriving the day I was meant to die. Maybe there was a miracle waiting for me in Porubka.

"My family will be waiting," I said. "Can you help me get home?"

CHAPTER 17

NOW

Mom sets a chocolate cake on the table and asks Dad if he's full.

"I can open another liquid supplement if you're still hungry?" she offers, draping a tea towel across his lap and reaching for a can.

"I'm okay," Dad says, eyeing dessert.

He doesn't tell us that he misses the taste of food. Perhaps because Willie is still here, whispering in his ear, telling him to fight; to not let the world see he's struggling. Maybe that's why Dad can keep telling his story as if it's someone else's broken childhood. Can talk about Willie's death without cracking wide open. Can tell us he'll never eat again without his voice going wobbly.

Everyone says I'm just like him. Maybe it's more than the eyes and the freckles. I'm good at keeping my feelings in check too. I used to think that was a good thing. Now I'm not so sure.

"So, when you got home, was there a miracle waiting for you in Porubka?" Tom asks.

"A miracle?" Dad smiles. "You'll have to wait till next week."

"But you *were* free?" Jack asks.

"Yes. The United States Third Army liberated Buchenwald and I was free. My hair grew back and I put on some of the weight I'd lost. I learned how to use a toothbrush again, how to use toilet paper and cutlery ..."

Dad had to learn how to smile, remember how to laugh. I think about all the words he had to re-shape – oven, selection, camp and gas. They meant different things to a boy who was free. And now his vocabulary is shifting again. Food is a drink fed into his stomach. Golf is something he watches on TV and saliva is something that can drown him.

I label tonight's recording *Day 7 – Freedom* and drop the tapes into the shoebox. I slide *Day 3* into my Walkman and add Dad's words to the story I wrote for Mr C, turning them into something I can hold onto, something I can give back to Dad. I need to do *something*. Mom feeds and washes him. Jack and Tom talk to his doctors. All I can do is give him back his past and tell him it's important, and that I've been listening.

Maybe if I had his words down on paper – if *we* remembered – *he* could forget.

I ring Deb's doorbell and wait. I have to tell her what's going on. I've lost a boyfriend. I can't lose a best friend. *She won't care that you're Jewish*, I tell myself. *Ludwig didn't turn his back on Dad when he found out.*

"Hey," I say, when she opens the door. "I was hoping we could talk ... about Adam ... and other stuff."

Deb stares at me, stony-faced. "You're unbelievable," she says, and not in a good way. "You want to talk about Adam?"

I nod. "You said to come over."

Still nothing.

"But if now's not a good time ... I can come back?"

"You weren't there."

"There?" I'm confused. "Where?"

She disappears inside. When she comes back she shoves a flyer at me. "*Here.*" It's a flyer for the school play.

My stomach drops.

"Oh my God. You forgot!" Her mouth hangs open. "I thought you'd come up with some lame excuse. But you forgot. You knew how important this was for me ... I mean it's all I talked about."

I try to speak but Deb is talking again, more to herself, than to me. "You know what? Screw it. I'm not going to feel bad about the play. I was brilliant. I killed it."

"I'm sorry. I can explain."

"You don't owe me anything ... I mean it's not like we're besties anymore."

"I *want* to be ..."

"Well, that's great," she says sourly, "but best friends are there for each other. And it's not just the play." She straightens her headband. "I just don't feel like I know you anymore."

"You're right," I say. "You don't …"

"Okaaay." Her mouth is a straight line. "So, I guess that's it. I'll see you at school."

She reaches for the door handle but I get to it first.

"My dad's dying."

"You serious?" Deb grabs my hand.

I nod. "Can I come in?"

We sit in her room, on the edge of her bed.

"He has amyotrophic lateral sclerosis."

"I'm sorry …" she shakes her head. "I don't –"

"It's okay," I say, "I hadn't heard of it either."

I swallow the tears and stick to the facts. "It attacks the nerves, the ones that tell our muscles to move. Once the nerves are shot, the muscles waste away." My voice wobbles. "It's about the worst way I reckon you can die. Dad's memory and his brain are working, but his body's giving up on him."

I look down at our coupled hands. "The doctors gave him six months."

"When?"

"Two months ago."

I let myself feel awful instead of running from it. "I'm going to lose him, Deb. Everything's falling apart and I don't know what to do." I don't try to stop the tears. "I'm losing Dad. I've lost Adam. I'm losing you."

"Firstly," Deb says, pulling tissues out of a box and handing me one, "you're my best friend. I was just talking trash before. I was hurt. I missed you. Secondly, I love you. I thought you knew that. I know sometimes it's hard to get a word in, but this ... your dad ... it's huge. You should have told me."

"I know," I say. "I'm sorry. I don't like talking about myself. And I don't like people feeling sorry for me ... and they will."

"Maybe," Deb says. "But we're not talking about *people*. We're talking about us."

"I know." My eyes slide to my lap. "It's not that I don't trust you."

"Then what?"

"I don't know. I don't want to be someone other people feel sorry for. I want to be strong, like Dad. He's been amazing, Deb. *He's* the one comforting *us*." I smile but it doesn't stick.

"You're the strongest person I know." Deb pulls a tissue from the box to blow her nose. "You have all this stuff going on and you're still keeping it together, keeping up an A average, killing it at the athletic leagues ..."

"That stuff's easy. It's letting go that's hard."

Deb's forehead wrinkles.

"Dad's let go of so much," I try to explain. "Driving. Dressing himself. Eating. He's sad for a bit but then he just ... recalibrates. I want to be that type of strong but it's like someone got the vacuum out and sucked up the future." I can't find the right words to fit my pain, but I keep trying. "It's just all going to shit. I hardly see you anymore. I miss *us*. I miss our Friday nights. I just wish everything could go back to how it was before. Before the stories and –"

"The stories?" Deb looks confused.

"I'm Jewish," I say.

I wait for the roof to cave in. I wait for Deb to stand and point me to the door, or at least say, *You don't look Jewish*.

"Dad survived the Holocaust." I look down at my lap. "He never told us about it. Now he is."

"Your poor dad." Deb is still holding my hand. This is not how I thought this would go.

"I thought you'd say I don't look Jewish."

"What does Jewish look like?" Deb narrows her eyes. "You? Your hot brothers?"

"Yew!" I grimace. "You did *not* just say that." And it feels like us again. Like Deb and Lis. "So, you're not mad that I didn't tell you about Dad and the Jewish thing?"

"No, I'm not mad. Maybe a little hurt. It's not the secrets, just the fact you kept them. I get why, I just wish you would've trusted that I would've had your back. This is *your* story. You can do whatever you want with it. You can tell people or not tell people. You're still my best friend. Who cares what God you believe in?"

"That's the thing," I say. "I don't know if I even do. Not that it matters. Half the people who died in the camps probably didn't believe in God, but they died anyway because some twisted guy with a moustache decided they didn't deserve to live. Sorry. I'm rambling."

"It's called talking." Deb smiles. "And please. Don't stop. I like talking, don't get me wrong, but sometimes it's exhausting when I'm the only one doing it. You're a great listener, Lis, but, I don't know, sometimes it feels like a counselling session, and I have Miss Evans for that."

"The school psych?"

Deb nods. "I saw her a couple of times before the play opened. I was getting antsy about opening night. You know, being the lead with most of the cast being in 11th and 12th Grade. It was a lot."

"Why didn't you tell me?"

"Says the woman who has so many secrets they need a postcode."

"I'm serious, Deb."

"I don't know. You had this perfect life. You're a straight-A student with a cute boyfriend and the perfect family. You're always so together. I mean today is the first time I've ever seen you cry. When I ask, you're always, *I'm great!* or you deflect with a question. You have a life too and I want to know about it."

"I'm trying."

"Good." Deb flings an arm over my shoulder.

"So, you won't tell?" I blurt. "I'm glad we talked, but I'm not ready to be the school cover story."

Deb extends a pinkie finger and I hook it with mine. "You planning on telling Karen and Tracey? What about Adam?"

Deb's eyebrows hitch. "Is that why you broke up?" She grabs my sleeve. "I think we better take this –"

"– to the bath," I finish her sentence.

We always talk boys in the bath. I kick off my shoes and climb into the pink clawfoot tub in Deb's bathroom while she raids the pantry. When she returns with a bottle of Sprite, two packets of Cheezels and a very excited Elle, I scoot to my end of the bath so they can both squeeze in. Elle climbs on top of me and waits for a Cheezel.

"Not happening," Deb tells the dog. "Here, you can have this." She pulls off her Reeboks and hands the puppy a sock. "So ... Adam?"

I tell her everything – how I forgot our anniversary, blew off his invitation to the soccer finals, bailed on Saturday night.

"I haven't told him about Dad, or the Jewish thing." I slide a Cheezel onto my ring finger. "I mean I was hanging on by a thread. He's way out of my league."

She lets me gush about the way his face lights up when he laughs and the notes he was always leaving in my locker. "He was a good boyfriend. A *great* boyfriend, even though I don't have a lot to compare it to."

"Coz he was the first boy you ever kissed?"

I shake my head and offer up Jason Matthews. Grade 6.

Deb snorts. "Truth and Dare doesn't count."

"Anyway," I say, "I thought if I dumped all my stuff on Adam, he'd split. Which he did."

"*Because* you didn't tell him."

I shrug. "Anyway, he's moved on."

"With Leanne? They're just friends. And he only hangs out with her because you aren't around."

"And I won't be, for a while. Dad's only going to get worse."

"Okay," Deb says, lifting Elle out of the bath. "Let's do this. You and me, we're done with boys." She grabs my hand and pulls me to my feet.

"A boy ban?" I climb out of the bath after her.

"Till the end of the year … or at least till formal."

"That's next week," I laugh.

And the laughter feels good. Being back at Deb's won't make Dad better but it hurts a little less when you're not alone.

My father was good with his hands. Those wide, freckled hands had made so many things – Mom's engagement ring, my treehouse in the backyard, a go-cart for my brothers. Now he needs help unzipping his pants. I slip my arm through his and guide his shuffling feet to the bathroom. I get him to the toilet safely, position him at the bowl, unzip him and turn away until his flow stops … my cue to flush the toilet and tuck him in.

Mom snaps a photo of Dad sleeping in his chair. She has hundreds of photos in piles around the house – Emil in bed, Emil being fed, Emil mid-suction.

"Do you really want to remember him like this?" I pick up a photo of Tom pouring Dad's dinner into his tube. "Doesn't it make you sad?"

"No," she says. "I want to remember every single day.

This is all I'll have when he's –" She swallows the last words. "I'm just documenting his life – the good and the sad – same as you."

I look at her dumbly.

"I've seen you at night, listening to the tapes and scribbling. You should tell him."

It's another Monday and Deb is offering me a bite of her pig in a blanket. We're sitting in the cafeteria with Karen and Tracey.

"Don't turn around!" Deb whispers, so of course I do.

Adam is sitting two tables away. Leanne sits next to him, fiddling with her necklace, hoping to draw attention to her cleavage, which is at least two cup sizes bigger than mine.

"Look away!" Tracey says. "Look. Away."

I turn back to the girls. "It's cool. I'm done with boys."

"We're *all* done with boys," Deb says. "The four of us. Starting now."

Karen looks scared. Tracey is shaking her head.

"I've got a better plan." Her eyes sweep the room. "How about instead of avoiding boys, we find Lisa a new one?"

"Hey." I wave Mai over, when I spot her searching for a seat. "You can sit here, there's space."

Tracey and Karen shoot me a curious look. Deb scoots over.

"Mai, isn't it?" Deb holds out her packet of Cheetos.

Mai settles her bamboo box on the table. "No, thanks,

I'm full." She lifts the lid and tips the box toward us. "I can't finish them. Want one?"

Inside are three deep-fried flaky rolls. Karen plucks one from the box.

"Omigod," she says between mouthfuls of pastry. "It's like chicken fingers, only better."

"Thanks for the loan," Mai says, sliding the library copy of *I Know Why the Caged Bird Sings* across the table. "I loved what she says about bigotry and loneliness. It was hard to read, must've been hard to write, being an autobiography and all, but I think it's really important." She blushes. "Sorry, I'm gushing," she says. "This is the first time I've eaten lunch with people ... so ..."

"You should review it," I say, sliding the book back to her. "They need book reviews in the school newspaper – stuff that doesn't make it onto the school booklists."

"And maybe some non-fiction too?" Deb says, her eyes cutting back to me.

Mai's face hardens. "Maybe I'll write something about what it was like coming over here by boat. Maybe if some of the boys read it ..."

"... they'd understand," Deb says, holding my gaze.

Deb stops outside my house. "Would your dad mind if I came in to say hi? I hate that the last time I saw him I told him to feel better. You told me it was the flu, so ..."

"Sure," I say, fishing for my key. "He'd love that."

"Me too," Deb says. "I like talking to your dad. He always grills me about university. We never talk about that stuff at home."

"I always feel bad when he corners you."

"Nah, it's okay." Deb follows me into the house.

We ride up the stairs, crammed into the chairlift. I tell her that she'll have to sit close to Dad to hear what he says. It's getting harder for him to speak now that the muscles in his tongue are weak. I tell her that she can ask him how he's feeling. "Asking doesn't remind him. He knows he's sick."

Deb sits in the armchair closest to Dad. "Hi, Mr K."

"Deborah! So nice to see you."

Deb shuffles closer. "I'm sorry about your illness. Lisa told me. How are you feeling?"

She doesn't raise her voice to compensate for his quiet answer or jump in to finish it. She tells him about the van and our gap year and the play she just starred in.

"It was a full house," Deb gushes. "Do you want to hear my monologue?"

Dad's slumped in his chair. There is spittle at the corners of his mouth, but he's smiling.

When we sit down to eat, the first stars are already blinking in the Friday night sky.

"I'm glad you told her," Dad says, waiting for Mom to feed him. "Letting others in, it's not dangerous – it's freeing."

CHAPTER 18

THEN

Those first months after liberation felt like a miracle. People called me by my name, they cared if I was hungry and wanted to know how I felt. My future was important to them. *I* was important. After all the years of hate, I felt like people finally saw me for who I was – a kid who'd survived three camps and wanted to be a lawyer. A boy who liked soccer and had lived through a death march. A boy who'd lost a brother and loved maths. They saw *all* those parts of me.

And when I finally stood in front of a mirror in one of the SS commander's rooms, I saw that boy too. A boy in neat clothes with all his teeth. A boy whose scalp didn't itch. Who was thin but not skinny. Small but getting strong. I'd learned to smile again, to look people in the eye. I didn't leap to attention every time the loudspeaker crackled and I didn't shovel food into my mouth or hoard it under my mattress.

I can do this, I said to myself. *I can start over. I'm a survivor*. And if I'd survived, maybe Tatte, Mamme, Max, Dita and Sari had too.

The train station was full. People stood on the platforms, swapping stories about the camps and the secret places they'd hidden. It seemed like everyone was heading home or scrambling to start a new life. Poles, Russians, Ukrainians and Hungarians pushed past each other to clamber onto the free trains that zigzagged through Europe, returning them to their villages and empty homes.

The train for Slovakia wheezed into the station and I vaulted up the steps before its wheels ground to a stop. I'd never been in a train with windows and leather seats. I flew down the narrow corridors, flinging doors open, but all the carriages were full, so when the train stopped at the next station, I followed a group of boys outside and clambered up onto the roof after them. The top of the train was crowded with people hunched against the wind. I found a spot on the cold metal and, ducking to avoid tunnels, spent the next three weeks clinging to the roof, following the curve of the tracks that would take me home.

They fed and watered us, but sometimes when the train stopped I'd climb down to scour the fields for cherries and plums. I was sitting on the roof one day, watching some boys shake pears from a tree, when a head popped up over the side of the carriage.

232

"Oszkár, psst."

The man sitting next to me looked up.

"So you've had enough of first class, Endre?" he joked. His smile came unstuck when he saw his friend's irritation.

"There's a man, down below." Endre's face darkened. "He's wearing civilian clothes and trying to lay low, but he's SS."

The man next to me got up slowly. I jumped to my feet and followed the men from the roof. There must've been a dozen of us by the time we stormed the compartment. We crowded around the suspect's seat, staring down at his blond scalp.

"What the hell –" He looked up as one of the boys whipped his newspaper from his hands.

A second boy jumped him and twisted his arms behind his back.

"Take his shirt off," Endre ordered, pulling the man's gun from his belt. He pressed the barrel to the man's temple.

"I think you've mistaken me for someone else," the man stammered. "I'm a farmer. The gun is for shooting rabbits."

Endre grabbed the man's hands and turned them over. His palms were smooth. "He's no farmer," Endre said, turning to face us. "Strip him!"

The boys flew at the man, tearing the shirt from his body, looking for proof the man was a Nazi. I'd seen the Americans drag German suspects into the camp and strip them. I knew what they were looking for.

"Lift your arm." Endre pressed the gun to the man's thigh. "Lift it," he spat, releasing the safety.

The German hovered his left arm and Endre grabbed his wrist. He twisted it so we could all see the letter A – his blood type – inked on the skin below his armpit. His SS stamp.

Endre drove his fist into the man's face and the next thing I knew I was on top of the Nazi, clawing and punching, swinging blindly until someone pulled me off.

"Let me at him!" I windmilled my arms.

I wanted to hurt him like they'd hurt Willie. I wanted to tear him to pieces. I wanted to break bones.

An inspector swung the door open calling for tickets when the train stopped to refuel and the SS man fled. I ran after him, the last in a long line of boys to jump from the train but by the time I reached the cluster of trees where the older boys had cornered him, they wouldn't let me at him.

"Then let me watch," I begged. "I just want to make sure he's dead."

"You're just a kid." Endre grabbed me by the collar and turned my head from the mess. "You've seen enough killing. Go home."

I stepped off the train in Ungvar. It was a Friday in early June and the sky was blue with possibility. *I can't be the only one who survived*, I told myself, breaking into a run. I ducked under some wire fencing to cut through a field, the hungry grunting of pigs making me homesick for our small barn. I'd lived through a barbed-wire hell surrounded by strangers. Whatever was waiting for me, at least I *knew* this place, these sloping hills and winding streams. I stopped to let a herd of cows pass. They were mostly black, but one or two had Minu's mottled brown and white coat.

"Minu?" I called out, just for the hell of it, just to remember how it felt to call for an animal.

A cow with brown smudges on its back lifted its head.

"Minu?" I croaked. "Minu, is that you?"

The cow stretched its neck and turned to face me. It had two brown ears, the left slightly smaller than the right.

"Minu! Minu!" I circled the herd.

Minu pushed her way through the pack, her pink tongue sandpapering my face when we met.

"What do *you* want?" a man called from the door of the milking shed. Warm milk splashed the sides of his pail.

"She's mine! The cow." I pointed. "Her name is Minulka." I scratched the cow behind her ears.

"And who are *you*?" The man's voice bounced off the tin shed. He dropped the bucket of milk and stalked toward me, grabbing the ring around Minulka's neck.

"I'm Emil. My father is Aaron Rosenfeld. From Porubka. Maybe you know him?"

The man's face was blank.

"He sells livestock."

"Well maybe your father *sold* us the cow then." He yanked Minu toward him and turned for the shed.

My legs ached by the time I reached the outskirts of Porubka, but when I caught sight of the village it turned into a different kind of ache. I hadn't let myself think about what I'd do if Mamme and Tatte weren't actually there. I shook the thought off and quickened my step. It was Friday. I had to get home before the first stars appeared. Tatte would be pulling on his best suit and making his way down the hill to unlock the synagogue doors.

That's the tree Willie fell from. That's the haberdashery where Dita bought her hair ribbons. That's the park I wasn't allowed to play in. I stopped and squinted into the sun. Two small figures were making their way up the hill ahead of me, crossing the creek that cut the town in two. I ran up after them.

"Mamme? Tatte?"

An old man turned around. He had small, black eyes and a flat face covered in stubble.

"Oh," I said, blinking fast to stop myself crying.

The man ran his eyes the length of me, turned and kept walking.

I continued up the street, feeling as much a stranger as I'd ever been. I walked past kids I'd gone to school with and men who'd bartered with my father. No-one asked where I'd been. No-one smiled or stopped to talk. I swept my hand along our front gate. Tatte's wagon was missing and there was a new welcome mat at the door but the house was unchanged; the sloping roof still covered in creepers and the plaster walls still in need of a paint.

I scanned the yard for Tatte's boots and saw a wire basket full of carrots; the fat orange ones Mamme liked to float in her soup. My heart beat harder. Someone was home!

I leaped over the fence and broke into a run, was almost at the front door when I heard a woman's voice. "That will be three koruna."

Coins jangled and dropped into Tatte's metal cashbox. I turned toward the general store butted up against our house.

"I'm home, Mamme!" I shouted, bolting for the shop door.

A young woman stood blocking the entrance. She looked as though she'd been expecting me.

"Hello," I said uncertainly.

She looked me up and down. "What do *you* want?" She lifted her eyes from my ragged clothes.

"I've been away," I stammered.

"And now you're back."

Someone called from inside the store. A customer wanting to pay.

"Things have changed," the woman said, and she didn't look sorry. "You left and we took over. We've been here for more than a year. You can't just come crawling back."

"But my parents, they own the shop," I heard myself say. "And the house. And the barn."

I scanned the street for someone who knew me, someone who'd bought onions from my mother or sat at our Shabbat table, but the houses either side of ours had both been owned by Jews. There was a man I'd never seen before pulling potatoes from the Goldblums' front yard and a pair of eyes behind Mrs Klein's drawn curtains, but they weren't Mrs Klein's.

The woman gave a short, barking laugh. "I know what you want. You people are all the same. You're not getting any money, if that's what you're after."

The front door of our house snapped back on its hinges. A man built like an armchair appeared in the entrance. He was wearing a pair of faded overalls and Tatte's fur-lined black boots.

Tatte was dead. Mamme too. I should've listened when Jacob warned me not to get my hopes up, when he told me that Mamme would've died the day she arrived at Auschwitz and Tatte after he failed selection. I didn't listen to him and I didn't listen to the aid workers who offered to send me to America.

I stared at Tatte's boots. The laces were fraying and the soles were caked in mud. My parents were dead and another man's feet were in Tatte's shoes, dragging mud and horse shit across Mamme's rug. They were sleeping in my parents' bed and eating off our plates. They were stocking the shelves in our store and clearing out the till as if they owned the place.

I thought about knocking the woman out. I thought about bringing the cashbox down hard on the man's head so I could yank off Tatte's boots while he lay sprawled on our porch. But all the anger leached out of me, and all I was left with was *sad*. Sad was easier to hide and less likely to get you locked up.

Better I find out now. I swallowed the sick rising up in my throat. *Better to face the sharp truth of it.* Mamme and Tatte were gone. My brother and sisters too. Better to face it now, so I didn't waste time wishing for things I couldn't have. I was alone, and my bed and the books I'd left behind wouldn't bring my family back.

"You causing trouble?" the man said, stepping off the porch.

I shook my head.

"He was just leaving." The woman's mouth twisted in disgust. "There's nothing here for you." She pointed a thin finger at the gate. "Go on, get out."

I wandered the main street, past the burnt-out remains of the synagogue and the boarded-up kosher butcher. My parents were dead, the synagogue was rubble, our prayer books were burnt and the small desks in the *cheder* were piles of ash. There was nothing to say my family had lived here, had walked these streets or worked the land. *I* was the stranger here, the one who didn't belong.

I looked around and saw the small-minded, mean, hateful town where I'd grown up. The people who lived here hadn't changed, they were still filled with hate, but *I'd* changed. I wasn't the same boy they'd shoved into a cattle car. I'd survived hunger and cold. I'd slept in the snow. I'd stolen food for my brother and traveled alone. I'd lost friends and made new ones.

"You can keep the business *and* our home," I yelled at the sky. "I won't be back."

I walked the neighboring villages and towns, to find the same gray, dour faces, the same disinterest. "Hitler didn't keep his promise. There's more of them now than before," I heard someone complain.

It was getting dark and I was tired and hungry but I didn't stop for the night. I walked through the emptying streets, crossing paddocks that turned from green to black, putting as many miles as I could between me and hate.

Others must have had the same idea because when I reached Ungvar it was impossible to find a bed for the night. The only place to sleep was the park. On the second night a stooped, silent man curled up on the grass beside me. He didn't talk, just hummed a sad song to himself, but when the first streaks of light appeared in the sky, he turned to me and said: "They stole my house."

I didn't ask who had stolen it. They were the same people who had stolen mine.

"They took everything," he said, his mouth tightening, "but they don't get to decide who I'll become. I'm getting out of here and I'm going to build a better life, a *bigger* life than I ever could've here."

A soup kitchen had been set up in the courtyard of the old Jewish community center. I was lining up for lunch when someone tapped me on the shoulder.

"You don't recognize me, do you?" A man in a crumpled suit stood behind me.

I shook my head.

"You were young when we met." He smiled, and I smiled back.

It felt good to be recognized. Good to be Emil Rosenfeld from before the war, a boy who had parents. A boy who had plans.

"Last time we met it was at your Mamme's table."

"Mm-amme," I stuttered, and the man nodded his small head.

"She was a good woman, Pepi Rosenfeld. Never turned me away when I came begging for a hot meal." He looked at me through a milky left eye. "Your mother gave me food *and* a seat at her table. I remember you because you always asked for a second helping. Your mamme would roll her eyes, but I saw her sneak you an extra plate of ... what was it?" He scratched his bristled chin. "Ah, yes, it was *cholent*. She made a good *cholent*."

I threw my arms around the stranger. "Mamme's gone," I blubbered into his wool coat. "Tatte too, and all my brothers and sisters."

He peeled my hands from his neck. "Not all," he said, his face suddenly serious. "Your brother Max ... he's alive." The man had seen Max on the street in Velke Kapusany. "I never met the boy before but he's the mirror image of your tatte, so I stopped him to ask after your father. We didn't talk long; he was on his way to work."

Velke Kapusany was a town in Slovakia, a little smaller than Ungvar and six hours walk from where we stood.

The streets of Velke were filled with survivors looking for their families. I joined the throng of ragged refugees trying to find their loved ones.

"Max Rosenfeld ..." The woman at the Refugee Reception Centre ran her finger down a list. "Rosenfeld, Max. Yes, here he is."

She scrawled my brother's address on a scrap of paper and passed it to me. I held it for a long time, that flimsy bit of paper that said I wasn't alone. I had a brother who knew what Mamme's *cholent* tasted like. Someone who had debated God with Tatte and chased Willie around the garden. Someone who had Sari's freckles and had teased Dita about boys. I shoved the small square of paper into my pocket.

"Emil?" Max stood at the door, his mouth hanging open.

"Max?" I whispered, my heart banging hard.

He was thinner than I remembered and his eyes were ringed with dark circles but he had that gap between his two front teeth – the one we all had – and our father's broad nose.

"Emil, you're alive!" Max shouted. "You made it. I knew you would." He cupped my face in his big, hairy hands. "I told them." His face split into a smile. "He's alive! Emil's alive!" he shouted over his shoulder. "Dita, come see! Sari, your brother's home!"

I stumbled backward. Max was calling my sisters to come see me. Either the war had driven him mad or Dita and Sari were in the kitchen making lunch! Something crashed to the floor and my heart started hammering. Feet pounded the timber boards and Dita flew at me, Sari on her heels, both of them shrieking.

"Elyuka!" Dita buried her wet face in my neck.

"Emil!" Sari cried, wrapping her arms around both of us.

Max smiled and joined the scrum and we stood there, in the entrance, laughing and crying and not letting go – a huddle of orphans singing each other's names.

"His hair is thick and curly." Sari turned to Dita.

"He's alive," whispered Dita, and we all held hands.

"You're so skinny," Sari said, pulling me into the kitchen. "Are you hungry?"

A table had been set for three but now Sari dropped cutlery onto the red tablecloth and slid a plate between the knife and fork. The room was warm and smelled of *challah*. I sank back in my chair and tried not to stare. Dita's flaming red hair had grown back a dull orange and was scraped off her head with an elastic band. She wore house slippers and an apron around her narrow waist. Sari had also been whittled by hunger and her hands trembled as she spooned pea soup into my bowl.

"Eat," she said, so we didn't have to talk. So she wouldn't have to ask about our parents and Willie, and hear me say that they were all dead.

I tore at the crusty *challah* and dunked it into the broth, licked the bowl clean, then asked for another. Then I told Dita, Sari and Max how Willie and Tatte had died and they told me about Mamme.

"We lost her after you left," Dita said. "The SS sent her off with the sick and the elderly and we were put to work. I took a job as a tailor. They gave me a needle and thread, and for every torn SS collar and loose button I repaired I got extra bread, which I smuggled to Sari."

"I was starving," Sari said, tearing up.

I had a mountain of questions I wanted to ask but I didn't know how, so I just held her hand.

CHAPTER 19

NOW

The room is quiet. I'm still in Porubka, wondering if the man who stole Tatte's boots is alive and living in his house.

Tom is worrying over something too. "The Americans stopped you ransacking homes." He looks at Dad. "And that man, Endre, he wouldn't let you finish off the SS officer. Did you ever get your revenge?"

I don't want Dad to answer. This is one secret I want him to keep because in three months, give or take a day, I'm going to be standing at his grave and I still want to think he was some kind of hero.

Dad looks at the three of us, then smiles at Mom. "You are my revenge."

Mom lets me look through her wardrobe for something to wear to my 10th Grade formal. I've been in her wardrobe before. When I was young and scared of thunderstorms I'd climb into her closet between floor-length gowns and hide until the blasts stopped. Now I'm here to find a dress. We'd planned to go shopping months ago, but then Dad got sick and Mom got too busy.

"How about this one?" Mom pulls an attention-seeking green dress from its hanger.

"Too green."

"This one?" She holds up a sequined mini dress. "I have boots to match."

She reaches into the back of the wardrobe and pulls out a pair of knee-high, Halloween-orange boots covered in a thin veneer of dust. She's kept everything. Every dress from the last three decades, every handbag and belt. My mother doesn't like to let go of things.

"It's not a dress-up party. Seriously, Mom. Do you have anything I can actually wear?"

She pulls out a paisley-print caftan and platform heels.

I throw my arms up. "We were meant to go shopping. It was just an afternoon. I only wanted a few hours."

Mom is shaking her head, somewhere between disappointed and baffled, and I get it, she has to focus on Dad, but where does that leave me? In a hand-me-down dress from her costume-department wardrobe, getting a lift to the formal because Mom can't drive me.

I want to say, *Dad's not the only one whose life has imploded.* Instead, I say, "Don't worry about it, I'll borrow something from Deb."

It's the night of the formal. I climb into Deb's pink taffeta dress, sweep some gold eyeshadow onto my lids, pull on her metallic bomber jacket, grab a clutch and stand in front of Mom's mirror. I want to see the same thing Dad saw when he gazed into the mirror at the SS officers' barracks – a person who can tell their story and let people in. Instead I see a girl with plastic hoop earrings and a plastic smile.

Mom appears in the mirror and I spin around to face her.

"Why aren't you dressed?" I ask, panicked. "And where's Dad? We have to leave soon."

"Dad's not coming. He's not feeling up to it. Nothing serious. He's just tired." She picks up a comb. "Want me to tease your hair?"

I nod.

"I'll drop you at school, but I can't stay for the photos. I'll ask Deb's mom to take some." Mom grabs a section of hair and gets to work.

"Okay," I say, worry butting up against relief.

If Dad doesn't come, I won't have to ask Mom to take off his neck brace and leave the suctioning equipment in the car. I won't have to explain why he's sitting in the corner and can't have a drink. I *will* tell my friends – I want to – but not tonight. Formals are about making out on the dance floor, drinking too much and finishing school. I don't want to be the sad sack stuck in a corner having a heart-to-heart.

"You look great," Mom whispers when the cloud of

hairspray thins. "I don't know when it happened – you growing up and becoming a woman."

I take a last look in the mirror. A tall, long-lashed girl in pink stares back at me. A girl who wants to drink and dance while her father does the hard work of dying.

"It's okay if I'm late," I tell her. "I want to sit with Dad for a bit."

Dad is lying in bed, his head propped up by pillows. His smile reaches his eyes when I show off the dress. I lift the cloth from his bedside table to wipe the dribble from his chin, but he shakes his head.

"Do you want the suction?" I glance at the machine.

"No. You've got a party to get to. Did I ever tell you that when I was younger I was quite the dancer?" He gives me a small smile.

"Does it make you sad, thinking you won't ..." My words dissolve.

"There are lots of things I'll never do again." Dad's smile falters. "Sunset walks on the beach, yum cha on a Sunday morning, soccer in the park. They're not the hardest things. The hardest bit is someone I love not understanding me when I speak. It's wanting to hug someone and not being able to put my arms around them."

I rest my head next to his. "I'm sorry you can't come," I whisper, and I'm only half-lying.

"Me too," Dad says, "but I'm okay, really. Now, get out of here and go have fun!"

"Oh my God," Deb shouts over the live band beat. She's wearing a purple organza dress with giant shoulders and rainbow-colored eyeshadow. "You look way better than I do in that dress! Keep it, it's yours!"

She drags me onto the dance floor and we dance till our hair droops.

"Need air!" Deb says dramatically.

I follow her from the hall. A group of boys are sitting on the steps leading down to the oval, sneaking sips from a bottle someone has smuggled in to school. Someone has set up a boom box and couples are slow dancing to Lionel Richie on the oval. Tracey and her blond surfer-boy crush are there, so are Adam and Leanne, who's eight-feet tall in silver heels.

Deb notices me noticing Adam's arms on Leanne's hips. She winks at me and lunges for Leanne. She's not drunk, but she does a good impression.

"Where did ya get that dress? It's cool," she slurs through metallic orange lips. She grabs Leanne's hand and pulls her from Adam. "And that makeup!" She stumbles, cupping Leanne's face in her sweaty palms. "How do you get the mascara to clump like that?"

Leanne twists around to look for Adam but he's looking at me.

"I like your dress," he says, his green eyes soft.

Lionel Richie sings into the silence between us. Something about a love that lasts forever. I don't know what to do with my arms and legs. Everyone around us is dancing slow, arms slung around necks, bodies swaying.

"It's Deb's," I say, cutting across the chorus.

He nods and we stand there fumbling for conversation.

"It's nice to hear though." I lean in and drop my voice to a whisper. "Things have been a bit rough lately."

"Because of us?" He catches my hand and pulls me to a quiet bench.

Act cool. He's with Leanne. "It's Dad," I say. "He hasn't been well." Adam's face is inches from mine. "That night I came over, I was going to tell you, he –"

"There you are, mate!" Paul burps loudly and collapses onto the bench. "I was just saying to Leanne –" He slugs on a bottle, tips it upside down and shakes the last drops onto his tongue. "I was just saying, I think the two of you ..."

I let go of Adam's hand.

"... I just love you guys and ... woah, why is the room spinning?" He slings an arm around Adam's shoulder. "I don't feel great," he says, eyes rolling back in his head until I can see the bloodshot whites. "I think I'm gonna puke."

His body judders and then he does. And it's fluoro green like the Midori he's been drinking. And I should've worn Mom's green dress because he's hurled all over me.

"I've gotta go," I say, looking up from my ruined dress, hot tears pooling.

Paul is on all fours on the grass, unloading his drinks, and Adam is trying not to gag while he wipes the sick from his friend's face. I run for the bathroom, past Leanne and Deb. I can hear Adam behind me – "Lis, I'm sorry.

Can we ...?" – but I'm already past the dark dance floor and taking the stairs two at a time.

The school year ends, so I don't have to see Adam. I meet Deb at the pool or the beach most days, and when Dad's done with appointments I hang out with him. We sit in the garden, reading and talking. Sometimes we meditate or watch TV. Sometimes I ask him questions about living and dying, scribbling his answers on the notepad Tom gave me.

Today I tell him that I'm copying down his story and he grins, spittle at the corners of his mouth. I like how the inked pages make his words feel important, make *him* feel important. His lids start to droop. I pull his blanket up to his chin and return to my room, to the tapes.

When Deb comes over later that day, I hand her a stack of pages – Dad's story so far.

"You sure?" she says, dropping onto the bed next to me.

"I'm sure," I say, pulling on headphones.

I write while Deb reads.

It's almost dark by the time she puts down the pages. "I can't believe he kept all this secret. He *never* talked about it?"

"Nope."

"Were there clues?"

"Like what?"

"I don't know." Deb shuffles closer. "Like does he hate trains ... and showers? Is he scared of dogs?"

I stare at her, realization dawning. "I don't know if he's scared, but he *is* kind of weird around dogs. I've never seen him pat one and he doesn't go near Elle. But really he was just an ordinary run-of-the-mill dad."

He took us camping and let us have water gun fights. He let us catch trains to the city and walk to the shops on our own. He watched us tip leftovers into the bin and whine about homework. He wasn't suspicious of strangers who came to the door and he never used the word *hate*.

I had an ordinary dad. And for the first time I realize how extra-ordinary that is.

Mom suggests I stay with Deb for a week. She says I deserve a summer holiday and that we all need a break. She doesn't say *from each other*, but that's what she means.

"Come in, darl," Mrs Cartman waves at the disappearing car. "Terrible news about your father." She pulls me toward her, pressing my face into the soft padding of her push-up bra.

"Mom!" Deb wails. "She doesn't want to talk about it."

We escape upstairs. Deb has made up a bed next to hers. There's a pile of *Cosmo* magazines on the bedside table and a pile of Kit Kats on the pillow. "I've planned the whole week. It's going to be epic."

We spend our days by her pool in neon bikinis. We go

to the movies and play mini golf and bedazzle Elle's collar with glitter and rhinestones. We bake chocolate cake, chocolate brownies and chocolate-chip cookies and eat them at midnight under the covers. We sleep in, read our horoscopes and do each other's nails. I try not to let my sorrow rub off on her. Some days we crank up the music. Some days we scream at the walls and some days we do both. The sadness is still there, but it's smaller.

Adam is away all of January but Deb won't let me mope. Her boy ban is over and she's organised a double date. 'It's Raining Men' blares from her speakers. She shimmies toward me, scooping my hair into a side ponytail and sliding a dozen jangling bangles onto my wrist.

"You can wear these," she shouts over the track, tossing me a pair of short shorts and a fluoro yellow tank top.

Deb's date, Greg, has long blond hair. He's eighteen and drives a car. He leans out the driver-side window, a cigarette dangling from his mouth.

"Your friend can sit in the back."

Deb climbs into the front passenger seat and I open the back door.

"Hey." A boy with brown eyes grins from under a cap. "I'm Ted." He scoots over. "And you're ...?" He looks up from my legs.

"Lisa."

Ted taps a cigarette out of its pack, leans back into the seat and lights up. I watch the smoke curl between us and try to stifle a cough.

"Want one?"

I shake my head and pull on my seatbelt.

"I've seen you around." He grins. "I went to Glenrock. Just finished 12th Grade. School. Is. Done." He fist-pumps the air. "You used to hang out with that kid from the soccer team."

I nod, unsure what to say.

"You broke up."

It isn't a question, so I don't answer.

Ted winks. "His loss."

I lunge for the front seat. "Can we play some music?"

Greg slides a tape into the deck and 'Highway to Hell' blasts through the speakers. I sink back into my seat. Ted is playing air drums. His eyes are closed so I sneak another peek at him. Tight acid-wash jeans, big shoulders and brown hair. He's good-looking and he knows it. *So* not my type. But then my type dumped me, so what do *I* know?

We get to the beach and the boys go hunting for branches that they can use to build a fire. Deb smooths a blanket over the sand.

"He's a hottie, right?" she whispers as the boys scoop up sticks.

"Greg?" I shrug. "Sure."

"What about Ted? Do you like him?"

"He's ... he's ..." I want to say *not Adam*. "He seems nice."

The boys dump their branches and Deb opens a packet of Cheezels and a half-finished bottle of vodka. I take a swig and pass the bottle to Ted.

"We need more kindling," Greg says, pulling Deb to her feet.

She looks at me, eyes pleading, so I nod and watch them walk away.

"So, it's just you and me?" Ted gives me a sideways smile.

A smile he's used before, I'll bet. Ted's eighteen. He's probably pashed a thousand girls and I've never even gotten to third base.

I push the worry back inside me. "Guess so."

"So, what do you do for fun?" He slides closer, close enough for me to smell the cigarette smoke in his hair.

"*This*," I say, tipping the bottle up and drinking.

I'm single, he's hot, the stars are out in their millions, and Adam is with Leanne. *Okay, let's do this.*

I let him lean in and tuck a stray hair behind my ear. "You're really pretty," he says. "Killer eyes."

I know it's a line, but I let the words hang there. I let him trace the curve of my cheeks with his thumb, let him lean in and kiss me.

I don't know his last name. I don't know anything about Ted-from-12th-Grade and that's exactly what I need – uncomplicated. I think about all the ways I've hurt and disappointed Adam. Ted doesn't know me so I can't let him down. We kiss and I let him walk his fingers up my legs because life is short and you have to grab it with both hands because bad things happen out of the blue.

His hands are on my waist now, my back, my bra. I let him unclasp it. I slide a hand under his T-shirt and run my fingers down his back, trying out this new *me*. But it doesn't feel like freedom and when I open my eyes all the

255

magic is gone, and there's just me and a boy I don't know, sitting on the sand.

"Sorry," I say, pulling away to do up my bra. "I'm not in the mood."

He looks confused. I could blame the vodka but I'm sick of pretending.

"It's not you or anything you did ... my dad is dying ... and I'm not over my ex."

Ted shrugs and grabs a stick to spear a marshmallow and we sit and watch the flames blacken the sugar so we don't have to watch Deb's and Greg's shadows making out on the sand.

"Want to smash something?" he finally says.

"Smash something?"

"I don't know." Ted shrugs. "You just look like you could do with a visit to the Johnson house."

I know the house. It's a dump. The doors have been torn off; the windows are broken. It's been derelict for years.

"Is that where you take *all* your dates?"

He laughs. "Nah. I usually go on my own. You know," his voice dips, "to let off steam. There's a heap of old junk there, empty bottles of booze, broken down TVs, stuff you can smash. Just saying."

"Sounds great, but I'm okay." I try for a smile.

"Well, if you change your mind."

He pulls the stick from the fire and tosses me the burnt remains of a pink marshmallow.

"So, Ted didn't work out." Deb slings an arm around me, the next day. "At least you put yourself out there. And now that's *two* boys you've kissed."

"Three," I correct her. "Jason Matthews. 6th Grade."

A car horn bleats below us in the street. "That'll be Mom," I say, grabbing my bags.

I don't want to leave. I want to order take-away fish and chips and talk about boys. I want long, lazy days and milkshake breakfasts. I want to hold onto the sunshine. But I kiss Deb goodbye.

CHAPTER 20

THEN

My sisters found husbands who made them feel safe. Dita was eighteen when she married Marek Hoffman, a short, serious man who smelled of old milk and was almost bald. Sari was seventeen, and with her sister resettled in Kosice she was lonely, so she married Samuel Kirshner, a thin, nervous man in his thirties. Maybe she thought she'd be half as lonely as part of a pair.

I didn't want to be pinned down. I wanted to finish school and reclaim the life Hitler had stolen from me. That would be my revenge. Not the few weak punches I'd thrown at that SS officer on the train. Being a lawyer and living a *big* life ... that would be my way to get even. I didn't think about what it would cost. I thought my sisters would *want* me to go to school.

"It's out of the question," Samuel said, holding out his bowl for another helping of chicken soup. It was a Saturday and Dita and Marek had traveled from Kosice to discuss the question of my future.

"I'm sorry, Emil," Sari said. "You're fifteen. It's time to take responsibility and start building your future. You'll need to start pitching in."

Dita stared into her lap.

"So, what work do you want to do?" Max asked.

I thought about Tatte and the money he'd squirreled away for my schooling. I thought about Mr Lukacs at the synagogue pushing past the guards to give me a book. Maybe my dream of becoming a lawyer could come true later. Maybe I could get a job, save some money and go back to school when I was sixteen.

"What about a motor mechanic?" I offered. Marek was always complaining that mechanics charged too much and if I worked as a mechanic I'd get to sit in a car, maybe even drive one.

"Are you kidding?" Marek laughed. "You'll never get the dirt out from under your fingernails and your clothes will be filthy. You'll freeze in winter and in summer you'll sweat. That's no future. What you want is a nice heated room in winter and a fan to keep you cool in summer. What you'll do is become a jeweler."

Dita clapped her hands. "Yes. You can come live with us. There are jewelers in Kosice. We'll find one to take you on."

Within a week of landing in the city I had a job as a jeweler's apprentice. My days started at 6 am. I cleaned equipment, counted stones and tagged jewelery. I bought lunches and ran errands. I sent the post. Whenever I could I'd wander the factory floor, watching men repair broken clasps and shape gold into rings. Sometimes the boss would test my knowledge by lining up tools and asking for their names. Sometimes his men would test me by making me find the gemstones they'd hidden between pieces of pastrami they'd left in the fridge.

When the boss started paying me a wage, I enrolled in 10th Grade at night school and began the long, slow climb to the top of the class, where I'd have to stay if I wanted to get into law school.

"I don't have anyone to help me at home," I explained, reddening at the *Can do better* comment scrawled at the top of my exam. "My parents died and I live with my sister, but she didn't finish school."

My teacher nodded. "I see. And how are you supporting yourself?"

"I'm working as a jeweler on Hlavná Street."

"Tell you what." My teacher picked up a pen. "How about I tutor you free of charge. If your grades improve, we'll continue. If not, we'll stop."

He drew a line through the *can* and wrote the word *will*. Emil *will* do better.

My grades improved. I studied whenever I could, on lunchbreaks at my bench and at night by torchlight under my blankets, scrambling to fill in the gaps in my learning, careful to keep my studies a secret. I didn't tell Dita I was learning to read English from the small library of children's books I hid under my bed. I didn't tell Marek I was enrolled in night school. He hated it when I read.

"Who is paying for the electricity for that lamp you're using? Enough with the reading!" he'd grumble, whipping the newspaper from my hands. "You know how to read. Go live your life."

"You need to make friends," Dita would say.

So I did. I made friends with their maid, accepting her invitation to join her in bed on Saturdays while the others were in synagogue, and sometimes early in the morning while they still slept. She taught me what to do between the sheets. The Jewish friends I made let me borrow their books.

"I need to catch up," I told my tutor. "I want to know what *they* know."

Marek was furious when he found out I was in school. "You should be focusing on your job and collecting pay cheques. What will a degree get you?" He threw up his hands. "It's just a bit of paper that's useless to the butcher and meaningless to your landlord. And those friends of yours ..." He wagged a finger at me. "I don't want them here again. Not in *my* house."

I was a disappointment to my family. I didn't go to synagogue. I didn't keep kosher and I wasn't looking to settle down. We butted heads, but I wouldn't budge. The more they tried to convince me to drop out of school, the harder I worked. The more they criticised my friends, the more often I saw them.

The plan was to sit my 12th Grade exams in June 1949. I was months from graduating, from getting that high school certificate I'd worked so hard for, when the communists seized power. I wanted to sit my final exams but I had to get out of Czechoslovakia before they made me a prisoner again. Every day there was news of another arrest. Marek knew a man who'd been beaten during an interrogation. Dita knew a woman whose husband had disappeared.

"I can't do this again, Emil." Dita dabbed her eyes with her apron. We were having lunch.

"Do what?" I asked, looking from Dita to Marek.

"Lose everything again." Marek's voice dipped. "They're forcing people from their homes." He stopped pacing and turned to face me. "People like us, people who have businesses and make money, we're the ones the secret police watch."

"We're leaving," Dita said, sliding her hand over mine. "We're moving to Israel. Come with us."

"Israel?" I said, pulling away. "I can't."

"You can't stay *here*." Marek shook his head. "You're a Jew, and sooner or later, they'll come for you. There's talk of shutting down the synagogues. That's how it starts ..."

"Come to Israel," Dita begged. "You'll be safe there. No-one will threaten to lock you up or deport you." She raised her hand to stop me. "I know, I know, you want to go to America. Maybe they'll let you in. But what's to say in ten years the same thing won't happen there?"

I'd barely survived one war. Nothing could get me to Israel to risk fighting another one. I took the next day off work and visited the American consulate. "Sorry, son." The American consular worker rose from his chair after hearing my story. "I'd like to help you out. You seem like a nice kid but you're Czech and that quota's been filled." He walked me to the door.

"Who else should I try?" I stopped at the entrance. "Please."

I must've looked desperate because he returned to his desk and grabbed a pad.

"Here," he said, scribbling something onto it. "I can't promise you anything, but it's worth a try."

I prepared a speech before phoning, not that it did any good.

"I have an aunt," I told the woman from the Hebrew Immigrant Aid Society. "My mother's older sister, Merele Rosner. She lives in New York. She married an American. We're close. She's like a second mother," I lied. "You wouldn't have to worry. She can support me. She's rich."

"I'm sorry," the woman sighed into the phone. "You're over eighteen. We only work with children."

There was no future for me in Czechoslovakia. The country was in chaos and if you complained about any of it, the authorities would find you and throw you in jail. No-one was putting *me* back in a cage. I dumped my schoolbooks onto my bed and crammed some clothes into my schoolbag.

"Where are you going so late?" Dita stood over the kettle in her slippered feet.

"I forgot something at school. I'll be back," I promised, hating myself for the lie.

Dita would worry when I didn't come back but I had no choice. When my brother and sisters were interrogated about my disappearance – and they would be – it was best they not know anything.

"So, what's the plan?" I asked Emanuel, when we met on the steps of the train station at midnight.

Emanuel was a friend from school who'd shared his plans to escape to Austria. I'd asked to come with him. It was April 1949. I was four months short of finishing my apprenticeship and two months off my final school exams.

"Get on," Emanuel said, flying up the steps of a train bound for Bratislava.

I climbed in after him and followed him to our seats. "The plan?" I reminded him.

"Give me your identification papers."

"That's your plan?" I grumbled, handing them over. "You're going to look after my papers?"

"The Israeli Government has struck a deal with the Czechs to let Hungarian Jews pass through Czechoslovakia to get to Vienna. From there, we can get to the American zone."

"But we're not Hungarian," I said, deflated. "We're Czech."

"Not anymore," he said, striking a match and setting our papers on fire. He lifted the smouldering papers from his lap and we watched them burn.

"So, we're Hungarian now?" I stared at him doubtfully.

Emanuel laughed. "Well, not yet."

"So, we're two boys on a train without papers in Soviet-controlled Czechoslovakia?" I waited for Emanuel to catch on.

His smile wilted. We grabbed our bags, found the closest toilet, and locked ourselves in until the train rolled to a stop.

We registered as Hungarian Jews with an underground organisation who moved concentration camp survivors across borders, caring for and feeding them, until they found new homes.

"Name?" the officer asked.

"Keller. Emil Keller." A new name to go with my new identity. A name that couldn't be traced back to my siblings and land them in jail.

"Nationality?"

"Hungarian."

"Your identification papers?" The officer held out his hand.

"I lost them," I said, trying to look ashamed, rather than scared.

"You lost them?"

I nodded.

"And I suppose your friend has lost his too?"

Emanuel smiled. "Funny story –" he began, but the man waved him away.

"There's a truck outside. It leaves in five minutes."

They drove us to a railway siding way out of town where we boarded a train for Vienna. From Vienna, we wrangled seats on another US Army truck and, camouflaged by night, using back roads we made it through the Russian zone to the American zone in Austria.

"This is where we say goodbye," Emanuel whispered as we climbed from the truck. He stuck out his hand and I stared at it.

"Goodbye?"

Emanuel nodded and slung his bag over his shoulder. "My uncle got me a permit for Canada."

"Canada?" I said. "I thought we were going to America?"

"Plans change." He shrugged, staring up at the sprawling brick building that would be my next home.

I walked through the doors of the displaced persons camp alone but unafraid. They'd feed us in the camp, as much food as we wanted, and there was a bathroom with basins and plenty of toilets. There were hundreds of refugees living out of backpacks and suitcases, but I didn't mind. I liked the noise. I liked that people argued, laughed, fought and made love without being hauled outside. There were no *kapos* here, no secret police. We were free, and I was on my way to America, a place untouched by death. A country still inventing its own history, like I would invent mine.

I waited a week before writing home. I wanted to tell Max, Dita and Sari that I was sorry if my leaving hurt them. I wanted to let them know that I loved them but I couldn't risk the authorities reading their mail, so I sent my train ticket stub instead.

CHAPTER 21

NOW

Mom helps Dad from his chair. He stands and tilts his face to us, waiting for each of us to give him a kiss goodnight.

"Goodnight, Dad." I kiss his clammy cheek.

"I love you," he says.

His words are garbled but I can still make them out.

"I love you too," I whisper. "To the Statue of Liberty and back."

I retreat to my room, to the family tree I began at Deb's. It was her idea. She wanted to know more about the dad she'd lost. I grab a green pencil and draw the outline of a leaf. Inside it, in small letters, I write *Merele Rosner, New York*. I stare at the leaves on the uppermost branches, the ones carrying Tatte's and Mamme's names. I've lost something too, and it makes my heart hurt. It's a weird feeling, missing something you've never had.

We are meant to spend the last week of the school holidays in Rosebud with my brothers but we don't get to the beach. Dad is in hospital. He has pneumonia. Laid flat on an emergency trolley, he's feverish and drowsy and struggling to breathe.

"He's burning up," Mom says, panicking. "Emil? Emil, can you hear me?"

Mom turns from Dad to stare at the screen. Dad's oxygen levels are dropping.

"Something's wrong!" She runs, screaming, to find a nurse.

I'm left alone in the cubicle and Dad is turning blue.

"Don't go!" I yell at him. "Please. Mom will be back soon."

I'm not ready for him to die and I don't know how to help him. I can feel my heart beating against my chest. A nurse shuttles the curtains apart and drags me from Dad. Mom is sobbing, an alarm is bleating and the nurse is bent over Dad, yelling, "Code blue!"

Doctors come running. One of them cuts my father's shirt away while another tears off his neck brace and straps an oxygen mask to his face. Dad's breathing returns to normal. After a few minutes, so does mine.

The doctors file out of the room and after a while the nurses leave too. The bed sighs when I sit down and take Dad's hand. It's a cloudless spring morning but the room feels like a coffin. Dad opens his eyes and looks down at his shredded shirt.

"They had to cut it away," I tell him. "You stopped breathing. What was it like?"

"Like?" Dad tilts his head.

"You know ... dying."

"Peaceful," Dad says. "I could hear myself struggling to breathe, but I wasn't scared. I was ready. But then I saw you guys and decided to stick around."

"Good," I say, threading my fingers through his. "Coz I'm nowhere near ready. I need to hear the rest of your story. You're just getting to the good bit."

Dad's doctor, a thin man with a cloud of white hair, closes the door to his office and invites us to sit down.

"Your husband is having trouble breathing. It's only going to get worse," he tells my mother. "He has a choice. He can have a tracheostomy –"

"Or?" Mom asks.

"He'll die."

"I don't understand," I say. "Where's the choice?"

"Some people choose not to get the trache," Jack says. "If Dr Irving cuts Dad's windpipe, he won't be able to speak."

Mom glares at Jack. "He'll *have* the procedure." Tom reaches for her hand. "It's not our decision."

We follow the doctor to Dad's bed.

"We can make your last days here comfortable, Emil, or we can perform a tracheostomy and insert a tube into your windpipe to help you breathe. It's not a cure," the doctor's voice dips, "but it will buy you some time. It's up to –"

My father cuts him off. "Doc, I want to live. Do whatever it takes."

It's only been a day and I already miss Dad's voice; the slurring consonants, the drunk vowels. The room is quiet, the only sound the sigh of the ventilator, breathing for Dad. He's half rubber, half man; plastic tubes poking out from his throat and his stomach. I scrape my chair closer, so close my knees are butting up against the hospital mattress. Dad's eyes flutter open. His mouth pulls into a smile, but then he remembers, and his face falls. Tears drip down his chin onto his blue hospital gown. It's the second time I've seen my father cry. If I tell him I love him, will it hurt because he can't say it back?

I watch my father's eyes drift and close. Who is he without his voice? Without his words and opinions? Dad was always the first at parent–teacher night to put up his hand. The one voice cheering louder than everyone else at sports day, the first at celebrations to raise a glass and make a toast. Whatever the size of the room, his voice was too big for it. And the louder he was, the less I listened. At dinners when he talked about raising money for refugees or his work on council, I tuned out. His life had nothing to do with mine. Now I'd pay to listen to him speak. To say the words, *I love you, pineapple.* Or *Kellers don't quit.* To hear him snort with laughter. And finish his story.

Mom brings me a can of Fanta from the cafeteria. Tom and Jack arrive from work. We sit without speaking, watching Dad's chest rise and fall as he sleeps, taking it in turns to hold his hand.

"What was it Dad said about Auschwitz?" Tom asks over the whoosh and click of the ventilator. "I learned to be quiet when all I wanted to do was cry and scream and run."

We eat trembling jelly in plastic cups filched from the hospital cart, and blink away tears. When Dad opens his eyes, a second time, it's almost dark outside. The hospital lights flicker on, bathing the room in a cold, fluorescent sheen. Dad looks lost. There are deep purple hollows under his eyes. He opens his mouth, then closes it. Mom lays her head on his chest and weeps.

"Let's give them a bit of privacy," Jack whispers, grabbing his jacket.

I follow my brothers out, and when we return an hour later Mom is curled up on Dad's bed. She sees us and gives an embarrassed smile.

"Everything will be fine," she whispers into the sheets, before climbing off the bed to grab Dad's glasses.

She slides the frames onto his face. Dad blinks a *hello, I'm still here* and we crowd his bed, trying to read the soft clicks and sucking sounds he makes with his tongue.

"Are you in pain?"

"Do you want the doctor?"

"You want me to sit here?"

He blinks when we're right and clicks his tongue against the roof of his mouth when we're not. Stealing someone's voice is a kind of erasure, but Dad refuses to disappear.

Jack and Tom are in Dr Irving's office, discussing Dad's discharge. Mom has gone home for a nap and I'm alone with Dad. He blinks three times.

"Do you want me to call a nurse?" I panic. "Are you tired?" I don't know what three blinks means.

Dad clicks his tongue. He is staring at my mouth. I lean in to kiss him, but he clicks again. He opens and closes his mouth.

"You want me to talk?"

He blinks.

It's awkward at first. I'm not the one normally doing the talking and I don't know what to say. "I've almost finished copying down your story. Ninety-eight pages so far."

Dad blinks.

It's not fair you can't finish it, I don't say. Instead, I tell him the subjects I've chosen for 11th Grade. Dad blinks twice. He likes that I've chosen Maths.

It's hard making conversation when it's all one way, but I try. I tell him that I've been elected sports captain. Dad's eyes are smiling, so I go on talking. I tell him about the TV ad Deb scored and I tell him about Mai and the boys who made fun of her. I tell him about Adam and all the ways I screwed up.

Dad is in his pyjamas, sitting up. There's a large laminated sheet of paper on his lap. A nurse is bent over him, pointing to the letter T on the alphabet grid. Dad blinks.

"Hot," she says. "Are you too hot under the blanket?"

Dad blinks again. She pulls the blanket away, folds it and sets it at the end of the bed. Dad sees me at the door and clicks his tongue. The nurse wheels around.

"Oh hi, you must be Emil's daughter?"

I nod.

"Your father is doing much better today. He's feeling stronger so we had a visit from the occupational therapist." She glances at the board. "Would you like to learn how to use it?"

The board is divided into squares. There are the twenty-six letters of the alphabet, a square for *Yes* and another for *No*. One for *Hello* and one for *Goodbye*, the numbers one to nine and a question mark. As soon as we're alone, Dad starts blinking.

I shuffle closer. "Do you want to tell me something?"

Dad nods.

I point to *A*, glance at Dad and when there's no response, slide my finger to *B*. He blinks when I reach the letter *O*. It takes a while to get the first word out: *Open.* Then I start on the second. By the time I get *Open curtains* Dad is exhausted.

I shuttle the curtains apart letting a rectangle of sky into the room. Dad turns his face to the light and I follow his gaze. Beyond the window there's a flowering tree.

We stare at the burst of purple-red blossoms.

Look. for. the ... I scribble down Dad's words; read them back to him when they form a sentence. *Look for small things. Small joys.* Dad sinks back into his pillow and closes his eyes.

"We can talk more tomorrow," I whisper, lifting the board from his lap.

I stare at the tree. By the time Dad comes home, it will have lost its flowers. Maybe that's what makes its beauty so powerful; the fact that soon it will disappear. Maybe knowing that death is around the corner makes the last months more beautiful.

When he wakes up I ask Dad about this. I drag my finger along the alphabet, quietly copying down his words. I stare down at the stilted sentences built of blinks. *Things that bring happiness change. Can listen. See you smile. Hold hands. Watch sky change.*

"I wish I'd starting asking you questions earlier," I whisper.

A nurse appears with a tub of warm water and a wet cloth. "Time to wash!" she says, in a sing-song voice, like my dad is a child who needs convincing.

"We're talking," I snap, dragging my fingers across the board.

Dad spells his reply while the nurse sets the tub down. *You learned what I needed to teach you.*

He's right. There were things he never talked about, but still, I listened. I worked hard at school, I worked hard to fit in. I didn't let anyone know who I was. Not really.

I have been shaped by the stories my father did and didn't tell me.

He's stopped talking now. But that's no reason to stop listening.

"My dad has a hole in his throat," I tell Deb. "The doctors said it'll give him a few more months, but he can't speak. Deb?" I call down the phone, "are you there?"

"Sorry," Deb says, "I'm listening." Long seconds drag by. "I can't imagine not being able to talk."

I want to hang up and climb back into bed, but I don't, because I want Deb to know what it's like. I picture Dad blinking at the alphabet, trying to fight his way through silence and then I think about all the things I don't say.

"It was awful." I force the words out. "That first day when he woke up after the anaesthetic. He opened his mouth to say something. I think he forgot that they'd taken his voice."

"Want me to come over?" Deb asks.

I fight the impulse to say no. "That'd be great," I say. "Maybe you can sleep over?"

Deb brings a sleeping bag, a backpack and Karen and Tracey, who are dressed in black spandex leggings with hair so big you must be able to see it from space.

"*Grease.*" Deb hands me the video and I hug it to my chest.

The last time we hung out with Danny Zuko at Rydell High, Karen was high on painkillers after having her wisdom teeth yanked. The time before that Tracey had been dumped. It was a guaranteed pick-me-up.

Deb tips the bag out and I pull leggings and a teeny black top from the mess of skirts and heels. Karen shoves the video into the recorder and we strut around the living room, singing into hairbrushes, watching Sandy and Danny fall in love, and I'm trying to forget the white-walled hospital room and the fact Dad won't ever speak again, because being with the girls is my happy place.

Deb's trying so hard, and Rizzo and Frenchie are belting out tunes, but it's not really working. I want to be here in these too-tight pants, singing off-key, but I'm still in room 256, searching Dad's face for a smile.

The days turn into weeks and Dad is finally allowed to come home. He sits in his tilting chair in a patch of sun in the living room.

"Hey, Dad," I say, dropping onto the couch next to him. I grab the alphabet board and slide my finger from A to Z.

Am lucky man.

I read his words out loud, my forehead wrinkling. By definition, if you can't say the word *lucky* – if you have to rely on another person to decode your thoughts – you are not lucky.

Still, he insists. *How many people get notice will die, time to plan?* He blinks out a question mark. *How many get chance tell family love them?*

"But you're dying," I blurt.

Dad shakes his head and blinks at the board. *Not dying of disease*. I run my finger along the letters. *Living with it*.

I pull out the notebook Tom gave me and commit Dad's words to paper, so I won't forget. I write slowly, trying to embroider his spirit onto the page. Dad just wants to connect sound to his thoughts. That's the hardest part, he tells me. Not the dead arms or heavy head. Not the exhaustion or the missed meals. What hurts most is being shut in. Shut up. Muzzled.

I try it one day: silence. I sit in Dad's study and let my arms hang by my side. The phone rings. I let the machine take a message. Dad's voice fills the room. "We're not home at the moment. Leave a message and we'll call you back." I tear up when I hear him but I don't reach for a tissue. I sit mute and let the silence tease. This is Dad's life – sitting with his hands tied behind his back and his mouth taped shut. This is what life's like for him; what it was like when he was fourteen, in the cattle train and at roll call, in the mines and the barrack.

I close my eyes and try to keep still. My thoughts wander to Adam and all the things I want to tell him, the things I need to say, but don't. The things I want to do, but don't. I close my eyes and imagine his long fingers on my skin. His mouth on mine.

"I'm sorry, Adam," I whisper, practising an apology, then realize my mistake. I look down at my watch. I lasted ten minutes.

I want to kick the walls in, but I can't. Not when my dad is being so brave about dying. I tell Mom I'm going for a run but after a few minutes I stop at the Johnson house, the place Ted told me about – the place where he comes to let off steam. I sneak into the backyard. There's a burnt-out car sitting next to the washing line. I pick up a splintering broom and bring it down hard on the rusted hood. The first hit is for ALS. So's the second and the third. I want to smash the disease to pieces. I want to break its bones. I'm beating the hood with the broom but I don't feel any better – I feel worse – because when I go home, Dad will still be dying. And my rage won't change a thing.

Mom is squeezed into Dad's electric armchair when I get home, her body nestled against his.

"Dad has a new toy," she says, climbing off the chair to lift a small computer keyboard onto his lap. "It's called a Lightwriter."

Dad grins and walks his fingers onto the letters. Words track across the small screen that faces out. I got my voice back.

The fluorescent green letters disappear and the screen goes blank.

"Wow!" I say. "Do that again!"

Dad's smile is huge. He drags his finger to a different button and sound fills the room. It's not his voice. The speaker doesn't sigh or pause. There's no rhythm to the speech, no hesitation, no thick European accent – but it's speaking his words. I got my voice back. Now try and shut me up!

"You can choose the gender," Mom says, "and it has all these greetings stored for when friends come visit."

Dad's sweating at the effort of moving his fingers across the keyboard but his eyes are shining.

Hello. So nice of you to visit, the robotic voice pulses. How have you been?

It's the Friday before school starts. Dad has been cooped up in his study typing all day. I rest my head on the doorframe and watch his fingers crawl across the Lightwriter's keys.

I've asked your brothers to come at six, the machine bleats. I've typed the next chapter.

The past won't be silenced, and neither will Dad.

CHAPTER 22

THEN

With Russia and the Western Allies vying for control of Europe, people in the camps started whispering about a third World War. I had to get out of Europe, fast. If the United States wouldn't have me, I'd just have to find a country that would. I'd never thought about Australia, not till Ernst mentioned it. I met Ernst Weiss my first week in Vienna. We shared a bunkroom and became good mates. But then Ernst left for Australia without a forwarding address. "If you're ever in the area, look me up," he'd said, his face growing serious. "You should think about Australia. Things are heating up here with the Cold War. Don't wait too long."

All I knew about the country was that it was big, full of kangaroos and about as far from Europe as you could get. It was a young country with a bright future, willing to welcome people like Ernst onto its shores. It's perfect, I convinced myself, heading to the consulate.

I'd heard that it helped to know something about the country, so I'd done some reading. Australians loved tennis and cricket, I found out. They cooked on something called a barbecue and on weekends they went to the beach. There were lots of sheep and outside of the city most of the country was desert.

The sandy-haired officer who welcomed me into his office didn't ask me what I knew. He looked at my blood tests and examined X-rays of my chest to rule out tuberculosis. He didn't want to see my apprenticeship certificate. He wanted to make sure I was fit enough to work.

"You speak four languages. Impressive," he said, sliding a stack of papers across his desk.

"Five," I said in English. "Slovak, Hungarian, German, English and Yiddish. I've picked up a bit of Russian too."

"Sit down, mate," he said, pointing to a chair, "and I'll translate the mombo jumbo."

I had no idea what mombo jumbo was, but I didn't interrupt. He continued for a while, flipping the pages and stopping every so often to explain, but I must've looked confused, because he slowed right down.

"This here is a contract between you and the Australian Government." He sat back in his seat, grinning. "What it boils down to is, if you want to be an Aussie we're happy to have you. On one condition. We'll let you into Australia if you agree to work for the government for two years at any job anywhere in the country. Sound alright?"

I grabbed the pen and signed.

Two weeks later I was on a train to Italy. I couldn't sit still. I paced the corridor, eavesdropping on conversations about Australia.

"The girls are blonde and tanned," I reported to the boy sitting next to me. His name was Arthur and he was headed to Australia too. "And the beaches are covered with the softest white sand. But the best part," I said, waiting for his smile, "is that you can make loads of money if you're willing to work hard."

I could see it all so clearly – a car in a garage, a house with a garden, sunshine and road trips and a wallet with a business card.

"What if no-one gives us a job?" Arthur fretted. "What if we hate it?" He slumped lower in his seat.

I ignored his questions and went in search of friends who'd fan my excitement. I approached two boys, asking if they knew when we'd arrive in Italy. The older of the two, an olive-skinned boy with dark eyes and black hair, lifted his face from behind a newspaper.

"Four hours to go." He smiled, pushing his spectacles back up his nose.

"And then two weeks in Bagnoli, a month on a ship and we land in Australia. You headed there too?" asked the second boy. "I'm Carl. This is my brother Andrew."

Andrew disappeared behind his newspaper and Carl and I swapped stories. The boys had survived two years in a concentration camp and were headed for Melbourne.

We were taken from the train to an army barrack in the suburb of Bagnoli. Carl threw his bag onto the stretcher bed next to mine, Andrew ditched his paper and, ignoring the camp commander's order to stick close to the barracks, we jumped the fence and headed to Pompeii to tour the ruins. We skipped camp most days, preferring Bagnoli's orange groves to the concrete towers of the camp. I tasted my first orange in Bagnoli, drank my first glass of wine and sank a fork into my first bowl of pasta.

I spent the last shillings of my refugee allowance wandering the hidden coves of the Amalfi coast, counting down the days until our ship set sail. Carl and Andrew had money tucked away from the sale of their parents' home and a diamond embedded in a false tooth in Carl's mouth. I left Bagnoli with a battered schoolbag and a second chance at being happy.

CHAPTER 23

NOW

Dad sits listening to the small computer on his lap spill his secrets. I listen to the robot voice too but I'm watching Dad's face for clues – a shy smile when he meets Carl on the train or maybe a cheeky grin when he jumps the camp fence to visit Pompeii. Something to make this *his* story, not the computer's. But Dad's face doesn't move and neither do we. Not until the glowing letters on the screen disappear and it's just the five of us again.

I lean forward to speak into the silence. "How did you find Ernst when you got to Australia?"

Dad's fingers move across the keys. No-one talks or leaves the room to grab a cup of tea. It feels like interrupting.

Dad clicks his tongue and presses play. I saw his name in an engagement announcement in the newspaper. He was marrying a girl called Barbara Rubin. I looked her up in the telephone book and told her that I had a great idea for an engagement present to surprise Ernst with – me.

"I never heard you two talk about the war," Tom says.

We didn't need to, Dad types. We'd been through a similar hell so we understood each other. Understood that we were here to start again.

I slide tonight's videotape into the shoebox. I can't watch it back. The camera is fixed on Dad, sitting slumped in his chair. I play the cassette tape instead, copying down the Lightwriter's clipped sentences. It's still early when I'm done so I grab a roll of clear contact paper and start covering my textbooks. School starts in a few days. I slap a sticker on a book cover and write my address and then my name: *Lisa Pepi Keller*. I rub the *epi* out and leave the *P*. *Lisa P Keller*. I like how it sounds, the weightiness of it, the *P* anchoring me to the past and the family Dad left behind. And if anyone asks, I can always say it stands for Penny.

I pull another book from the bag and an invitation flutters out. It's on school letterhead and is addressed to my parents. I'm the 11th Grade girls' sports captain and Mom and Dad have been invited to assembly to watch me shake the principal's hand. I think about binning the invitation or burying it inside a book. If Dad rolls into the hall in a wheelchair with a tube sticking out of his neck and an oxygen machine on his lap, Adam will know – everyone will know – that he's dying.

I don't want Adam to find out that way, but I also can't hide Dad away like a secret or steal this moment from

286

him. He loves assemblies and parent–teacher nights. He never got to finish school. He's going to want to see the principal hand me that gold badge.

"Dad?" I tiptoe into his room. "You awake? I have something for you." I reach for his glasses and slip them onto his nose, holding the invitation up so he can read it. "Do you want to come?"

His mouth stretches into a smile.

"I'm taking that as a yes."

I leave the invitation on Mom's pillow. Dad blinks three times. He does that when he's happy.

"I'm glad you're coming," I say, and I mean it.

I'm tired of caring what other people think. I want to care less. I want to be more like Dad. He doesn't ask his friends to leave when Mom feeds a catheter into his tube to suction his lungs; he asks them to speak louder so he can hear them over the buzzing. He invites them to feed him and help him from his chair, refusing to be ashamed of the tubes, the spit, the blinks and the clicks. He doesn't apologise. He just needs looking after.

It must be liberating not seeing yourself through other people's eyes.

The bell rings and we file into class for the roll. The loudspeaker crackles and Principal Blackwood's voice bounces off the walls.

"Would all students who have guests attending

this morning's assembly meet them in the carpark and accompany them to the hall."

"Is your dad coming?" Deb keeps step with me.

I nod.

"Is it going to be weird?"

I stare at her.

"No, not your dad. I mean is it going to be awkward, you know, you and Adam being sports captains?"

I shrug. "I haven't seen him."

Deb spots her mom wielding a video recorder and pulls me into a hug. "I'll come say hi to your dad later."

"Hey, there's my drama queen!" Mrs Cartman calls across the carpark.

"Drama *captain*, Mom," Deb shouts back.

I find Mom's car and reach in to undo Dad's seatbelt.

"You nervous?" Mom asks, and there's something about the way she says it that makes me think she knows how big this is for me – not the captaincy, but having Dad here at school.

I help Dad from the car and guide him to the wheelchair Mom has hauled from the trunk. "Let me," I say, pushing the chair up the ramp.

Mom has the suctioning device, the Lightwriter, her handbag and a camera to juggle.

We roll into the hall past an infinity of kids, and I can feel the sweat prickling at the back of my neck. My hands are clammy and I'm staring hard at the wheelchair handles but I can feel the room tracking us. Dad wants to sit in the front. He blinks and Mom shuffles chairs to make space, and half the front row are offering up their seats and everyone's staring. I beat back the nerves. *You can do this. Dad's doing it. If he can, so can you.*

Dad doesn't care that there are a hundred sets of eyes on him, or that other parents will have to squeeze past him to get to their seats. I try to look oblivious.

Names are called, badges are pinned to collars, students smile for photos and parents clap politely, except for Deb's mom, who catapults out of her seat for a standing ovation halfway through Deb's Academy Award-length acceptance speech.

I'm on stage for less than a minute. You can hear a pin drop. People are looking from me to Dad and back at me, unsure whether to clap. I shake the principal's hand but I'm looking down at Dad and the happy corners of his eyes and his lopsided smile. The Lightwriter's screen is flashing and the volume is turned up high. Dad's robot applause is louder than Deb's mom. I take a bow.

Mom lifts the wheelchair into the trunk while I buckle Dad in and slide the Lightwriter onto his lap. I rest my head on his shoulder. He smells like alcohol wipes.

I'm so proud of you. The machine spits the words out. I imagine my dad trumpeting the words, dragging out the *so. I'm soooo proud.*

"It's nice to see you, too." I hear Mom say. And then more words. A boy's voice. Adam's.

"I'll see you at home, later," I tell Dad, swinging the door shut.

Adam is talking to Mom, lifting the camera bag from the ground and passing it to her.

"Hey," I say, trying to read his face.

"Hey," he says back.

We're both tongue-tied.

"Okay," Mom says, brightly. "We've got to go." She blows me a kiss and turns to Adam. "Thanks for coming to say hi. And yes, Emil would love a visit." I glare at her but she doesn't notice. "We all would."

Adam waves at Dad as they pull out of the carpark. Dad can't wind down the window so he blinks his hello.

"He can't talk," I say, quietly. "That blink was him saying hi."

"Is he ..." Adam can't say the words.

"The doctors gave him six months ... back in August."

We stare at the ground.

"Do you want to talk?" Adam whispers.

I nod and follow him from the carpark to a quiet rectangle of grass behind the sports oval. We sit. Our legs don't touch but he's looking at me – looking *into* me.

"I'm sorry," we say, at exactly the same time.

"Why are *you* sorry?" Adam is shaking his head. "You were going through this enormous thing and I wasn't there." His mouth sags. "I didn't try and find out what was ..." He stumbles over the words. "I just tapped out."

"You didn't know. I didn't tell you." I try to cross the miles of silence. "I didn't want to dump it on you, especially after your grandma died and, I don't know, sometimes it's easier *not* talking." I pull at a clump of grass. "Talking makes it real, and school's the one place I can escape that and be the same as everyone else."

"So why ask your dad to come today?" Adam's brow creases. "What changed?"

"Dad," I say. "Me." Fear muscles its way in but I shove it aside. "Watching Dad disappear, I realize I've been doing the same thing. Making myself ..." I need to say the words out loud. "Invisible."

"You couldn't be invisible if you tried." Adam smiles. "Or maybe that's just me."

We both blush.

It feels good to talk about Dad, to share him with Adam, so I keep talking. "He's incredible. He eats and breathes through tubes. His arms don't work and he needs a brace to hold up his head but he's completely himself. A *better* version of himself." The tears start up.

Adam slips his arms around me and I bury my head in his shirt.

"My mom said something after Gran died and it kinda stuck with me." He sorts the words in his head. "The thing about knowing that bad things can happen is that good things can happen any time too." The bell rings but he doesn't move to go. "Don't shut me out," he says.

He says something else, but the school sounds drown it out – the pounding of feet on asphalt, bottles landing in metal bins. Adam doesn't pull away, so I do. There are tears pooling in his eyes.

"How do you do it?" I whisper.

"What?"

"Not care what everyone thinks?" I glance at the girls watching us from the stairs.

"Is *that* what you think? Is that why you couldn't tell me about your dad?" He pulls his hand from mine. "Because you think I have everything sorted and my life is so perfect?"

"It kind of is," I say, dropping my voice to a whisper. "You kind of are."

And then I remember we're not together. He's with Leanne. And maybe I've read this all wrong. Maybe this is pity. Maybe he's just being a good friend. I backtrack. "I mean, you're captain of the soccer team. You've got a black belt in karate. Everyone likes you and you ace all your exams."

"I have to." He cuts me off. "You haven't met my dad."

I wait until he has the words. Another thing Dad has taught me.

"He's not around much. He has a job in tech. An *important* job," Adam says. "Offices all over the world, different time zones. He's hardly home and when he is, he's either too tired or too busy to talk. Unless I've aced a test or won a medal or captained a team to the finals. Then he'll want a play-by-play. Dad was valedictorian and sports captain of Glenrock back in the day." There's a thin sheen of sweat on Adam's forehead. "Pretty sad, huh? Living your life to get a smile from your old man."

I pick at my hem.

292

"Maybe if I'd talked about it, you would've told me about your dad?"

"Maybe," I say, and the storm clears on his face.

"So, no more secrets?" he says.

"No more secrets."

"And we're friends?"

I force a smile. *Friends.* Great.

The bell rings and we grab our bags.

"I'm that way." He points left. "Chemistry."

"English," I say, pointing in the opposite direction.

"I know you probably don't care," he says, walking away backward, "but Leanne and I ... we're not a thing."

Hearing those words is like being handed a box of chocolates. I take a deep breath and rearrange my face. I can't walk into English with a crazy smile, not after Dad's appearance at assembly.

I brace myself for the sad looks and slide into an empty seat behind Deb. "Need to debrief," I whisper to the back of her head.

She slides me a note. *Your dad?*

I tear a page from my notebook. *Adam.*

She spins around just as a crumpled note lands on my desk. I scan the room. Kids look away or smile sadly. No clues about the note. I smooth the paper with the palm of my hand.

I thought we were friends. T.

293

It's awkward at lunch. Tracey won't look at me.

"I'm sorry," I say, sliding my Twix toward her. "It's been really hard at home and you guys, you're my happy place."

Tracey shunts the Twix back at me, refusing the peace offering.

"I should've told you about my dad."

"You think?" Tracey sniffs.

"It wasn't because I didn't trust you, Trace. It's just hard asking for help."

Karen elbows Tracey in the ribs.

"Okay, okay." Tracey holds her hands up in surrender. "I'm sorry about your dad." She swallows her hurt and lays her head on my shoulder. "I really am."

"And?" Deb frowns.

"And I'm sorry I made it all about me."

"Okay," Karen says, relief spilling out of her. "We all good?"

Tracey nods.

"Great," Karen says, wrapping an arm around my shoulder. "You're always listening to our problems, Lis. We just want to do the same for you. So, anything you need … you just name it."

Deb grabs the Twix, snaps off a piece and tosses it to me. "So, what's the deal with Adam? Are you back on?"

"I don't think so. I don't know." I lick chocolate from my fingers. "Maybe."

"Apparently," Tracey says, holding her hand out for her share, "Leanne told Paul that Adam told *her* he wasn't ready to jump into another relationship."

We're about to debate whether Adam getting back with me would be jumping into *another* relationship or just revisiting an old one when a girl with short hair and a rash of pimples stops by the table.

"My mom has MS," she says. "If you ever want to talk ..."

I blink at her, then remember to smile. Wherever I look, people are looking back at me, sadness stuck to their faces. And it feels okay. Kind of comforting even.

"Your dad is so brave." Mai pulls her bag from her locker as the final bell rings.

I nod. "He is."

"How long does he have left?"

"A month, maybe two," I say, grateful for the question. It's easier to answer than, *How are you?*

"I don't really remember the boat trip from Vietnam," Mai says, lobbing a sesame ball into her mouth. She offers me one, says there's something called mung paste inside, and I pass. "I remember feeling sorry for myself," she continues, "and I remember my dad lifting me onto his lap on a quiet night and us looking up at the moon. He said, 'When you think you have nothing left, there's always the moon.' I thought he meant that literally. But watching your dad smiling up at you today, I think I know what he meant."

"Thanks," I say.

I'm his moon. Me and Mom, Jack and Tom, we're the

reason Dad gets up every morning and takes his meds and types his story. He's sticking around for us.

Mom is waiting for me at the front door when I get home from school.

"I won't be long. I just have to grab a few things for dinner. Your brothers will be here at six." She flies out the door.

Dad is sitting in his tilting chair, in a square of light by the window.

"Do you want me to put some music on?" I dump my bag. "It's so quiet in here."

He shakes his head. I'm getting to like the quiet. It's when you're quietest that you can really hear yourself. His fingers crawl across the Lightwriter's keyboard. How was your day?

"Actually, it was good. People were ... kind. And some of them were going through stuff I didn't know about."

We're both quiet until the Lightwriter speaks. Carl came over today. He asked how you were all doing. I said you were good, but it got me thinking. Maybe the reason none of you ever complain is because you think you don't have a right to be unhappy. The words trickle out slowly. I didn't tell you about the camps when you were young because I didn't want you to be contaminated. He closes his eyes and rests his fingers. I also didn't want you comparing your childhood to mine. He keeps tapping. I don't want you to think your problems aren't worth talking about. He looks up from the keyboard to give me a small smile.

"I know," I say.

There's been something I've wanted to talk to him about, something nagging, but there's never been the right time and I don't want to disappoint him. Whenever he looks at me, it's with so much pride, like I'm some miracle child. And I guess in a way I am. I'm a living, breathing thing. A piece of his past, carried into the future. Proof that Hitler didn't win. And if I *am* this miracle child, this child that wasn't meant to be, shouldn't I *do* something with it? Something important? I picture my life as a lawyer sitting in a windowless room behind a big desk, buried in paper ...

"Dad?" I say, forcing my eyes to meet his. "Do you think I'd make a good lawyer?"

You'd be a brilliant lawyer. Dad watches my face fall.

Minutes slide past before he returns to the keyboard. You'd be good at anything you set your mind to. Lawyer was my dream. You need to work out yours.

"What if I don't have one?" I whisper. "What if I don't know?"

Dad thinks on this for a moment. His fingers comb the keys. Whenever I have a decision to make – and maybe it's because I've been near death more times than I'd like – I always ask the same question. If I'm not here tomorrow, what would I wish I'd done? You get to choose what to do with the rest of your life. Don't choose for me.

The doorbell rings and I let my brothers in and grab my notebook. It falls open on the list I wrote soon after

Dad was diagnosed; numbering the things I didn't want to forget about him. The gap between his two front teeth, skiing between his legs, his size 11 feet. I pick up a pen and add two more.

9. Our chats and the way he talks to me now. Talks *to* me, not *at* me.

10. This. Him digging up his story; every last bone.

CHAPTER 24

THEN

I stood on the dock with my mouth hanging open. A ship wider than a city street towered over me. Carl pointed at the black letters painted along the ship's flank – *General WC Langfitt*. Our home for the next thirty-five days. We stood there for a while, looking out at the Bay of Naples, breathing in the briny, wet air, transfixed by the water.

There must have been a thousand people on board. They crowded the decks and leaned over the ship's rails, waving wildly, holding handkerchiefs like flags. They wiped away tears and yelled their goodbyes to the fathers, mothers, lovers and friends who'd come to see them off.

"I won't forget you, Willie," I whispered to the wind. "Goodbye, Tatte. I love you, Mamme."

The ship's siren sounded and people started singing; the words to a dozen national anthems joining into one sad love song to the continent we were leaving. I didn't sing our national anthem. Czechoslovakia wasn't home anymore, and I was glad to leave Europe.

"Want to stay above deck and watch Europe disappear?"
I asked Arthur.

He shook his head, and ducked under a low doorway.

I didn't follow him into our hold. It was 20 December 1949.
My life was about to start and I didn't want to miss any of it.
Not the new stars in the sky or the smell of the salt air or the
crashing waves that were nudging us toward Australia.

I found Carl at the railing as the ship's engine rumbled to life
and flung an arm around his shoulder. A foghorn blared. "The
future's out there," I pointed at the open ocean, "and it's all ours."

For thirty-five days it was just sea and sky. We didn't leave
the ship except to wander the dusty harbors while the ship
refueled. I didn't have money to tour the pyramids or take a
camel ride through the desert, but I bought my first banana
from a man wearing jeweled slippers and a red felt hat. I
peeled the skin from the fruit and took a bite, then bought the
bunch. I ate so many I was sick for three days. I recovered by the
time we crossed the equator and, sailing the warm currents of
the Indian ocean, spent my last days on board trying to make
out the coastline.

It's all anyone talked about – our new home down under – a
place that didn't harbor ghosts. On board it didn't matter if you
were Jew or Gentile, Hungarian or Pole. We were all heading
across the ocean to reinvent ourselves. To build businesses and
buy houses and fall in love so that one day we might have a
family of our own.

For some, starting over meant leaving their old lives behind; leaving *God* behind. I didn't know if I even believed in God. Tatte had taught me that God had created the universe and everything in it – the trees and the sky, the rivers and lakes, man and woman, and every animal and plant. "God is with us," Tatte had said. "Everywhere. All the time."

All the time made it worse. If God was everywhere, all the time, then he'd been with us in the cattle train. He'd been standing next to Mamme in the gas chamber when she took her last breath, and had watched Tatte burn. How could I pray to a God like that?

A God who let pregnant women die.

And gypsies and Jehovah's Witnesses.

And men who loved men.

And girls who limped.

And boys with epilepsy.

And babies with Down syndrome.

How could a God who knew how kind Willie was let a bullet end his life?

How could I honour a God like that?

Do they keep koalas as pets? I heard the toilets flush backward. They have spiders as big as your hand and snakes that can kill you. We traded facts about our new home as we waited in line for the ship's doctor to give us a clean bill of health.

"You've been approved." The nurse smiled, handing me a piece of paper signed by a doctor. "You can get dressed."

I folded the sheet and slipped it into my pocket. Here was proof that I was healthy, proof that I was healed.

"Next!" the nurse called, shooing me outside.

I stood on the deck in the January heat, staring at the Australian coastline. The past couldn't touch me here, a thousand miles from hunger and hatred. I stared at the people standing on the dock and something loosened inside me.

"Look, they're waving!" I shouted to Arthur as we stepped off the ship. I dropped to my hands and knees and kissed the ground.

"They're not waving at you." Arthur pulled me to my feet. "They're waving away flies!"

A woman in uniform checked my papers and handed me a yellow button.

"Yellow for Bonegilla," she said, pointing to a railway siding. "The train is over there, unless you have family or friends waiting?"

I shook my head. I didn't have anyone waiting, but that was okay, because one day I would. In the meantime I'd look after myself. I'd been looking after myself for years.

I scanned the pier crowded with sunburned faces – Australians grabbing at bags and loading trolleys, people holding signs and hawking drinks. They looked happy. It was like I'd been living underground and was seeing color for the first time.

"God, it's hot! No-one said it would be this hot …" Arthur undid his top button, "and the flies …" He swatted an army away. "In Budapest …"

"This is the happiest day of our lives and you're worried about a few flies?" I cut Arthur off.

Here was our chance to become whoever we wanted, and Arthur wanted to stay exactly who he was.

Up ahead a boy with a biscuit-brown face licked the sweat from his lips and lifted a dozen cellophane bags. "Candy, chocolates, get them here!"

I stopped to stare at the glinting packets.

"Here." Andrew pressed a coin into my palm.

I ran to the boy and held out my shilling.

"G'day, mate." The boy smiled with all his teeth. "If you're here to sweeten your day you've come to the right place. So, what'll it be? Choc-nut? Honeycomb? They're all going cheap."

I stood, riveted, by his gap-toothed grin.

"Here, take a choc-nut then. Take two. Just don't hang on to them too long or they'll melt." The boy prised the coin from my palm, winked and moved on.

I followed Carl to the platform where our train was waiting. The doors opened and we climbed inside. Carl grabbed the window seat opposite mine. Neither of us mentioned the cattle trains that had transported us to Auschwitz or the icy open carriages that took us to Buchenwald. We were here now, and that was all that mattered.

I stared out the window. Street lamps and cars and small weatherboard houses sped by in a blur, replaced by the faded greens and browns of the Australian countryside. It was nothing like the Australia I'd seen in books and ads – a place of golden beaches and rolling hills. I tried to spot a kangaroo or a black man with a spear, but there was nothing but yellow grass and scrubby gray trees. The countryside was burnt and the summer heat more oppressive than any I'd known. Still, the country's rawness appealed to me – the endless flat fields, the intensity of the sky. It was new, and for that I was thankful.

Eight hours after we set off we were deposited with our worn coats and battered bags at the gates of Bonegilla, a tin-barrack town in the Australian bush framed by strange-smelling gum trees. I breathed out the musty hours cooped up in the train, and breathed in the sky. We were miles from the nearest town. There was space here. And light.

"How long will they hold us here?" a Hungarian protested as we were led, single file, through the gates of the camp.

"They can't be serious," someone muttered.

A Dutch boy swore and swatted at flies.

"We're in the middle of nowhere," an Italian complained.

They saw flat, barren ground and dry, dusty streets. They saw ants crawling up rusted pipes and rows of corrugated-iron huts. They saw a depressing refugee town surrounded by scrub. I saw a welcome banner blowing in the breeze and the end of my wandering.

"Welcome to the Bonegilla Migrant Training and Reception Centre," a voice over a loudspeaker bounced against the low buildings. "If the new arrivals can make their way to the main hall for the commandant's welcome, we'll get everyone processed and settled in."

"The commandant? Did they say commandant?"

"Do you think he's German?"

"I can't do another camp."

Worried voices from Prague, Vienna and Budapest coursed through the line of migrants. Heads turned and looked for an escape route. A frail woman sweating under a trench coat broke from the line and ran toward the open gate.

"He's not SS," I called after her in German, Polish, Slovakian and Hungarian. "There are no *kapos* here. No barbed wire." I raised my voice so it would carry down the line of whispering refugees. "This is Australia. We're safe."

CHAPTER 25

NOW

I'm not surprised Dad left Czechoslovakia. If he wanted to forget, he had to bury the past and those who'd remind him of everything he'd lost. I picture Dad on the deck of the *WC Langfitt*, squinting at the coastline of his new home. A place to start again.

It's Saturday. Dad wants to go to synagogue.

"Why?" I ask. "You don't believe in God."

I know, but I still feel like a Jew. The Lightwriter dispatches Dad's thoughts. Not because I survived the Death March or have a tattoo. All those mornings in *shul* with Tatte, baking *challah* with Mamme, that's what being a Jew meant. It was more about home than about God.

Dad waits by the door, buttoned into a suit.

Mom points to my tank top. "You can't wear that to synagogue. Or that." She glances down at my shorts. "You can borrow one of my long skirts and grab something with long sleeves to cover your arms."

I return in a hideous burgundy corduroy skirt and a white ruffled shirt. I sprint to the car and hunker down so no-one can see me. I'm not a fan of the seventies. I'm not a fan of religion either, but here I am.

When we get to the synagogue Dad disappears behind a heavy wooden door with my brothers and I follow Mom upstairs to where the women sit. There are girls my age with neat, pinned-back hair and billowing skirts. They hold worn prayer books and sing softly in Hebrew. And it's strange but familiar.

From up here I can see Dad wedged between my brothers on the benches below. Pools of jeweled light spill from the stained-glass windows, coloring their faces blue and red. I lean over the balcony rail and stare down at them, at Dad's curly hair trapped under a crocheted Kippah and Jack, beside him, holding up a prayer book. Dad's lips are moving and I wonder if he's praying to God – asking him to take care of his dead parents and brother. Or maybe he's talking to Willie; telling him it won't be long.

Adam is sitting cross-legged on our front lawn. I invited him for one o'clock, knowing I'd be late and he'd ask where I've been.

I open the front passenger door and help Dad from

the car. "Sorry. We were out," I say to Adam, lowering my voice. "I'll explain later."

"Hi, Mr Keller." Adam follows us into the house, settling himself on the couch, next to Dad's tilting chair. "I got you something. I know you're a mad soccer fan so ..." He pulls a wrapped gift from his backpack and holds it out.

Dad stares at the present, then at me.

"Why don't *you* open it?" I say to Adam, because Dad can't.

Adam blushes and pulls off the paper. "My dad was in Italy for the World Cup," he says tentatively.

The Lightwriter's robot-voice cuts through the awkward silence. Did he see Paolo Rossi? Best forward soccer has ever seen.

Adam laughs. "Did you see the penalty shootout?" He relaxes back into the cushions.

Dad nods and clicks his tongue.

I take the striped soccer top from Adam and pull it over Dad's head.

"My dad bought me a heap of gear and I remembered you follow Juventus," Adam says, grinning.

I want to kiss him. Instead, I watch the curve of his mouth as he asks for Dad's opinion about Melbourne University. Dad smiles. He likes to dispense advice. He likes the sound of his own voice, even if it's computerised.

I wait for a break in the conversation and blurt, "Want to go outside?"

We head to the garden. I lie on the lawn, wishing I'd swapped the mood-killer skirt for a pair of shorts. Adam drops down next to me and we lie side by side, staring up at the washed-out sky. Dad can't lie on the warm ground or sit on the grass, but he spends lots of time staring out at the garden. He likes to listen to the cicadas and watch the wind ripple the leaves. He notices stuff like that now. Small things. He makes time for them.

"You were great with Dad. I could tell it meant a lot to him."

I can feel Adam's eyes boring into me and I want him to see how much I've changed, but how can he? I haven't let him in, not completely. *Here's your chance to become the person you want to be*, I imagine Dad whispering from behind the glass.

"I'm sorry for all the lies." I turn to face him. "I'm sorry for not trusting you enough to tell you about Dad. I don't know why I was scared." The words come out in a rush. "I'm ridiculous."

"You're not ridiculous. You're –"

A liar? A coward?

I cut him off. "You know what your gran said about knowing bad things could happen? Well, my dad grew up at a really shitty time, when terrible things happened."

Adam looks confused.

"I was late," I blush, "because we were in synagogue."

He sweeps the hair from his eyes. "Yeah … okay."

He's waiting. Maybe he didn't hear me. Maybe he doesn't know what a synagogue is?

"I was in synagogue," I say again, slowly, "because I'm Jewish."

It's too late to take it back. *Jewish*. It's the first time I've said the words out loud.

Adam doesn't look disappointed or disgusted. He doesn't get up and leave. He says, "Okay," like what I've told him isn't the hand grenade I thought it was. Like there needs to be something else to explain my stammering.

"You're not ... surprised?"

I swallow hard.

"No. I figured." He grins. "From the synagogue comment. Mom brought me up Anglican, but I'm an atheist now."

He says it like we're even. Like we're playing a game and next up is our favorite ice-cream flavor. *Mine's cookies and cream, what's yours?*

"It's not the same," I say, stiffening. "Have you *heard* of the Holocaust?" I don't mean to snap.

"Yeah," he says. "My soccer coach – he was born here – but his parents are Romanian. They were both in Auschwitz. They talk about what happened a lot." His mouth sags. "They're pretty messed up by it."

"My dad's the opposite. He *never* talked about it. I didn't live under the shadow of the Holocaust; I lived under a fucking rainbow." My face prickles with heat. "I'm sorry, I'm not angry, I'm grateful. It's just, he's finally opening up and ..." I can feel the tears pooling, but I force the words out. "He's been telling us about it for the last five months and –"

"That's why you stopped coming over."

"Yeah." I smile an apology, but he bats it away.

"I thought it was me. I thought you didn't want to see me." He shakes his head as if to empty it. "Turns out *I'm* the one who's ridiculous."

"No ..." I reach for his hand but he pulls away.

"You didn't tell me about your dad being sick because ..." He throws up his hands. "I don't know ... because you didn't think I'd be there for you? Because you didn't trust me?"

"No." Now it's my turn to shake my head. "I told you. I just wanted to –"

"And then –" he cuts me off, "– we said no more secrets. You promised. And here's another one. Did you really think I'd care that you were Jewish? I don't," he says, softening. "I don't care if you're Jewish or Hindu or a Born Again Christian. Okay ... maybe a Born Again might be a deal-breaker." His white smile reappears.

He takes my hand and his is clammy; he's nervous too. "You're the same as you were yesterday. Nothing's changed. I don't need to know your dad's story. None of that matters."

"But it does," I say, pulling away.

We sit without speaking in the deepening dark.

"So, *tell* me," Adam says. "Tell me the story."

I don't tell him that night, but when he walks me home from school on Monday, I tell him everything and he doesn't leave.

"We're taping it all," I say. "I've been listening back to the tapes and writing everything down. You know, to give him something he can touch and feel so he knows it will survive him."

Adam throws me a smile. "That's amazing," he says, feeding his fingers through mine.

But I'm *not* amazing and I need him to know that, to see all the broken bits of me, and still choose to stay. "I didn't want to listen," I tell him. "Not at first. I hated Friday nights. I knew something really bad had happened when he was young, but I didn't want to know. Maybe if I'd starting asking questions earlier ..."

"You're asking now." Adam draws me into a hug, even though my face must be all snot and blotches.

I nod and pull away. "Yeah, that's the only upside. The silver lining to this shitstorm. We've become friends. I know what Dad's scared of. I know the name of his first girlfriend and where he learned to ride a bike." I wipe my face with my sleeve. "So, that's it. You know everything. No more secrets."

And just like that the lies come to an end.

CHAPTER 26

THEN

There weren't enough chairs in Bonegilla's main hall, so we stood in rows of ten, listening to the camp commandant welcome us to our new home. He had cropped yellow hair and a light brown uniform plastered with medals. His face gave away nothing. I couldn't tell if he was pleased to see us or annoyed. He grabbed a microphone and told us that they'd house and feed us, and in return all we had to do was attend English lessons and accept whatever work they found us.

Someone wheeled a blackboard into view and the commandant pointed to a dozen rules. I didn't bother translating them for Carl and the boys. We wouldn't stick to them anyway.

Our tour guide walked us from one block to another, from the mess to the camp shop to the post office and laundry. There were classrooms and kitchens, a rec room and a hospital block.

"After the hard times you've had," our tour guide said, "Bonegilla must seem like a paradise."

The tour ended at our barrack, an unlined corrugated iron hut among the gumtrees. Some of the stretcher beds had

313

mattresses, some didn't. Arthur spread his blanket across the wires of his cot and slumped on his bed.

"Did you see the toilet? It's just a pit in the ground. And the showers don't have doors and …" Arthur leaped up, aiming a finger at a redback spider, "… they didn't mention those in the ads selling us the Australian dream."

We woke early the next day to the strains of 'God Save the King'. Arthur refused to leave the hut until I'd checked outside for wild animals. Breakfast was porridge with milk, lamb's fry and spongy white bread.

A voice over the loudspeaker directed all new arrivals to the social services building. I lined up to collect my weekly allowance of two shillings, dreaming about the chocolate and books I'd buy. I took my brown paper bag rattling with change and lined up again, this time for the camp nurse.

She asked about previous injuries and health problems, ticked some boxes on a form and pointed to the scale. "You're slight," she said, noting my weight, "but nothing out of the ordinary."

I didn't like being called ordinary, but here in Bonegilla ordinary was good. Ordinary meant I was like everyone else. Ordinary would get me a job in Melbourne.

She picked up a stethoscope and asked me to take off my shirt. "You, too?" She stared at the black ink on my arm, A7639. Her face softened.

I didn't want her pity and I didn't want to talk about the

needle or the men with razors or the tub I'd been dunked in which burned like hell. "So," I asked her, "am I fit to work?"

"I'm healthy," I pointed to the nurse's signature on the medical form, "and I already speak English, so I don't need to take lessons."

"That may be," the employment officer said, "but here in Bonegilla you have to be over eighteen to work, and you ..." he glanced down at the form and found my name, "... Emil Keller, are seventeen." He pointed to *10 May 1932* with a fat forefinger. "Says right here, plain as day."

"I'm sorry," I said, "I don't understand. I *want* to work. *You* want us to work. Why does it matter —"

"You're seventeen, right?" The man blotted the sweat from his face.

I nodded. Keller wasn't really my last name and I wasn't seventeen. I was nineteen, but I couldn't tell him the truth; that I'd changed my name to escape the Soviets and lied about my age so America would accept me.

"I am," I said. Seventeen meant I hadn't surrendered two years to the Nazis. Whatever happened in those two years didn't happen to *me*. "I'm seventeen but I'm also a jeweler —"

"And I believe you son, but —" the officer looked past me, down the long line of migrants waiting their turn, "to be honest, when you signed up, it was for a labouring job. That's what we need here – builders, cane cutters, farmhands, rail workers. Anyway," he said, picking my papers off the desk, "it's all irrelevant. You're underage."

"They won't give me a job!" I stripped down to my underwear and wrapped my towel around my waist. "They say I'm too young to work."

"How old *are* you?" Carl pulled on a pair of shorts and flung a towel around his neck. We were going swimming in the weir.

"*They* think I'm seventeen. But I'm nineteen," I said, waving away his question. "But that's not the point. Point is, I'm going to spend the year collecting trash. That's all they think I'm good for, cleaning the streets."

The days slunk by. We spent the empty hours playing soccer, climbing gum trees and floating around the weir on old truck tires. Sometimes we'd chase rabbits through the red bottlebrush, or fish for tadpoles. We were supposed to ask for permission to leave the camp, but we never did.

The loudspeakers called us home for lessons. They taught us English by making us recite songs until we knew them by heart. You had to concentrate hard to catch the words flying out of the teacher's mouths – words I'd never heard in English before, like swag and billy and didgeridoo. I wrote them all down. There was so much to learn.

We lay on our fold-out beds and made grand plans for the future. One by one the men in my dormitory found jobs. Former doctors and engineers cut cane and built railways. They picked grapes, milked cows, sheared sheep and dug dams while their wives worked as housekeepers and kitchen hands.

I emptied trash cans and swept the streets while Carl and Andrew took their turn at the job placement office. It was like entering a race and being held back at the start line.

I wanted a job. I'd been told in Australia I could be whatever I wanted and I wasn't about to let anyone – not a jobs officer or a camp commandant – tell me who I could be.

Over the next two months everyone got jobs. I missed sitting at a workbench and working with gold. I missed Carl and Andrew who'd both got jobs while Arthur and I were still on trash duty. So I called a meeting of all the in-between kids – kids too old for school but too young to work, kids without anyone looking out for them – and within minutes we'd decided to ask the camp commandant for our release. I was to be spokesman.

We filed into the commandant's room, twenty orphaned teenagers in scrappy clothes, our faces coated with sweat and dust.

"What can I do for you boys?"

Arthur and the others stood behind me, half in, half out the door.

I cleared my throat. "Commandant Williams, sir." I looked him in the eye. "The twenty of us have been here for a number of months and, well, we'd like to talk about our jobs, sir."

"Your jobs?" The commandant's eyebrows arched in surprise.

"Yes," I said, starting to sweat. "We're too young to be assigned jobs so we're left cleaning the camp." I heard shuffling behind me. "We want to work, sir." I forced the words out, aware that the commandant's hands had balled into fists. "We want to leave, sir." I swallowed. "As soon as possible, s-sir, to make a life in Melbourne."

The commandant's face looked like thunder. Fat veins stood out on his forehead. I heard feet scuff the floor and turned to see the last of the boys back out the door.

"Step forward, boy!" the commandant hissed.

I took a step toward him.

"You ungrateful shit!" The commandant's face was so red he looked like he might burst. "We bring you here to this beautiful country from starving Europe where you lived off the smell of an oily rag, and what do you become? You become a rabble-rouser and a troublemaker. One more squeak out of you and you'll be on the next ship back to Hungary. Or wherever it is you came from."

I nearly shat my pants. Back to Europe? The words stung like a slap.

"No, sir, you misunderstand," I backtracked, "must be my English. Please forgive me. I love Australia. Please don't send me back."

The commandant looked me up and down, his mouth a closed slit. I knew what he saw – dark hair and a dark past, a skinny boy with a strange accent, a new Australian, a refuge.

"Okay," he said, his words clipped. "You can stay. For now. But one more outburst and you're gone. I'll see to it personally."

CHAPTER 27

NOW

"You speak six languages?" I ask, realizing my stupidity too late. Dad can't speak at all, can only type with the cooperation of his fingers.

Dad nods.

"Why didn't you ever speak Czech or Yiddish with your friends?"

He lifts his fingers onto the Lightwriter. Slovak was the language my classmates used when they called me names, and the begging and abuse in the camps was all Yiddish, Slovak, Hungarian or German. Even now hearing those languages shakes the memories loose. Dad's fingers hover over the keys, then start tapping again. English feels safer.

Deb arrives for our sleepover. She empties her bag onto the kitchen table and pulls a hair crimper and a flask from the debris.

"Okay, so I was thinking either makeovers or homemade cocktails?"

I grab the flask and shove it under my waistband before Mom can spot it and reel off her non-negotiable rules: *No drinking. No smoking. No boys in the bedroom. No piercings. No fake ID. No nightclubs or bars.* It's a long list but you get the picture – I'm not meant to have fun until I'm eighteen.

"We can do both."

We head to my room and Mom pokes her head around the door. "Goodnight, girls!"

I wave from the mirror, my hair clamped between the crimper's zigzag plates.

"Hey, Mrs K. I hear it's your anniversary soon?"

Mom nods. "Twenty-eight years on Wednesday."

"Wednesday?" Deb grins. "I happen to have an opening on Wednesday. Should I book you in for a blow-dry?"

Mom runs her fingers through her limp, greasy hair. She hasn't washed it in weeks. "That'd be lovely," she gushes. "We're having a special dinner."

She uses the term *dinner* loosely. Mom and Dad haven't eaten together in months. Mom feeds and gets Dad ready for bed, then eats alone, pulled from her plate by his buzzer to adjust a pillow or dim the lights. She rarely finishes a meal. She's lost eight kilos. She was skinny to start with.

Dad's buzzer is ringing and Mom's already out the door by the time Deb calls out, "Appointment's at four." She takes another handful of hair and traps it between the irons.

"Your poor mom. She looks exhausted."

"We're trying to convince her to hire carers," I say to the mirror, "but she won't. She doesn't want to share Dad."

"Must be so hard." Deb's voice flattens.

We talk while my hair fries. I tell her that Mom's world is the four walls of our house. That she loved work but quit her job to care for Dad. That she picks flowers for his desk to bring the outside in, and develops reams of color film – Dad in bed, Dad being fed, Dad mid-suction. She reads medical journals instead of magazines and smiles when friends remark on Dad's courage and strength.

"How's *she* doing?" Deb asks.

But I can't answer. I don't know. I've never asked.

I hug Deb goodbye. I don't want her to go to dance practice and leave me alone in the kitchen, watching Mom feed Dad. I pull out my homework and watch them over the top of my books. Mom tucks a cushion behind Dad's neck, unbuttons his shirt and trickles medicine down his feeding tube, before serving him breakfast, a diet supplement from a can. Feeding tires him and he asks to be put to bed.

Must be so hard for your mom. Deb's words bounce around in my head.

"Let me help," I say, following them to the bedroom.

"Maybe just watch the first time."

Mom lays Dad down, lifting legs and dragging arms into position. She pulls on a pair of sterilised gloves and drops a plastic piece of my father into my palm – the tracheostomy filter – so she can feed a catheter down the hole in his throat to clear his lungs. After that she massages vitamin E cream onto his face, tracing the line of his mouth with her finger, trying to encourage a smile. It works.

Curtains drawn, glasses off, a towel under his chin, the bed control and buzzer under his fingers, blankets smoothed. Mom recites the checklist as she fusses around Dad. *This is what love looks like*, I think, wondering if I'm capable of it. Wondering if, fast forward thirty years, I'd do the same for Adam.

Twelve. That's only twelve times I've thought of him today. *Better.*

It's the morning of Mom and Dad's wedding anniversary. Twenty-eight years. I've done the maths, that's ten thousand two hundred and twenty mornings they've woken up next to each other. Mom's washing her hair. Dad's in his study, bent over the Lightwriter. I sidle up next to him.

"I got the photo frame you asked for." I keep my voice low. "Mom will love it. Want me to wrap it?"

I show Dad the silver frame holding a black-and-white photo, the one of Mom and Dad holding hands at the beach. Mom's head is on his shoulder. She's thin and dark-skinned with sea-sprayed hair. Dad is wearing a white singlet tucked into high-waisted pants. His blue eyes are smiling behind thick black frames.

We'd just got engaged. I still can't believe she agreed to marry me, Dad types. He adjusts the volume on the Lightwriter so it drops to a murmur. I'm writing Mom a message to play after dinner. Can you type it and have it laminated so she can keep it after I've ...

We're saved by the doorbell. Tom and Jack arrive and we get to work transforming the dining room into a restaurant while Mom dresses and Deb does her hair. Tom sets the table with candles and wine glasses. I cut flowers from the garden and drop them into a vase. Jack has picked up pasta from Mom's favorite Italian takeaway, and we grate parmesan and warm a loaf of bread.

I help Dad into a tux and walk him to the living room where Mom waits in the wedding dress she married him in. Dad's glasses mist up. I'm feeling weepy but I don't want to ruin the night, so I get busy feeding Dad while Jack lowers the needle on a Frank Sinatra record. Tom serves Mom pasta, dressed as a waiter with a curling moustache.

When we return an hour later with dessert, Mom's sitting on Dad's lap.

"How did you pop the question?" Tom carves up the chocolate cake and slides a piece onto a plate for Mom.

Dad lifts his fingers onto the keys. When? The first time I asked her? Or the time she said yes?

323

I knew the basics of their love story, or at least I thought I did. Mom grew up in Hungary, hid from the Nazis, and escaped the communists at nineteen. They met in the Elsternwick boarding house where Dad lived and a year after she moved in, he proposed. I didn't know she'd turned him down.

"Both proposals, please." I wait for Dad to answer.

I'd wanted to marry her since the day I laid eyes on her. The first time I asked, we were at Sandringham beach and she lifted her sweater and explained why she couldn't be my wife.

"Her sweater?" I'm confused.

The scar on her belly, Dad says. She told me she couldn't have children. "It doesn't matter," I told her. "You're the only family I need." It wasn't the answer she wanted. She said she liked me very much, but she wasn't ready for marriage.

"I was twenty!" Mom protests. "I wanted to finish school and go to university. Your dad wanted a family and a house in the suburbs."

We broke up, Dad drags his fingers across the keys, but eight months later we got back together and a few months after that I proposed and she said yes.

"Why didn't you just tell the truth?" I turn to Mom.

We all stare at her. Secrets and lies. Runs in the family.

"You're right," Mom says. "I shouldn't have lied. It's just that after the war everyone was in such a rush to get married. I had to know your dad was marrying me for *me* and not just to attain some goal – a wife, three kids, a white picket fence – a family to replace the one he'd lost."

"I get it," I say, offering Mom a small smile.

She had her reasons. Her own sad history I know nothing about. I make a mental note to buy another stack of tapes and a notepad. For Mom.

I don't care about the lies – not anymore. Sometimes we keep secrets from the people we love because we want to protect them. And sometimes we need to protect ourselves.

Dad clicks his tongue; my cue to give Mom his gift. I pass Mom the wrapped frame, slide the Lightwriter onto Dad's lap and press play.

We listen from behind the dining-room door.

My darling, Eva. You asked me yesterday what I wish for you. You wanted to know how to live your life. How to build a future to honour my memory and keep us close. I know you love me. I see how much you care. Nothing you do can diminish that.

I don't want you to mourn me. Your life has been on hold for too long; jump back in. We have lots of good friends, people who love you. Say yes when they invite you out. Work if you want to. Travel. Study. Watch the kids' games and have them over on Friday nights. Take them for pancakes.

I want you to be happy. If our home feels too big or too lonely, sell it. If you meet a man and he is kind and good to you, let yourself love again. You're young and beautiful and your life mustn't end with me.

It's not easy to recreate yourself. But I did it. You can too.

Mom is a puddle on the floor. Dad is clicking and blinking and shaking his head. He didn't want to upset her; it was meant to be a gift. She didn't need his permission to find happiness without him – to laugh and love again – but he knew that without those words she'd grow old alone.

"You look like shit." Deb pulls a tube of lip gloss from her locker, but I wave it away.

"I was up till three. Mai's article in the last school newsletter about the boat trip from Vietnam made me want to write something ... I don't know ... something important. I mean does anyone really care that we beat Davenport High in the table tennis finals?"

"We did?"

"Exactly."

"So, you're going to spill?" Deb pulls the wand from her watermelon lip gloss and leans into the mirror tacked to her locker.

"Not about the Jewish thing." I pull a piece of paper from my bag. "It's about Dad. And losing him."

It's been six months. Dad has outlived his doctor's gloomiest predictions and he's back into the unknown and that's a better place to be, because that is where the maybes live. Maybe his doctors got it wrong. Maybe he has another month. Or a year.

Deb holds out her hand. "Give."

I wait quietly while she reads.

"It's good, Lis." Deb looks up from the page. "Sad, but good."

"I should've asked more questions. That's what I'm trying to say. Don't wait until it's too late to get to know your parents. You might actually like them."

"I'm proud of you, Lis." Deb hands it back. "This is big."

"Is it?" My heart is drumming against my chest. "Maybe I just needed to get my thoughts down. I don't need to hand it in."

Deb grabs the sheet off me. "Or maybe you do. Maybe there are dozens of other kids who are going through something like this. Or maybe kids who are about to get some bad news, who'll wish they'd read this and got to know their mom or their gran before they had a massive coronary or were run over by a tram or –"

"Okay! I get it," I say, letting her drag me to the secretary's office.

She waits while I read through the article one last time before knocking on the door.

"So, can I get your autograph?" Adam is standing at the school gates, the school newsletter open to the page with my article. And Deb's right, it's big, literally. It takes up half a page.

"Deb made me do it."

I scan the words. *I get to say goodbye ... no regrets ...*

"Deb said it was a big deal, but it's not, is it? I mean, no-one actually reads this thing ..." I grab the paper off him. "Do they?"

"That's a trick question, right?" Adam plucks the newsletter from my hand and drops it into his bag. "Walk you home?"

I don't know what we are right now, but I want to find

out, so I nod. Last time he was over I spilled all my secrets.

"No more secrets," I said, and he'd smiled, a big half-moon smile, but he didn't kiss me. In the re-write he kisses me. He tucks a strand of hair behind my ear and kisses me and the world goes quiet. This is why I love writing.

"Anyway," I say, walking out the school gates with him, stopping the soccer ball he passes me, and sending it back, "I wrote it for Dad, so it doesn't really matter if no-one else reads it."

Except that it does. I *want* people to know Dad and miss him, as much as I will. I want his life – and what happened to him – to matter.

"I call bullshit," Adam says, kicking the ball straight up and catching it with one hand. His smile reaches his eyes. "You're scared, but you want people to read it, and they will, and their brains will explode." His smile wilts. "I wish I'd asked my gran more questions. Mom's telling me all these stories about her now, and she was pretty cool."

We turn off the main road onto a quiet street.

"She went to university instead of marrying her boyfriend. Was the only woman in her accounting class and captain of the university women's hockey team."

We pass the ball between us, and it's easier to talk like this; not looking at each other.

I tell him I'm thinking of asking Miss Evans if I can set up a lunchtime group for kids who've lost someone. "You know, just to talk. Everyone's got stories they're afraid to tell."

He fumbles for my hand and we stand at my front gate in the long shadows thrown by the setting sun. And I don't know what this is – or if I'll ever get him back – but for now, it's enough.

I'm out here floating in the middle of the *maybes*, in the right-now, just like Dad.

I type up Dad's latest instalment. All up it's now almost a hundred and forty pages. A book that holds my father close, but not close enough to stop time. I want to give him the pages, but there's still more to tell.

There's one last chapter, Dad had said, and I've saved the best for last.

CHAPTER 28

THEN

The first time I saw your mother's face was in a photo. I'd moved into a boarding house with Andrew, Carl, Arthur and a bunch of other migrant boys after my stint at Bonegilla.

Mr Drucker, our landlord, told us the nineteen-year-old girl from Budapest was a distant relative who'd be staying in the spare room. I remember staring at her dark eyes and long black hair. She was the most beautiful girl I'd ever seen.

I let one of my housemates, George, pick her up from the station. I didn't think a girl like that – a girl with movie-star looks who'd grown up in a city with music and art – would look at a guy like me. Best to hang back and play it cool, let George, Stephen and the other boys fall over themselves to impress her. But then the car door opened and your mom tumbled out clutching a small battered suitcase and I was a goner. She was the type of girl who made your heart beat harder, who stole sentences from you. The five of us boys watched her unbutton her coat and sit down to eat. Then we sat, five sets of eyes on her, five chairs pulled close and no-one saying a word.

She's just a girl, I told myself. *She was born in a big city but she came here alone. She must have left family behind. Or lost them. She's probably lonely, just like you were.*

"*Jó estét*, Emil, *vagyok*." I introduced myself in Hungarian, reaching across the table to shake her hand.

She put down her fork and smiled, and my stomach turned inside out.

"*És én*, Stephen, *vagyok!*" Stephen's hand shot out and then Mark stuck his hand out and Philip too and someone knocked over a glass and your mom laughed and let go of my hand and that laugh, it was full of warmth.

"Eva *vagyok*," she said in Hungarian, shaking hands with the boys, "but if do not mind," she switched to English, "I want learn English. Can please we speak English?"

She reached into her coat pocket – it was a tattered old thing she'd been given in Bonegilla – to pull out a small dog-eared Hungarian–English dictionary, and she thumbed the pages until she found what she was looking for.

"Slow. Can we speak slow?"

"Yes. Of course," I said, watching her search the dictionary again. I hoped it wasn't for the word *goodnight*.

"Thank you the dinner," she said, pushing back her chair. "It was –" she checked the book again, "delicious."

Stephen was the first to get to her the next morning. I think he might've camped outside her door. He stammered something about taking her on a tour of the city. She took the map he offered and spread it open on the small table, a smile lighting up her face.

"Maybe another day," she said, studying the map. "I have to

find a newspaper-selling shop. Is there one, a small walk?"

"A newsagent," I said, stepping into the hallway. "There's one around the corner. I can walk you?"

"That's alright. I walk myself." She handed me the map. "You show me on here?"

She returned an hour later, disappearing into Mr Drucker's study where the telephone lived, her Hungarian–English dictionary tucked under one arm, the jobs section of the newspaper under the other. She started work soldering electric cord at the Astor Radio Factory the next day.

I was waiting at the dining table when she returned that evening. She was wearing a pair of stained overalls, her arms were blistered and her hair smelled of smoke, but she didn't change her clothes or run a brush through her hair.

"I starving," she said, splashing soup into a bowl.

I'm going to marry that blistered, beautiful girl, I said to myself. *And one day I'm going to be brave enough to ask.*

Our first date was a tram ride to St Kilda. I'd waited so long, waited until she'd been to the movies with George and the botanical gardens with Mark and the zoo with Stephen. There was so much I wanted to tell her, so much I wanted to know. There weren't enough words in that Hungarian–English dictionary for all the things I wanted to say.

We sat on the sand watching the sun disappear, and it felt like there was no-one but the two of us, like I'd booked the sand and the sky just for her. We talked about our families and why we'd escaped to Australia and left them behind. We didn't dwell on the war years, preferring to fast-forward to the month at sea and our time at Bonegilla. We were both in a rush to get to *now*.

She didn't ask how Willie had lost his life; she wanted to know how I planned to live mine.

She had plans of her own. She wanted to finish school and go to university. She wanted to be an engineer; she loved maths.

"The radio factory is just a stone to step," she said.

"A stepping stone," I corrected her, dragging a stick across the sand to add the words to our beach dictionary.

"Beach. Seagull. Crumbs. Stepping stone." She read the words out loud, her smile fading.

"Why are you sad?"

"I am no sad," she said, settling a plate of food on her lap. "It's just ... no person has given me thing like this."

"*This?*"

I was confused. It was just the two of us, a scratchy towel and some cheese and crackers on a paper plate.

"Yes," she said, looking up at the stars. "The sky and the moon and this ... this ..." She pointed to the plate on her lap.

"Cheese?"

She laughed and shook her head. "This –" She pointed to the blanket.

"This picnic?"

"Yes! This pic-a-nic." She smiled. "Thank you for the pic-a-nic, and for all your stories, and the words. Thank you for my new words."

I was in love with her. It was crazy. I'd only known her for six weeks but I found myself listening for her footsteps in the morning and telling jokes just to hear her laugh. I waited for her at the tram stop so I could walk her home at night and helped her dry the dishes because those were the times we got to talk. I didn't tell her that I lay in bed at night imagining my

333

arms around her or that I practised saying the words *I love you* out loud but I told her things I'd never told anyone. I told her that I was scared of dogs and that I missed Willie and that one day I was going to do something big, something good, something Tatte would be proud of.

She didn't care that I was still living in a boarding house and not my own home. Maybe she knew that a house was just four walls and that you needed someone to love you before it became a home. She made every small moment feel like an adventure. Like life was an adventure and we were just at the start. It didn't matter where we went – to the post office, a town hall dance, or shopping for fruit at the Vic market – she made the world bigger just by being in it.

It took me eight weeks – and seventeen dates – before I worked up the courage to hold her hand. We were hiking in the hills on a Sunday afternoon.

"The view is meant to be spectacular from here." I pulled myself up onto a ridge and turned to offer her my hand.

She didn't need help scrambling up the rock. She'd climbed most of the steep sections ahead of me, but I held out my hand and she took it. And when we were both safe on top of the rock, she didn't let go.

I was too scared to look at her so I stood looking out at the rolling hills, her small hand in mine, my heart exploding. I wanted this startling, brilliant brown-eyed girl to be my family, my four walls. She'd given me her hand but I wanted her heart.

I brushed the hair back from her face. "I love you," I said. "I've been in love with you since the day you dragged your suitcase through Mr Drucker's door."

I can't remember what she said next – you'll have to ask your mom – but I remember that she smiled, and I remember our first kiss. It felt like home, like I'd been found. The world went quiet and the past fell away. It was just me and her and the rest of our lives.

CHAPTER 29

NOW

Dad's mouth splits into a wide smile and then he remembers. The *rest of their lives* is almost over.

"Should we call it a night and head to bed? You must be exhausted," Mom says, trying to read Dad's face to spare his hands the effort of typing. His fingers used to glide over the keys. Now they crawl.

Dad nods, his smile deepening the lines around his eyes. After all these years, she's still in a rush to get me into bed.

Mom rolls her eyes and we laugh and watch her shuffle closer to Dad to plant a kiss on his cheek. I used to cringe when Dad pulled Mom onto his lap when we watched TV. I hated it when I tried their bedroom door and found it locked; the thought of them playing tonsil hockey made my skin crawl. Now I'd give anything to see Dad drop a Frank Sinatra record onto the turntable, grab Mom by the waist and spin her around.

Dad is asleep, a mask strapped over his nose and mouth. I watch the rise and fall of his chest. He looks peaceful in sleep. I tiptoe out and find Mom in the kitchen, mopping the floor.

I put the kettle on. "Want a cup of tea?"

"Sure." Mom tips the gray water into the sink and sets the mop down. "I've got to prepare Dad's meds for tomorrow. You can keep me company while I do it."

I pour us two cups. "What was Dad like when you first met?"

"Handsome," Mom says.

"No, I mean, was he okay? You know, after everything that happened?"

Mom stares into her teacup.

"How much did he tell you? Did you know about the Death March and how Willie died? Did he talk about his parents?"

"We didn't really talk about it."

"What? At all?"

Mom looks up from the tea-leaves. "We swapped a few stories about where we grew up and who we lost. We didn't talk about the camps. If friends brought it up, he'd say, 'The past is behind us.' He wanted to focus on what was in front of him." Her eyes cut back to the tea. "He was just so excited about life. I didn't want to drag him back there."

Mr Curlew stops at my locker. "I read your article in the school newsletter."

My eyes drift to the socks trapped under his sandals, pineapples playing tennis.

"It's a really powerful piece. You might want to think about swapping one of your other subjects for English Lit?" He hands me a change of subject form.

"Thanks," I say. "And you were right."

Confusion slides across his face.

"The writing," I say. "It helps."

I think about it all the way home, about writing Dad's story and why I've been putting off finishing it. I lost grandparents, cousins, uncles and aunts to the Holocaust. Maybe Dad's words are my way back to them. Or maybe they're just a big F-you to Hitler. I know one thing for sure, I feel closer to Dad – and closer to the person I want to be – when I write. I don't want to study Law.

I drop my schoolbag at the door and head to Dad's bedroom. *He doesn't want you living someone else's life*, I remind myself.

"Hey, Dad." I grab the Lightwriter from its charger and settle it on Dad's lap. My hands are shaking. "You know how we talked about me studying Law and finding out what my dream is?"

Dad clicks. He remembers.

"I think I want to write," I say, searching his face for

disappointment. "I want to be a writer."

To my surprise, he smiles. He can't wrap his arms around me. He's too tired to type. He can't speak his happiness, but I know he's good with it. I pull the bound pages from my bag and rest them on his lap.

"Thank you," I whisper.

For what? Dad's eyes ask.

I try to order my thoughts. For slipping coins under my pillow when my teeth fell out so I could make-believe. For introducing me to my grandparents and the small boy who lost them. For never giving up hope. For trusting me with his memories.

"For opening my eyes," I say.

Dad presses a button and a question mark flashes across the screen.

I try to explain. "You know how you used to hoist me onto your shoulders so I could see across the park to the rest of the world?"

Dad nods.

"I can see further now."

My father is sitting at his desk the next day, a scrapbook of newspaper clippings open before him. I drag a chair next to his so we can flip through the pages, proof of a happy life. The second-last page boasts a photo of Dad holding up his Citizen of the Year Award. Carl and Ernst are blurred in the background behind him.

"Don't you want to talk about any of this stuff?"

Dad drags his fingers to the keys. You want to know who I am?

I wait, wait, wait for the next words. Dad types out another slow sentence and presses play.

I can tell you in less than a minute: a lucky man. Sweat beads on Dad's forehead as his fingers roam the keys. The man your mom chose. A man with three incredible kids.

I don't know if Dad's fingers are giving up on him. Maybe he doesn't want to talk about his achievements because the times he was away from us don't matter as much as the times we were together. Or maybe he doesn't need to because we were there to witness them.

Except, I wasn't. I didn't want to hand out how-to-vote cards on street corners for him, or miss the latest episode of *Happy Days* to sit through another boring council meeting. I didn't want to spend the night on the phone, calling strangers to beg a few dollars for an orphanage, or eat goulash with sixty year olds at the social club he helped found. I knew Dad did all these things and I knew that they were good things. I just didn't see how they related to me.

Silence settles on the faded pages. The last page is empty and I wonder if Dad's thinking what I'm thinking: *Space for the death notice.*

Adam is not going to kiss me while my dad is dying, but I want him to. I want to be us again. I want to rewrite our story. Dad waited seventeen dates before he kissed Mom. I'm not that patient. We have the stars to ourselves and his hair smells like the beach, like coconut and sunshine. And I've been thinking about him – about love – all day.

"This looks amazing," Adam says, spearing a square of cheese with a toothpick.

I look at the nest of blankets and the food and the moon and think, *What are you doing? This was Mom and Dad's first date.* I don't tell *him* that, because it's weird, and because I don't want to kill the mood by talking about my parents, but then I talk about my parents.

"Dad's getting worse. I don't know how long he'll be able to type for and Mom's exhausted ..." I shake my head. "But she never complains."

The tears start and Adam slips his hand into mine. We sit with our foreheads pressed together. I'm an ugly crier. Red nose. Bloodshot eyes. Not a face you want to kiss.

"Anyway," I say, not making eye contact, "Dad has finished telling us his story, so my Friday nights are free."

I kick off my sandals and dig my toes into the sand so I don't have to look at him. Neither of us know what to say next.

"So, I saw your flyer about the meeting." He offers a smile.

I set my plate down. "Yeah. After I wrote that article about Dad, kids kept coming up to me. Some of them just wanted to say, 'Hey, hope you're okay,' but there were others who wanted to tell me they'd been through it too, lost a brother or a mom. One kid in 10th Grade told me her dad walked out on them last year, so he wasn't dead but it felt like being left, like she had all this heaviness and nowhere to put it. So I asked Miss Evans if we could set up a sharing circle for anyone who's lost someone."

Adam is studying me.

"What?" I say.

"This might be way off base," he says, "but can I –"

He leans close, so close I can smell the butterscotch on his breath. He's going to kiss me. After eighty-two days and seven hours he's finally going to kiss me.

"Yes," I whisper, my heart drumming hard.

He smiles, opens his arms and wraps them around me. In a hug.

Miss Evans has stacked the library chairs and dropped beanbags and cushions onto the floor. Adam is sitting on a small pink puff with his eyes closed and legs crossed, hands steepled in front of his chest. He opens one eye and winks at me.

"I thought we might try a seated meditation until the others arrive," Miss Evans whispers. "If you'd like to close your eyes ..."

The clock ticks. I listen for footsteps.

Miss Evans rests a hand on my shoulder.

"It's ten past one. I think we might have to make a start."

"But there's no-one ..." I glance at the door. The corridor is empty. "Sure." I shrug. "Whatever."

It was a stupid idea, forcing people to dig up old wounds. What do *I* know about sharing? I'm a secret-keeper, a wall-builder. A hypocrite.

"Is this cushion free?"

I vault off my beanbag at the sound of Deb's voice.

"Oh my god, you didn't have to come." I wrap her in a bear hug. "This is so embarrassing," I whisper into her neck. "Let's just go to the cafeteria."

"What, and let all these people down?"

I drag my head from Deb's neck. At the door a girl in a netball uniform mombles her hellos to two girls in 12th Grade. A boy with a buzzcut tears open a packet of ginger snaps and passes them around.

Miss Evans introduces herself and asks who'd like to go first. She's looking at me. *I* called the meeting and wrote the article in the newsletter. I should go first but my legs don't seem to be working, and suddenly there's no air in the room.

"What about you, Trevor?" Miss Evans eyes slide to the boy with the buzzcut.

He gets to his feet, slowly. "My dad died a few weeks ago." He looks up from his shoes. "It was sudden," he says, "a heart attack. He was away, on duty. He's in ... he *was* in the army. Anyway, after they buried him, I got out his shaver and took it all off." He runs a hand over the bristles on his head.

"I'm still wearing my mom's scarf and it's been seven

months," the girl in the netball uniform pipes up. She raises a thin wrist, wrapped in a silk headscarf.

"Do you want to go next, Vanessa?" Miss Evans asks her.

Vanessa nods, burying her nose in the silk. "I don't want to forget what she smells like." She looks up at Miss Evans. "Is that weird?"

Miss Evans rests her hand on the girls' shoulder. "No, it's not weird. There's no right way to grieve, just *your* way."

She scans the room, and I want to say something because no-one else is, but the words catch in my throat.

"Okay," Miss Evans, says. "Why don't we try something else."

She lifts a piece of chalk from the board and starts a list: Stupid things people say at funerals.

The boy with the ginger snaps swipes the crumbs from his lap and walks to the board, shoulders sloping. He writes: *God must've needed your dad in heaven.*

He hands the chalk to Vanessa and she scrawls: *I told your mom to stop smoking.*

The chalk is being passed around and people are talking and I can tell they're as surprised as I am.

It's not a big deal because literally everyone dies.

I don't want to sound mean, but you need to move on.

Call me back when you've stopped crying.

A girl with sad eyes asks for the chalk and writes: *I know how you feel. My pet fish died last year.*

And then someone laughs, and the bell rings.

CHAPTER 30

NOW

Dad has convened a family meeting. We wait quietly while he types. He's been having trouble lifting his fingers and the letters are slow to form words.

I want to die on a Friday.

Mom recoils as if she's been punched.

The funeral can be on the weekend. No-one has to miss work.

I stare at the crooked smile under Dad's ventilator mask and think the roof might cave in under the weight of all this sadness.

Dad battles on, his words clipped, his fingers too weak for whole sentences. The instructions continue but none of it feels real – the talk of turning off ventilators and wills and burial rites.

Tom has been taking notes and Dad asks him to read them back. It's *his* story – *his* life – and he wants to control the ending. He wants to decide when it's time to turn off the machine. When Tom reads the words out loud, they're spoken between sobs.

A tear slides down Dad's cheek. It's the third and last time I'll ever see him cry. We arrive at the big question no-one wants to ask. I break the silence and invite death into the room.

"When will it be enough?" I can't look Dad in the eye.

He presses a single button, linked to a pre-recorded message. He's thought about this.

My fingers are weak. Soon I won't be able to type. You'll have to ask questions. I'll blink once for yes. Twice for no. Ask me how I feel. Ask if I'm ready to go. He repeats the code. I'll blink once for yes. Twice for no.

Mom's pacing now. "I can't do it. I won't." Her face is wild with worry. "You might just be having a bad day. You can't make me –"

They argue and she negotiates a painful compromise. The ventilator will be switched off if Dad blinks *Yes, he is ready* seven days in a row.

He makes us give our word. Tom writes the code down – once for yes, twice for no.

Dad touches his tongue to the roof of his mouth and draws it away sharply, making a clicking sound. His approval. One click, precisely delivered. It's a language. His language. One sound capable of expressing so many emotions. Anger – a round of clicks fired off like a shotgun. A cry for help – slow, loud, repetitive clicks. Thankfulness – one click, blown soft and full, like a kiss.

Dad makes each of us repeat his instructions. I stare at the inky words.

"I'll tell you when I'm ready. One click for yes. Two for No," I say.

I pass the notebook to Jack. He repeats the words and passes the book to Mom. Her eyes are wet, brown pools.

"One for yes. Two for no." Her voice sounds ragged and far away.

Thank you, the Lightwriter bleats.

I look at Dad's face. I can't tell if he is scared.

When I get home from school the next day, Dad's still in bed, attached to the ventilator. He wakes when I sit on the edge of the bed.

"Want to talk?" I lift the Lightwriter onto his lap.

He blinks twice. Twice for no, but he's staring at the machine. He's been typing and saving messages over the last few weeks.

"The save button?"

He clicks his tongue and I press the button.

Sorry, Dad's robot voice apologises. My fingers won't do what they're told. Typing this message – and others – for when I can't type. I know you have questions. You'll have to figure out the answers on your own. It's not important you know everything about me. What's important is you remember everyone has a story, and no matter who they are, their stories are important.

Dad presses another button and a message scuds across the screen: There's a present for you on my bed.

It's fluffy dice. For my gap year van.

A week later we are huddled around Dad's bed. He can't drag his fingers across the keyboard so I press play.

It's nearly time.

Dad blinks at the machine. There's another pre-recorded message.

Death makes more sense.

I bend down to hug him. It's getting harder with all the electrical cords, tricky to land a kiss on his cheek with the mask. His eyes are closed. He's too weak to sit up.

My brothers go get food and Mom slips away to shower. I perch on the edge of Dad's bed. It's hard talking when nothing comes back but I stay a while longer, holding his hand. I don't want to let go. He feels so far away when we're not touching. I know he feels it too – the connection being cut. He knows he's close to being locked in. He's not scared of the end, just the silence. He wants to go before we're totally lost to each other.

Death makes more sense.

"We have to give him permission, Mom. I don't want him to feel like he's letting us down," I tell Mom over pizza that night.

Tears gather at the corners of her eyes. She doesn't want to have this conversation; doesn't want to let him go. But later that night I walk in on her washing Dad's hair. He's sitting in a plastic chair, naked from the waist up. It feels more intimate than walking in on them in bed. Dad's eyes are closed, his head tilted over the basin. Mom sponges his face and neck, and the arms that once held her.

"It's okay," she whispers, washing the suds from his hair. "I don't want to lose you, but I understand why you have to go."

CHAPTER 31

NOW

Dad's lungs are infected. He's in bed all day. He hasn't touched his Lightwriter.

"He wants to die," Mom says, scraping away tears. "In a week. He told me yesterday."

Tom and Jack come over and we camp out in Dad's room. He sleeps most of the time, the ventilator breathing for him. But when his eyelids flutter open, he smiles at us with so much love it's like the sun is rising.

We eat meals and cancel plans from the safety of our parents' bed, too scared to leave and miss a smile or a blink. We take turns pulling up childhood memories, rewinding the decades to a time when Dad could hold us and shape our world. Now he speaks with his eyes because his arms don't work but there's still feeling in him. When we laugh, he smiles. When our sadness spills out, his eyes leak too.

"You're so brave," I say, lying down next to him.

He seems so unafraid. I follow the curve of his Roman

nose, the small bump on the bridge, just like mine.

I wonder if I have his courage.

Jack shakes me awake. It's still dark. He is wearing pyjamas. Tom is standing behind him, rubbing sleep from his eyes.

"Come quick," Jack says. "Dad's worse."

But I can't. I can't move. I know if I get out of bed and walk to his room, I'll see my father die.

Tom pulls off my blankets and I follow him down the hall, wading through quicksand.

"Seven days." I tug on Tom's sleeve. "He was meant to wait a week."

Dad opens his eyes at the sound of our voices but he doesn't move. His face is gray, sunken in on itself.

"He's struggling," Jack says, "even *with* the ventilator."

Dad's eyes flicker to the calendar pinned to the wall. I follow his gaze.

It's Friday.

"I'll call the doctor." Jack turns to Mom. "Call his friends."

Within half an hour the house is full. My father's oldest friends line the corridor, their faces smudged by shock. The sun is up but the house feels dark.

Mom ushers them into the bedroom to say their goodbyes. Dad never got to say goodbye to his parents or Willie, never got to thank the Polish woman for saving his life. This is *his* idea. He can't shake their hands or turn to look at them, so he blinks, and in that small, deliberate gesture says *thank you* and *I love you* and *goodbye*.

The last of the visitors leave and it's good to have Dad to ourselves again. Mom sets the Lightwriter on the bed and presses play. My father's instructions, recorded weeks ago, fill the room.

Invite everyone back to our house after the funeral, he has typed. Remember me. Don't mourn for me. There will be tears, but I hope also laughter.

The doorbell rings. Jack answers it. Mom is squeezed in next to Dad on the bed, whispering in his ear when a rabbi walks in. Dad's eyes flicker open. He's not a religious man, but he smiles when the rabbi pulls up a chair.

"You've done good, Emil," the rabbi says. "You go to God pure. He will look after you."

How does this bearded man dressed in black know what God will do? And does it matter? He begins to sing a soft, mournful song, something in Hebrew. Dad's eyes are closed, but his head is tilted toward the music, and I think, *What a nice way to leave, even if you don't believe.*

The rabbi departs and the doctor arrives. My mother had put off calling the palliative care team because calling them meant Dad was dying. Now the doctor sweeps into the room with a bag full of death's helpers. Dying is her day job, but she's not grim.

"I'm here to help," she tells us, before turning to Dad. "Do you want the ventilator switched off today?"

Dad blinks once. *Yes.* We all know the code.

Mom jumps in. "Are you sure, Emil?"

He blinks once.

"You won't change your mind?" She's begging now.

Dad blinks twice.

The room is full of the rattle of his chest. I escape to the bathroom. *My father is going to die. He is going to die and leave behind slippers, half-used shampoo bottles and a toothbrush.* I lift his dressing gown from the hook on the door and shrug it on. It took so long to find out who he was, and now he's leaving.

"I'll be in the living room. Take your time. Say your goodbyes," the doctor says as we pass each other in the hallway.

I can't look at her.

"The last sense to go is hearing." She touches my shoulder. "When someone is dying, they'll lose their taste, their sight and their sense of smell but they can still hear."

I look up from my shoes.

"He can hear you. Go talk to him."

We take it in turns. I go last. I shuttle the curtains open, letting shafts of afternoon sunlight into the room. I wish I could see inside Dad's head, but all I can do is show him what's inside mine.

"You told us you were lucky." I bring my face close to his. "But really, it's the rest of us who are lucky."

Dad's eyes flicker open.

"I know you have to leave and I'll miss you like crazy but I'll still be your little piece of pineapple, and I'm going to keep talking to you. Talking and asking questions."

Everyone pours back into the room.

"There's one last message." Mom presses *play* and nestles in next to Dad.

Don't be afraid of growing old or getting sick. Even trapped in this wrecked body, I wouldn't trade the last eight months for anything. Every single day, every conversation, every smile, and all the tears and hugs. Every night of storytelling and all the questions and answers. I'm taking them with me. I know you'll keep them close too. I love you all to the moon and back.

We are all crying now. Mom nudges closer to kiss Dad. She doesn't expect anything in return. Not a kiss, or a word. He might smile if he has the energy. Still, she rests a cheek against his lips, just to feel their warmth on her skin. He hasn't kissed Mom – kissed any of us – in months. He couldn't physically manage it. But now, seconds from death, he presses his lips to her cheek and kisses her. I hear it. Jack does too, and now he's hovering above Dad, holding his breath. He gets a kiss too. I watch Dad's lips rise up to meet Tom's stubble and then I'm on the bed, bent over Dad, the whisper of his breath on my skin and then his soft mouth.

We all get kisses.

The sky through the bedroom window is darkening when the doctor gently explains what will happen once Dad gives the order for the ventilator to be turned off. My brothers are tilted over, sobbing. Mom's face is hidden in her hands.

"Oh my God, oh my God, oh my God," she is saying, and I feel it too, the hurt, almost like a physical burn.

I look at Dad. His eyes are dry, his breathing even. He knows he is going to die in hours, maybe minutes. I've imagined it so many times, but now that the moment is here, it feels far away. I hold my breath. Dad's sleepy now, sliding away. It is like a light going out very slowly. The morphine the doctor has given him is starting to work.

"You'll be asleep soon, Emil, and then we'll turn down the machine," the doctor says quietly.

We're running out of time. We lob promises at him.

"We'll never forget you."

"We'll look after Mom."

"We'll tell people your story."

Dad's body is engulfed by blankets. His face is moon-pale but his mouth is moving. We scrabble closer to read his lips, to watch them form words.

"I. love. you."

"I love you too," I whisper as Dad's eyes close to the rush of morphine.

And then a chorus of *I love yous* erupts around me. We repeat the words over and over, trying to coax him back, but we can't stop him drifting.

The doctor looks at my mother and nods.

Dead? He can't be.

I reach for Dad's hand. It's still warm. I look over at my brothers. They're still waiting for the end, the last gasp, the struggle, but Dad looks exactly like he always has – sky-blue eyes and curly hair, his skin loose and lined. Except it's tinged gray and his eyes look empty. Like he's dead. A few seconds ago, he was alive and breathing. How can he not be alive and breathing now?

"He's gone," the doctor says, and Mom howls out her grief.

She buries her face in Dad's neck, the moment stretching out between us until I'm sure it will break. And then I feel it – a slipping away.

He's free. Mom is still talking to him, trying to tempt him back. She touches her cheek to his lips and waits. She wants me to touch him too.

"He's still warm," she whispers. But he's not anymore.

I hold his hand – for her – but when I look for him, it's through the window, outside in the buzzing dark. I slip my hand from his and head for the door, pushing it open to gaze at the stars; the first stars in the Friday night sky. I make a mental note to tell Mom that Dad will need his good suit. Tatte and Willie will already be dressed and on their way to *shul*. I hope they save a seat for him.

I fall asleep in Dad's wheelchair and wake to the doorbell. The men at the door are in black. Black shoes, black pants, black coats, black hats. They're carrying a stretcher.

"We're sorry for your loss," they say. "We're from the Chevra Kadisha." They slip off their shoes and pick up their buckets. "We're here to clean the body and prepare it for burial."

The body? It takes me a minute.

I don't want to go into my parents' room. I want to remember Dad breathing, but I show them in, apologising for the scene. Mom is under the covers, body curled around Dad.

"She wanted one last night ..." I try to explain. "They always fall asleep holding hands, so ..." I stare at Dad's bluish fingers caught between Mom's.

"It's probably best if you both wait outside." The men pull on rubber gloves.

I hold up a dressing gown and wait for Mom to step into it. The sun is up, and Dad is not Dad, and the room already feels strange without him snoring in it. We pad to the hallway.

An hour later the men wheel a green body bag past the kitchen. Mom cries out when she sees the dad-shaped bag.

"He's not in there," I say, looking toward the front door. "He's out there, somewhere, telling his story."

CHAPTER 32

NOW

I can only remember the funeral in snatches – our stiff black clothes, the hole in the ground waiting for Dad's bones and a wooden box the size of a grown man. The men in overalls lowered the box with ropes and someone dug up a load of earth and emptied it on top. The damp thud made my knees buckle. Another flood of dirt hit the wood, and then another, and bit by bit the box disappeared.

The days after are a blur. I feel bruised and empty. Mom wanders through the house touching Dad's things. She doesn't make the bed; doesn't want to disturb the imprint of his body on the wrinkled sheets or scare away the familiar soap-smell of his skin.

I don't know how to do the grieving-remembering-healing thing, but I want my friends close. Deb, Karen, Tracey and Adam come over. Karen asks about the service and how Jews mourn and I do my best to explain the sheets hanging over the mirrors and the seven days I'll be staying home to sit something called *shiva*.

"I'm not really into religion," I tell her, "but Dad was raised religious and I think toward the end he reconnected with it. So all this stuff ..." I point to my black skirt and the torn collar of my shirt, "... I don't know, it makes me feel closer to him."

We spend a week in the *shiva* bubble, listening to Sinatra tunes and looking through old photos. We cook Dad's favorite food and drag our mattresses into the garden to sleep under the stars. We take turns reading chapters of his story out loud. We cry a lot, but Deb and Adam come every day after school with bunches of flowers and bags of chocolate and we watch cheesy sitcoms that aren't about dads.

I'm a mess – laughing one minute, weeping the next. Wanting to talk about Dad, and not wanting to talk. Wanting to be left alone, and wanting company. It's not easy letting people hold your heart, hoping the scared, sad sides of you won't scare them off. I think about Dad being fed and wiped and how he never hated any of us for it. And how this last lesson was perhaps the most important one he taught us. It takes guts to be vulnerable.

On the last day of *shiva* Deb comes over, pulling a plastic pocket from her backpack to share the latest additions to her family tree – two small leaves clinging to the branches of a towering oak.

"Grab yours," she says, settling herself on the floor.

I open a drawer and pull out the tree I started at her place. Dad always wanted me to know I was part of something big.

"I spoke to my dad," she says, cutting leaves from a block of green paper, "and I have *your* dad to thank for that. Last time I saw him, he told me to try silence. 'Don't be afraid to disappear for a while and see what happens,' he said." She gives me a smile. "So I did. I stopped talking and Mom started." She glues a leaf to the tree. "She told me dad moved to Sydney after she got pregnant. He said he was too young to be a dad. He'd just started a job, didn't think they'd get by. Anyway, he's married now. I've got a half-sister. I spoke to them."

"Oh my God. A mini Cartman. I don't know if I could handle *two* of you."

Deb elbows me.

"Are you going to meet her?"

"Dad's agreed to keep talking." She shrugs. "So, yeah, maybe." She points to a canopy of green on my family tree. "Who are they?"

"Cousins. Aunts. Uncles." I trace the names on the leaves. "One of my cousins – Sari's daughter – sent me the names. We're going to meet up once I've finished school. Want to head to Europe after our road trip?"

Deb gives me a smile. "I reckon your dad would like that."

"Me too."

360

I climb into bed but I can't fall asleep. I'm supposed to go to school tomorrow. I promised Dad I wouldn't grieve for long. I didn't promise to stop missing him. I didn't promise to stop writing. I reach under the bed, pull Dad's story from the shoebox and turn to the last page. It's time for an ending.

I write about Dad's last day and our last kisses. I write about the funeral and Dad's escape and the friends who gathered to remember him. I write that it helped; the pots of soup and the stories and everyone telling us how much they loved him. And Dad there too, or at least the idea of him, shimmering at the edges of things like a hologram.

The words come out in a rush. I want to get everything down, everything Dad told us. When the words dry up, I draw pictures – a tattoo, a jeweler's workbench and a thirteen-year-old boy with the same face as my father.

Mom looks in from the doorway. "It's late. You've got school tomorrow." She pauses. "Is that Dad's story?"

I nod. "I'm just finishing up."

Mom pads to my bed.

"I was going to photocopy it at school tomorrow. Deb asked to read it. Is that okay?"

"I think Dad would like that."

I reach toward her and finger the buttons on Dad's cardigan.

"I don't want to forget," she says, pulling it close around her like a hug.

"You won't," I say.

And neither will I. I won't get to sleep under the stars or kick a ball around a park with him, but I have his past on spools of tape and A4 paper. I have every day up to right now. All his secrets and small joys burned deep in my memory. I have that.

I loop my arms around my knees. "Dad let go of the past," I whisper. "He *had* to. We don't."

I call Adam as soon as I hear Mom's bedroom door close.

"Can you come over and bring the car? I want to go out."

Adam turns up in a beat-up Honda he bought secondhand, and we drive past Elwood beach to the tattoo parlor where Dad buried his number under a spray of purple flowers.

"That's it!" I yelp, when I see that Black Ink is still open for business.

He pulls up at the kerb and I tell him about Dad's number and how he buried it.

"He had this way," I tell Adam, "of making ugly things beautiful. He did it after the war, with the number the Nazis branded on his arm, and he did it again, when he got sick. Every time he found himself somewhere dark, he searched for a blade of light."

Adam brushes his fingers across the pale skin of my arm. His face is inches from mine. I want to make up for all the time I was supposed to be kissing him, but I reach for the door. There's something I still have to do.

CHAPTER 33

NOW

I grab my schoolbag and let Deb slip her arm through mine and we walk into the blue day together. I'm at the beginning of the rest of my life without Dad.

"You ready to do this?" Deb asks, and I nod.

The last seven days were crowded with dying but also with the best bits of living – friendship and food and hugs and love.

"I'm ready," I say, turning the corner for school.

"And the sharing circle?" Deb slows. "You know you don't *have* to spill. You don't have to go."

"I know," I say. "I want to. The talking helps."

"Helps?" Deb says, staggering backward dramatically. "Does this mean from now on, *you* do all the talking?" She pulls a face of mock horror. "And *I* have to listen?"

"God, no!" I say. "I need my daily fix of melodrama. Please don't ever stop being a self-obsessed diva."

"Done." Deb holds up a hand and we high-five.

"Okay, so there's this family who've moved into our

street," Deb says, keeping up her end of the bargain, "and I kid you not, their son is Rob Lowe. Not actual Rob Lowe, but if Rob Lowe had a better-looking twin brother, this boy would be him."

"Hotter than Rob Lowe?" I shake my head. "No way."

"Yes way," Deb says, "and I plan to bump into him after school so I need to workshop some lines. As soon as you're done with sharing circle I need you in the cafeteria."

Deb doesn't need boy advice, especially from me. She wants me in the cafeteria after the bell so I'm not sobbing in a toilet stall after confessing my secrets. I stop at the school gate.

"I'll be okay," I say, scanning the treetops for Dad. "I want to talk about it. I need to."

Deb follows my gaze to the cloudless blue. "You know all those things you shared with me that your dad taught you?"

"Yeah." I look at her.

"You forgot one." Deb grins. "The one where he taught you to be a total boss."

I shrug my schoolbag onto my shoulder and walk through the school gates. I hope I'm as brave as Deb thinks I am.

I'm about to shove my bag into my locker when I notice a crumpled scrap of paper stuck in the door's metal grille.

Adam.

I wave Deb goodbye and pull it out.

Three words in blue ink: *Our usual spot?* Could be the library behind the stacks but we're not officially back together so I choose something safer – the hidden patch of lawn where we ate donuts, a million lifetimes ago.

"This from you?" I toss the note onto the table Adam has dragged from the chem lab and try to dim the fireflies lighting me up from the inside. I wonder if he can he see me blaze.

There are no donuts today, but the table is covered in glass beakers and the beakers are filled with water and the water holds flowers, dusky pink, long-stemmed roses.

"You know the last kid who stole a rose from the principal's garden got trash duty for a month?"

Adam smiles. "Do you want to sit down?"

"Sure. I've got a few minutes." I drop into a chair. "Just got to be in the library by 10.15. I promised Miss Evans I'd share with the group."

He nods, not taking his eyes off me. "I thought you could use a few minutes away from the madness before we head there."

"We?"

"Yeah." Adam pushes his hair off his forehead. "So, if it gets hard, if you want to stop, just shoot me a look, and I'll jump in. Can't guarantee I'll say anything worth listening to, but I'll be ready with an inane comment if you need a breather."

"Thanks," I say, wondering how he can see straight through me to my beating heart. "I'm mega nervous but I really want to do this. I'm just not sure how much to say."

"What do you *want* to say?" Adam lowers his head so his chin rests on his crossed arms. "If you could tell me one thing about your dad, right now, what would it be?"

I shrug. "I don't know. Maybe something about hope and miracles, something about forgetting but not letting go. Something about love," I say to my shoes. "Maybe the real miracle was that Dad could love again." I force myself to meet Adam's gaze. Dad's words whirl in my brain: *At the end of the day, it's all about who you love and who loves you back.*

"Since we're being honest," Adam says. "You know when we broke up?"

"When *you* broke up with *me*."

"Okay, when *I* broke up with *you*," he offers an apologetic smile, "and said I was falling in love with you?"

I nod, my face filling with heat.

His smile widens. "I never stopped."

We fly at each other. I don't want to waste another fraction of a second not kissing him. Our mouths collide and it's like electricity sparking. A kiss so hot it melts me. Hours pass – or maybe it's seconds – before he pulls away. We're both grinning. We're going to be okay.

"We better go," I say, untangling myself from him.

I scoop up the flowers and reach for his hand.

Miss Evans offers me a smile and a chair.

"Okay, we're all here. Adam, there's an empty seat ..."

She casts around for a chair. "Nope, all taken. Just find a spot on the floor."

Everyone who turned up to the last sharing circle is here, but also Karen, Tracey and Mai. Plus Gavin from the school newspaper and Kim with a few 12th Graders. Deb is curled on the floor like a cat.

"Lisa?" Miss Evans says gently. "Would you like to go first?"

"Sure," I say, standing. And even though I think they will, my legs don't give way.

I look at Deb, Mai and Adam, telling me with their eyes that I can do this. Dad is outside, hovering. *My time is up but* you're *still here*, I imagine him saying. *You can be whoever you want to be, do whatever you want to do. You have that freedom. What are you going to do with it?*

"My dad had so many secrets. I don't want to live with one. I'm Jewish," I say, "and my dad survived the Holocaust."

The words spill out of me, filling the bewildered silence, my big, banging voice too loud for the room.

"I thought I was going to talk about my dad's last hours and how his dying changed me but I think I'll talk about his life, if that's okay?"

Miss Evans nods.

I tell them about my dad's childhood and the bullying. I tell them about the cattle truck and the tattoos and the colored triangles of cloth that prisoners had to fix to their striped uniforms. I tell his story for the dead and the living. But mostly I tell it so there won't be more stories like his.

"Hitler wanted to mould a race of blue-eyed, blond Germans. Anyone who didn't fit that description – anyone who was different – he wanted dead. I'm not saying there aren't differences between us. We're *not* all the same. But that's okay." I look around the room. "It's okay to speak with a foreign accent, eat dahl or dumplings and believe in a different God ... or no God at all. I've spent so long thinking that being different was bad but my grandpa, Tatte ..." I wait for the snickers, but the room is dead quiet. "He told my father to be proud of our difference. And I am."

I feel Dad reach across the room and squeeze my hand. I close my eyes so I can remember him better and there, sitting next to him, is an old man with a silver beard. Tatte. And they're both smiling. Two wonky half-smiles that make a whole.

"I lost my dad," I say, rolling up my left sleeve, "and one day soon there won't be any Holocaust survivors left to say, *I was there. It happened.* No-one with a number etched onto their skin."

The tattoo on my forearm isn't big. The pale purple rose Phil inked is smaller than a thumbnail, but it's a big deal because it's *me*, the *least* likely person in our year to use a fake ID to get inked.

"My dad trained us to forget history. He didn't want to live in the past but the past lived in him. And now," I trace the inky petals, "it lives in me."

Deb grabs my arm for a closer look. Then Karen, Tracey and Mai pile in.

"Who *are* you?" Deb says, marvelling at the tattoo. "And what have you done with my best friend?"

She flings an arm around my shoulder, her face shiny with pride, and I wonder if it was *always* this easy – telling the truth.

"Did it hurt?" Tracey touches the petals tentatively.

"Heaps," I say. Dad's sickness, his stories, his secrets, his leaving us. It hurt big time. But *this* – the small unfurling rose and my friends' arms around me – they help.

Miss Evans thanks me for sharing and asks if anyone else wants to speak. Kim raises her hand and asks if I could tell them more about the camps. I talk until the bell rings and kids file out of the room in twos and threes with red eyes and secrets they want to share.

"There it is," Adam says, and I know he's talking about my smile. The hand-me-down half-smile I stole from Dad. I'm grinning at him stupidly and he's smiling back.

There's no-one left in the room, except Adam and a few ghosts – girls with yellow stars stitched to their sleeves who never got to kiss boys. Boys who were forced onto cattle cars before they had a chance to fall in love.

"I missed that smile," Adam says. "I missed *you*."

He draws me close and there's nowhere to hide, no more secrets, no shame. I smile, and I couldn't turn down the wattage, even if I wanted to. There's a light burning bright, deep inside me. And it's the past, the future and the right now, all rolled into one.

AUTHOR'S NOTE

My father never talked about the Holocaust. If he battled ghosts, I never saw them. There was the past – the camps, the loss of his family and his home – and then there was us. We didn't talk about *before*. We focused on *now*. And that suited me fine. I didn't want to invite death into our home either.

But then my father got sick and everything changed. Suddenly he *wanted* to talk. *Inkflower* is the fictionalised story of what he told us, and what I learned while watching him die. Nearly all of what you've read is true. My father was diagnosed with amyotrophic lateral sclerosis and given six months to live. My mother cared for him at home, my brothers are doctors, Dad told us his Holocaust story and I wrote it down. Everything in this book that happened to him as a child, everything he witnessed in the camps, on the ship and in the refugee camp, mirror events in his real life. He built a business. He fell in love. He was happy. And when he said his final goodbye, it was just as I rendered it on the page – awful, beautiful, shattering.

I've rounded out the facts and added dialogue and color. My father only told us what he thought we could bear. He used the word 'hunger', not 'starvation', and 'death' instead of 'murder'. He never talked about being beaten or hopeless or hurt. The challenge for me was to convey everything that he left out, all the silences and empty pauses, the tears he blinked back and the stories he never told. The challenge was to convey the chaos of war when that war is recounted by someone who refuses to be broken by it.

The challenge was also revisiting the feelings his death stirred in me twenty years ago. My father raised us to build walls. To let go of pain, disappointment and sadness, and cling to hope. This book was my chance to dig deeper and examine my own personal hauntings. To imagine my father's pain and the weight of his buried memory, and let myself grieve. To be the same age he was when he lost his father. To be a Jew in hiding, a girl with her own secrets. That's where I blended truth and imagination.

I didn't go to Glenrock High or have a boyfriend called Adam. I didn't have a best friend like Deb. I wasn't seventeen when my father died. I was thirty-seven with a child of my own. I worried these embellishments would obscure the truth, but this story is more personal, more true, than anything I've written. I'm younger on the page as Lisa – angrier and more unsure of myself – but it's still me.

I did leave out one thing – the vow I made just before my father died. I promised him that I'd use his past to rewrite the future. I told him I'd pass on his warning that we mustn't forget, and that difference should be celebrated. I kept that promise when I wrote *The Wrong Boy* and *Alexander Altmann A10567*, but something continued to draw me back to the past.

My father taught me that we have to talk about the things that scare us before we can change them. He's gone now, and soon there won't be any survivors left to say the Holocaust was real. Maybe that's why I can't let it go.

Why I continue to write about my father's dark past in the hope that his story will act as a warning so future generations don't repeat the same mistakes.

ACKNOWLEDGEMENTS

There was so much in the writing of this book that made me smile, but there were long months spent in the dark too – back in Auschwitz, and beside my father's hospital bed. Reliving and writing about loss and grief can be lonely, so I'm especially indebted to all the people who kept me buoyed with their enthusiasm, support and love.

To my beautiful mother, thank you for allowing me to reimagine your love story and your pain for a new generation of readers. To my brothers, thanks for sifting through your memories and adding to mine. To Shaun, my husband, who helped me convert our bathroom into an office during the long months of lockdown (picture a trestle table over the bath and an office chair shoved up against a basin) – thank you for making space for all my stories. To Tanya and Remy, for ordering takeaway when I was too wrung out to cook, Leyla for never saying no to a game of Monopoly Deal, and Josh, my first reader, whose kind words gave me hope that I might pull this off. Thanks, guys.

To my writer's group – Sian Prior, Clare Strahan, Yannick Thoraval, Ilka Tampke, Fiona Scott-Norman and Mel Cranenburgh – who spent time with my characters and nudged them in the right direction. You made this book so much better. And to all the friends who walked along the windy beach track with me before I sat down to write each day. Thanks for the laughs and the 'what if she did XYZ?'

My cousins and their children, some of whom I only met through the writing of this book, told me stories about my father and sent me bundles of old photos that helped fill in the blanks. Martin Weiss gifted me a sprawling family tree and photos of my father's first home. Andrea Braun Katzav, Ernest Braun and Lorene and Mikulas Rottmann unearthed a black-and-white photo of my dad at thirteen. Eva Shulman shared her recollections and Mary Pfeffer revisited some dark times to shed light on my father's early years in Australia.

So many important organisations allowed me to comb their collections. The Motor Neurone Disease Association of Victoria, the Bonegilla Migrant Reception Centre, the USC Shoah Foundation's visual history archive, the Lamm Jewish Library of Australia and the Melbourne Holocaust Museum shared their resources and wisdom. A special shout-out to Sue Hampel for generously offering to be my expert reader, Moshe Lang for talking me through repressed memory, Irene Krauskopf for her insight into second-generation trauma, and Julia Reichstein for her exhaustive research and Covid book delivery service. And to Robbie Simons who gave me access to a videotaped testimony my father made years ago, one I'd never seen. Thank you for the gift of more time with my father.

To Irma Gold, my brilliant editor, for believing I was too good for cliches and demanding I do better. Her sensitivity and intelligence helped shape the story. Big thanks to Linsay Knight for believing young adults ought to hear this story, and to the amazing team of bookish people at Walker Books Australia including Clare Hallifax, Christina Pagliaro, Steve Spargo, Candace Stuart and Sarah Mitchell for bringing the story to life. Thank you!

But mostly, enormous thanks and endless love to my father. It's been twenty years but I still miss you, Dad. Thanks for teaching me how to live, love, grieve and celebrate. Thanks for letting the walls come down and trusting me with your story. And especially for showing us all what it means to be human.

LEARN MORE ABOUT THE HOLOCAUST

Resources recommended by Melbourne
Holocaust Museum (suitable for 13+).

MEMOIRS

Gary Gray, *A Spoonful of Soup and Other Stories*
recommended for readers 13+
Guta Goldstein, *There will be a Tomorrow*
recommended for readers 14+
Phillip Maisel, *The Keeper of Miracles*
recommended for readers 14+

HEAR FROM A SURVIVOR

Understanding Through Testimony
Meet 26 of Melbourne's survivors in this curated program that
focuses on five different phases in the Holocaust.
https://jhc.org.au/education/virtual-learning/
understanding-through-testimony/

Ask a Survivor
In this interactive experience, you will have the opportunity
to ask four Holocaust survivors one of 18 commonly
posed questions.
https://jhc.org.au/education/virtual-learning/ask-a-survivor/

The Eyewitness Project
A project to preserve the talks given by survivors to school students at the Melbourne Holocaust Museum since 2002.
https://jhc.org.au/education/for-students/eyewitness-project/

Lala
In this 360-degree VR blend of animation and live action video, Holocaust survivor Roman Kent shares the story of his time in Nazi-occupied Poland with his beloved dog, Lala, who taught him that love is stronger than hate.
https://iwitness.usc.edu/sites/360/lala?clip=859&entry=0.734cpui1

LEARN ABOUT GHETTOS AND AUSCHWITZ

Who Will Write Our History
https://www.facinghistory.org/resource-library/
who-will-write-our-history

The Jewish Letter Carrier in the Warsaw Ghetto
by Peretz Opoczynski
https://www.yadvashem.org/education/educational-videos/video-
toolbox/hevt-opoczynski.html

Animated map
https://encyclopedia.ushmm.org/content/en/
animated-map/the-holocaust

Timeline – Auschwitz key dates
https://encyclopedia.ushmm.org/content/en/
article/auschwitz-key-dates

LEARN MORE ABOUT AMYOTROPHIC LATERAL SCLEROSIS

Prepared with the assistance of the
Motor Neurone Association of Victoria.

BOOKS

Mitch Albom, *Tuesdays with Morrie*

BOOKLETS

Talking About Motor Neurone Disease for Teens
https://www.mndaustralia.org.au/getattachment/
efdf398a-8b02-474b-8f80-2d93b7bfe990/
Talking-about-MND-for-teens.pdf?lang=en-AU

Talking About Motor Neurone Disease
A resource for young people who have a friend
whose parent lives with motor neurone disease,
https://www.mndaustralia.org.au/getattachment/
97a24e2b-cda4-4a37-b3fb-26fd0ca9935a/
Talking-about-MND-for-young-friends.pdf?lang=en-AU

MOVIES

The Theory of Everything

In the 1960s, future physicist Stephen Hawking (Eddie Redmayne) falls in love with fellow collegian Jane Wilde (Felicity Jones). At twenty-one, having learned that he has amyotrophic lateral sclerosis, Hawking begins an ambitious study
of time, of which he has very little left.

You're Not You

An American drama starring Hilary Swank about a classical pianist who has been diagnosed with amyotrophic lateral sclerosis and the college student who becomes her caregiver.

Gleason

A hit documentary from the 2016 Sundance Film Festival that goes inside the life of Steve Gleason, the former New Orleans Saints defensive back who, at the age of thirty-four, was diagnosed with amyotrophic lateral sclerosis, and given a life expectancy of two to five years. Weeks later, Gleason found out his wife, Michel, was expecting their first child.

ABOUT THE AUTHOR

Suzy Zail has worked as a litigation lawyer, specializing in family law, but now writes full time. Among other titles, she has written *The Tattooed Flower*, a memoir about her father's time as a child survivor of the Holocaust, the story which inspired this novel. Her first novel for young adults, *The Wrong Boy*, was shortlisted for the Children's Book Council of Australia (CBCA) Book of the Year Awards, the Adelaide Festival Awards for Literature, the WAYRBA, United States Board on Books for Young People and YABBA awards. Her second novel, *Alexander Altmann A10567*, was a Notable Book at the CBCA Awards. Her previous YA novel, *I Am Change*, was written after a trip to Uganda and tells the story of a young Ugandan girl's struggle to stay in school. In 2022, Suzy published her first picture book, *Arabella's Alphabet Adventure*. Suzy's books have been published in Europe, the UK and US. You can visit Suzy online at suzyzail.com.au and on Instagram @authorsuzyzail

Want your own mixed tape of 1980s hits?
Scan the barcode using your Spotify app and
listen to Lisa and Deb's favorite tunes.

CHAPTER 28

THEN

The first time I saw your mother's face was in a photo. I'd moved into a boarding house with Andrew, Carl, Arthur and a bunch of other migrant boys after my stint at Bonegilla.

Mr Drucker, our landlord, told us the nineteen-year-old girl from Budapest was a distant relative who'd be staying in the spare room. I remember staring at her dark eyes and long black hair. She was the most beautiful girl I'd ever seen.

I let one of my housemates, George, pick her up from the station. I didn't think a girl like that – a girl with movie-star looks who'd grown up in a city with music and art – would look at a guy like me. Best to hang back and play it cool, let George, Stephen and the other boys fall over themselves to impress her. But then the car door opened and your mom tumbled out clutching a small battered suitcase and I was a goner. She was the type of girl who made your heart beat harder, who stole sentences from you. The five of us boys watched her unbutton her coat and sit down to eat. Then we sat, five sets of eyes on her, five chairs pulled close and no-one saying a word.

He fumbles for my hand and we stand at my front gate in the long shadows thrown by the setting sun. And I don't know what this is – or if I'll ever get him back – but for now, it's enough.

I'm out here floating in the middle of the *maybes*, in the right-now, just like Dad.

I type up Dad's latest instalment. All up it's now almost a hundred and forty pages. A book that holds my father close, but not close enough to stop time. I want to give him the pages, but there's still more to tell.

There's one last chapter, Dad had said, and I've saved the best for last.